MW00931054

THE COSMIC BURRITO

A Transcontinental Adventure of Discovery and Decadence

By

David Shiffman

© 1998, 2001 by David Shiffman. All rights reserved.

No part of this book may be reproduced, stored in a retrieval system, or transmitted by any means, electronic, mechanical, photocopying, recording, or otherwise, without written permission from the author.

ISBN: 0-7596-6586-9

This book is printed on acid free paper.

1stBooks – rev. 11/12/01

This book is dedicated to my loving parents, Gail and Milt, who taught me to keep an open mind, gave me the opportunity to travel the world and have always allowed me to express myself and live life to the fullest.

Acknowledgements

First and foremost, I give love and infinite thanks to the Most High.

Over the years, I have met many incredible people that have greatly influenced my life and helped to shape the message within this book. Though I never even knew the names of some of them, others I would like to thank here for their time, opinions, openness, wisdom, kindness, and/or precious friendship. Heartfelt gratitude to: Lascelles "Trainer" Adams, Rocco Appio, Jim Berryman, Ras Alan and Deanna Childres, Paul Davis, Ron Fein, Mike Hicks, Larry Isip, Sally Johnson, Mark "Elmo" Jordan, Christopher DePinto, Sarajane Ledewicz, Laurie Mitchell, Papa Pilgrim, Quino, Jill Leigh "Bean" Shiffman, Milt and Gail Shiffman, Kevin Tolnai, Scott Tolnai, Slike Valinski, Stan and Joanne Valinski, Luis Violante, Frankie Wilmot and Diana Yellen.

Love and hugs to Kezia Meagher for her support (which includes her unbelievable cooking).

I would also like to acknowledge the Grateful Dead and the Deadhead community whose music and spirit of the open road equally inspired the writing of this tale.

Finally, I would like to give huge thanks to reggae musicians universally for the joy and hope they give to me through their uplifting words and soothing music.

CHAPTER 1

Crosby Graves spit out a grain of rice as he spoke through a mouthful of Mexican food. "Forget Kansas." With the back of his hand he wiped away the salsa that had accumulated in the corner of his mouth. "Nothing happens in Kansas. It's flat." Crosby burped. "Flat and boring."

"That's not the kind of attitude we are encouraging on this trip," replied Tosh Tyler, disdainfully. Tosh scratched the straw-colored peach-fuzz goatee forming on the edge of his chin. "This isn't some prolonged ride, Crosby. This is our *journey*, our odyssey, subject to nothing but our whims and desires."

Crosby stopped chewing momentarily and looked at his best friend.

"We are exploring this awesome country," said Tosh, leaning in closer to emphasize his point. "Exploring doesn't mean visiting places that we already know about. That would be a tour."

"Tours are cool. Look at the Dead. Grilled cheese, nitrous, patchouli. What could be more fun?"

"Tours are for tourists."

"But Kansas?" refuted Crosby. "Do we have to explore Kansas? Look at *The Wizard of Oz*. Why do you think Dorothy spent the whole entire movie trying to get out of Kansas? 'Cause it sucks."

"Cros, Dorothy spent the entire movie trying to get back *to* Kansas."

"Oh." Crosby stared mournfully into his guacamole. "O.K. Tell me, Tosh, in all honesty, what could Kansas possibly have to offer — besides corn?"

"How will we know if we just blow through the whole state without getting off the highway? Let's stop somewhere, anywhere, and really experience Kansas."

"We'll experience nothing," Crosby cracked, polishing off his last bite of food.

Tosh smiled and replied with a pseudo-Jamaican accent, "It what yuh mek it, mon."

*   *   *   *

Corn — the versatile vegetable.

Aspiring for a life beyond the husk, it has leapt from its cob and become quite ubiquitous.

Corn has born cornstarch, corn flakes, cornbread, corn oil, cornmeal, corn muffins, corn dogs, corn salad, corn chips, corn whiskey, corn chowder, Corn Pops and Corn Nuts.

Corn is a third of succotash, half a hush puppy and the cornerstone of polenta.

In fact, corn makes an appearance in roughly half of the available food-products, disguised as a high-fructose syrup.

1

The only vegetable to venture into other sectors of the English language, corn has become a verb (corned beef) and an adjective (corny).

Corn has even made it in show business. It has a bit part in "Frosty the Snow Man," guest-stars in "Jimmy Crack Corn" and steals the show in *Children of the Corn.* Knowing how to play the Hollywood game, it's no coincidence that corn is served in every movie theater in America.

Speeding along the highway, Crosby and Tosh sliced straight through an endless cornfield like a paper cut in a sea of skin. Gazing out at the horizontal mass of husks whizzing by, Tosh recognized that Crosby had accurately assessed the topography of Kansas.

It was flat.

And saturated with maize.

"I feel weird eating this," said Tosh, dipping his hand into a bag of microwave popcorn recently purchased from a roadside mini-market.

"Why?" asked Crosby. He took his eyes off of the highway and turned to Tosh in the shotgun seat. "It smells good."

"I don't know," replied Tosh, turning his gaze out the van's window. "I feel very self-conscious, like the 18 million corn plants out there are watching me."

"What the hell are you talking about?"

"I feel like the corn has its eyes on me. Or should I say ears?"

"Don't be silly. That's why corn is on this planet. To be eaten."

Tosh peered deep into the bag, searching for the few remaining pieces of popcorn resting among the un-popped kernels at the bottom. "I feel stupid. There's all that corn out there, grown naturally under the sun, watered by the rain, sprung from the fertile loins of the earth. We could just pull over and I could grab an ear off the stalk and chow down, but I'm eating the stuff processed by some corporation, covered with this buttery goop that's probably just a mess of chemicals, and then zapped with radiation in the microwave. I'm sure the Indians never ate corn this way."

"The Indians never had microwaves," Crosby pointed out. "Besides, the rain doesn't water all that corn. They have massive irrigation systems nowadays."

"I guess. I mean, if we water our yards with sprinklers in New Jersey, The Garden State, they probably don't rely on Mother Nature for H-two-O in Kansas."

"Are you kidding?" said Crosby, turning to Tosh again. "Of course they don't. They have a whole network of garden hoses that makes the power lines in New York City look like a tic-tac-toe board."

Crosby took his hands off the steering wheel and spread them wide in the air, illustrating his point. He stared at his suspended hands for an exaggerated moment as the van motored along at double nickel. (Its maximum speed on flat land, sans tail wind.) The point Crosby really cared to illustrate with his look-ma-no-hands gesture, Tosh realized, was how straight the highway ran. In other words, Kansas was dull territory.

"Crosby," Tosh scolded, snatching up an un-popped kernel from the depths of the bag and popping it in his mouth. After sucking the buttery flavor off of the little nugget, he bit down into it. The kernel fractured and took residence in his upper molars.

"Damn!" muttered Tosh, shoving his fingers deep into his mouth. Trying to pry the little bastard loose from his teeth, he glanced at Crosby and realized his friend still had no eyes on the road and no hands upon the wheel. Immediately, he asked Crosby what he was doing as best as he could with a mouthful of fist. "Whuh ah u uin'??"

"The road's straight as an arrow," Crosby said, without even looking at it.

Tosh removed his hand from the cramped confines of his mouth. "Yeah, but somebody could be crossing it!"

Crosby returned his faculties to the control of their vehicle and Tosh focused his attention back on the un-popped kernels resting at the base of the bag. He yanked one out and held it in his hand. "I never learn *not* to eat these things," he said, and tossed it out the window. "Why is it that some kernels never pop?"

"Don't know," said Crosby.

"If all of the kernels would pop, I wouldn't fall into that trap."

"What trap?"

Tosh tossed the rest of the unborn corn out the window. "Be free! Go join your brothers and sisters!" He crumpled the empty bag and threw it down by his sandaled feet. "The trap of eating the unpopped kernels. If all of the kernels would pop, I wouldn't still be hungry after eating the entire bag."

"It's meant to be a snack, Tosh. Microwave popcorn is not supposed to serve as an entire meal for a grown man. Especially one who has hunger compounded by the side effects of pot."

"Do you think there's something wrong with those kernels, and that's why they didn't pop?"

"Maybe," said Crosby, running his hand through his short brown hair, scratching his scalp. He needed a shower. "Maybe it has something to do with The Clam Principle."

Tosh wiped his greasy hand on his bare calf. "The Clam Principle being that you are not supposed to eat clams that do not open up when you cook them?"

"Exactly."

"That those clams are not meant to be eaten, for a reason known only to a higher power, and eating them could be like fucking with fate?"

Crosby crinkled his brow. "I don't know about that, Tosh. I just kinda thought it was because they were diseased or something."

*   *   *   *

In almost twenty years of friendship, Tosh and Crosby had only one fight. It occurred during the summer between second and third grades, when Crosby took Tosh's Mets hat and threw it high in a pine tree, claiming the Mets were a second-rate franchise, a perpetual expansion team doomed to forever hobble in the shadow of illustrious Yankee baseball tradition. Crosby had lifted the quote from the sports section of the New York Times, and though he did not understand all of the verbiage, it was nevertheless an impressive recitation for an eight-year-old.

Though on the surface it seemed like an act of aggression, Crosby acted mainly in jest, hoping to initiate a little horseplay by getting a rise out of a usually mild Tosh. His ploy worked. Tosh responded by tackling Crosby, which led to a good-natured wrestling match with false threats, laughter and mock cries of agony.

The exact moment was unclear, but somewhere during the course of things, it became serious. Somehow, someone crossed a line. Suddenly, the smiles had disappeared and Tosh and Crosby started throwing punches. A bloody nose and a black eye later, the two former friends parted with calls of "asshole" and "baby," not to mention, "fucking jerk-off." (For the record, a referee would have awarded the fight to Crosby. He had gotten the better of Tosh, but not by much. T.K.O., tenth round.)

Soon after the episode, the Graves visited the Tylers, and by the end of the day, Tosh and Crosby had shaken hands and patched together their relationship, a friendship that would approximate brotherhood and lead to many shared preferences, dead brain cells and meaningless quarrels, but no more fisticuffs.

*   *   *   *

Tosh and Crosby had left home only a week ago, but their journey had essentially begun back in junior high when they first conceived the notion of a cross-country trip after watching *Cannonball Run,* a Burt Reynolds b-movie about an illegal transcontinental race that featured a lot of fast cars and fast women. T & A might have been their initial motivation, but Tosh and Crosby had genuinely yearned to get away from the bland and boring suburbia of New Jersey. They ached to get off the east coast and see what else was out there.

The call to the road persisted in their nagging souls and they talked about it from time to time. Over beers and hockey, they had speculated about the travel vehicle. Lying on the beach, they had sketched possible routes in the sand. It sounded like a great idea but that's all it was for a long time— an idea.

Then Tosh and Crosby graduated from college.

*   *   *   *

College graduation — a bittersweet occasion.
For Tosh, bitter.

4

For Crosby, very, very sweet.

*   *   *   *

For Tosh, graduation meant the end of a carefree, decadent lifestyle that featured four years in a fraternity with an extremely active social life. Aside from an exam now and then which required only a moderate amount of mental application, Tosh's stress level remained as worrisome as a speed bump in a car wash. Like many of his fraternity brothers, Tosh lived predominantly on junk food, cheap beer and psychedelic drugs, managed to seduce quite a shameful amount of coeds, and finished with a very respectable grade point average.

He did *not* want to graduate. Not yet, anyway.

Tosh's college years were not altogether devoid of growth and maturity, however. By the end of his sophomore year, he had sworn off computer video games for life; at the end of his junior year, he decided to forego a summer of lifeguarding and fast-food cooking at the New Jersey shore to do some international traveling.

As luck would have it that year, Tosh had inherited several thousand dollars from a distant uncle. Contradicting his parents' push to invest the wad, Tosh jumped at the opportunity to join a couple of college buddies on a global excursion. Instead of rescuing drunk vacationers at high tide and preparing fried-clam sandwiches at 2am (for drunk vacationers), Tosh would be swatting malaria-carrying mosquitoes and fighting dysentery.

Shunning Europe as one huge tourist trap, the boys hit random, less popular countries, without rhyme or reason. The trip would end, they had said, when the summer was over or when they ran out of money, whichever came first. Conveniently, they both occurred at the same time.

Tosh's summer of travel made him more aware of the wealth of diversity in the world, introducing him to different cultures and other ways of thinking. Tosh cursed himself for not paying attention in previous social studies classes, and vowed to make up for it his senior year.

He took "Varieties of Religious Tradition" and earned a C. Tosh enjoyed the class very much and the mediocre grade displeased him, for he had held an A average until he missed two days of studying for a mid-term when he accidentally overdosed on acid, trying to have an out-of-body experience. Instead, he ended up convincing himself he was a mango, refusing to get down off his top bunk because he "did not feel ripe."

Nevertheless, Tosh's mind had been pried open.

*   *   *   *

As Tosh's college years flew by, Crosby's crawled.

5

Throughout high school, with the exception of his art classes, Crosby had customarily displayed a general disinterest and lack of effort. Instead of working out the trigonometry problems on the blackboard, he'd sketch the teacher trimming his nose hairs at his desk. While others scoured the card catalogs in the public library and hustled to type their term papers, Crosby would reword an older cousin's research and rig up the windsurfing equipment.

Aware of this, his parents refused to fund his college tuition. Crosby's high-school grades did nothing to insure a return on his parents' investment and Crosby's father did not want to see his hard-earned cash wither away in the form of Ds on a college report card. He would rather use his money productively, like bet it on football.

If Tosh's college experience likened itself to dollar nachos in the sports bar, Crosby's path through post-high-school academia was like a cafeteria serving wax beans.

While Tosh tailgated at Big Ten football games and ogled sorority girls, Crosby worked at a deli to pay his way through an art major at a local university. With few friends around and a low cash flow, Crosby kept his nose pretty well to the grindstone. He'd go to class, put in a shift at the deli and then retire to his bedroom to smoke a bong and hit the books. (Sketchbooks, that is.) The cheesy Jersey bar scene rarely distracted him, with the exception of an occasional jaunt to the go-go, and the high points of his social life were road trips he took to visit Tosh and his other friends.

For Crosby, graduation meant an end to a disciplined routine, integral and rewarding, but not exactly fulfilling in the fun department.

*   *   *   *

Following his senior year, Tosh graduated from college and returned home unemployed and, even worse, aimless. He had no idea what he wanted to do with his life. Furthermore, after the previous summer of trekking through Borneo jungles and sleeping in Buddhist monasteries in the mountains of Taiwan, life in suburban New Jersey seemed exceptionally boring.

The double-whammy transition killed him. Dark clouds gathered over Tosh's unplanned future. Suddenly, the "real world" confronted him like a faceless beast.

*   *   *   *

Without school in the way, Crosby reasoned, he could get a job that didn't leave him elbow deep in egg salad, earned him some decent money and still gave him time to recreate. Unfortunately, he had not been prepared for the demanding job-search process — deciphering the cryptic jargon of the classified section, thinking up lies for his resume, writing cover letters, going on interviews. (If he got that lucky.)

Crosby's dedication to his low-key routine enabled him to graduate in four years, but it drained him of his lust for life. He approached his jump into the nine-to-five world like walking the plank. His youthful exuberance nearly petered out, he needed a break.

Crosby decided he did not want to get a job. Not yet, anyway.

*   *   *   *

Two friends, two different paths, same result — wanderlust.

Tosh had visited many parts the world, yet he had seen very little of his own country. Like a bear cub that had acquired the taste for blood and now favored a diet of flesh, Tosh had witnessed the bounty of travel and he yearned for more knowledge and experience. No longer satisfied to forage for berries, his craving burgeoned and began to gnaw at him.

On the other end, Crosby had been stuck living with his parents in New Jersey, surrounded by Taco Hells and Pizza Sluts. Like a bear that had not eaten at all, the only new landscapes he had surveyed were the latest strip malls and condos going up. Sick of pavement and tired of traffic, he starved for a glimpse of something stimulating, a nibble of adventure.

*   *   *   *

Memorial Day Weekend, the dawn of summer, normally a festive occasion. This time, however, as they prepared for their annual holiday beach bash, Tosh and Crosby had felt mutually apathetic.

Crosby handed Tosh a large bottle of Captain Morgan's Spiced Rum and opened the refrigerator. Grabbing a twelve pack of Budweiser, he said, "I just don't feel as pumped up as usual. Summer used to be great. We used to live for summer. Now, it's like back-to-school time."

"I wish I could go back to school," lamented Tosh.

The guys shuffled a few steps to the end of the checkout line, which had wrapped itself around the corner and down the aisle. Genesis pumped through the speakers in the liquor store's ceiling.

Crosby covered his ears. "If I hear another Phil Collins song on the radio, I'm going to take hostages at Gold's Gym."

"Tell me about it." The line moved forward a of couple feet. "So, how's the job search going, Cros?"

"Don't ask."

Tosh nodded. "You know, this summer doesn't have to suck."

"Why not?"

7

"Technically, summer is supposed to be vacation. That's the way it's always been growing up. I mean, we are programmed for leisure in the summer. Not motivation."

Crosby took a hand off of an ear, making sure that Phil Collins no longer filled the air. Relieved to hear an old Kinks tune, he took his other hand down. "That's what makes it so hard."

"Well, why should we fight it? Let's not get jobs yet. I don't even know what I want to do."

"Me neither. But what am I supposed to do? Should I stay at the deli and just fuck around all summer? I'm sick of the smell of tuna salad, Tosh." Crosby put the Budweiser back in the fridge and grabbed a pack of less expensive Rheingold. "Besides, what the hell am I going to tell my parents? That I'm just going to fart around all summer because I don't feel like getting a real job?"

"Let's take our cross-country trip."

Crosby dropped the twelve-pack of cheap swill to the floor. "Now? Are you serious?"

"Of course I am. What better time? We have no commitments, no plans."

"No money."

"Oh come on, we've got some dough. You don't have to start paying your loans for like another five months, right?"

"True."

"We could do it really cheaply. We'll camp out the whole way. The only thing that will cost us is buying a vehicle — we'll find a cheap old van — gas money and beer."

Crosby picked the twelve-pack up from the floor. He opened the fridge once again and exchanged the Rheingold for generic Beer in solid white cans with bar codes. "I'll think about it."

*   *   *   *

Tosh poked his head into the old Dodge van he and Crosby had bought the day before.

Crosby tightened a screw on the newly-installed blinds on the rear window and turned around. "Whassup?"

Tosh climbed in and sat down on the van's carpeted floor. He opened the bag of Taco Hell he had brought along and handed Crosby a burrito. "So, we all set?"

Crosby tucked the screwdriver in the side pocket of his cut-off carpenter pants and sat down next to him. "Just about. Got tint on the windows and blinds up for privacy. My old man installed a fan for additional ventilation."

"Good thinking. I got the paperwork all squared away — registration, insurance — we're good to go. Hot sauce?"

"Definitely. These so-called burritos can use all the help they can get. I can't believe we make ourselves suffer through this generic fast-food slop disguised as Mexican food. Can you please tell me why?"

"Because there's no place better?"

"There has to be. I mean, think of the concept of a burrito – it's a beautiful thing. A tasty, well-rounded meal made up of meat, cheese, vegetables – all kinds of goodies – wrapped up in a convenient, fun-to-eat tortilla. Look at this – this is just a pound of refried lard bean sludge with a few itsy-bitsy mealy tomato pieces and some wilted brown lettuce. This is inexcusable."

"They forgot the chicken?"

"I believe in the burrito, just not *this* burrito!" Crosby made a face like he was about to hurl.

"Don't look so glum, chum."

"I can't help it. I got average grades at an average school. I have no idea what I feel like doing with my life and I am about to spend every last dime I own taking a pointless trip to nowhere against the will of my parents who do, thankfully, still provide me with shelter, though I am not so sure after this."

"Dude, chill out." Tosh reached into the cooler underneath one of the van's beds, pulled out a pair of cold beers and handed one to Crosby. "Here, wash down that pasty motherfucker. First of all, you are so not average. An average guy does not have the balls to spend the rest of his savings on a cross-country journey in a cruddy old van – though I must admit this is a charming, cruddy old van. Secondly, most people at our age don't know what they want to do with their lives. That's all the more reason to take this trip now. Thirdly, don't sweat your parents – they are all bark and no bite. They love having you live at home. You take out the garbage, vacuum the pool. And even if they do give you the boot, you will never have to worry about finding a place to live again, because now we have this puppy."

"Oh great," Crosby lamented, "I can live in a van down by the river."

"And finally, this is not a pointless trip to nowhere. Just because we have no specific destination doesn't mean we're not going somewhere. On the contrary, we're going everywhere. We're exploring."

"Yeah, but…"

"The point is discovery," Tosh interrupted. "That's what explorers do – they discover. Like Lewis and Clarke. They didn't know what they were looking for. They were just *looking,* and they discovered half the country."

"Yeah, well, news bulletin, Tosh, the country has already been discovered."

"Cros, we are exploring for *ourselves.* There are so many places out there we haven't seen. There are people to meet with stories to tell. This is about discovering things about life and about ourselves and —"

"Don't feed me your new-age hippie shit, Tosh. I don't need to discover anything for myself. I'm all set."

"Oh, you don't, eh, Mr. Know-it-All? Just a minute ago you told me how nice it would be to find a good burrito."

Crosby sat and pondered that for a moment. As was often the case, Tosh was right. Crosby knew he was just being closed minded and cantankerous. This trip would be good for him. And of course it would be a hell of a good time. Why was he fighting it?

Crosby smiled. "We leave at daybreak, bro." He slid out of the van and sauntered over to his mutt, Scrappy, sitting on the lawn. Depositing the remains of his burrito at Scrappy's paws, he turned back to Tosh and said, "And not only are we going to find a good burrito, we are going to find the best burrito ever made!"

CHAPTER 2

The Wet Spot sat just past the John Deere dealership, set back off the main drag in Buford, Kansas. A large cloud of dust shrouded the old pile of lumber and neon and kept the raucous music inside from spilling out onto the street.

Crosby finished his last sip of beer, crushed the empty can and hopped out of the van. "You coming?" he called to Tosh, who was rummaging through his backpack.

"Go ahead, I've just got to find some underwear."

"What do you need underwear for?"

"To shield people from my smell."

While Tosh changed his clothes inside the van, Crosby choked his way through the dirt parking lot in front. Armed with sunglasses and a bandanna tied over his mouth and nose to filter each precious breath, he searched the roadside bar for an entrance. His keen vision enabled him to read the neon beer signs, although it did not help him locate the door. With squinted eyes he groped his way along the front of the building, feeling for an opening.

Suddenly, from inside The Wet Spot, someone pulled the hidden door open.

Crosby stumbled into the void, tumbling right onto the floor. *Great,* he thought. *Drunk college asshole making a scene in a biker bar. I'm a dead man.*

He quickly jumped up, slid the shades to the top of his head and brushed himself off. Trying to keep a low profile, he slithered through the crowd and found an opening at the bar.

Crosby ordered a beer from the bartender, a muscular but haggard woman with an eyebrow ring. Grabbing the nicely frosted mug, he thanked the bartender and turned to lean back against the bar.

On stage, four young men in T-shirts and shorts tuned their instruments in front of a bass drum that read "Corn Sucks." To his left, Crosby overheard two men discussing the latest line of manure spreaders. To his right, an ancient man sat with his head hung low over his scotch.

He had short white hair, wrinkled skin and liver spots on his face. Eyes drooping heavily, the guy wavered slightly in his seat, like a flag swaying in a stiff breeze. It seemed like he might keel over onto the bar at any moment.

Crosby spoke loud enough to be heard over the din of the bar. "Hey buddy, what's happenin'?"

The man's eyes perked up slightly and he glanced at Crosby.

"How're you doin' tonight?" Crosby asked.

"I'm all right, suppose."

"What's with the band? They called Corn Sucks?"

"Yep. Punk rock," said the man, turning to get a better look at Crosby. "You not from 'round here, huh?"

"Nope." Crosby took a sip of his beer. "You here to see punk rock?"

"Naa. I'm here to drink. Just happens to be Thursday."

Crosby nodded. Then he said, "It's Tuesday."

The man considered Crosby's statement. Becoming aware of his slumping posture, he straightened himself out. "Whoah Nelly," he said. "It *is* Tuesday, ain't it?"

"Yep."

"Corn Sucks plays every Thursday night, see. On Tuesdays, Jumpin' Jim Crow usually plays the blues." The man coughed, cleared his throat and spit on the floor. "Sorry about that," he continued. "If I recall, Mr. Jim had a batch of that bad moonshine goin' round and he come down ill. So Burt had the punk boys fill in tonight. Burt's the owner."

"That's cool," said Crosby. "What other types of music does Burt get here?"

"Lots. Wet Spot's the only bar in town with live music. Gotta make everyone happy." The man spit on the floor again. "Actually, it's the only bar in town."

"Does Burt get reggae?" Crosby asked, thinking of his friend in the parking lot. *Where the hell is Tosh anyway?* he wondered.

"Does he get what?"

"Reggae."

"Reggie? Never heard of 'em."

Not worth the explanation, Crosby thought. "What kind of music do you like?"

"I like all types — country *and* western," said the man, taking a sip of his whiskey. "We get that here on Friday nights."

"That must be pretty wild."

"Hoo, yeah. It is. But that's nothin' compared to Saturday nights. Boy, you should come here on a Saturday night." The man downed the rest of his drink and his eyes grew wider. "Saturday night's a grand old shindig. Burt breaks out this new-fangled entertainment system. It's called Carry Okie. Everybody gets up on the stage and sings. Possum on a gum bush."

The man reached down the bar for a half mug of beer someone had abandoned. "I reckon I'll adopt this little orphan," he said, taking a few large gulps.

"You ever sing?" Crosby asked him.

"They tell me I sang a frightful Loretta Lynn one night. I don't remember it none." He finished off the mug of beer and placed it down on the bar with a thud. "That was one a them nights." Leaning in close to Crosby, he whispered, "Wet Spot sold outa whiskey, both legal and illegal."

He leaned back again and hiccupped a "'Scuse me."

Crosby watched the man slide off his bar stool and shuffle off into the crowd.

Noise picked up in the bar as the drummer had begun his warm-ups. Crosby scanned the mix of people filling the small tavern. College-aged people gathered around the stage, mingling energetically. In the corner, a couple of Harley dudes shot pool. Around the bar sat mostly old timers, drinking quietly and keeping to themselves.

"What're you searchin' fer?"

The raspy voice came from Crosby's left where the manure-spreader guys had been. In their place sat a slender, almost gaunt man with long, graying hair pulled back in a ponytail.

"You talking to me?" Crosby asked him.

"Sure am." The man tipped his tattered hat. "What're you searchin' fer?"

"What am I searching for?"

"That's right. Everybody's searchin' fer somethin'."

"What are *you* searchin' for?"

The man furrowed his forehead and pursed his lips. He scratched behind his ear. "I asked you first."

Crosby thought for a moment about the cryptic question and then realized he actually had an answer. "I'm searching for The Ultimate Burrito."

"The what?"

"Me and my friend are looking for the best burrito we can find." Pleased with his decisive answer, Crosby emptied his brew.

"A burriter? That's it?"

"Yeah," said Crosby defensively. "Why, what're *you* searching for?"

"I've already found it."

"Oh yeah?"

Just then, Crosby felt a hand squeeze his shoulder. He turned around to a face full of smoke. The bartender, cigarette hanging out of her mouth, winked at him. "Can I get you another beer, hon?"

"Oh, yeah, please." Crosby handed her his mug and fished a five from his front pocket. He put the crumpled bill on the bar and smoothed it out with the side of his hand as she topped off his beer.

"So what have you found?" Crosby asked, turning back around with a refilled mug.

"Excuse me?" A petite, Asian girl sat on the bar stool to Crosby's left.

"Hey, what happened to that guy?"

"What guy?"

"What are you doing here?"

"I just sat down."

"There was a guy sitting here. I was just talkin' to him. He looked like Willie Nelson. Did you see him?"

"The seat was empty. I didn't see him."

Crosby peered around the tavern and saw no sign of the Willie Nelson guy. "Musta split."

"Do you want me to leave?" the girl asked him.

13

Crosby sat down. "No, not at all." He looked at his new neighbor. She had smooth, golden skin and bright, perky eyes. Her head askew, she brushed her long black hair behind her ear and smiled alluringly.

"Make yourself comfortable," said Crosby.

*   *   *   *

Through the thick cloud of dust, tinged pink from neon, Tosh followed Crosby's progress. As his buddy crossed under the large Jayhawk Beer sign, the bar seemingly swallowed Crosby up. In return, the edifice spit out a young woman. Running out of the bar with her head down and her hands covering her face, she almost smashed right into Tosh.

"Sister, are you all right?"

The girl stopped in her tracks, her face still concealed by her hands. After a moment, she slowly removed her hands and revealed a big smile.

Her expression caught Tosh by surprise and he responded with a snicker. "I guess so," he said. "You had me worried there. I thought maybe something bad happened."

"Oh, how *swee-eet,*" she replied with a mid-western twang. "Don't worry darlin', everything's great. Even better now that I'm out of that stinkin' hole." The young lady threw the mass of blonde hair off of her face. "My name is Sally."

"I'm Tosh."

"Well it's nice to meet you."

"Same here." Tosh started to hold his hand out to shake, but quickly withdrew. He felt awkward for a moment, never knowing what to do in this situation. Some girls preferred handshakes while others didn't. Which category did Sally fall in?

Sally just smiled contentedly, so Tosh opted for no handshake. It didn't seem like she needed any more of an introduction. "Hey Sal, would you like some company for the rest of the evening? I'm not really in a beer-chugging, tequila-burping mood right now."

"Well, what did you have in mind, darlin'?"

The way she said that made Tosh's toes warm. "I was hoping maybe you know some place cool where we can kick back and hang out."

"Are you kidding? That's all we do 'round here. This is Buttfuck, Kansas, honey. Not much else to do." Sally pinched Tosh's arm. "Come on."

She grabbed Tosh's elbow and led him through a maze of motorcycles and pick-ups parked in no semblance of order. The Wet Spot's dirt lot did not offer the luxury of parking spaces neatly mapped out with white paint.

"Must be tough to park," Tosh commented.

Sally raised an eyebrow and said, "Especially when you're already drunk."

At the end of their roundabout path, Sally led Tosh to a big old Ford Flatbed truck.

"I like your wheels."

"Thanks. It's my Uncle Bob's. He lets me use it while he's away," she explained as she hopped up into the truck. "It's temperamental. Sometimes it won't turn over for me. I think it's just a moody son of a bitch."

"Yeah, I know what you mean," said Tosh. "Sometimes Jo does that too."

Sally pumped the gas a few times and turned the key. The Ford sputtered, but started right up. "Who's Jo?" she asked.

"My van, Josephine. I'm driving cross-country with my buddy, Crosby, and we named our van Jo." Tosh rolled down the window. "She's a '73 Dodge Sportsman."

"Oh, how cool," said Sally, revving the engine. "Wish this was a Dodge." Sally listened closely to the sound of the motor until she felt satisfied it wouldn't stall. "Is your van a nice ride?"

"Well, we didn't really buy it for the ride," Tosh explained. "It's got space. You know, we can sleep in it, it holds all our stuff. It's like an apartment on wheels."

"Why'd ya name it Jo?"

"When we took off, the first song we heard on the radio was "Ride on Josephine." It's about a car, you know, so we just figured, how appropriate."

Sally nodded. She pulled the Ford out onto the road and they listened to its mufflerless howl for a minute.

"So why did y'all come to Kansas?"

Tosh's fingers dug through his dreadlocks to scratch his scalp. "Well, we're exploring this great country of ours and Kansas is part of it."

"A big, flat part, darlin'."

"Well, we didn't exactly come *to* Kansas. We're kinda just passin' through it."

Sally stopped at a liquor store on the edge of town. "I hope they're still open," she said. "You like red wine?"

Hopping out of the running truck without waiting for an answer, she hustled up to the door of the store. Already locked, Sally banged on it.

Inside, an old man pointed to his wrist, indicating they were closed. Sally jumped up and down furiously and then theatrically mimicked a temper tantrum. After completing her little act, she flashed Tosh a quick grin and then presented a prize-winning smile to the store clerk. He shook his head with disgust and moseyed on over to open the door.

In a minute Sally returned with a large jug of red wine. "This stuff is the best. He orders it just for me."

Tosh removed the wine from the crinkled brown paper bag. The burgundy booze inside the green bottle made it appear black. Grabbing the built-in handle, he gazed into his reflection on the smooth surface.

This bottle holds a lot of warmth and relaxation, Tosh thought.

"You drink a lot of wine?" he asked.

15

"Ever since I read *Tortilla Flat* in high school. They try to teach us Steinbeck and I learn how to become a wino," Sally laughed.

"I read that. All those dudes did was sit around and drink red wine and think about how they could get more."

"Well, this gal never had a sip a red wine before that book."

"Hey, I can't blame you," said Tosh. "It made the stuff seem like nectar."

"Darlin', it is."

Outside the truck, the moon cast a serene glow on the fields passing by.

"So what was that deceitful exit all about?" Tosh asked Sally. "You looked like you had just seen someone die when you came running out of that bar."

"Oh, yeah," Sally giggled. "There was this guy there who has a crush on me..."

Sally told him about love notes and flowers and other failed baiting gestures as she turned off the paved highway outside of the town. Tosh listened only partially as she related her tale of the badgering romantic — part of his mind focused on Sally's appearance. Taking advantage of the fact that her eyes were on the dirt road in front of them, Tosh coyly sized her up.

His heart began to beat faster as he fell for her. Sally had large blue eyes, full cheeks and swollen lips shaped in a constant pout. Her thick, wavy locks fell forward, framing her adorable face. She had a full-figured body, just the kind Tosh preferred. He always favored sturdy women over the whole emaciated, figure-like-a-pencil look. Tosh liked girls he could hug without feeling as if he would crush them.

Sally wore black leather cowboy boots and tight blue jeans. Her thin white blouse, unbuttoned just enough to drive Tosh crazy, allowed peeks at her healthy cleavage when she looked away. To top it all off, she adorned herself with silver — twisted and molded and carved into a necklace, rings and bracelets.

And the accent. Her country-fried accent just melted Tosh.

As Crosby would say, she was a nugget. Through and through. A solid gold nugget.

Tosh wanted to kiss her.

"...and I just didn't feel like dealing with him. He's nice and all, but he's just not my type. You know, he's a dork. I don't know what it is, but I'm such a geek magnet."

"Well you attracted me, and I don't consider myself a geek."

"Most geeks don't," Sally kidded. She put the truck in park, gave Tosh a pinch and killed the engine. "This is my father's farm."

"What's that smell?"

"Oh, that's the pigs."

"Whoa."

"You get used to it." Sally hopped out of the van. "I'm gonna take you to my special place."

"Your special place?"

"Yeah, darlin'. Round here, everyone has their own special place."

"What's special about it?" Tosh asked.

"Well, what's special about it is that it's no one else's place." Sally smiled.

Tosh wasn't sure he understood. "So, do you, like, have to lay claim on some place as your special place?"

"No, silly, no one *knows* that it's your special place!"

"Hmm."

Sally laughed. "It's where people go when they want to get away from it all."

This is away from it all, thought Tosh.

*   *   *   *

The petite Asian cutie introduced herself as Dorothy.

"Nice to meet you," said Crosby, lighting her cigarette. "So, Dorothy, what do you do around here?"

"I'm a cocktail waitress."

"Oh, what a coincidence." Crosby downed the rest of his drink. "I love cocktails."

*   *   *   *

Sally led him by a tidy old farmhouse, around a big red barn, past some junked cars and a tractor and over a small, weathered, wooden fence. There, they climbed to the top of a huge pile of hay. Sally took the quilt she had brought from the truck and spread it out for them to sit on. The haystack was molded into a sort of reclining lounge chair so they could lean back and stretch but still remain sitting upright.

"You like the shape?" Sally asked. "I custom designed it that way so I could drink my wine while staring up at the sky."

"Very comfy."

A few silent minutes passed as the two sipped the wine from the bottle. Tosh listened to the crickets, the rustling of the reeds, a small airplane passing overhead. Tosh liked this spot, especially the haystack. It was true – Sally had structured it so that they could sip their wine while gazing at the stars. Tosh felt kind of bad he had been down on the whole *special place* thing.

A breeze picked up and Sally crossed her arms and snuggled deep into the quilt. Noticing her chill, Tosh took the flannel shirt he had wrapped around his waist and handed it to her.

"I was glad to get out of that bar," Sally said. "I'm not much into punk rock anyway."

"It's pretty cool. It's a release." Tosh handed the wine to Sally. "When it comes to music though, for me, nothing beats reggae. I love reggae. I live for it. Do you know reggae?"

17

"Not really."

"Did you ever hear Bob Marley?"

Sally lowered the bottle from her lips and said, "Nope." She handed the wine to Tosh, singing, "Red red wine."

"There! That's a reggae song!" Tosh said excitedly.

"It is?"

Tosh suddenly felt stupid. He was thinking UB40, 1980s.

"I have a question," Sally announced.

"Shoot."

"I've never heard that name before, Tosh. How'd ya get that name?"

"Well, actually, it's a nickname that I got because of my love of reggae. See, my real name is Joshua Tyler, but since I'm so heavy into de reggae scene, mon," Tosh explained as he slipped into his Jamaican accent for effect, "all mi friends, mon, dey call mi Tosh. Afta Petah Tosh."

"So, this Peter Tosh guy is a reggae singer."

Tosh relished the opportunity to describe his favorite artist and namesake. He chose his words extra carefully, trying to relate the magnificence of such an extraordinary man. "Peter Tosh was a visionary musician. He had a mystical aura, this, like, transcendental energy."

Sally looked at Tosh with intrigue, but barely a hint of understanding.

"He was a spiritual man who sang for the righteous upliftment of humankind, a warrior of the downtrodden who strove for equal rights and justice for all people."

"He sounds like a rebel."

"Right on," said Tosh. She was getting his drift. "He also sang about the legalization of ganja."

"Ganja?"

"Yeah mon, you know, pot, weed, herb, buds, hooch."

"You mean marijuana?"

Tosh nodded his head.

"Got any?" Sally asked.

"Not with me," Tosh laughed. "Why, you smoke it?"

"When I can. Usually when someone else has it. I don't really know where to get it. But I always liked it. It makes me feel very relaxed. Kinda like my wine. But it makes me very perceptive-like. Does that make sense?"

"It sure does," Tosh replied, grabbing the half-finished bottle of wine from Sally. "So what type of music do you like?"

"I am a Jimmy Buffet freak," Sally giggled.

"You are? Me too! I love Jimmy Buffet!"

"The man drives me wild. I have all of his records."

"My buddy, Crosby, he's a Parrothead too. We love Jimmy!"

"His music makes me feel so good."

"No doubt. He's definitely one of a kind." Tosh breathed a sigh of relief, happy that Sally wasn't as musically unenlightened as he feared. "I love the stories he tells in his songs."

"Do you know the song, 'The Great Filling Station Hold-Up?'"

"Yeah! About ripping off a gas station with a pellet gun!"

"They take a big old jar of cashew nuts and a can of STP."

"Don't forget the Japanese TV."

Sally took another sip of wine. Using the back of her hand to wipe the burgundy marks from the edges of her mouth, she posited, "I got one. Do you know 'Peanut-butter Conspiracy?'"

"I don't know," Tosh replied. "How's it go?"

Sally bobbed her head and shoulders as she sang. "You go steal the peanut-butter, I'll get a can of sardines, Runnin' up and down the aisles of the mini-mart, stickin' food in our jeans..."

Tosh chimed in: "We never took more than we could eat, There was plenty left on the racks, We all swore if we ever got rich, we would pay the mini-mart back!"

"You know it!"

"I love that song!"

"What about Frank and Lola?"

"On their honeymoon in Pensacola."

"Billy Voltaire?"

"The piano player up from Miami a ways."

"Wow, you really do know Jimmy Buffett," said Sally. "I'm impressed."

Tosh could almost *be* Jimmy Buffet, if Jimmy had dreads. He had sun-drenched light brown hair, sparkling eyes and a warm smile and was of average height and build. He wore cut-off corduroy shorts, a Miller Beer T-shirt and faded black Chuck Taylor's with red, yellow and green striped laces.

Tosh reflected on the good times he had shared with Jimmy Buffet and how his music had just enhanced those experiences. He could picture hanging on the beach with Crosby and some friends, sipping beers during the late afternoon, the intense heat of the day faded but the sand remaining warm and spilling over their bare feet.

In other instances, when the going got ugly, he had called upon Jimmy Buffet for an attitude adjustment. If Tosh was down in the dumps or stressed, he would put Buffet on to soothe his soul. His music always cheered him up and helped him deal with his obstacles.

"Buffet's music is like a painkiller," he rationed.

"Yes, but it's better than any drug you could take."

Sally played with Tosh's hair. "My favorite Jimmy Buffet songs are the ones about the sea. I love hearing about tropical islands and boats and sailing adventures."

"Yeah, the pictures he paints in your mind are so vivid. On the coldest, darkest winter day, he could bring the tropical ocean to you."

"My dream is to go and live near the ocean. I've never seen one," Sally lamented.

"You've never been to an ocean? Man, that's weird."

"Not if you're from Kansas and you don't have a lot of money."

"Aw man, I guess I do take it for granted. Where I live in New Jersey, the beach is only an hour away. I usually live at the shore during the summer."

"Lucky duck." Sally took another guzzle of wine, sticking her tongue down the neck of the bottle.

I wish she'd stick that tongue in my mouth, thought Tosh.

"The only way I can get to the ocean is through Jimmy. Otherwise, I'm stuck here."

Tosh grabbed her hand and held it.

"Sometimes I just lie on my haystack and stare at the stars," continued Sally, "and pretend that I'm lying on a boat at sea, sailing to some exotic island."

Tosh thought of his trip the previous summer. He'd seen exotic lands and oceans all around the world. Poor Sally couldn't even get to the coast.

They remained silent for a little while, peering up into the clear sky. The wine had sunk in and feeling mellow, Tosh put his arm around Sally.

It was a crisp night, kind of cool for summer. The stars sparkled bright in the heart of Kansas.

"Do you know where the stars came from?" Sally questioned.

"I wish."

"Well, your wish is my command. I'll tell you."

"You'll tell me?"

"Hush. This is where the stars came from," whispered Sally. She took another sip of wine to wet her whistle and then began her tale.

"There were five wolves who hunted together every night. They were brothers. They would share their meat with Coyote. One night, the wolves were all staring at the sky. Coyote wanted to know what they were looking at but they wouldn't tell him, 'cause they were scared he may interfere. After like a week of this, the wolves decided to let Coyote in on it. They told him that they were staring at two animals way up in the sky.

"'Let's go see them!' said Coyote. He shot an arrow into the sky and it stuck. He then shot many arrows, one after the other, and each one stuck in the one before it, making a very long ladder.

"For days and nights the wolves and Coyote climbed the ladder. Finally, they reached the sky. At this point, they could see that the two animals were grizzly bears.

"'Don't go over there. They may be dangerous,' Coyote warned them.

"But it was too late. The youngest wolf brothers had already headed over. Then two more wolf brothers followed, leaving the oldest wolf brother with his dog and Coyote. When the oldest wolf brother noticed that it was safe, he went over with his dog and sat down with them. Coyote still didn't trust the bears so he remained behind. He thought to himself, 'They all look pretty good sitting there together. That makes a real nice picture. I think I'll leave them there for everyone to see.'

"He then climbed down the ladder, taking the arrows out as he went. From down on earth, Coyote looked up and admired his work. Today we can still see them. They're the Big Dipper. See? Up there?"

Sally leaned her cheek against Tosh's and pointed to the Big Dipper. "Three wolves make up the handle. Then, in the middle, sits the oldest wolf brother and his dog. The two youngest wolves make up the bottom of the bowl and the two grizzly bears make up the other side. Coyote liked his work so much he made pictures all over the sky."

Tosh smiled at Sally. "That's one I've never heard. Did you make that up?"

"Naaa. It's an old Indian myth. I can't remember which tribe, though."

"You know, it's interesting that these Indians recount the origin of the stars as having no purpose other than their beauty. I would think that they would have something to do with spirits or prophecy or creation."

"Hmm. Actually, I never thought of that."

Tosh held the wine bottle up to the moonlight to see how much remained. Not much. He took another big swig and rolled the wine around in his mouth as he played with this idea.

"Well," said Sally, "the Indians really lived in tune with nature. They worshipped the earth and cared for the land, kinda like someone would nurture a pet. I guess it makes sense that the beauty of their environment would be important to them. Heck, the Indians probably valued the aesthetics of the earth more than anyone!"

"Not only is she beautiful, but smart too."

Sally smiled. "So you liked my story?"

"Definitely. And I don't usually like to think about the stars."

"Why not?"

"The stars make me nervous," replied Tosh.

Sally giggled. "What do you mean they make you nervous?"

Oh no, thought Tosh. *Here we go.* "Just the whole idea that space goes on forever really freaks me out. I can't conceive how outer space can go on infinitely. I mean, it's gotta end *somewhere*, doesn't it? How can it go on forever?"

"I don't know. I never really thought about it." Sally grabbed the wine and polished it off. "Thanks for the buzz," she said to the empty green bottle as she gave it a good toss. She grabbed Tosh, hugged him hard and gave him a big kiss on the cheek.

"I just wish it ended at some point. The whole concept of infinity and outer space really upsets me. I just don't get it. It genuinely upsets me." Tosh hated that feeling, the knot forming in his stomach

"Let me take your mind off of it, honey."

21

Sally got up and straddled Tosh. She edged her face closer to him until her lips pushed against his. They remained like this for a moment until their mouths opened slightly, letting their warm, wet, grape-flavored tongues mingle.

*   *   *   *

"I was named after David Crosby. You know, from Crosby, Stills and Nash. My mom was a hippie," Crosby explained to Dorothy.

Corn Sucks had just completed their last set and The Wet Spot offered dollar drafts for the final half hour of the night. After a sweaty night of moshing, Crosby was cooling down with a few more frosty pals.

"I like Crosby, Stills and Nash," said Dorothy, sucking on the straw in her rum and coke.

Crosby told everyone the David Crosby/hippie Mom story when explaining his unconventional name. It was much easier than explaining the truth, and much less embarrassing. In reality, though, Crosby's name came from his grandfather's cat.

The story begins when Crosby's mother, Amanda, was a little baby. The family cat, an affectionate Siamese named Crosby, would often jump up into her crib while she slept. Crosby would harmlessly lick the infant's face until Amanda awoke, terrified by the awful Brillo tongue scraping her tender pink skin. Paralyzed by her fear, she would stare into the two large feline eyes until tears flooded her vision. This continued throughout Amanda's youngest days until she learned how to clutch and pull. Shortly after that, Crosby learned to keep a safe distance. Nevertheless, the scars left by these calamities never healed.

Twenty years later, they resulted in a strange paradoxical complex; Amanda loved animals but intensely feared cats.

Perhaps not following her best instincts, she nailed down a job as a veterinarian's receptionist. Things went well for the first couple of weeks until the first feline patient came through the door. Amanda had a seizure and passed out cold. The incident remained a mystery until it happened again four days later. The staff deduced that Amanda must have some type of adverse reaction to cats.

Luckily, the veterinarian, Dr. Dalton, had a kind heart. He knew how much Amanda loved her job and how much she needed the money with a child on the way. So, instead of firing her, Dr. Dalton put Amanda on temporary leave and suggested she see a psychiatrist to overcome her phobia.

After a few excruciating Freudian analysis sessions, the psychiatrist uncovered the root of Amanda's problem. The dignified doctor offered a solution — Amanda should give something "very dear to her" the name Crosby. This beloved item would replace her caustic subconscious memories of the kissing cat, alleviating her fear.

The beloved item, of course, turned out to be her precious son.

"Just for the record, you have the tightest, most beautiful little ass I've ever seen. And I've seen quite a few."

Dorothy pulled a pack of Camels out of the cigarette machine. "Thank you," she said.

"You probably hear that all the time, huh?"

"Not really. At least not when I'm wearing clothes."

Dorothy told Crosby the truth about her "cocktail waitress" job. She was actually a topless dancer. She earned big bucks having horny men stuff dollar bills in her thong, copping a feel of her precious butt as she pranced around the disco stage of the Half-Way Go-Go. She indeed received plenty of compliments, but usually from smelly truck drivers with bad teeth, not attractive boys like Crosby.

Crosby looked like a Dennis the Menace. His hair, though short, was always unkempt. (Just like Tosh with his dreadlocks, Crosby found no need for a comb.) Dressed in a pair of worn khaki shorts and a faded old golf shirt, his checkered Vans sneakers added a touch of California to his preppy attire. His ancient baseball hat read Cocks, after the University of South Carolina Gamecocks. A real conversation piece, Crosby's favorite cap had started many chats while sitting awry atop his messy dark brown hair. The once-white hat now needed a wash pretty badly, but Crosby rejected this notion for fear of bad luck.

"I want to lick you," Dorothy said to him, compliments of a heavy buzz, a night of dancing and Crosby's irresistible charm.

Crosby did not waste time. He reacted instinctively. Taking her hand, he quickly led Dorothy out of the bar and proceeded to engage her in a kiss — a sloppy, face-sucking extravaganza up against a 1971 Chevy Nova.

Passion filled the air, but this was only the beginning. Just ahead would come a night of invigorating sexual activity unlike anything Crosby had ever experienced before.

And he thought Kansas was going to be boring.

*   *   *   *

Tosh opened his heavy eyes and without sitting up, scanned the van. He could see rumpled clothing, empty beer bottles, ashes and sunflower seed shells, but no Crosby. Wearily, he rose from the back bed and put on a pair of shorts that had been lying on the floor. Opening the side doors of the van, Tosh greeted the new day and then began to sweep out the sunflower seed shells with the side of his hand.

At that moment, an old Cutlass pulled up. Crosby stumbled out of the car and gingerly shut the door, as if the noise from slamming it would have agitated his aching skull. The car drove away quickly and noisily, air rumbling out of the hole in its muffler.

Crosby's hair was completely disheveled. His shirt was torn and he had some kind of dried substance all over his face.

"Please tell me you didn't get raped," said Tosh.

Crosby smiled.

"I got laid on a haystack last night," cracked Tosh, "but why do I get the feeling it didn't compare to your night?"

*   *   *   *

The Dunk n' Dine had a pleasant country charm. Red and white checkered, vinyl tablecloths covered the small round tables. Two huge spider plants dominated the front window, while tamer plants hung along the side. A yellow linoleum floor and powder blue curtains gave the decor a *Pee Wee's Playhouse* feel. Scattered throughout the small cafe were photographs of local barns, most in some state of disrepair. Tidy and well kept, only numerous burn marks left in the tablecloths by sloppy smokers scarred the Dunk N' Dine.

Tosh and Crosby sat exhausted but extremely satisfied at the counter.

"Tapioca pudding and a *what?*" asked Tosh.

"A reticulated python."

"That sounds disgusting."

"Trust me," said Crosby. "It was amazing." He sipped his black coffee and opened the Buford Digest.

"Probably get some type of reptilian disease," Tosh murmured. He felt a little jealous that his romp in the haystack with Sally didn't measure up to Crosby's bizarre carnal adventure.

The waitress placed Crosby's order in front of him. "Here ya go, darlin'. The 'Three Mushroom Omelet.'"

Though Crosby would hardly be considered a gourmet, his years of working in the deli taught him a thing or two about food and gave him a particular yen for mushrooms. Crosby folded up his paper and put it down beside him. Salivating, he pondered the steaming egg creation on his plate. What types of mushrooms were in that omelet? Truffles from France? Shitakes from Japan? Portobellos?

Excited that this little hick diner in the middle of Kansas could proffer three distinct types of 'shrooms, Crosby cut into his omelet. But inside, to his despair, he found just what the menu had read — three mushrooms. Three ordinary, run-of-the-mill mushrooms plopped right in the middle of his Plain-Jane breakfast.

"I should have known," Crosby mumbled.

"Hash browns and coffee make a man feel fine," said the waitress as she placed a huge plate of the golden fried potatoes in front of Tosh.

"Among other things," Tosh snickered.

The waitress shot him a shameful glance, but Tosh had already dug his fork in. Always conserving their precious cash, this was the first real meal Tosh and Crosby had eaten in a while. They had been dining on the many canned goods they had stuffed into the van, things like Campbell's Chunky Soup, Cream of Broccoli, Spaghetti-O's, Chef-Boy-R-Dee Raviolis and Pepper Pot. (Whatever that was.)

And plenty of re-fried beans. It might not have been the wisest meal choice for two guys spending lots of time together in a car, but nachos was one of their favorite dishes and Tosh and Crosby were not about to deny themselves. Hedonism was a theme of the trip, they declared, not prevention.

They left home with 18 bags of nacho chips, chips made from red corn, white corn and blue corn, chips flavored with lime and chili, black bean and sour cream. They had giant chips and bite-size chips. Their selection of salsas was no less impressive.

Making nachos without an oven was no easy task, but why eat boring every night? Accepting the challenge, they used their campfires and small propane stove to the best of their abilities.

It began with a pile of corn chips in a skillet. After heating up the beans in a can, (stirring frequently,) they'd scoop them on top and add some grated cheddar. Then, they covered the pan and let it sit over the fire for a few minutes. Once the entire concoction was warm, they'd pour a whole mess of salsa over it. They didn't have meat, but it sure beat another can of soup.

*   *   *   *

Tosh drove the van while Crosby hung his bare foot out the passenger side window. "Where are we going?" he asked.

"Why are you concerned?" retorted Tosh. "We don't need to be anywhere, right?"

"We are heading east. We just came from the east. What, are we going home? Trip's over already?"

"We're going to Sally's farm. She wants to show me the pigs."

"The pigs?"

"Yeah."

"Why?"

"I don't know, because she loves pigs. The pig pen is one of her favorite places."

"Why didn't she just show you last night?"

"'Cause it was dark and they were sleeping."

"And she was too busy playing with your little piggy." Crosby ran his fingers up Tosh's arm and tickled his neck. "And this little piggy ran all the way home."

"Something like that."

"Come on, dude," Crosby urged, "let's hit the road. We've got no time for pigs."

"What are you talking about? We've got nothing but time."

"There's a whole country out there and you want to play the fucking farmer in the dell, man. Hi ho dedario..."

"Listen, Mr. 'Nothing Ever Happens In Kansas — Kansas Is Flat And Boring.' Kansas wasn't too boring last night, was it?"

"It wasn't flat, either."

*   *   *   *

Tosh drove the van down a dirt driveway to where Sally stood waiting.

"Let me get this straight. We're here to see pigs?" Crosby said without even introducing himself.

"Yes-sir-ree-bob," Sally responded cheerfully.

"Sally, this is my friend, Crosby."

"Howdy, Crosby."

"Howdy."

Tosh and Crosby hopped out of the van but Crosby landed in a puddle, splashing brown liquid up his leg. "Oh, shit."

"No, I think it's just mud," Sally chided.

"Now you'll look like one of them," laughed Tosh.

"What is that *smell?*"

"That's pigs!"

"You get used to it," said Sally.

Crosby grimaced. "I don't think I want to."

"I can smell 'em, but I can't see 'em," said Tosh. "Where are they?"

"Behind the barn. Follow me."

Sally led the guys past two cylindrical feed towers and around the barn to a corral that had an open-walled shelter and troughs at the near end.

"So, Sally, this is one of your favorite places?"

"Yes, Crosby. It is."

"May I ask why?"

"You may."

"Why?"

Sally explained that she loved to see the affection the pigs showed each other. "You have to see how they sleep," she said. "They all pile on top of each other. It's so cute."

"Sounds uncomfortable," said Crosby.

"No, they *cuddle,*" said Sally. "And I love to watch the mothers care for the babies."

"The piglets?" asked Tosh.

"Yes, the piglets!" Sally screamed. "They're so cute!"

"You're pretty passionate about pigs, huh?"

"Pigs are beautiful creatures. They are so gentle and caring."

"I've never seen a real live pig before," Crosby said, as if he had just realized it.

"The only pig I've ever seen was pulling someone over on the side of the road," cracked Tosh.

Or on my plate, he thought. Tosh remembered one Homecoming at the fraternity a few years earlier. Many alumni had come to visit and to celebrate, they held a pig roast.

At sunrise that morning, Tosh greeted the hog "chef," arriving to set up the rotisserie. The man resembled the animals he bred. At six and a half feet tall and a rotund 375 pounds, Jeremiah wore a very wide pair of overalls and big old boots. His straggly hair poured out from under his grimy Caterpillar hat. A long beard hid his crusty mouth where rotten teeth spit out brown wads of tobacco juice.

This man is going to cook for me, Tosh had thought.

Despite his appearance, however, Jeremiah turned out to be a cool guy. He knew the words to every Hank Williams Jr. song and he even liked to "burn one down" every now and then. Tosh and Jeremiah struck a little bargain. In return for a constant supply of cold drafts, Jeremiah gave Tosh the best cut of pork.

All day long, the pig had roasted. Turning over and over, the juices dripped into the fire, causing a constant sizzle. Every hour Tosh would check on its progress and, every hour, more and more curious and hungry men would join him. Finally, by five or so that evening, the skin had browned and cracked and the men were at last allowed to taste the smell that had been wafting under their noses throughout the day.

The hog farmer sliced the pig into tons of tender, juicy, fresh ham. Tosh never ate so much pork in his life. Up until then, he had never even really *liked* pork.

"Uh oh," said Sally. "It's feeding time."

"Oh man," gawked Crosby.

The pigs did not, in any way, resemble what Sally had described. They ate frantically and spastically, like sharks during a feeding frenzy. Literally throwing themselves into their food, some of them climbed *into* the feeder. While snorting and/or farting loudly (Who could tell?), in addition to the grain in their bin, they ate the slop off of each other's faces and out of the mud. They ate the mud too.

Some of the pigs were defecating as they ate. "In one end, out the other," said Crosby.

"*Gentle* and *cute* are not words I would use to describe these pigs," said Tosh.

"It's because they're eating. They're only like this during mealtime," Sally reasoned.

Mealtime for swine compared to nothing in the human world, they determined. It went beyond a celebration, deeper than an orgy, partly utter bliss and partly a fight for survival.

The madness continued, the pigs wolfing down whatever came within reach of their mouths, including mud, manure and other pig parts.

"I've never seen anything like it. It's a shit factory," said Tosh.

Sally cringed. Even for a veteran, it was a tough sight to behold.

"Oh my God!" yelled Crosby, laughing. "Look! That one is eating the other pig's shit right out of his ass! He's dining on his ass!!"

Tosh shook his head in disgust. "What a *pig,*" he said.

*   *   *   *

After getting intimate with the pigs, Tosh and Crosby were treated to hot showers at Sally's house. They needed it too, for they hadn't bathed for a few days.

Tosh got the first shower. It felt so good. He stood in the hot water for a few minutes, letting the steam build up. The soothing water shot out of the nozzle forcefully, hitting the back of his neck and running down his back.

Already, life on the road made Tosh and Crosby appreciate things they usually took for granted. A clean bathroom, for instance. They had become accustomed to an indefinite bathing schedule. Most urban areas offered an opportunity to cleanse themselves, whether it be a YMCA or a public shower. Otherwise, they took a dip in a lake or river, which usually proved to be more refreshing than cleansing.

Still, they tried their best to maintain their hygiene. They washed their faces and brushed their teeth daily, always in some highway restroom offering bizarre French condoms or Exxon Kamasutras. Some were reasonably clean with breathable air, some toilet paper and maybe a hook for a towel.

Most restrooms, though, produced a rancid stench that reached them even before entering. Tosh and Crosby didn't mess around in those babies. They kept it all business. Don't touch anything except the sink nozzles, keep your towel around your neck and probably hold in your shit till the next stop.

One joint outside of Clarksburg, West Virginia was too disgusting to even piss in. They had actually found a whole load on the back of the toilet seat. By the looks of the petrified turd, it had been there for a while.

Luckily, neither Tosh nor Crosby had a problem with defecating in a public restroom. Crosby never thought twice about it. He could lay an egg on national TV. It wasn't always that way for Tosh, however.

Growing up, he had always been bashful when it came to moving his bowels, afraid to give it a go if there were people even *near* the bathroom. But a college education goes a long way.

Tosh had been forced to overcome his shyness when he joined his fraternity, because there was no such thing as privacy in the frat house. Traffic flowed constantly through the bathrooms, and to make matters worse, they had no stalls around the toilets.

Eventually, the whole experience became as banal (not anal) as shaving, shitting right next to his buddies, sharing the sports page, passing the lone role of toilet paper back and forth.

After all, they were fraternity brothers.

* * * *

"What's your best burrito?"

"That would probably be the Deluxe, sir."

"What's in it?"

"Well, ya got yer re-fried beans. Ya got yer cheese. Ya got yer choice of meat and ya got yer salsa."

"What about guacamole and sour cream?"

"Oh yeah. Sour cream is extra."

"No guacamole?" said Crosby, a little perturbed.

The zit-faced teenager behind the counter just stared at him blankly.

Tosh ordered the chicken burrito for comparison. They both sucked.

"How can you charge extra for sour cream?" Tosh asked Crosby under his breath as he washed down the pasty food with a lemonade.

"That *is* nervy," Crosby responded, refusing to finish his burrito. "Damn, these fools don't even know what guacamole *is!* How can you call that Mexican?"

"Disgraceful," Tosh agreed.

"We should have known. We shouldn't have even wasted our time and money in an amateur place like this. We're in the middle of Kansas, for God's sake."

Tosh took a deep breath and offered Crosby some lemonade. "Cros, if we're searching for The Ultimate Burrito, we've got to give every place a fair shot. You never know — we may find it in the weirdest place."

* * * *

In the evening Tosh and Crosby had some time to kill. That night, they and the girls had plans to have dinner at Dorothy's, get drunk and play Twister naked.

The guys used the time to straighten out Josephine. Things had become a mess. Sunflower seed shells, empty soda cans, ashes, junk food wrappers and newspapers littered the van. Tosh made Crosby throw out the Snapple bottles filled with his spit from chewing tobacco.

"What do you save that stuff for?" Tosh asked him.

Their clothes, some dirty and some clean, were strewn about, so Crosby combined all their dirty laundry and took it to the laundromat. Tosh used the time to put everything back in order and sweep out the van — the first housekeeping session since they had left home.

The guys had been on the road for a week. They didn't have anything mapped out and the only place they knew they wanted to explore was the west coast. Other than that, they figured they would just wing it.

29

For the first few days, they just drove. If it were up to Crosby, they wouldn't have stopped until California. Crosby thought anyplace else would be a bore and a waste of time, but Tosh pointed out that the whole trip was about discovering new things and how would he know what kind of things went on in Kansas unless they stopped to hang out? To finally convince his friend, Tosh had offered to let Crosby choose the place where they would stop.

"Oh, like it *matters!*" Crosby had exclaimed sarcastically. To emphasize his skepticism, he made his decision by closing his eyes and bringing his finger down on the map.

His finger had landed on Buford.

*   *   *   *

Coed naked Twister never materialized. After a huge lasagna meal, a couple of bottles of burgundy and a good-sized spliff, no one felt up to stripping down to their birthday suits and assuming complex acrobatic positions. Instead, they opted to fast forward to where the night inevitably headed – fornication.

*   *   *   *

The next morning, Tosh and Crosby found themselves at the counter of the Dunk n' Dine once again. Sally was waiting on tables this morning, so she put their breakfast on the house.

"Altoids? The breath mints?"

"Yeah," said Crosby. "The 'Curiously Strong' ones."

"How many?"

"A handful of 'em."

"Damn." Tosh took a bite of bacon.

"Yeah," said Crosby. "I'm still tingling."

The guys ate the rest of their breakfast silently, except for occasional little groans of pleasure.

After devouring their foot-high stacks of flapjacks hot off the griddle, Tosh and Crosby sat back and washed them down with refills of hot black coffee.

"Dude," Crosby began, "this is too good to be true. Free breakfasts, hot showers, a clean, private crapper and two gorgeous girls that totally dig us. Basically, it just doesn't get any better than this."

"And you didn't want to stop in Kansas," Tosh reminded him.

"I don't want to hear it."

They relaxed a bit more in the warm sunshine that filtered through the two large front windows. Tosh watched Sally joke with one of her local customers. She giggled and pushed back the blonde curls that had fallen in her face. She was beautiful.

"I can't believe there are girls this good-looking in Kansas. We should just hang here for the rest of the trip," he remarked, half-jokingly.

While Crosby attempted to do the *Buford Gazette's* crossword puzzle with little success, Tosh folded up the rest of the paper. He neatly piled up their empty plates and utensils and pushed them to the edge of the counter for Sally to pick up.

There he noticed a small, colorful cardboard box. It read, "Celestial Seasonings Herb Teas."

Where did this come from? he wondered.

The front of the box displayed a detailed picture of a forest setting. Evergreens, birch trees and ferns grew abundantly. A squirrel and rabbit joined an owl and bear watching a boy and girl pick blackberries with their docile white horse. Their faces held pleasant expressions as they filled their wicker baskets with the plump berries. In the background stood a quaint cottage with a red chimney. Birds and butterflies flew by.

Tosh studied the enchanting scene for a minute. *I'd like to go there,* he thought. Tosh inspected the rest of the box and found, on the back, the following quote:

"As you think, you travel; and as you love you attract. You are today where your thoughts have brought you; you will be tomorrow where your thoughts take you. You cannot escape the result of your thoughts, but you can endure and learn... You will realize the vision (not the idle wish) of your heart, be it base or beautiful...for you will always gravitate towards that which you, secretly, most love. Whatever your present environment might be, you will fall, remain or rise with your thoughts, your vision, your ideal. You will become as small as your controlling desire; as great as your dominant aspiration."

— James Allen

"Let me borrow that pen," said Tosh.

Crosby, focused on the paper, answered without looking up. "I'm doing the crossword."

"You only have three words. Just give me the pen for a second."

"It's hard," said Crosby, passing Tosh the Bic ballpoint.

Tosh grabbed a napkin and wrote:

Sally,

I'm so glad I met you. Thanks for making our brief stay in Kansas so pleasurable. You are a great hostess. Drop me a line some time. Maybe you can come and visit the ocean. It's worth the trip.

Love,
Tosh

31

He added his address and phone number and left the note under the Celestial Seasonings box.

"Give me the pen, Tosh. I think I got another one."

"Take it with you," said Tosh. "Come on. We've got traveling to do."

CHAPTER 3

After a full workout wrestling with a stubborn, nearly drained lighter, Crosby's thumb had become sore. Fed up, he threw the lighter down in disgust.

Josephine had lost her dashboard lights just outside of Ogallala, Nebraska. In order to view the gauges, the guys needed light provided by the instant flame.

A flashlight would have been a lot more practical, but they didn't have one. What planning — a cross-country journey without a flashlight. They had everything from a dartboard to glow-in-the-dark rubber dinosaurs, but no flashlight. They did have a lantern, but Crosby reasoned that it would be unsafe to have burning kerosene inside the van.

Tosh picked up the lighter and tried to coax one last spark. "Oh Precious Flame. Director of the Dashboard, Creator of the Campfire, Commander of the Coleman, Master of Marijuana, Giver of Light and Heat. Where would we be without you?"

"Shut up Tosh. Just try to dig up some matches. If we can't get that joint lit, I'm gonna eat it."

Tosh searched the glove compartment. Brushing aside the van's legal documents, a pen, condoms and a brown paper bag containing money for beer and gas, Tosh found a lone match.

No book.

No cover.

No way to light that spliff.

He put the joint down among the hodgepodge on top of the engine cover and got up to search his backpack for matches. Located between the two front seats, the engine cover served as the van's only "table" and naturally accumulated an assortment of crapola.

First and foremost it held the van's stereo, which Crosby had yanked out of the dash in order to repair the tape-deck. He failed to fix it and, making matters worse, failed to reinsert it, leaving an unattractive rectangular vacancy in the center of the dashboard. Keenly suspecting that radio reception throughout the majority of their travels would yield only static or country music, Tosh and Crosby refused to drive cross-country without a functioning tape deck and so brought along a portable boom-box as well.

Cassettes, loose change and empty bottles further cluttered the engine cover, and overlooking the mess were Fred and Barney — the miniature dinosaurs Crosby had brought for good luck.

Finally, on top of the engine cover sat the alarm clock. That damn clock! It had terrorized them throughout their first few days on the road.

Late the first night of their trip, the alarm announced itself with a startling ring. Tosh and Crosby, unable to locate where the muffled sound came from, tore apart the innards of Josephine. They searched underneath the beds, below the seats and in the hollows along the rear sides of the van that functioned as cabinets.

Aggravatingly, they could not find it.

During the next few days, the alarm would shriek like a screech owl at completely random and usually inconvenient times. At these moments, the boys stopped whatever they were doing and searched frantically, honing in on the shrill ring for guidance.

It was to no avail.

Finally, later in the week, Crosby was digging deep in his backpack for a clean pair of underwear when his hand grabbed something solid. To his surprise, he pulled out a small travel alarm. As if mocking him completely, the nervy clock went off in his hand.

Crosby did not remember packing the item, and chalked it up to his trusty mom throwing it in along with some extra boxer shorts. Good old Mom. An alarm clock. She just didn't get that the whole point of the trip was to get away from such restrictions.

Having found the source of their ire, the boys had celebrated immediately by diving into one of the coolers and cracking open a couple of Bud nips. Crosby laughed, remembering he had actually searched in the cooler a few days earlier.

Now, the alarm answered to them. After subduing the brazen clock, they forced the brass and glass critter under their control. It sat silent atop the engine cover, telling them the time whenever *they* desired, only jingling its siren if Tosh and Crosby gave it the command, which they didn't plan on doing.

While Tosh searched for matches, Crosby grew impatient and began rummaging through the odds and ends on the engine cover, looking for the joint.

"Keep your eyes on the road!" shouted Tosh.

"What the hell for? Josephine can drive herself. This road is as straight as the Brady Bunch."

"Just do me that favor. Look at the road."

"There's nothing out here, man." Crosby spit his tobacco juice into an empty Gatorade bottle. "If we had cruise control, I'd catch some zees while Jo drove us straight to California. Granted, she may take out the occasional rodent. But shit, buzzards gotta eat too."

$$* \quad * \quad * \quad *$$

Crosby looked at Tosh lying on the back bed. How content he seemed — sleeping pleasantly, probably dreaming about sexual escapades with some exotic woman he encountered overseas.

Sleeping pleasantly, deep in slumberland, while Crosby fed himself another cup of stale, black, truck-stop coffee.

Sleeping pleasantly, spread out on the back bed, while Crosby tried to stretch his cramped legs and aching back at 60 miles per hour.

Sleeping pleasantly, warm and comfy, while Crosby rolled the window down a crack, hoping the cool night air would revive his heavy, bloodshot eyes.

Sleeping pleasantly, oblivious to everything around him, while Crosby futilely searched the radio on the engine cover for some type of entertainment to pass time on the endless road.

Sure, Crosby could have pulled the van over, said "To hell with it" and caught some shut-eye. He did not have to flirt with the fringes of fatigue, push himself to the edge of exhaustion and let the highway lull him into the lower levels of lassitude.

After all, they didn't have to be anywhere. They didn't even know where they were going. They were just driving. Destination wherever.

But that didn't matter.

The point was that Crosby was now a traveler. He was a beatnik nomad, crossing this great land at his own whim, searching for adventure. He was a drifter, living on the road.

For this reason, he could not let the road get the best of him. What kind of voyager would he be if he gave into the travails of the highway? He had to be in control, master of his domain. For Crosby, this was not just a drive but also a contest of wills, a test of endurance.

It was the darkness versus his vision. The monotony against his sanity. The hours versus his strength.

But he did not fight this battle alone.

Crosby had Josephine on his side.

It was pavement versus rubber. The elements versus performance. Mileage versus durability.

It was small, winged insects against headlights.

Crosby intended to prove that they were worthy of this trek, if only to himself. He would continue until...until...until when? Crosby, like a seasoned journeyman, figured he would know when he got there.

*   *   *   *

The time had come to wake up Tosh.

Lowering his face towards his friend's until they were nose to nose, Crosby spoke ever so softly. "Boo."

Tosh sprang up, startled and sleepy-eyed. "Wha— What? What is it? What happened?"

"Take it easy, dude. It's morning."

"What time is it?"

"Five forty-five."

"That's not morning. I'm going back to sleep."

"C'mon, dude. You gotta see this."

"Where are we?"

"Just come look."

Tosh threw on a hat, sweatshirt and flip-flops. He cleaned the crusties out of his eyes and took a swig of Crosby's orange juice. The day's first light filtered through the blinds that provided Josephine with a little privacy.

Crosby opened the side doors and Tosh jumped out.

"Holy shit!" Tosh could not believe his eyes. He had seen nothing but cornfields for the past few days. "I thought the Grand Canyon was in Arizona."

"It is."

"How did we get to Arizona?"

"We didn't. We're in South Dakota."

Tosh studied the magnificent cliffs that he stood above and gazed at the wide-open plains in the distance. "What is it?"

"It's the edge of the world," Crosby said with a far-away look.

"South fuckin' Dakota. Damn. I never knew anything like this existed in South Dakota."

Crosby seemed lost in contemplation. Finally, in a reverent tone, he said, "*This, my friend, is the Badlands.*"

They stood silently, side by side. Daylight crept through the sky though the sun was not yet visible. A cool breeze whistled past, disrupting the awesome silence. Not a creature stirred, not even a mouse.

The Badlands were a series of small canyons carved into the earth, forming an endless maze of jagged clay hills that stretched as far as the eye could see. Though every hill had a different shape, it seemed impossible to distinguish one from another. They all had a pale rust color with dark horizontal lines. Only an occasional tumbleweed graced the barren mounds left standing by raging water many centuries ago.

Tosh peered down the bluff he stood upon, making sure he kept a safe distance from the edge. *No need to have a close-up look at the texture of the cliff,* he thought, wincing at the idea of his flesh being scraped from his bones as he slid and bounced all the way down the rocky precipice.

It's strange how distance affects perception, he thought, looking down a couple of hundred feet to the scrubby valley below. He knew the ravines were all roughly the same depth. Yet, as he surveyed the immense land, the more distant the ridge, the flatter it seemed. This common optical illusion amazed Tosh at that insane hour of the morning.

Crosby gaped far into the distance. As the orange sun peeked over the flat horizon, he took a deep breath. The vista looked like a canvas. Was he really part of this beauty surrounding him? Canyons, plains, a river in the background. Gorgeous land that, throughout the better part of time, has withstood geological shifts, blizzards, floods and droughts. Earth that has seen millions of lives come and go. Ground that will endure until the planet ceases to exist.

Suddenly, Crosby felt very small and meaningless. He adjusted his filthy cap and skipped over to Josephine. He pulled the sleeping bag and blankets off one of the benches and pried it open. While propping open the lid with his left hand, Crosby reached into the cooler with his right and yanked out two icy cold beers.

"Here, Tosh."

"Ho! Beer — it's not just for breakfast anymore." Tosh cracked the lid and took a healthy swig. "Here's to a beautiful day."

Crosby touched his bottle to Tosh's. "It's good to be alive."

*   *   *   *

Tosh and Crosby got some exercise by hiking up and down the mounds of earth, searching for secret paths and Indian artifacts.

After stretching their legs for an hour or so, they decided to get back on the road and see more of the enchanting area. Tosh cranked up his namesake — Peter Tosh's *Mama Africa* — and with the driving reggae beat filling the fresh South Dakota morning air, they slowly followed the winding highway through the Badlands.

As Crosby guided their way through curve after curve, Tosh augmented his breakfast of hops and barley malt with some delicious sunflower seeds.

Sunflower seeds were a staple of their existence. Tosh picked up the habit in college when he would go through a bag every study session. Crosby chewed the little buggers as well, frequently in left field during his soft ball games or while he worked on his art projects.

A seasoned chewer did not have to think about deshelling the seeds. The process became instinctive.

First, Tosh would suck the seed to taste the salt and moisten the shell. Next, he'd maneuver the kernel onto his molars, lean it on its side and bite down just enough to crack the shell without crushing it. Then, he used his tongue to move the opened shell under his top front teeth, which pried the seed out. Finally, ushering the liberated seed beneath his agile tongue, Tosh would discard the remains of its casing by spitting it into a cup.

Or, in this particular instance, out the window.

Because seeds were natural and biodegradable, Tosh did not consider this littering. He justified his expectorating of refuse into the environment by rationalizing that the seed shells had come from the earth and he was simply returning them. It didn't really matter, anyway, since the majority of the shells were blowing right back in the window and landing on and around Crosby's backpack.

At this precious point in the seed-eating process, Tosh would bring the tiny treat out from under his tongue and eat it. Sometimes, feeling ambitious, he'd build up a collection of seeds underneath his tongue and eat them all at once. This enabled him to obtain a true taste of the sunflowers' germ. The most he had ever hoarded away at once was thirteen, while studying the Yanomami Indians of the Orinoco River Basin for his anthropology class.

Tosh and Crosby didn't really chew the sunflower seeds for dining purposes. More like chewing tobacco than eating a meal, the seeds had little nutritional value. In fact, they were extremely fattening. And they hardly curbed hunger — they certainly didn't satisfy the craving for a cheeseburger.

Ooh, a cheeseburger! Tosh could go for one of those babies in a big way. He hadn't eaten one in weeks. His mouth began to water as he thought back to the best burger he had ever consumed — the day he truly understood how Jimmy Buffet felt when he praised America's delicacy, the day Tosh had his "Cheeseburger in Paradise."

The event occurred a couple of summers back when Tosh and Crosby and some buddies had rented a house on Long Beach Island. It had been a gorgeous summer day, and Tosh sat on the deck enjoying the serene evening's last light.

Taking his plump burger with cheese (white American) off the grill, he gingerly placed it on a sesame seed bun. He added Gulden's Spicy Brown Mustard and the incomparable Heinz Ketchup, creating a funky crimson and gold swirl. To wash down this feast, of course, Tosh popped an icy cold brew.

He sat shirtless at the picnic table overlooking the rippled bay. The cool, gentle breeze kept the pesky skeeters and greenheads away. No one intruded. It was just Tosh and his burger.

As Tosh slowly bit into the meaty treat, he could feel the warm juice ooze out of the beef onto his lips. He smiled and the natural gravy dribbled from his lips down onto the tip of his chin. He let it hang there on the edge of his chin for a minute as he gazed into the succulent, pink meat, cherishing every moment of the experience.

The juice dripped from his chin onto his bare stomach and rolled into his belly button. It didn't matter. He was alone. Just him and his burger and his greasy lips.

He chewed the cheeseburger, taking time, savoring the flavor of the beef. Tosh tasted the cheese and enjoyed the softness of the bread.

His stomach rumbled, wanting that beef, that luscious beef! That cattle bred, butchered, processed and packaged for human consumption.

Agghhh! How did that thought creep into his tasty recollection?

It made sense, though. Lately, Tosh had, once again, been considering becoming a vegetarian. As one who truly loved animals and respected all forms of life, eating meat had become a troubling question of ethics. It bothered him that his eating habits supported death.

Tosh had heard all the arguments. He knew the animals were raised for culinary purposes; the industry provided many jobs.

It was true — *animals* ate animals. Yes, if humans did not regulate the populations of cattle and chickens and pigs, the animals would starve to death anyway.

Still, whenever Tosh ate chicken, he couldn't help but think about the little motherly hens sitting on their (scrambled, over-easy, hard-boiled) eggs. Whenever Tosh dined on steak he thought of the docile cows chewing grass on the side of the road, lazily eyeing him as they shooed the incessant flies away with their long, stringy tails.

These frequent feelings of guilt had prompted Tosh to try to give up meat. If he had any kind of will power, he would have been a vegetarian by now. But, time after time, the damn cookouts got him.

He could make it as much as two weeks eating only salads and pasta and soups and cereal. Then, his friends would fire up the grill. Burgers, dogs, steaks, chicken. A warm sunny day. A keg of beer. Wiffle ball.

Tradition.

Watching his friends happily gorge themselves on sizzling beef and spicy, barbecued poultry, Tosh's mustard and cucumber sandwich just didn't cut it. A couple of Budweisers coupled with the hissing sound of the meat's juices dripping onto the hot coals of the grill got him every time. He always broke down.

Soon Tosh would be basting breasts and flipping burgers, his mouth watering, his stomach growling impatiently. "Screw it," he'd say. "Meat's a treat. Buffet would be proud."

Tosh's moral will had lost the war, but it did manage to win one small battle — veal. Tosh renounced veal cold turkey after, late one night at school, he saw an alarming documentary on the ranching process.

Wedged deep into his shabby yet comfortable couch, high on weed, Tosh had flipped through the cable stations. He settled on the Discovery Channel, hoping to catch an interesting piece on the clouded leopard or the reticulated python. Instead, he became entranced and then appalled by the graphic depiction of veal ranching.

Little calves lie cramped, bound in chains, in dark, dingy little stalls. They were fed nothing but a milky gruel. The ranchers completely restricted the animals' mobility from birth up until the end of their hellish, brutal lives. *How horrible*, Tosh thought. Never seeing the big blue sky. Never stretching your legs. Never feeling the warm sun on your back while grazing on fresh grass as the breeze blew over your snout.

How unfair. Inhumane. Cruel.

It's one thing to slaughter a steer or pig after he has lived the good life — having the run of the pastures, chowing on unlimited tasty hay and stuff — but to prevent an animal from even enjoying the fruits of his pre-destined life?

Tosh cringed at the scrawny young cattle with sad sunken eyes and swore he would never eat veal again. He did not take too much pride in this decision, however, for he knew it was not much of a sacrifice; his friends never barbecued veal.

The sun burned bright at 7:37am and Josephine purred like a kitten. As she rounded one turn, Crosby pulled on to the shoulder and braked to a stop. Nearby, in a field off the road, stood three pronghorn deer.

A couple of families with U-haul trailers had stopped along with Tosh and Crosby to view the wildlife.

Two male deer were dueling. With lowered heads, they crashed their antlers together like battering rams. One deer drove the other back until the other returned the favor. Back and forth, the two deer jostled while the third, a female, watched on, seemingly unimpressed by this display of bravado.

"This is cool! They're dukin' it out," said Crosby excitedly. "Do you think they're fighting over the female?"

"Definitely", Tosh answered. "*Does,* you can't live with 'em, you can't live without 'em."

"Two guys fighting over a woman. Just like the bars back in Jersey."

Tosh wondered what the doe was thinking. Was she rooting for a specific buck to win? Would she go home with the victor, awed by his machismo? Or was she a compassionate doe? Maybe she would mate with the loser as an act of consolation, a sympathy fuck, stressing that he gave it his best shot and that's all that counts.

Who knew — maybe she was a promiscuous little doe and she'd end up doing them both.

"It's like they're putting on a show for all of us," Crosby commented.

At that moment, the two male deer stopped wrestling and scanned the area, as if they had suddenly become aware of their audience.

"What the hell are they looking at?"

The deer casually walked away from each other.

"No more fighting," said Tosh. "Cops are coming."

The guys watched the pronghorn a little longer and then determined that the bout was indeed over.

"That's it," Crosby concluded. "They're grazing."

*   *   *   *

Just beyond the Badlands, Tosh and Crosby stopped in the tourist trap of Wall, South Dakota. They brushed their pasty teeth and shaved in the fairly sanitary bathroom of the Mobil station. A quick dip in a motel swimming pool took the place of a shower.

Crosby, reading a newspaper spread out on the ground in front of him in the motel parking lot, scoffed down some glazed donuts and chocolate milk. "Yanks won," he said. "Three in a row now."

Tosh ran a towel over his head, his dreads heavy with the weight of water. "I love the smell of chlorine," he said, climbing into the van to change out of his wet shorts. Reaching into his backpack, he found some Umbro shorts and his beloved Jamaican Style T-shirt.

Tosh grabbed the journeyman's Bible, the road atlas, and tossed it on to Crosby's newspaper. "Where to?"

Crosby opened the road atlas. "Let's see here. Hmm. We're close to Mount Rushmore. We should check that out."

"Mount Rushmore? Isn't that the place with the faces carved into it?"

"Yep. Four presidents."

"Damn, I didn't know that was in South Dakota. This state's got everything."

"Whaddaya think? Shall we do Rushmore?"

"Rushmore it is."

*   *   *   *

"What is that? Is that a nose?" Crosby questioned.

They caught glimpses of Mount Rushmore as Tosh drove through the Black Hills National Forest.

"Maybe it's a chin."

As the highway wound through the mountains, Crosby ran around the inside of the van trying to get a good look at the granite mug shots. Finally, the road allowed them to get a full view of the presidents preserved in stone.

"That is tremendous," said Crosby.

"Respect to the dude that did that," Tosh added.

They arrived at the entrance to the Mount Rushmore National Memorial along with hundreds of Winnebagos, trailers, vans and station wagons full of families with screaming children. It seemed like a major production to park the van, wait on line and trek through the park, all the while wading through the hordes of annoying tourists.

"All this and we've already seen the damn thing," lamented Tosh.

"Plus we have to pay."

"Do you want to deal with all this?"

"Not really. But I'd like to find out a little bit about how the guy did this, you know? It's pretty crazy."

As they sat in the van and decided what to do, a young boy passing by wet his pants and began crying hideously. A heavyset woman, probably his mother, lifted the damp lad by the armpit and carried him quickly ahead of the rest of the family.

Crosby looked at Tosh, who leaned his head on the steering wheel, disgusted.

"Screw it. I'll read about it in an encyclopedia."

Opting to pass on the crowds and hassles, they drove on.

The Black Hills were beautiful and rustic. Old mines dotted the landscape. They passed over Harney Peak, elevation 7,242 feet, the highest point in South Dakota.

The driving was slow because of the curvy mountainous roads, but they had no hurry.

Soon, Tosh and Crosby itched to get out of the van and do some exploring. As if they had a psychic tour guide, a sign reading **RUSHMORE CAVE – 5 MILES** appeared at a junction in the road. Without even thinking about it, Tosh turned off the highway.

"Good call," said Crosby, showing his support.

They drove on listening to a bootleg tape of the Grateful Dead. Jerry Garcia ripped his way through a "China Cat Sunflower/I Know You Rider" from Red Rocks, Colorado — August 12th 1982, Set II. Tosh and Crosby sang along enthusiastically.

"This is my favorite part!" Crosby shouted. "Jerry gets *so* into it!"

They sang, "I wish I was a headlight, on a northbound train! I'd shine my light through the cool Colorado rain!"

As the Dead slowed down into an intro of "Women Are Smarter," Tosh and Crosby realized a significant time had passed since they had left the highway.

"Could we have missed a turn?" Crosby asked.

"There hasn't been any. Here's a sign."

It said **RUSMORE CAVE – 5 MILES**. Tosh and Crosby looked at each other.

"Great," said Crosby. "What, did all that road we just covered *not count?*"

"Maybe we went in a circle or something."

Crosby looked behind them and saw nothing but a cloud of dry dust kicked up from the road. They drove on throughout "Women Are Smarter" until they saw another sign, reading **RUSHMORE CAVE – 3 MILES.** Tosh slammed on the brakes.

"What are you doing?" Crosby shouted as he peeled himself off of the dashboard.

"At the rate we're going, those next three miles could take an hour."

"Yeah, but we've got nothing *but* time."

"Including gas."

"Ohhh." Crosby hadn't thought about that. "I don't suppose there's a truck stop out here, do you?"

"Nuh-uh."

"It can't be that much farther. We've come this far. Ride on," Crosby commanded.

Tosh followed Crosby's suggestion. It took them the better part of "Terrapin Station," but eventually they arrived at Rushmore Cave. Tosh figured, since they left the highway, they had driven about 15 miles total. "Good deal," he said, "I just hope we have enough gas to get out of here."

Crosby dismissed his concern. "We'll worry about that when the time comes."

They went into the office and learned that the next tour departed in forty-five minutes. The pictures of the cave mounted on the walls looked intriguing so they went back to Josephine to smoke a bowl and have a couple of cold ones to pass the time.

"I can't believe we're in the middle of the Black Hills of South Dakota," Crosby said, more to himself than to Tosh.

"We'll probably never be back here as long as we live. Maybe South Dakota, but not this exact spot, right *here.*"

"I guess we better live it up then, huh?" Crosby cracked open another beer and handed one to Tosh.

They drank their beers and played a little hackey sack, listening to the rest of the Red Rocks bootleg. While Tosh and Crosby volleyed the little broken-in leather sack on their knees and feet, Jerry Garcia, Bob Weir and company cranked out a "The Other One," a "Dear Mr. Fantasy," a "Wharf Rat" and a "Lovelight." Just as Tosh and Crosby had broken into a full sweat, it was time for their tour of Rushmore Cave.

About five families and a few couples, from young children to senior citizens, accompanied the guys on the tour, presumably the overflow of tourists Tosh and Crosby had wanted to avoid at the monument.

A nerdy scientist type of guy, probably around 20 years old, led the tour. He introduced himself as Cliff and no one saw the humor in this except for Mr. Tyler and Mr. Graves, who tried unsuccessfully to stifle their stoned laughter. Tosh and Crosby brought up the rear of the group.

The cave was interesting but lacked excitement. Colorful lighting accentuated some cool stalagmites and some funky stalactites, but overall, the half-hour journey failed to present anything extraordinary. Much of the original beauty had withered away over the years due to a heavy flow of tourist traffic.

Unfortunately, the best part of the whole tour turned out to be the very beginning when the group had to squeeze and twist their way through a narrow, man-made stairway descending into the first chamber of the cave. Most of the tourists squealed and gasped, exaggerating the thrill and inflating their anticipation of the adventure to come.

That had been the extent of any strenuous activity, though. After the group made it into the first chamber, they walked uninhibited and upright the rest of the way. The tour proved to be more of a geology lesson than a challenging scenic venture. It was probably better that way, for the majority of the tourists would have needed a few sessions with Richard Simmons before attempting anything even remotely physically demanding.

At one point, Tosh found himself alone at the back of the line. *Great,* he thought. *Crosby is probably sneaking around in one of the sections that are roped off to the public.* (With good reason.) Tosh hastily backtracked, looking for his unruly friend.

He found Crosby a few rooms back, happily relieving himself on an unlucky stalagmite.

"I couldn't help it," Crosby apologized, noticing Tosh's disgust. "Those beers went right through me."

"This thing took thousands and thousands of years to form, and you're pissing on it. Don't you have any respect for nature? Cliff would go apeshit if he saw you."

"It's just a rock."

The boys hurried back to the group and, luckily, no one had even noticed they'd left. When the tour ended, they thanked Cliff and tipped him modestly. (A lukewarm beer.)

Their cave expedition had ended, but it was a beautiful afternoon and the boys really didn't feel like getting back into the van. Instead, they opted to go for a hike in the surrounding hills.

Crosby could smell the leafy trees and foliage as he stopped to take a deep breath. The sun felt warm but not hot on his face, and a breeze dried the little bit of sweat he worked up climbing the rigorous terrain.

Suddenly, he thought he heard a girl's voice: "What're you gettin' into, silly?"

Up on an extruding bluff, Crosby saw the owner of the voice.

"Tosh, c'mere!" he whispered. With Tosh following, he climbed up to the girl's level but remained hidden in the trees. Grungy but girlish, she wore old sneakers, baggy jeans and a faded T-shirt with an iron-on of Casper the Friendly Ghost. She had her short brown hair in pigtails.

"Who's she talking to?" Tosh asked.

Crosby shrugged.

She looked like an adorable *Denise*-the-Menace. The girl stretched her arms to the sky and arched her back, revealing a belly ring. "Julio, where are you?"

"Julio?" Tosh asked loudly, cringing when he realized he had ruined their cover.

The girl jumped and turned around, surprised to have company. "Who's there?" she asked, as a playful old hound bounded up to her side. "Julio, *get them!"*

"No!" Crosby called. "We come in peace!"

They joined her on the small clearing looking out over the valley.

"We come in peace?" Tosh mocked.

"It was the first thing that came to me. I must have seen it in a movie or something."

The old hound ran to them and sniffed them intensely, wagging his tail.

"Hi," said Tosh as he removed the dog's snout from his crotch. "How are you?"

"Fine," the young lady giggled. "What are you doing here?"

"We were just hiking," explained Crosby. "And we heard your voice. We were wondering who you were talking to."

"Oh. Just my dog."

"Your dog's name is Julio?"

"Yeah. What's wrong with that?"

"Nothing. Nothing at all," said Crosby. "I just never met a dog named Julio. And I've met a lot of dogs."

"He's named after Paul Simon."

This one stumped Crosby. He looked at Tosh, who was trying to make sense out of it himself.

"Oh, *the schoolyard!* 'Me an' Julio Down By the Schoolyard.'" Tosh said after a long moment. "Very cool. Paul Simon is great."

"He's a musical prophet," she said matter-of-factly. Then, after a thought, she added, "And cute too."

"We just came from the Rushmore Cave," Crosby said. "My name's Crosby, by the way, and this is my partner-in-crime, Tosh."

"Oh," she smiled. "My name is Betty-Lou. But you can call me Lulu. Everyone else does. What'd you think about the cave?"

Delicately, so as not to hurt her feelings, Crosby said, "It was nice, but it kind of bored us. We were hoping for something a little less touristy."

"Anything that has signs posted from here to Rapid City will draw tourists. If you want adventure, you should try a cave that doesn't advertise."

"Wish we could."

"Well, you can." Lulu bent down and retied the bandanna around Julio's neck. "It's called Demon's Lair. I run it all the time. My brother and I used to play there when we were kids. Now it's just me and Julio."

"Your dog goes in the cave?"

"No, he just hangs out at the entrance. If for some reason I don't come out by dusk, Julio barks his head off. If no one hears him after a while, he'll run home for help."

Tosh did not want to know what "some reason" for not getting out of the cave might be. He hated the thought of being stuck underground. Like most reggae lovers, Tosh liked sunlight. And the sun sure didn't shine down there, baby.

CHAPTER 4

Lulu led the boys down into a valley. They trekked a couple of hundred yards and then gradually started hiking up a ridge until it became too steep to walk. With still no cave in sight, Tosh feared they might have to actually start climbing the vertical rock face.

Then, he saw it. In a little nook about ten feet away, a storm pipe protruded from the cliff.

"Welcome to my cave!" said Lulu with a Transylvanian accent.

"This is it?" said Tosh, astounded.

"You sound like Count Chocula," Crosby cracked.

"Count Chocula?"

"I mean Dracula," Crosby corrected. "Count Dracula."

"Don't worry. You'll see him and his family soon enough."

"What's that mean?" Tosh asked with concern.

"Bats."

"There're bats in here?" asked Tosh. He hated bats.

"Of course there're bats in here. Where do you think bats live?"

"I don't know. I never really thought about it."

"Don't worry, they're harmless." Lulu reached inside the pipe and pulled out a small burlap bag. She emptied its contents — two flashlights, rope, a lighter, matches and an old pair of work gloves. "They won't bother you if you don't bother them."

That sounds cliché, thought Tosh. "Well, aren't we kind of bothering them just by being in their cave?" He wasn't satisfied with Lulu's lackadaisical estimation of the bats' possible aggressive tendencies.

"Yeah, I guess. If they bite you, bite them back." She put the lighter in her pocket and pulled the gloves on. Lulu checked the power of the flashlights. Both worked. She put the rope back into the burlap bag and threw the bag on the ground at their feet. Julio curled up on top of it.

"What are you worried about, you big baby! You're with an expert!" Lulu winked and handed Tosh a flashlight.

This was true. Tosh felt a little better. "After you, ma'am."

Lulu squeezed into the storm pipe. Tosh went next and then Crosby.

"When you said cave, I pictured its entrance as a huge hole in the cliff," said Tosh. "Something we could walk right into, you know? Like the cave from *Land of the Lost.* I had no idea I'd be squirming through a drain pipe." Tosh's thin nylon shorts were not providing much comfort against the hard rippled steel of the pipe, adding to his anxiety.

"You ain't seen nothing yet."

They all crowded into the first chamber, about the size of a Volkswagen Bug. Tosh searched the walls with the flashlight, looking for bats.

"They're in deeper," Lulu explained. "Bats are nocturnal, so they should be sleeping now anyway."

Tosh hoped they were deep sleepers.

They slipped through a little passage and dropped a few feet down into the next room. Stretching back about thirty feet, it had a lot more space. They could stand straight up and walk around easily. Graffiti covered the walls. Some of it read: Led Zeppelin, The Rat Bastards and Anarchy. A large portrait of two smurfs copulating filled one wall.

"Who's the artist?"

"My brother Barney. He was in a band called The Rat Bastards. They'd hang out here and write songs."

"Wow, how weird."

"They said you could hear Demon's Lair in their music — that the cave influenced their creativity on a subconscious level. I think it was a load of shit."

"What kind of music did they play?"

"Mostly hardcore — but they had a few ballads." Lulu thought for a moment. "They never used to go past this point in the cave, though. They were always too stoned."

They continued on. Lulu moved confidently, giving directions on how to move through the difficult parts of the cave. She would say things like: "Go feet first on your back," "Step here and grab that crack" and "Grip this and squirm on your belly."

Crosby heeded the advice and fared well, keeping up with her.

Tosh had the jitters but his curiosity pushed him. Never in his life had he been in such a place like this. Demon's Lair was a vacuum. The cave was impervious to everything that happened outside — wars, famine, droughts, acid rain, riots, tornadoes, slash-and-burn agriculture, the Oscar Awards and the Super Bowl. The only evidence linking the cave to the outside world were the materials used in its self-construction. Demon's Lair took morsels from the environment and incorporated them into its own unique structure — drops of water and minerals that seeped through tiny cracks in the layers of rock.

All of this occurred, of course, over millions and millions of years. This gave the cave an unchanging appearance, rendering even the ages powerless. With the past and future irrelevant, Tosh felt locked in time. There was a compulsory focus on the present. A profound awareness of the now.

"There're some of the bats."

Bats? That word alerted Tosh. Lulu was pointing her flashlight at a niche a few feet above their heads. Three small brown spheres about the size of hand grenades hung from the ceiling of the cavern. No perceptible features could be discerned.

"That's *them?*" Tosh asked, relieved at their innocuous appearance. He whispered, so as not to wake them.

"They look like brown tennis balls," commented Crosby.

"They're sleeping with their wings wrapped around themselves. A self-made cocoon," Lulu explained. "I wish I could sleep with that kind of privacy. The damn rooster wakes me at sunrise."

Lulu held her hands about nine inches apart. "When they're flying around they're about this big with wingspan."

"Well, let's not wake them."

They spelunked further, passing through extremely narrow crevices — climbing, sliding, jumping. Lulu stated she wanted to take them to a special room about halfway through the grotto.

"We're almost there," she declared as she came to a ten-foot drop.

Tosh was thankful to hear that; he had been noticing more and more bats on the ceiling as they got deeper into the cave.

"This part is kind of tough. Just take it slow and be careful."

A rope, wrapped around a boulder and knotted tightly, hung over the drop. They each grabbed the cord and lowered themselves at their own pace.

Once down the miniature cliff, they turned a corner and found themselves in a fair-sized cavern. A little opening at the back led to Lulu's special room. They had to crouch when entering the hole, an entrance to a tunnel that narrowed as it continued.

Tosh and Crosby wriggled on their stomachs through the very tight passage. The dampness lubricated the cold abrasive stone brushing against their bodies. With their arms outstretched in front of them, they slithered slowly, hoping the end of the tunnel would come soon.

"I feel like I'm being born," said Crosby, inching forward into the darkness.

"Funny you should say that," Lulu replied. "This part of the cave is called the Birth Canal."

They continued on until the tunnel opened suddenly. Pushing themselves out of the tight confines, they stretched their muscles.

Lulu shined her beam.

"Holy shit," gasped Crosby.

The chamber was immense — about the size of a high-school gymnasium. The flashlights showed many great stalagmites hanging from the ceiling. Each structure had many tiers, every one smaller than the next. Like massive icicles with distinct layers, some of the stalagmites stretched all the way down to the floor. Others met stalactites half way. Giant flowstones covered the floor, resembling a rushing river frozen in stone.

"This is the Wedding Cake Room," Lulu said proudly, like a real estate agent displaying a newly finished basement with a hot tub, bar and entertainment center.

"The stalagmites look like upside down wedding cakes! Ain't that cool?"

The three explorers laid down to rest, their flashlights scanning the splendid surroundings. Already caked in rich brown clay, they didn't mind the damp floor.

Demon's Lair matured patiently, musky and still.

Crosby registered the cave's effect on all his senses. The air felt thick and cool around him as his clammy cotton clothes clung to his body. He could hear only the steady splashing of a drop of water over the sound of his breath, so Crosby synched up the pace of his breathing with the rhythm of the dripping.

Up until this point, he had not really acknowledged the full personality of the cave. He had been too anxious to see what awaited them beyond each turn. Was it a huge cavern or tiny chamber? A climb or a drop? Serving as their collective eyes, the flashlights' piercing beams revealed very little at a time, giving the journey added suspense.

At Lulu's suggestion, they simultaneously killed their flashlights. Without the lights, the cave became pure darkness; darkness so thick and final they couldn't see their hands right in front of their faces. No *trace* of illumination existed, the total absence of light rendering their eyes completely useless. They would have been able to detect more with their eyes closed in a bright area than they could in the cave with their eyes wide open.

"This room makes me think of my brother," Lulu said. "We used to hang out here all the time. It was our secret fort. Our hideaway from home."

The pitch of Lulu's voice changed slightly as memories filled her head. "Now I come here when I'm missing him."

"Where's your brother now?" asked Tosh.

Lulu remained silent for a moment. As her eyes began to tear, she spoke softly. "He's dead. He was killed in the Gulf War."

Tosh had not expected such a morose answer. "I'm sorry," he replied hoarsely.

"Luke was a mixed-up kid, but a good person. He went into the Marines to get his shit together. Instead, he died." Lulu tried to stifle the tears. "He just deserved better than that. To die in the desert on the other side of the world. What for?"

Hearing the pain in Lulu's voice made Tosh feel awful. He sat up and without turning his light on, found Lulu's hand to grab. She welcomed his compassionate gesture and squeezed tightly.

"I come here when I want to feel close to him. I'm sorry. They say time heals all wounds, but I guess I just haven't gotten over it yet."

"Don't be sorry!" Crosby remarked. "He was your brother. Crying is the right thing to do."

"My old man doesn't like to see me cry. He says 'It don't help none.'"

"I think it does. If it's what you feel, then let it out. Let it out until it just stops. If you keep your feelings stuffed up inside you, they don't go away. They eat away at you in bits and pieces until you're totally unhappy and you don't even know why. Let your feelings out and they don't bother you constantly."

Crosby thought about it. "Kind of like a pet cat. If you keep him all locked up in the house, he's gonna be stir crazy. He'll scratch the couch and eat the plants and cause all kinds of hell. But if you let him out when he wants, he'll be in control of himself. He'll have the freedom to come and go as he pleases, and when he's around he'll be more pleasant. You can't try to repress your feelings, because they'll end up controlling you."

Crosby knew this from experience. He had always been close to his grandfather. The hard-working, kind man with the big bushy beard shared a lot of time and love with Crosby. After he died, Crosby would fight the sadness and ignore the thoughts of his grandfather that desperately searched for a place inside him. For a short while, Crosby successfully avoided the pain, but stifling the memories of his grandfather caused him to become cranky and angry. He didn't realize it until the day he finally gave in.

He had been searching for a tool in the family's messy garage when he came across an old plastic case. Curious, Crosby opened it up. It was his grandfather's tackle box. Filled with countless stories and acquired wisdom, the box had accompanied Crosby and his grandfather on all of their many fishing trips.

Ashamed he hadn't recognized the keepsake, Crosby immediately broke into tears. But this time he didn't stop himself. He cried for hours until he could cry no more — gut wrenching sobs that covered his face in snot and pounded his throbbing head.

When his tears finally ran out and his eyes dried, Crosby could clearly picture his grandfather. A floppy green fishing cap sat crooked atop his head, pieces of bologna sandwich caught in his beard.

Crosby grinned and then he laughed. He actually felt good.

Lulu cried. Lulu opened herself up and let the emotions she had bottled up for months pour out. Tosh and Crosby listened to her, knowing her cries spoke of many special memories. Memories that were part of her. Memories that will never leave Lulu, but one day may bring her smiles instead of bitter tears.

*   *   *   *

The Gulf War. Tosh remembered staying up late every night with his fraternity brothers, getting stoned and watching the war on television. *Operation Desert Storm* rated second in popularity only to *Monday Night Football*. It might have even beaten out ABC's classic football games if the boys could have bet on it; it had more excitement than a lopsided 37-10 blowout.

They would watch *Sportscenter* on ESPN and then switch over to catch the war highlights on CNN. The two shows went hand in hand. With all of its animated diagrams, interviews, analysis and live-action reporting, CNN's television production of the Gulf War seemed like a sporting event. A classic drama complete with good guys and bad guys, the bout featured a feisty underdog Iraq pitted against the favorite and reigning champion United States.

Tosh wondered about CNN's ultra-slick television coverage. Was it to provide useful information or just to keep millions of viewers glued to the moneymaking brutality? Did the armchair generals at home really need to see through the U.S. pilots' infrared vision? Did they need to hear the effects of land mines described poetically: "Step on this baby and you'll be nothing but a red mist." Did they need to watch Stormin' Norman, Colin Powell and Dick Cheney enthusiastically discuss their battle plans like Dick Vitale breaking down college hoops with Xs and Os?

The overzealous reporting sadly sensationalized the violence in the gulf and reduced the tragedy to a petty contest like a computer video game.

It was pathetic, Tosh knew, but entertaining.

So, in the comfort of their old stone house, Tosh and his fraternity brothers entertained themselves at the expense of the American troops and thousands of dead Iraqis. Alternately fascinated and horrified by the demonstrations of highly advanced, war-mongering technology and the detailed, visual depictions of the turmoil in the sand, the guys would watch bombs drop over a pile of Buffalo wings and a pitcher of draft beer.

Tosh felt guilty about watching the conflict, cozily lying on the couch, while his peers fought for their lives, scared shitless in the desert. For Tosh, the war ended each day when he shut off the television. The young men and women in the Persian Gulf did not have that luxury.

But what could he do? He certainly wasn't going to volunteer for the armed services. Tosh had definite pacifistic tendencies. He hated to see anybody or anything die for any reason.

Yet, he also had the sense to know that this idealistic attitude often didn't apply to our world. Unfortunately, sometimes war was necessary. Or at least unavoidable.

But was the War in the Gulf?

Tosh wanted to believe the government would not send troops into battle unless it was imperative, but he did not trust the government.

The issue confused him. Was this a strategic move necessary to insure the freedom of our country? Were we fighting to protect ourselves from the maniacal leader of Iraq? Should the lives of Americans have been risked to police the Middle East and protect Kuwait?

Tosh wondered if his country were really fighting the war for humanitarian reasons. The motives for sending troops to the Middle East could have been purely economical. Was the United States trading blood for oil?

And ultimately — whatever the reason for the fucking war — is it *worth* it?

Witnessing the war solely by television, these questions seemed almost hypothetical. Now, though, sitting in the thick darkness of the Demon's Lair, Tosh knew the questions were as real as the tears flooding Lulu's eyes.

He also knew the answer.

*   *   *   *

The group made their way back through the Demon's Lair. After resting in the cool Wedding Cake Room for a while, Crosby was raring to go. His zeal catapulted him past Lulu to the front of the group. Feeling drained after her cry, Lulu relinquished her guide duty to the avid rookie spelunker, trusting Crosby would stay out of trouble.

This turned out to be a bad idea.

While Crosby forged ahead, Lulu paused in one dazzling chamber to point out its sparkling walls. Tiny deposits of calcite glittered as she splashed her stream of light over them.

The splendor enclosed in the dark hollows of the planet awed Tosh.

"There is beauty even in the center of the earth," Lulu said.

Crosby's distant voice called out in excitement. "Cool! A secret passage!"

Lulu laughed at Crosby's youthful exhilaration, like a kid exploring a haunted house. All of the sudden, she stopped.

"Whatsa matter?" Tosh asked.

"Secret passage..." Lulu murmured, thinking aloud. "Oh no! Follow me!" She squealed, grabbing Tosh's hand. Lulu quickly led him through the narrow corridor into another chamber and climbed into a small passageway that sat about five feet high. "Wait here," she said, passing her flashlight to Tosh.

Tosh waited uneasily while Lulu bravely crawled through the cramped tunnel, clawing through the dense darkness and calling Crosby's name.

Getting no responses, Lulu felt panic setting in. Then, she saw Crosby's flashlight flickering ahead. The beam bounced off the ceiling and walls but its reflected light did not reveal Crosby's profile. Where was he?

"Lulu?"

"Crosby?"

"Yeah," he said hesitantly, "I'm down here."

As Lulu proceeded, the ground quickly became muddier and very slippery.

"Actually, Lu, you better stay where you are. I think I'm stuck."

Crosby's sagacious words of advice came seconds too late. At that moment, Lulu lost her grip on the slick and suddenly sheer surface and cascaded down the chute at a high velocity. Her desperate clutches slowed her enough to prevent serious injury, but she couldn't stop herself, bumping and sliding all the way down into Crosby's waiting arms.

"Well I guess I'm down here, too," quipped Lulu, aggravated that Crosby didn't warn her earlier and shamed by her own carelessness. She had been too anxious to locate Crosby. Lulu had wanted to march up to him, scold him for being

52

irresponsible and resume her guide duties like a seasoned veteran. Instead, she lost her poise and now shared a very tight pit at the bottom of a steep, slippery shaft.

There Lulu and Crosby sat like two kernels of corn stuck in the colon of Mother Earth.

"What now?" croaked Crosby, flustered by Lulu's annoyed silence. He knew his own juvenile negligence got them into this predicament. "I'm sorry."

"Oh, it's okay," said Lulu, frustrated but forgiving. "You didn't know. Are you all right?"

"I hit the ground pretty hard. I'm sore, but it's just bruises. No broken bones. What about you?"

In the beam of Crosby's flashlight, Lulu saw the scrapes on his face. He had taken some pretty good licks. "Same here. Just some black and blues. Nothing I ain't had before. Thanks for catching me."

"Yeah, well, it was the least I could do. So...uh...what's next?"

"Next?"

"Yeah. How do we get out of here?"

"We don't."

"Whaddaya mean, *we don't?*"

"We're stuck, fella. Better sit yer butt down and relax. Save your energy for the ropes, which is the only way we're gettin' outa here."

Lulu explained that Tosh would eventually have no choice but to come after them. When he came within earshot, they would yell for him to stop before he got too close and then they'd send him back to the entrance of the cave to get the ropes.

"I don't know," said Crosby, "Tosh is not gonna love walking through the cave alone."

"He doesn't have a choice."

*   *   *   *

Tosh stared into the black crevice Lulu had entered. How long had she been gone? Every silent second agonized him. How far did that tunnel stretch? Had the tube swallowed her up?

The deafening silence unnerved him and Tosh called out for his missing companions. Then, Tosh remembered the snoozing bats. *I'll give Lulu some more time,* he thought, opting for the eerie tranquility instead. The last thing he wanted to do was arouse those blood-sucking varmints.

Scratch that.

The last thing he wanted to do was go into that hellhole after Lulu. He told himself not to let his imagination run away from him but he knew that as time ticked on, that prospect became more and more probable.

The thick air became chilly, as Tosh, underdressed for the impromptu caving expedition, remained static. Sitting down and leaning back against the hard jagged wall, Tosh pulled his arms inside his shirt for warmth and hoped the devilish cavity would spit up his lost friends.

*   *   *   *

"I dropped the flashlight as soon as I lost my grip in the tunnel. It's funny," Crosby said, "as I was falling down that chute, I shut my eyes. I shut them even though I was already blinded by the darkness."

"It's instinctive."

"It's fear."

"Fear is instinctive."

"You think?" Crosby contemplated Lulu's statement. "Animals operate on instincts. They look and listen and if they detect something, their intuition alarms them of danger and makes them stay away from it. It's not so much a reasoning process as it is a self-preservation instinct. Fear has nothing to do with it."

Debating in the dark. Anything to pass the time and keep their spirits up while in their sketchy predicament.

Lulu thought about Crosby's hypothesis. "People analyze their situation and then react emotionally to their crisis. These emotions — fear — help keep them out of hazardous situations. It's the *human* self-preservation instinct."

"Then how do you account for some people being more fearful than others?"

"Better instincts," said Lulu as though she had nailed it down.

"Yeah, but you define fear as the end result of a logical thought process. The fundamental characteristic of instinct is that it doesn't require thinking. So fear is not an instinct but a learned behavior."

Out-reasoned, Lulu frowned. "You suck, Crosby."

*   *   *   *

How long had they been gone? Tosh had no sense of time. He knew he had to go in after them, but he kept procrastinating.

Ten more minutes, he thought.

I'll give her five more minutes, and then I'll go in.

It reminded him of all those cold rainy mornings he would lie in bed, miserable, knowing he had to get up to go to school. The sun had barely risen and Tosh could feel the winter air biting at his nose. His scratchy throat ached and his eyes fought to stay open.

When his alarm went off the first time, he would decisively pound the snooze alarm for an extra nine minutes in the snug cocoon.

The second time it blasted its annoying siren, Tosh would let the bastard run. He'd tell himself he'd get up in one minute, and then count to sixty — slowly.

When he reached sixty, Tosh, pathetically still procrastinating, would grant himself thirty more seconds.

When they expired, ten more.

Then ten more.

Then he'd be late to school.

Now, Tosh found himself reverting to his weaker high-school behavior. He had gotten to thirty second segments when he finally put his foot down. After all, his friends might be in serious trouble. He could not let his fear of the foreboding tunnel prevent him from helping them.

Tosh stood up, stretched (it might be a while until he could do that again) and took a deep breath. Without further hesitation he entered the abyss.

*   *   *   *

Cramped in the compact crater, Crosby and Lulu repositioned themselves for maximum comfort. Tired of standing inches apart, Crosby slumped down, leaned back against one side of the pit and stretched his legs as far as the close quarters permitted. This left his lap as the only remaining place for Lulu to sit.

They passed the time by singing Paul Simon songs, alternately choosing tunes.

Crosby wondered if they were ever going to escape from the subterranean prison. He pictured his face on the side of a milk carton and his distraught mother receiving a letter years later saying that her son's bones were found in a cave in South Dakota.

He began to sing, with Lulu joining in after the first line. "No, I would not give you false hope, on this strange and mournful day..."

"Mother and Child Reunion" made Crosby think of Tosh, because it was his favorite Paul Simon song. (Most likely because of its reggae beat.) Maybe the song's acoustic vibes would help guide Tosh to them.

While waiting for a sign from their rescuer, Lulu and Crosby shared heartfelt renditions of "Slip Slidin' Away," "Loves Me Like a Rock," "Boy In the Bubble" and "The Sound of Silence." During a boisterous version of "Late in the Evening," they heard Tosh's call.

The adrenaline flowed at both ends of the cascade. "Don't move Tosh!! Don't come any closer or you'll be trapped here with us!!"

After briefly explaining the situation, Lulu instructed Tosh on how to get them out.

"You want me to *what?*" Tosh could not believe Lulu's command.

"Go back to the entrance of the cave and get the rope! Bring it here until you feel the first sign of dampness! Stop there and tie the rope around yourself and throw the rest as far as you can down the shaft!"

"You want me to go all the way back by myself? *And then return??*"

"You won't be alone!" Crosby replied. "The bats will keep you company!"

Lulu slapped Crosby. This was no time for humor. Besides, Tosh was obviously terrified already.

She laid it on the line for Tosh. "You have no choice, Tosh! You're our only hope of getting outa here! Suck it up, you big baby!!"

*   *   *   *

Lulu sighed, confident Tosh would get them out. From that point in the cave, she explained to Crosby, there were not many ways Tosh could get lost. She believed Tosh would make it out and back, and help pull them to a safe escape with the combined strength of their own climbing efforts.

She shifted her weight, still sitting on Crosby's lap, and shined the light into his face. Crosby squinted but retained the slight grin upon his face. "What are you thinking?" she asked.

Crosby did not answer but his sheepish grin turned into a big smile. Lulu leaned forward and inserted her tongue into his mouth. Crosby's hands soon found Lulu's chest as her hand massaged his crotch.

Crosby's hand touched the side of Lulu's face. Stroking her cheek gently, he put his finger on Lulu's lips. She opened her mouth and took his muddy finger in. "I don't believe this," he moaned.

"There's nothing else to do," said Lulu, unzipping his shorts.

*   *   *   *

While Lulu and Crosby thoroughly enjoyed carnal pleasures, Tosh carried on through the Demon's Lair. Trying to maintain his courage and a positive attitude, he sang Bob Marley's "Three Little Birds" to himself while scanning the ceilings with his flashlight for bats.

Things went smoothly, at first.

Then, to Tosh's horror, an awakened bat flew past him. He barely saw it as it flashed in and out of his beam of light. When the bat returned to his vision, Tosh tried to keep his eye on it by following the thing with the flashlight, but its erratic flight pattern made it impossible. The bat fluttered, dipped and dove into his shaft of light for seconds at a time, and then disappeared into the complete darkness that surrounded him.

Bad enough that this thing is awake, thought Tosh. *Even worse that I can't keep an eye on it.* Not allowing Tosh to consistently observe its whereabouts, the creepy mammal tortured him.

Tosh thought back to his recent travels in Malaysia and realized the bit of irony presently occurring.

Visiting an Iban tribe in the jungle of Borneo, Tosh and his weary tour group rested with the natives in the early evening. The tour guide described some of the local wildlife they might encounter on their nature hike the next day, including warthogs, cobras and spiders so big "you can hear their footsteps."

The guide knew the chances of coming into contact with any of these pests were slim because the noise made by twenty people trekking through the jungle would scare off any wildlife that might be in the area. But he couldn't resist the tourists' awe and intrigue, so he milked it for all it was worth.

To demonstrate, he fired a shotgun into the air several times.

Shortly thereafter, giant bats towered above their heads. Their long wings flapped at a slow, steady rate as they traversed the sky, one after another. They eerily flew in a straight line, in regular intervals, as if mesmerized by some omnipotent force.

It had reminded Tosh of *The Wizard of Oz* or some old, black-and-white horror movie. He stared at the bats for a long time, his fascination unmolested by even a shred of fear because the bats remained at a safe distance, flying high in the sky.

Unfortunately, a completely different story now unfolded inside the cave. Tosh not only observed this bat, but the close confines of the setting forced him to *have a relationship* with the damn thing. Thank heavens this bat was much smaller than those he saw in Malaysia.

Every time he caught a glimpse of the critter, Tosh instinctively covered his head with his arms. This made for extremely slow progress, so he paused for a moment and tried to figure out a better game plan.

I can take this one step at a time, thought Tosh. *I'll shine the light in every direction with every foot of progress. Then again, the longer I take, the more I risk running into more bats. Maybe I should just haul ass through the rest of the cave without even looking up.*

Tosh settled on a compromise of the two options. When he first entered a chamber, he scoped the whole thing out with his flashlight. If his searchlight revealed no winged critters, he'd turn the beam to the floor, put his head down and bolt.

"Shine, then sprint," he repeated to himself.

This system worked effectively and for most of his remaining journey, Tosh successfully avoided the bat. Destiny, however, brought them together again.

The incident occurred in a short but extremely tight passage leading to a chamber near the entrance of the cave. Knowing he was almost out, Tosh excitedly flashed his light through the shaft into the next room. To his despair, though, a bat fluttered in the other end of the passageway.

Tosh gulped in trepidation.

He sat back, covered his face with his hands and waited for the bat to fly by. Minutes later, he shined his light through again, only to see the bat reappear in the same place.

This routine continued for another ten minutes or so, but the bat never took advantage of the ample opportunities Tosh provided for it to come through. It seemed Tosh and the bat were equally vexed by each other's presence.

What was he going to do?

Tosh thought of his friends stuck in the mucky pit. "Screw it," he said. "This is ridiculous."

He grit his teeth and made like a human cannonball. Clutching his flashlight like it was his only friend in the world, Tosh squirmed through the snug canal with his arms pinned over his head. He felt extremely vulnerable.

Then, horribly, in the shaft of light made by his flashlight, the bat appeared. Evidently, the bat must have also acquired some courage or lost its patience.

It flew toward him.

Tosh stopped, frozen in terror. He pictured the hairy ball of rabies impaling itself in his face, its razor-sharp teeth scraping away his tender flesh. He could feel its spiny claws tearing his awestruck eyes from their sockets, the optical nerve ripped from the back of his brain left to swing in the dank breeze. He closed his eyes and scrunched his unprotected face.

As the bat squeaked by him in the tiny available space between his head and the wall, Tosh could feel the flapping wings brush past his cheek. He wanted to vomit.

*　　　*　　　*　　　*

"Uh, ahh."
"That felt good."
"Yeah, it did."
A moment of silence.
"Now what?"
"Do you have a cigarette?"
"No."
"I wish I had a cigarette."
"Me, too."
"Do you smoke?"
"No."
Another moment of silence.
"Me neither, actually."

*　　　*　　　*　　　*

Tosh counted his blessings. The bat had safely passed him and he could hear Julio barking. He quickly made his way through the storm pipe and gratefully jumped out into the delicious dusk. Tosh sucked in the fresh air and peered into the sky. He wanted to hug the newly risen moon.

Then he realized he had only completed half of his mission. No relief yet. He had to go back through the whole damn cave again, past the stupid bat.

Tosh reminded himself that the bat was probably more scared than him. Well, maybe scared, but not *more* scared.

Once again, Tosh mustered his fortitude by reflecting on his worldwide travels. He had faced worse things than bats — things way more potentially harmful — like that crazed night in Kenya. Tosh and his traveling partners must have been lunatics.

Tosh and his two college friends, Bob and Jeff, had gone on a three-day safari on the Masai Mara plains of East Africa. One night, a couple of hours before sunrise, a loud splash in the stream behind his tent awoke Tosh. It took him a moment to regain his whereabouts, for he had a few too many Tusker beers that night before turning in. After locating his flashlight in a semi-panic, he shined it around his tent to refresh his memory. He heard nothing more in the next few minutes and wondered if he had actually heard anything at all. Could he have dreamt it?

It was not a dream.

At that moment, Tosh heard the most incredible sound. He sprang up in his cot, his senses keen. Tosh sat like a statue, waiting to hear that uncanny noise again as the nocturnal insects carried on their placid drone.

About a minute later, he heard it again - a low, guttural grunt. *That could only come from a large animal,* he had reasoned. Without speaking, Tosh quickly awoke his buddies by shaking them furiously in their cots. He put his finger to his pursed lips and cupped his ear. Gathering their wits, they remained stone-like, practically holding their breaths in anticipation.

Again the mighty animal spoke, this time louder. The growl, a bit closer, conveyed an awesome sense of power. They knew it had to be a cat.

Bob glued his face to the small screen window on the zippered door of the tent, peering out.

"Maybe the leopard," Jeff suggested, his whisper barely audible.

A freshly butchered goat had been hung from a tree in a clearing about 100 yards from camp. A night watchman employed by the camp periodically checked the bait in case a leopard, the only tree-climbing African cat, had taken advantage of the free meal. If, indeed, the hungry feline fell for the ruse, the watchman would alert the campers.

Stumbling out of their tents with their binoculars, cameras and sleep-encrusted eyes, the campers would scurry through a ramshackle, man-made tunnel to a beast-proof viewing room at the edge of the clearing. Everyone would secure a position that enabled him or her to gaze out the Plexiglas windows of the viewing room as the watchman flicked on the powerful floodlights, exposing the carnivore in the tree. Cameras would click and people would ooh and ahh and the leopard would continue grinding bones in his jaws until he was satiated and could barely climb down the tree. Both parties would be satisfied; the leopard would return to the jungle, no longer famished, and the campers would retreat to their tents with an unforgettable experience and pictures to prove it.

Who did this grunt belong to? Tosh analyzed the sound.

It wasn't a snarl, like the mountain lion cry that bellowed from the scoreboard speaker at his high school's football games.

It wasn't a roar, like the MGM lion after the credits of a film.

This wasn't a sound of distress or aggression, but more a visceral bark — a habitual display of ferocity to announce the animal's domineering presence.

The intruder continued its signals for about ten minutes until they became less frequent and more distant. The boys, adrenaline rushing, eventually found themselves listening intently to only creaking crickets.

What happened to the mysterious animal?

"Let's go out there," said Bob.

"Are you kidding?" replied Tosh, joining him at the screen window. Nothing moved in the moonlit campsite. "Whaddaya think, Jeff?"

Without saying a word, Jeff grabbed his flashlight, unzipped the tent door and walked out into the wild African night.

Bob and Tosh hurriedly threw on their boots, found their flashlights and followed. Bob also grabbed a hunting knife from his backpack.

What kind of beast were they searching for? Every animal on the African plains was equipped with frighteningly efficient self-defense mechanisms that could make short work of a human.

"Especially a weaponless human," Tosh had pointed out. "What are we going to do if we see it? Blind it with our flashlights and then beat if over the head?"

A leopard would leap for their throats, crushing their necks in its mighty, destructive jaws.

An elephant could shatter them with one accurate mammoth footstep if its piercing tusks didn't spear them first.

They could be accidentally crushed by a careless rhinoceros, rolling on the dry, hard clay to scratch his itchy, parasite-ridden back.

Even an ostrich could fuck them up.

Was it a big hairy orangutan?

A bushmaster python?

A really pissed-off llama?

Jeff, Bob and Tosh painstakingly crept around the camp, huddled together, frenetically shining their flashlights in all directions. Tosh breathed heavily as he illuminated the weeping trees above with his shaky hand. Companionship gave them the aplomb to push on — not really confidence that they could overcome their adversary, but more so hope that the fiend would attack one of the other two guys.

They inched along right up to the edge of camp, gaping into the darkness across the stream and beyond the dirt road. At every moment, Tosh thought he was going to turn around and see a hungry, four-legged marauder sizing him up.

It's funny, thought Tosh. *Adventure has no logic.* They had been searching for a creature that would probably eat them if they found it.

Tosh and his buddies never did find anything, but retired to their tents fulfilled nonetheless. Their experience had no climax, but they would never forget that rush of adrenaline and sense of adventure.

As it turned out, they learned the next morning from the night watchman that a pair of lions had walked right through the middle of camp. It was probably best that their story went without a climax. Had there been one, they most likely would not have been around to tell it. Three flashlights and a hunting knife against two hungry lions would not do the trick.

So Tosh had chased the king of the jungle, but now feared a measly bat. What was the deal with that?

Tosh realized he had more bravery in the company of others. Maybe it had something to do with the "misery loves company" theory. Maybe Tosh really had no courage, but simply leeched off of others and hoped for the best.

This was a test, Tosh believed.

He had a choice. The easy way out would be to follow Julio home for help. The more difficult way would send him right back into the bowels of the earth to face the awakening bats and other cave vermin.

Crosby and Lulu would be happy either way just to get out of the cave, but Tosh knew the former choice would be like getting an *A* on a trigonometry exam by cheating off of the brainy kid in the next row. Tosh had to prove to himself that when it came down to the buzzer in game seven of the playoffs, he could sink the three-pointer to propel his team into the next round.

With the grit of a junkyard dog, he snatched the rope and reentered the storm pipe. Bat or no bat, Tosh was going to tackle the Demon's Lair and rescue his friends.

CHAPTER 5

Never, in his twenty-three years of existence, was Tosh Tyler so happy to be alive. With his shirt off and the windows rolled down, he drove barefoot along Route 90 in Eastern Wyoming, headed west into natural splendor. The deep orange glow of the setting sun spilled from behind the jagged Bighorn Mountains and splashed across the purple sky.

"Yee-haah!" Tosh screamed, an exaltation from deep within his gut, expressing his abounding joy.

Tosh had the gorgeous twilight to himself as Crosby slept peacefully in the back, worn out from his subterranean sexual exploits. The balmy, sun-roasted air blew through his shoulder-length, dirty-blonde dreads, over his smiling face and across his bare chest.

"Blue Sky" wailed from the stereo, Dickey Betts' magical swirling guitar resounding off the metal frame of Josephine. The Allman Brothers' exhilarating music reverberated through the steering wheel into Tosh's fingers, hands, arms and torso — saturating the old Dodge van as it filled Tosh with rapture.

Part of Tosh's passion for life at the moment came from the absolute freedom he was experiencing. Ever since his first day with a driver's license, Tosh had wanted to take advantage and venture beyond his everyday domain. Many times, heading west on Route 80 on his way to school, Tosh tempted himself with the thought of an impromptu escape. He told himself if he really wanted to, he could simply keep driving all the way to California. He could go all the way to fucking Alaska, if he so pleased. Nothing or nobody could stop him.

But, in reality, that was not the case. He couldn't bail out of school. Plus, what would he do for money, sell finger paintings out of the back of his Buick? Although he had experienced a taste of freedom during his travels with his college buddies the summer before, it was not pure, but tarnished, because of their dependence on public transportation. Too young to rent a car, their mobility was restricted by flight schedules and train routes.

Nothing compared to this moment.

Today, nothing held him back. There were no responsibilities, no engagements, no obligations. No plan. They were crossing the country at will, following their own desires, their own vibes.

What the hell — Tosh could make a left and head down to Texas. He could bang a right and drive to Saskatchewan. Mississippi, Nevada, New Mexico. It didn't matter.

Tosh and Crosby answered to nobody. They explored their homeland at leisure, surveying the varied landscapes while meeting cool, interesting folks along the way.

And, to top it off, that stinking Demon's Lair Cave was out of the picture.

Tosh was out of that crappy hole in the ground and it could kiss his ass. No more choking darkness or claustrophobic quarters. No more crawling, squirming and squeezing. No more blind winged mammals with teeth.

Just the wide-open Wyoming grasslands and the freshest air Tosh had ever tasted.

Man, Tosh was glad the whole cave episode was over. And not only had they escaped the pit, but Tosh had proved to be the hero. He had shunned his fear and overcame the adversity.

After crawling back through Demon's Lair, Tosh had thrown the rope down to his friends. He tied one end around his waist and used every ounce of his strength to aid Crosby and Lulu in clambering up the cascade. Tosh had even suggested they might gain stability by climbing sideways, bracing themselves on the walls of the chute with their feet and backs. "A very clever idea," Lulu told him.

Tosh had found valor, and prevailed in the menacing face of trouble.

The sight of the splendid setting sun behind the admirable Bighorn Mountains, combined with the Allman Brothers' magical music, gave Tosh goose bumps. Feeling a genuine bliss, he filled his lungs with the pure, clement air and let out another hearty roar.

*   *   *   *

Stars were shining brightly in the darkening evening sky. The breeze chilling, Crosby shifted in the back bed and pulled the Dacron sleeping bag up to his chin. Tosh continued driving as he pulled a faded Georgia Tech sweatshirt over his head.

Further on up the road, a red pickup truck appeared. Tosh, maintaining a steady sixty miles per hour, gained on the fellow traveler. Could this be the first vehicle that they pass on their transcontinental journey?

Since they had left New Jersey three weeks earlier, Tosh and Crosby had been right-lane patrons, victimized by Dale Earnhardt wannabes cruising by in their trendy sports cars, luxury sedans and high-tech, four-wheel-drive, utility vehicles.

They were passed by Cutlasses, Caprices, Cadillacs, Novas, Dusters, Pacers, Regals, Range Rovers, Amigos, Accords, Eclipses, Thunderbirds, Firebirds, Sunbirds, Skylarks, Impalas, Rabbits, Mustangs, Lynxes, Cougars, Colts, Camaros, Corvettes, Caravans, Celicas, Centuries, Preludes, Prisms, LeBarons, Jettas, Jimmies, Samurais, Renegades, Cherokees, Troopers, Pathfinders, Broncos and Blazers.

The Japanese passed them in droves, as did the Germans. The French, the Italians and the Swedes all fed them dust. Tosh and Crosby were even passed by the Slavs. (Damn Yugos!)

Finally, Tosh and Crosby's turn had come. Trucking along in their weathered 1973 Dodge Sportsman Van, Tosh neared the battered red pickup. It was a Ford, probably as old as Jo. From the looks of it, though, it had lived a much tougher life.

Tosh noticed a funky sticker on the bumbling jalopy. *Very odd,* he thought. *Stickers usually do not grace the bumpers of clunkers like these.*

If they do, they say something like "If guns are outlawed, only outlaws will have guns" or they advertise some right-wing conservative politician. Of course, the gamut of religious bullshit always pops up, "Jesus Saves" the most popular. Other than that, stickers were usually reserved for Winnebagos and Deadheads.

Tosh leaned forward for a better look. His eyes had not betrayed him. Without punctuation, in thick black letters printed on a white background, the sticker read **NEVER DIE WONDERING.**

What kind of character was driving this oddity?

Slowly passing the red pickup, Tosh studied the driver, an old man with graying brown hair that hung down past his shoulders. The man gripped the steering wheel with two hands at the top and kept his eyes on the road. A tattered suede cowboy hat dipping below his brow and a long silver beard concealed a face wrinkled with wisdom. Torpidly, the man turned to face Tosh.

Suddenly aware his scrutiny had been detected, Tosh found himself staring blankly into deep, soulful eyes. Completely expressionless, the man nodded slightly. Then, as with great effort, he returned his gaze to the road upon which they traveled.

After about thirty seconds, Tosh left the curious hippie cowboy behind in the dry dust kicked up from their van, but he continued to ponder the curious statement scrawled across the old pickup's bumper. *Never Die Wondering — what the hell does that mean?*

*   *   *   *

The '73 Dodge van rolled to a stop just after Lodge Grass, Montana. It was dinnertime, according to their stomachs, and the guys found a nice little rest area atop a grassy knoll. A few wooden picnic tables circled a small rest room and vending area. Crosby cooked their canned cuisine on the Coleman portable stove while Tosh scrounged for change to seduce the soda machine.

After securing the necessary coinage, Tosh dropped a shiny bicentennial quarter into the slot. The soda machine contained their favorite soft drink, and within seconds it released two A&W Root Beers. Tosh wished he had a frosty mug to hold the sweet brown liquid. Unfortunately, life on the road did not offer such luxuries. Their drinks, just like their dinner, would have to come from a tin can.

After a satisfying dinner of vegetarian chili, saltines and gummy bears, a well-rested Crosby took the wheel. He put in a Jane's Addiction tape as he pulled Jo back onto the highway.

Montana is a huge, empty state. The night ahead, like many others, promised many dark miles with nothing to look at except dotted yellow lines.

And a fuel gauge reading empty.

*   *   *   *

Somewhere outside of Big Timber, flatulence set in.

Man, Crosby stunk like shit. He must have blown a hole in the driver's seat, not to mention his pants. Crosby hoped Tosh didn't notice because he would open the windows and it was freezing outside. It had been a hot day, but when the sun went down in Montana, it got cold, no matter what the season.

"Jeez, dude! Did you bust ass?"

Crosby denied farting.

"Yeah, right. Sure you didn't. You got bad ass, dude. That is *nasty*. I gotta open the windows."

They rode with the windows open, the icy night air whipping through the van.

Damn, thought Crosby. *What did I do to deserve this?* "Tosh, close the windows, man. I'm cold as hell."

"No. You stink."

"It's not my fault. I'm human. Humans fart. If it smells that bad, light a match or something."

"A match? You know how hard it is to find a match in this van."

"We've got a lighter."

"What's a lighter gonna do?"

"Shit, you're right. Make a note — we need matches." Crosby took his left foot off the dashboard and placed it next to the other foot that was doing all the work. "What was in that chili, anyway?"

"Well, beans, obviously. That's probably the culprit right there. Some peppers."

"Why do beans make you fart?"

"I don't know, Crosby. I'm going to sleep."

After five minutes with the windows open, the van felt like an icebox. Tosh closed the windows and curled up in the warmest sleeping bag. He turned on the flashlight Lulu had given him as a souvenir from Demon's Lair and grabbed the road atlas.

He opened up to the two-page spread of the United States. How exciting! The country was spread out in front of them. All Tosh had to do was choose a place and they could drive there.

There were blue interstates, red state highways, gray county roads. Indian Reservations, Wildlife Refuges, swamps, parks, campgrounds — even foot trails! What a map!

There were towns like Opportunity, Friendship and Wisdom. Riddle, Jackpot and Muleshoe. Vamoosa, Oshkosh and Kooskia. All these roads and towns were not merely lines and names. Each had a distinct personality. They all had stories to tell.

Tosh wondered what stories Climax, Happyland and Intercourse could tell.

"Oh my God, Cros, there's a town called Happyland."

"Happyland? Are you serious?"

65

"Yep."

"Let's go there."

"We'd have to backtrack."

"Wouldn't it be great to live in a town called Happyland? I would give anything to be able to fill out forms and list my city as Happyland. That would just make me so happy."

"They probably have a nice little plantation on the outskirts of town," said Tosh. "Constant buds, homegrown ganja. Happyland."

"The name of the city would be like a, what do they call it, *self-fulfilling prophecy.*"

"Good word, Crosby!"

"I didn't just study art in college, dude."

"Self-fulfilling prophecy."

"Yeah. You know, when something happens precisely due to the fact that it was predicted to happen? People would be happy just because they lived in Happyland. How could you help it? The signs would say 'Happyland General Store' and 'Happyland Post Office.'"

"I couldn't imagine the Happyland Police Department though. It's just not that intimidating. What do they arrest you for, frowning?"

"Yeah, they dress like clowns."

Pondering that image, they laughed.

"Hey by the way, Cros, where are we heading?"

"West."

"The west is the best."

"West by...west."

"That's good, but maybe we should come up with a more specific destination? Like maybe a city or at the very least a state or province?"

"Province?"

"Yeah, like in Canada."

"Yeah!"

"Yeah, what?"

"Let's do Canada!"

"Yeah, mon," Tosh chirped in his pseudo-Jamaican accent. "Mek we go to Vancouver."

"So Vancouver it is! Get some shut eye, Tosh buddy, and when you awake, we'll be on the road to Canada."

With that in mind, Tosh closed his eyes and drifted off to sleep, wondering what adventures awaited them in the Great White North.

*   *   *   *

Most of the problems that could be encountered while passing through Montana in the dead of night are self-inflicted. The problem that plagued Tosh and Crosby certainly fell into that category.

As Tosh slept obliviously in the back, Crosby's hindsight tortured his grieving conscience. "Why? Why didn't I stop for gas in Bozeman?" He spoke to himself, reprimanding his earlier bad judgment.

Unaccompanied nocturnal drivers often speak out loud for company. There is no need to keep thoughts inside when no one else can hear them anyway. The sound of a voice — even if it's your own — soothes the relentless, midnight highway drawl.

"I could have grabbed a cup of coffee and topped off the tank and we would still have plenty of fuel. But no, I had to cruise right past Bozeman because 'All Down the Line' is such a great driving song and I didn't feel like stopping."

Indeed, stupidity and carelessness were self-imposed obstacles.

For the past forty miles, Crosby had been checking the unlit fuel gauge on a regular basis. The process had become much easier with the advent of their latest technology — the flashlight. This, to Crosby's delight, rendered obsolete the lighter that had been running on fumes.

The needle dipped just below the old **E**. It had seemed like an hour since the last exit. Something had to appear soon, Crosby thought.

But there was no sign of any life on that dark, lonely highway. In fact, there were no signs at all.

Didn't people who live in Montana have any need to know where they were going? Crosby wondered. *Didn't people want to know how much longer they had to go?*

Crosby thought of the eternities between each exit. Then again, maybe most people didn't want to know how much monotony awaited them crossing the vast western state. Ignorance was bliss, right? Mileage signs would only rub in the boredom.

"Boredom," said Crosby. "I would welcome boredom at this point."

Boredom would beat the anxiety that turned his stomach. Would they run out of gas in the Godforsaken prairie?

They might be stranded for days before they found a considerate trucker or friendly farmer to assist them. What would they do?

They could read. Eventually, though, they would run out of reading material.

Then what? Play cards? Tic-Tac-Toe?

Maybe they wouldn't survive long enough to enjoy meaningless time-killing activities. Who knew what kind of danger lurked in that turgid darkness?

Suppose nature called Crosby. An appropriate place to piss would not have to take him far from Josephine. But a huge rattler seeking heat from the van may be resting just outside. It could seize Crosby's ankle and puncture his bony flesh with its venomous fangs. He'd writhe in agony as he waited for medical help, facing certain amputation and possible death.

Possibly, a crazed bald lunatic with an axe might scope the two docile dudes from New Jersey as his next victims. Crosby would be horribly awakened from a deep sleep by the smashing of a window. Limb by limb the maniac would deconstruct their bodies, all the while drooling and laughing uncontrollably.

Crosby considered he and Tosh stranded along the shoulder of the deserted highway. The Montana night would conceal them, shrouding the van in its unforgiving darkness. Along the interstate would speed a huge eighteen-wheeler, trying to make up lost time on its way to Yakima. The bleary-eyed old man at the wheel, wired on amphetamines, would watch the needle split the nine and zero and continue to rise. He would fuck with the radio. He would fiddle with the C.B. He would masturbate. Anything to get his mind off the straight, flat road. Gradually, the ill-fated rig would veer ever so slightly off its course. Leaving the confines of its lane, it would straddle the shoulder, spitting gravel for miles in all directions. Before the inattentive trucker could steer the tractor-trailer back onto the highway, it would barrel through he and Tosh. Their bodies would be pulverized by tons of steel, chrome and rubber racing along at a perilous velocity.

Crosby shuddered at the image and tried to think of something else.

Some call him Sasquatch. Others call him Bigfoot. Legend has the mysterious giant hairy beast roaming these parts frequently. It is known that the brute's most desired victuals are tasty young men from New Jersey...

Enough! The night and the road had gotten to Crosby. His imagination had run away with the running-out-of-gas scenario. *I gotta calm down,* he thought. *I need companionship. Tosh would kill me, though, if I woke him up to tell him that we were about to run out of gas.*

"Hey, Tosh, wake up."

"Give me my cat."

"What?"

"My cat! Give me my cat!"

"Your cat?"

"Lambada."

Annoyed, Crosby turned around. "What the fuck are you talking about?"

Tosh was talking in his sleep.

"Easy on the cantaloupe."

"Tosh wake up! We're about to run out of gas!"

Tosh stirred in his sleeping bag. "Five more minutes."

"It could be five. It could be one. I don't know how much fuel we have left."

Tosh mumbled unintelligibly without lifting his head from the fluffy pillow.

Crosby knew how to wake the lazy bastard. Pressing the brake pedal, he howled in terror.

Tosh screamed, jumping up in panic.

Crosby laughed at Tosh's fearful complexion in the rearview mirror, made even paler by the light of the moon. Tosh's look turned to an angry scowl as he realized he'd been duped.

"What'd you do that for?"

"I had to wake you up."

"You're nuts. A certified jackass."

"Maybe so. We're about to run out of gas."

Tosh joined Crosby up front and shined the flashlight on the darkened dashboard to see for himself. "How did you manage this, Einstein?"

"There haven't been any gas stations."

"Oh, I'm just sure there are no gas stations in all of Montana."

"Well, not since we've needed gas."

"Dude, have you ever heard of planning ahead?" Tosh was cranky from being awoken and unthrilled at the prospect of getting stuck in the middle of nowhere. "There's no law against filling the tank when it's still got some gas left." Crosby didn't reply because he knew Tosh was right.

"How long till the next exit?"

"Beats me."

"So we don't know if we'll make it to the next exit and if by some miracle we do, we don't even know for sure if we can refuel there."

"That about sums it up."

"So then, Cros, why the fuck did you wake me up? What could I possibly dot to help us out? Piss in the tank?"

"I just thought you should know."

"You really are a knucklehead sometimes."

Something green flashed up ahead along the side of the road — a sign for an upcoming exit. The next stop, Lost Creek, provided gas, food and restrooms.

"Oh, thank you thank you thank you thank you!" Crosby offered his palm to Tosh, who sighed and slapped him five.

"Hoo-fuckin'-ray. Let's not let it get this close again."

They pulled off the highway and came to a stop sign at the end of the ramp. Crosby turned left, following the arrow that pointed towards Lost Creek. After a minute or two, they entered a small, sleeping town.

"Oh, no."

"I don't believe this."

The entire town was closed and dark.

The guys sat in the gas station lot, weeping.

"I don't believe this," Tosh repeated.

"I do. Why would this station be open all night? We're in the middle of Montana, for Chrissakes. This place makes Buford look like a booming metropolis." Crosby took off his baseball cap and ran his hand through his short, straggly hair. "Now what are we gonna do?"

Tosh thought for a minute. "Let's just stay here. First thing in the morning we'll gas up."

"I would say that's a good plan, but look." Crosby pointed to a sign that read **NO GAS.**

In despair, Tosh placed his forehead on the dashboard.

"There's got to be another one," said Crosby. He pulled the van back out on to Main Street. As they slowly made their way through Lost Creek, they spotted an oncoming Chevy Blazer.

"Let's ask these guys," said Tosh.

"No way. They're gonna think we're idiots."

"Well, we are. Stop here."

"What do you want me to say?"

"Ask 'em if they know of another station."

The truck stopped alongside of them. Inside were two men. The driver looked about thirty while the other man had about 25 more years under his belt. Crosby rolled his window down to converse. "Uh...howdy...uh...I reckon there's no other fillin' station 'round here?"

The two men looked at each other and then spoke quietly amongst themselves. Tosh nudged Crosby and whispered, "Very good. You used their lingo. I like that."

The two men finished their discussion and the driver replied plainly, "Follow us."

Crosby turned the van around and fell in behind the rusty Blazer. Just past the edge of town the men turned off the road onto a dirt trail. Crosby looked at Tosh with concern as he tried to maneuver Josephine around the ruts. The Blazer kicked up the dry dust, clouding his vision and making him sneeze. He rolled up his window to keep the smothering sand out of their home.

"Where the fuck are they takin' us?"

"I have no clue."

"Get out my scuba knife, Tosh. It's in the top pouch of my backpack."

Tosh dug out the knife. His heart quickened as he grabbed the sturdy black handle. Six inches of solid stainless steel gleamed in the moonlight beaming into the van.

Crosby felt better with the scuba knife by his side, their only weapon for self-defense. Both sides of the fierce blade were extremely sharp — one side conveniently serrated for filleting. In addition, the handle served as a hammer and the blade contained ruling marks to measure the size of a catch.

He had packed it for camping purposes, but in the back of his mind he knew security had something to do with it. That knife could be devastating, although thankfully Crosby never had to use it violently.

Crosby's uncle lived up in Rhode Island and they would practically live in the water during the summer, whether it be sailing, wind surfing, fishing or diving. Crosby carried the knife with him whenever he dove. It primarily served as a way to get out of a tangle underneath the water. The serrated edge worked well cutting fishing nets and rope. Also, Crosby occasionally hunted flounder with it.

Flounder are bottom fish and lay on their sides in the sand. To successfully hunt these critters, Crosby had to stab them with the point of the blade sideways through the head. If the blade of the knife ran parallel with the body of the fish, the flounder could squirm free, slicing itself in half in doing so. The poor escaped flounder eventually would die and Crosby would be left with no seafood, turning an intimate fishing experience into useless killing.

Now, the knife protected them from harm. Whatever stunt the guys in the Blazer tried to pull, Tosh and Crosby would be ready.

Unless, of course, the fiends had a gun.

The Blazer stopped.

"What's happening? Where are we?" asked Tosh.

"I can't tell."

Except for the brake lights of the Blazer, they couldn't see a thing. The van's headlights reflected off the dust kicked up from the road and the rest of their surroundings were shrouded by the rural darkness.

Then, the taillights of the Blazer disappeared.

"Where did they go?"

"They might have shut off the truck. Hang on."

Tosh and Crosby sat tight, wide-eyed and alert, while the dust settled.

"The Blazer's gone."

In the beam of the van's headlights stood a lone gas pump. Behind it sat a plank-board shanty with a sign out front that read, **BUCK'S GENERAL STORE & BEER GARDEN**. A light burned inside.

Feeling a little better but still with an air of reserve, Tosh and Crosby entered the shanty. In the back of the store sat three old men and a woman playing cards. Beers lined the table. Their laughing conversation ceased when they noticed Tosh and Crosby, standing unsure in colorful surfing shorts, sweatshirts and flip-flops. Tosh's dreads spilled out from underneath his tam.

Crosby smiled uncomfortably. Not the usual midnight visitors in Lost Creek, Montana. Fer sure.

"Can we help you, boys?" the largest man said, getting up from the table.

"Would it be possible, uh, sir, to get some gas?"

The man looked back at his friends. The woman sipped her bourbon stoically while one of the men fingered a poker chip.

"Sure," he said. "And how about a beer while yer at it?" He smiled and grabbed two cold ones from behind the counter. "G'head. Fill 'er right up, son. Then take a load off fer a few and join us for a brew."

Soon, Crosby and Tosh found themselves sitting at the table with the old timers, drinking coffee and beer and bullshitting about their cross-country journey.

71

While Crosby told their hosts of how they almost ran out of gas in the lonesome Montana night, Tosh noticed a collection of plants in the corner of the store. Among them hung a large birdcage housing a couple of scarlet macaws. The large, bright red birds must have been the only two of their kind in the state of Montana.

Living in the jungles of the South and Central American tropics, the beautiful vibrant plumage of macaws has been sought since the beginning of time. As a result, the birds have always been hunted and victimized, coerced into domestication from the days of Blackbeard's shoulder to this very cage in Lost Creek, Montana.

The birds reminded Tosh of an experience he had had while traveling in Venezuela. He had sat in Canaima Camp, a jungle resort near Angel Falls in the Amazon Basin, relaxing with a late afternoon beer after a day of hiking. Noticing two of the colorful parrots quietly landing in a nearby tree, he blinked in amazement, as if to say, "What are *you* doing here?"

There he sat, drinking a cold one, listening to the jungle, facing a pair of genuine scarlet macaws. After a few minutes, the birds left as quietly as they came. Tosh's eyes never once left the birds until they flew out of sight.

Basically, he couldn't believe the birds were wild. The whole time they sat tranquilly on the tree limb, Tosh had half-expected some guy to appear and whistle to the birds, calling his pets back home.

Not these birds. Free to roam as they pleased, they had just dropped in for a leisurely break. There were no steel bars caging them in. No speech lessons. Only the serene tropical twilight to enjoy soaring among the treetops.

How sad, thought Tosh, that he only connected these magnificent creatures with captivity. Growing up, his sole encounters with tropical birds had occurred when they sat caged in pet stores. Never even having seen films of them in the wild, he regarded them merely as curious pets and couldn't even picture them as wildlife. (Toucan Sam did nothing to dissolve this image.)

That is not right, he thought. Tosh wondered how many other creatures would get the same treatment. Maybe twenty years from now, children will only picture lions as large cats kept in cages, rather than the mighty kings they once were.

"Tosh, I see you've noticed my birds."

Tosh looked at Bill, the man who first greeted them. "Yeah. I was admiring them. Where did you get them?"

Bill lit a cigar. "'Bout a month ago, I was in Billings. I had just bowled the best game of my life and I was feeling pretty good. As I was walking down the boulevard, this hombre dressed in one of them long overcoats poked his head out of the alleyway.

"'Pssst,' he said.

"I thought he was gonna flash me his privates or something. But then he said ever so softly, 'Wanna buy some birds?'

"I says to the guy, 'Birds? What kinda birds? Ya mean chickens?'

"He says, 'Ya can't eat *these* birds. Looky here.'

'Then I seen the most beauful critters I ever seen. Two big birds that looked like they been painted or something. Just like on the Froot Loops box."

Bill gazed proudly at his pets perched in the corner of the room. "This one's Howard, here. And that one's Neville."

Tosh could sense the man's admiration and affection for the birds by the tone of his voice and the look in his eye.

"Yeah, these birds helped me deal with the passing of Woody."

"Who's Woody?" asked Crosby.

Tosh glared at him. So not tactful.

"Woody was my pet hamster."

"How'd he die?" Crosby inquired.

Tosh covertly punched his arm. How could he be so inconsiderate?

"Woody took his own life."

"He committed suicide?!" Tosh blurted incredulously.

"Yeah."

"How does a hamster kill himself?" Tosh had to know.

At this point Bill started to choke up.

The woman, Madge, said, "You tell it, Kermit." Then, to Tosh and Crosby, she said, "Kermit has a flair for words."

Kermit took a few puffs on his pipe and a sip of his whiskey. "Woody used to live in a cage up on that shelf over there," he said, pointing to a shelf above the refrigerators.

Tosh and Crosby both turned to look.

The plastic home was of modest size. It had the usual hamster amenities, namely the exercise wheel.

"Most hamsters would be content to live a simple existence — running the wheel, burrowing in wood chips, chewing cardboard. But Woody was different. He wanted more."

Kermit spoke like he was narrating an episode of *60 Minutes*. "Day after day Woody would try to escape from his penthouse abode, pushing the screen off the top of the cage and attempting to climb out. Bill wouldn't have it though. A general store is no place for a hamster to be running wild. To prevent Woody from getting out, he kept a phone book on top of the screen. Problem was, even a hamster could move a phone book from Lost Creek — not many listings. So we had to get the yellow pages from Billings.

"Anyhow, forced to live in his enclosed quarters, Woody became disgruntled. The hamster began to pull out his fur. Tiny little hairballs littered the wood chips and cardboard bits. The doctor, or veterinarian, I suppose, said he'd never seen this before, but he figured it was a sure sign of stress. Unfortunately, the good doctor had no suggestions. Therapy was pretty much out of the question. He said there's not much you could do for an overly ambitious hamster.

"Then, one day, someone used the yellow pages and forgot to put them back. That night, without the weight of the phone book, Woody managed to move the screen and escape from his cage. He jumped to his death. About twelve feet."

"That's about 432 hamster feet," added the other gentleman who had been playing cards.

"That's right, Jed," Kermit continued. "The next morning, Bill found Woody on the floor, broken and bald. To this day, it's a mystery who moved those yellow pages."

Kermit raised his glass, acknowledging his friend Bill Buck, and guzzled the rest of his beer.

"I think we gotta get going," said Crosby.

*   *   *   *

"Brick Red."

"Lemon Yellow."

"Canary Yellow."

"It's just Canary, I think."

"Whatever."

"Maize."

"What's that look like?"

"It's a dark yellow. You know, like corn. Maize means corn."

"Yeah, yeah, I know. That's bullshit," complained Crosby. "Corn isn't dark yellow. It's bright yellow."

"Well I didn't name the fuckin' things!"

"All right...let me think." Crosby stared at Interstate 90, racking his mind. Finally, a name came to him. "How about, Thistle?"

"Ohhh, he pulls it out! I thought you were done."

"Hey, I had a 64-pack when I was a kid. I didn't only use *your* crayons, you know."

"Bittersweet."

"Damn! You give me no time! I gotta think again..."

Tosh and Crosby's contest to see who could name the most Crayola colors began soon after Tosh awoke from a strange, acid flashback-induced nightmare, blurting nervously, "Turquoise!"

As Crosby motored through the endless Montana night, Tosh had slept restlessly, tormented by indecisiveness in his head. He had dreamt: If I was a Crayola crayon, what color would I want to be?

Magenta, Maroon, Mahogany. Salmon. Violet. Pine Green. Midnight Blue. Orchid. He analyzed every color intensely.

Sky Blue was gentle and easy, but too passive. Infant-like. Just another dispassionate baby blue. It reminded him of the Montreal Expos away uniforms of the 1970's — doomed to lose.

Peach had flavor, but Tosh ruled it out because he had always used it to color Caucasian skin. Thinking back in his dream, he realized Peach more closely resembled a white man's bare ass in the dead of winter than natural skin tone. If he ever had that unnatural, pinkish cast, Tosh swore he would die himself like an Easter egg. He preferred a nice healthy-looking tan. More like a Burnt Sienna.

White was boring, black was too dark and depressing and Olive was flat-out ugly.

Tosh had narrowed it down to two colors — turquoise and silver – before making up his mind.

Turquoise — a rich, cool shade of blue. Distinct, refreshing, vibrant. Turquoise reminded Tosh of tropical waters. The Caribbean. Reggae.

Silver was unique; it did not extract its color from the spectrum but forged itself from the earth. Sparkling, regal, enchanting, silver shone proudly, but without the pretension of its counterpart, gold. It enveloped all the other colors as well, reflecting the ordinary greens, reds and blues.

But was silver an actual color? Perhaps silver tried to be something that it really wasn't, a poseur. Did silver surreptitiously eke out a niche in the Crayola universe? Besides, when silver smeared, as crayons are apt to do on occasion, it lost its luster and became more of a dull gray to the untrained eye.

"All right," Crosby moaned after a few minutes of pondering. "I didn't wanna have to do this. I'm gonna have to pull out my ace in the hole." He looked Tosh straight in the eye and said haughtily, "Periwinkle."

"Shit. Good one."

Tosh couldn't believe it. He didn't want to let on, but Crosby had him against the wall. He usually had a color on the tip of every finger, but at 4:30 am, he did not feel like the sharpest crayon in the box.

Damn, he thought. *Crosby will gloat all the way through Washington if I don't come up with one more color. After all, I'm the odds-on favorite.*

Tosh looked out the window. The immense darkness paled ever so slightly on the fringes of the sky. He concentrated, visualizing the gold and green flip-top box. He recalled various coloring books and pictures he made as a kid. No luck.

The next and final hope was to retrace their hard-fought contest. Sometimes a previously mentioned color will trigger one that remains unnamed.

In the pre-dawn hour, Tosh smirked. "Cornflower."

"Cornflower? What the fuck is that?"

"It's a color."

"My ass it's a color. You make this shit up."

"It's a pale blue!"

"It's a pale blue," Crosby mimicked. "All right, you swine. You win. And for a prize, you get to drive!"

On that note, Crosby pulled off Interstate 90 and maneuvered the van into an all night mini-market and gas station. Time to stock up on sunflower seeds, coffee, orange juice, gum and other necessities of the road.

Tosh looked out the window of the van and noticed something strange about the service station. Its bright, convenience-store glow had attracted millions of light-hungry insects.

From many miles of wilderness surrounding the fabricated fluorescent oasis, countless moths and mosquitoes flew in search of The Light. Arriving at their mini-mart nirvana, the pests plastered themselves to every square inch of window, squirming and wiggling. The clinging bugs gave the store an active, breathing appearance.

They even covered the door.

"Gross," said Crosby.

"Maybe I'll just pass on that coffee."

"We have to fill up on gas, though."

"You're right. We'll flip to see who goes into pay."

Tosh grabbed a penny off of the engine cover and told Crosby to call it in the air.

He called tails.

The penny landed with Honest Abe gazing at the clouds.

"Two out of three," declared Crosby.

Tosh flipped the copper coin again and this time Crosby was victorious.

"Rubber flip. This one wins it," said Tosh, throwing the penny up.

Crosby called heads.

Abe's face met the van's beige carpeting.

"Three out of five,"

"You've got to be kidding," exclaimed Tosh. He got out of the van and inserted the gas nozzle into the van's tank.

"Come on. You won the crayon contest," called Crosby from the van.

Tosh hopped back into the front seat. He threw the penny into the air and Crosby guessed correctly.

Once again, the match came down to a single toss.

The bugs squirmed, the tank filled, Tosh flipped, Crosby called tails.

The coin landed.

"Tails it is," Tosh claimed in disgust.

He tucked his dirty blonde dreads up under his hat and ran like hell for what he figured to be the door. Squinting his eyes and keeping his mouth shut tight, Tosh delved his hand into the layer of moths and grabbed the handle. The door would not budge. For a nasty second, Tosh stood there frozen, elbow deep in swarming insects. Thinking quickly under pressure, he pushed the door open and fell into the sheltered mini-mart, a flurry of winged marauders following him.

Shaking off a few of the cotton-eating scum, Tosh walked straight up to the counter and said with firm authority, "I'll have a bottle of anything and a glazed donut! To go!"

The overnight employee, an older gentleman wearing a 'Muff Divers — No Muff Too Tuff' cap, kept his nose buried in an issue of *Juggs* magazine.

"Cancel that. I just always wanted to say that."

Tosh grabbed some coffee and o.j. to wash down his Hostess Ding Dongs and beef jerky. He paid for the gas and breakfast, tucked his head down and made a beeline for the van.

Crosby settled into the back bed as Tosh put in an old ska tape. Belting out, "A Message to You Rudie," he pulled Josephine back onto the highway to polish off the rest of Montana.

CHAPTER 6

At 8:45am, the sun shined brightly over the northern tip of Idaho. Huge Rocky Mountains scattered pine green all over the tumbling landscape. The morning breeze already felt warm, but it lacked the humidity that made air feel so uncomfortable. Tosh and Crosby cranked Jimmy Cliff to welcome the day.

They crossed the border at Lookout Pass, elevation 4738 feet, surprised to be in Idaho. They had anticipated Washington to come next, unaware The Potato State poked its narrow head up into their path.

Tosh did not know what to expect from Idaho. He had never given the state much consideration. Once, he saw a cool Idaho license plate at a Dead show, but other than that one occasion, he had never muttered the name.

Tosh certainly did not expect the invigorating, sky-scraping peaks they soon descended. Rolling down the backside of the awesome hills, Tosh kept repeating aloud to himself, "We're in Idaho! We're in Idaho!"

He had done the same thing the night he, Bob and Jeff had visited the headhunters in the rain forest of Borneo. Determined not to waste one precious moment in their remote location, they had banned sleep. They wanted to gain as much as possible from their short stay in the jungle.

Tosh and Bob and Jeff sat and watched and listened. The jungle lived at night. Warthogs cried in the distance. A lone bat paced back and forth, its mouth open to catch any unfortunate insect. An unrestrained dog would occasionally stroll by.

As they soaked up the Borneo rain forest, the guys discussed their recent traveling experiences. They talked about life and death and the past and the future. They talked about Scooby Doo.

Then, randomly, as if some subconscious urge overcame them, they'd raise their arms above their heads, gape at the South Asian moon and howl in unison, "I'm in Borneo! I'm in Borneo! I'm in Borneo!" No matter how many times they repeated this consummating ritual, the reality of their isolated locale would not sink in.

The memories of Borneo and the rest of their international journey begat a dreamy feeling, for the unusual places they had visited dished out perpetual amazement. Idaho evoked similar feelings, albeit not quite as strong.

Tosh did not want to blow through this underrated state. When would they be in Idaho again? They might never return to Idaho the rest of their lives. He wanted to stop and spend a little time there. Have an experience.

As the Rocky Mountains grew smaller in his rearview mirror, Tosh spotted the deep blue water of Coeur d'Alene Lake and knew that was the place to have their experience.

*   *   *   *

"You've got to spit on the worm," Crosby Graves said as he rummaged through his tackle box for a Hula Popper. "My grandpa always used to tell me to spit on the worm for good luck."

"Did it work?"

"Hell, yes! It's one of those myths that circulate among fishermen. A bit of tradition that the old timers pass on to the younger guys."

"You used to go fishing with your grandfather a lot, huh?"

"Yeah." Crosby stopped what he was doing for a moment and reeled in a recollection of his younger days. "I can picture him right now in his old fishing cap. Man, it was great. We'd wake up at the crack of dawn. The sun would just be rising and everything would be covered with dew. We'd both get dressed in flannel shirts and my grandfather would pack a bag with sandwiches and drinks. He'd take the bait out of the fridge and we'd grab the poles lined up against the cottage and off we went."

"What kind of bait did you use?" asked Tosh.

"Night crawlers. You know, those fat juicy worms?"

"Ugh, you kept them in the fridge?"

"Yeah. In a container with dirt."

"That's disgusting."

"Where else are you supposed to keep it?"

"I don't know," said Tosh. "A cooler?"

"Well, there was a cover on it."

Crosby found the lure he was searching for and tied it on to his line. "Anyway, I was so excited just to be awake at that time of the day. Everyone else was sound asleep and me and Grandpa were about to start our little adventure. We'd be the only ones out on the lake."

Crosby, satisfied with his pole preparation, set it aside. Next, he picked out a lure for Tosh. "We'd get in the boat and quietly row out to the middle of the lake. He'd bait our hooks with the night crawlers and we'd drop our lines in. We fished with bamboo poles back then. No casting."

Crosby tied a shiny silver lure with an orange dot on to Tosh's line. "We would just sit there and wait. When that bobber would dip, we'd grab the pole. You'd have to know when to yank it up. Sunnies and perch usually nibble at the bait, barely tipping the bobber. A catfish will take it straight down. A few seconds later it'll resurface in another spot. Down again and you know he's chewin' on the run."

Crosby finished up with Tosh's pole and admired his work. "You get a big bass and that bobber just disappears."

"Did you catch a lot of fish?"

"Most of the time, yeah. We'd get a lot of sunnies. Sometimes we got catfish. That was always exciting. Those ugly bullheads would eat anything you put on that hook. They gave you a hell of a fight, too, and not just in the water. Those bastards

79

have some kind of stinger or something. You have to be very careful when taking them off the hook, 'cause they'll get you. I remember my grandpa's hand being all bloody. I'd say, 'Gramps, doesn't that hurt?' And he'd just shake his head and smile and say, 'Naaa.' But I think it probably did hurt."

"They have a stinger?"

"They have these two horns, like, protruding from underneath the head. If you're not careful, they prick you and inject you with some type of venom or something. Your hand will swell up and stuff. It's their defense mechanism."

"Sounds horrible."

"It's not bad. You just have to hold them underneath the horns. You can't grab them around the head."

"What happens if we catch one now?"

"We eat it. Catfish are good eatin'."

"Yeah?"

"They're a very sweet fish with very few bones. Not much guts either. I'll let you clean 'em."

Clean them — what a euphemism, thought Tosh. "You mean gut 'em?"

"Yeah."

"No way."

"It's easy," said Crosby. "Put your finger in their mouth, slice below the neck and peel back their skin with the knife. Pluck the backbone and you got a tasty dinner — catfish fillet. Put that critter in a pan with a little butter and lemon, some corn meal. Yum."

"I'll eat 'em, but you can clean 'em."

"Bass was the prize catch. The elusive large-mouth bass," he said with a hush. Proudly, he added, "We caught our share."

They packed up the van and headed toward the lake.

Crosby continued. "One of my favorite memories is our 'fish that got away' tale. My pole was bent so far I thought it was gonna break. My grandpa had the net waiting and when I pulled the sucker up we saw this huge black fish with a touch of orange. It was a perch. Probably the biggest perch to ever live in the lake, and it would have been ours."

"What happened?"

"He fell off the hook right before my Gramps could get the net under him." Crosby mimicked their actions. "We were like, 'Did you see that?' We couldn't believe it. It really happened, you know, but to everyone else, it's just another tall tale about the fish that got away."

The guys walked along the shore, searching for a convenient spot to fish. Not wanting to stray too far from the van in the unfamiliar surroundings, they settled on an old dock that jutted sufficiently out into the lake.

"Did you guys always catch a lot of fish?"

"Naa. There were times when we wouldn't get a single bite."

"What would you do?"

"That's where the sandwiches and beers came in. Well, my grandpa would have the beer. I'd have a soda or something. We'd chow on ham and cheese, bologna, salami, corned beef. No turkey or anything, all the fatty, unhealthy meats. It was before the world was health conscious." Crosby cast his line far out into the lake.

Tosh followed suit in the opposite direction but on his first try became snagged on an unknown object beneath the surface. He yanked and yanked in frustration until finally the line snapped. Embarrassed, Tosh held the pole pretending as though he were waiting for a hit and listened to Crosby's continuing monologue.

"I remember I would wash my hands off in the lake and then wipe them on my shirt before eating my sandwich. My grandpa, though? He'd just grab a sandwich and munch away, worm slime and fish guts and blood caked on his hands. He didn't care."

Crosby glanced over to see what Tosh was doing. "Are you gonna reel that in, dude?"

"I was waiting for a bite."

"Ya gotta reel it in. Slowly."

Tosh hesitantly reeled in the lureless line. Acting surprised when nothing but string rose from the water, he exclaimed, "What the fuck?"

"What happened?"

"Something ate my whole lure! Bit the thing right off!"

"You lost the lure?"

"It looks that way," Tosh said, spuriously inspecting the line.

"Man, that was a brand new lure!"

"Sorry." Tosh laid back on the dock and took off his shirt. "I'll just relax and watch you fish."

"Fishing *is* relaxing, Tosh."

"I'll fish vicariously," he said, dangling his bare feet in the cool water.

To Tosh, fishing was nothing but an excuse to drink. The two activities went hand in hand. Waking up at the crack of dawn to drop a line in? Not unless beer was for breakfast. Those were prime sleeping hours to pass up.

Fishing ranked right up there with bowling — utterly unentertaining unless beer became incorporated into the activity. Same with miniature golf.

And regular golf, for that matter.

"Hey, Tosh, why don't you get the radio or something? Make yourself useful if you're not gonna fish."

"The radio? Won't that scare away the fish?"

"Naa. That's just a myth."

"It is?"

"Sure it is. Next time you're swimming, stick your head under the water and tell me if you hear anything. Shit, I don't even think fish have ears. I've never seen any."

81

"They've got to have some type of ears."

"Maybe, but I still think people overestimate the intelligence of fish. How big could a sunny's brain be? The size of a pea? I'm not talking dolphins or whales here."

"Dolphins and whales are mammals, anyway. Mammals that swim."

Crosby reeled in his line and removed some algae that had gotten caught on the lure. "They're still fish."

*　　*　　*　　*

After a fruitless fishing expedition at Coeur d'Alene Lake, (a couple of bluegills, no keepers) the guys left Idaho behind and began their long journey through the Eastern Washington desert.

Air conditioning would have been nice but it was not an option. None of the clunkers that Tosh and Crosby looked at when shopping for a vehicle to take them cross-country featured such a luxury. So Tosh had to settle for a hint of relief from the warm, dry breeze blowing through the windows of the van as they drove through the sweltering heat. With his sweat-soaked shorts sticking to his butt, he felt like the floor of Madison Square Garden after a Rangers game — grimy, wet and smelly.

Tosh had to get out of the van. Josephine needed a rest, too. The past four hours rolling through the steaming desert took its toll on the van – inside and out. Her engine had been running hot and her faded blue paint was coated with dust. Spotting a scenic lookout along the highway, Tosh pulled the van over.

It felt great to jump out of the van and stretch. The breeze picked up to a steady wind as Tosh and Crosby walked to the edge of the cliff that towered over the wide Colombia River. The mighty Colombia, carved deep into the brown rock, stretched far below them like a giant black snake. Barges silently crawled up her back.

"This is wild," said Crosby, leaning over a man-made stone wall. "The river is so far away."

"Wanna jump?"

"Yeah, right. You go first."

"Whaddaya say we make a pit-stop. Give the van a rest and maybe grab some grub."

Crosby nodded.

Back into the van they jumped, headed for the next town.

*　　*　　*　　*

Vantage, Washington, sat perched high on the banks of the Colombia. Although it had a favorable location, the town featured nothing special. Vantage resembled every other small American town except for one thing — massive wind.

A strong wind blew through the sleepy town incessantly, not a fleeting breeze, but a constant gust. It was as if God placed his electric fan — not the portable oscillating variety but the big-ass window kind — on the edge of town and cranked it up to obtain some relief from the desert heat.

Tosh wondered if this were a passing windstorm or a permanent characteristic of Vantage. From the nonchalant attitudes of the townsfolk, the latter seemed more probable. Except for many squinted eyes, people went about their business routinely as the whipping wind messed their hair and disheveled their clothes.

The merciless gusts spared nothing in the town. Everything not nailed down and some things that were blew down the streets of Vantage. Like a perpetual, whirling rummage sale, random objects danced through the town.

The wind blew napkins. It blew scissors, Schnauzers, basketballs, radial tires, watches, junk mail, money, Budweiser bottles, eyeglasses, five-irons, fence posts, glue-sticks, tarps, cushions, milk cartons, hats, prunes, signs, sticks, stones, jack-o-lanterns, vases, soup cans, tuna fish casseroles, remote controls, Bic razors, chains, chickens, sisters, hoses, horses and #2 pencils.

Fighting off the wind and their hunger, Tosh and Crosby almost stooped to dining at McDonald's for lunch when Crosby sighted Paco's Tacos.

The decor deserved two thumbs up. Paintings of cacti and lizards and other desert life graced the walls. The interesting menu offered the usual Mexican dishes but it gave them cool names like: Lizard Lips Nachos, Scorpion Enchiladas and Cactus Needle Tacos. The Rattlesnake Shake sounded good, but it cost almost three dollars. Too expensive for a non-alcoholic drink.

Paco's Tacos did not serve quesadillas, chimichangas, or fajitas.

They did have one type of burrito, however, and were therefore subjected to the discerning taste buds of the two grimy gringos from New Jersey in their search for the Ultimate Burrito.

"I'll have The Iguana Burrito," requested Tosh.

"Ditto," added Crosby.

"Would you like anything to drink with that?" asked the pubescent girl with her hair pulled back in a ponytail.

"We'll have dos aguas," Crosby said cleverly.

The girl froze, confused by the beverage request.

"We'll have two waters, please," Tosh clarified, sarcastically disapproving Crosby with a mock glare.

The friends took their burritos and waters to the booth farthest from the counter. Crosby grabbed a bottle of hot sauce and a bunch of napkins along the way. Digging into the modest feast spread before them, the review began.

"Employees of a Mexican restaurant should at least know minimal Spanish," stated Crosby.

Tosh swallowed his first bite. "Oh, come on. Give her a break. She's like fourteen. Just judge the food, man."

"Once again, no guacamole," Crosby complained.

"At least this has sour cream."

"Yeah. It looks like we have beans, beef and cheddar."

"No onions, no peppers."

"Better than Buford, but bogus."

They chowed the rest of their mediocre burritos and bailed. Tosh started the van and waited for Crosby, who kindly instructed the young employee in a few basic phrases of Spanish before he left.

"I don't really feel like hitting the road just yet."

"Me neither," said Crosby, picking his teeth.

"I've got an idea," Tosh said excitedly.

"What's up?"

"Remember that giant car wash we passed on the way into town? Maybe we actually wash the van!"

Bath time for Josephine.

*   *   *   *

The car wash, of the self-help variety, gave customers access to auto shampoo and a power wash stream of water for $1.50. Tosh and Crosby took turns carefully hosing down Josephine and scrubbing her clean, inevitably soaking each other in the process. At first they forgot to close the windows and mistakenly washed some of the interior as well.

After her bath, they wheeled Josephine out into the lot to dry. "Might as well clean her out while we're at it," Tosh suggested. They hadn't had a good cleaning since Kansas.

"Might as well, might as well," Crosby responded, singing the chorus to the Grateful Dead song by the same title.

Tosh and Crosby put a lot of care into Josephine's "housekeeping." The van was not only their transportation, but also their home.

Finding a vehicle worthy of this trek had been no easy task. For weeks, Tosh and Crosby searched the want ads. With pens and markers they highlighted the best possibilities and took turns calling strangers to inquire about their merchandise.

It dawned on Crosby that every one of the people they called was essentially a used car salesman. This made their quest a risky proposition, especially since they were looking for a van.

"You never know what they've been used for," Crosby had pointed out. "Hauling meat? Chemicals? Illegal aliens? Could be drugs stashed somewhere."

Tosh and Crosby knew they wanted some type of van or Volkswagen Bus. They did not want to spend countless hours on the road cramped in some Japanese import. Never once did Tosh Tyler sleep soundly in the back seat of a car. Would the trunk of a Buick Regal hold their clothing, camping gear, cooking equipment, food supplies, plus various other useless belongings?

A van also provided privacy. They could sleep undisturbed by the sun, cops or snooping, immoral hoodlums. Furthermore, Tosh and Crosby could dress, smoke pot and drink whiskey and beer whenever they felt like it. A Honda Accord could not measure up to a Dodge Sportsman Van when it came to an apartment on wheels.

Tosh and Crosby scoured the farthest corners of New Jersey for their special cross-country vehicle. Sometimes they drove up to three hours to look at an available auto.

They found a 1971 VW Bus in Bedminster that fit the bill, but it carried a price tag too expensive and the ham-bone selling it wouldn't budge.

They tracked down a 1977 Ford Econoline Van in Waldwick, but it had more rust than a notable home-run-hitting first baseman from the New York Mets.

A 1975 VW Camper in Cherry Hill needed engine work.

A 1980 Chevy in Brunswick required interior construction.

In Kinnelon, while test-driving an olive green VW Bus, the sliding door fell off as Crosby maneuvered around a turn.

Maybe their hopes were too high, but Tosh and Crosby did not want to put additional cash into someone else's refuse. Besides, they could not do any of the necessary auto work themselves.

Tosh had no sense when it came to technology. He struggled with Legos. The phrase "Batteries not Included" frightened him. Programming the VCR was a far-fetched pipe dream.

And he had far less knowledge when it came to automobiles. The anti-mechanic, Tosh thought a transmission problem had something to do with the radio.

Crosby had a little more savvy, but not much.

They needed to find a vehicle already capable of making a sustained road-trip.

After two months of this hopeless hunt, they became doubtful. Wondering if their time and energy had been wasted, frustration began to take the fun out of the project. Then, at a particularly sad point when they considered bagging the whole damn trip, they inadvertently found Josephine.

Tosh and Crosby had just driven an hour to look at a VW Bus that had great promise. On the phone, the owner sounded cool. He had just installed a new clutch and he had offered to put on new brakes and tune it up for them as well. When they arrived, however, the dude turned out to be an asshole and the bus a hunk of crap so nasty it hurt their eyes to look at it.

They cursed their bad luck and drove back towards the highway, moping. Along the way, they spotted a blue van with a "For Sale" sign parked along a side street. With nothing to lose, they checked it out.

The owner had just put the 1973 Dodge Sportsman up for sale that morning. With only 72,000 miles on it, the old van looked younger than its age. It had new tires, wires and plugs and a fresh battery. No rust weakened its unblemished, extra-long frame.

On the inside, beige carpeting covered the floor and two beds, which sat aligned in an L shape with the bottom of the L along the rear of the van. It had plenty of storage space under the beds and the door cavities along the side and in the rear served as cabinets or shelves.

Finally, they had hit a stroke of good fortune.

The owner was asking $1100, but the guys would have paid more. With Tosh and Crosby's desperation boosting their excitement about the van, bargaining became a lost cause. They obviously wanted it bad, so their feeble attempt at haggling did not suffice. The owner stood firm.

The van drove about as well as could be expected from a 1973 vehicle — not very well. It had little power and manual steering and brakes. Driving the big lug required strength and sense. It would take some practice before the two of them felt completely comfortable behind the wheel.

But that practice would have to come on the road. Tosh and Crosby had wasted enough time and they were anxious to get going. They took one day of preparations before leaving New Jersey.

After registering and insuring the van, Tosh and Crosby converted it into an apartment on wheels. They tinted the windows and added pull-down blinds for total privacy. In return for a six-pack of Heineken, Crosby's dad mounted a small oscillating fan in the rear corner to provide ventilation when the van was parked.

Then came the Tosh Tylerization of the van. He covered the van in posters and pictures, leftovers from his bedroom in the fraternity house. Reggae and other hippie paraphernalia blanketed the bare metal walls, while Crosby's psychedelic drawings filled in the empty spots.

After adding a roof rack to hold Crosby's wind surfing gear, the guys topped off the transformation by dotting the windows and rear of the van with surfing, Rasta and Grateful Dead stickers. Lastly, they placed a giant Steal Your Face smack dab in the middle of the van's hood.

The Dodge Sportsman was ready for travel.

*   *   *   *

So far, the miles had been kind to Josephine.

With the desert dust cleansed away and an hour of rest under her belt, she felt refreshed and eager to move on.

As Tosh and Crosby finished up at the car wash, Vantage's ever-present wind increased, picking up pebbles from the ground. The tiny rocks felt like pricking needles as the wind whipped them into their bare legs.

"Ow! What the hell?" shouted Crosby.

"Damn! This hurts!" added Tosh, looking for the evil bugs that were attacking his exposed leg flesh.

Quickly they piled their bags, radio and coolers back into the van. They headed back to the highway, back into the Eastern Washington desert.

Vantage was history.

*   *   *   *

Tosh and Crosby continued trekking west across the arid sand. As the sweltering afternoon mellowed into a mild evening, the interminable desert finally gave way to the towering Cascade Mountains, the flat brown landscape abruptly changing to luscious peaks of dark green pine.

About 100 miles east of Seattle, the two worlds collided, each as unforgiving as the next. If the choking dust and heat of the desert hadn't made life miserable enough, the isolation did. This made the Cascades, full of natural splendor, a welcome sight. Yet their beauty could be deceiving; the harsh hills provided a tough fight for many travelers.

Josephine's engine began running dangerously hot. Tosh and Crosby had really pushed her, crossing the desert during the heat of the day. Now, it caught up to the van as she slowly tugged her weight through the steep mountains.

Horizontal light peeked under ominous thunderheads, prompting the guys to find a campsite before the stormy nightfall.

Crosby pulled off the highway into a huge truck stop that doubled as a vacationer campground. Featuring loads of gas pumps and even a cafeteria, the sight attracted a multitude of tourists.

Tosh and Crosby did not want to spend their night in the Cascades surrounded by a horde of RVs and station wagons. They wanted to experience the gorgeous mountains, not a small city of shitting dogs, arm flab and snot-nosed, fudgicle-coated rug rats. They might as well camp in the parking lot of Giants Stadium during the summer carnival.

"This is bogus," moaned Crosby.

"An ugly nightmare," retorted Tosh.

"We're not staying here. No way."

"Yeah, but we really shouldn't drive on. The van needs a rest. So do we. Besides, it looks like there's gonna be a wicked storm."

The darkening clouds piled higher as they spoke.

Crosby nodded and quoted a Bob Dylan song. "A hard rain's gonna fall."

"Don't wanna get caught pitchin' tent in some bad ass mountain storm."

"There's got to be other campsites around here. Look at these mountains!"

Tosh put the decision on Crosby's shoulders. "You're driving. You make the call."

Crosby started the van and pulled out of the lot. "Later, clowns," he muttered, eyeing the knucklehead circus in his rearview mirror.

Instead of getting back on the highway, Crosby chose a local road that ran parallel to it. After a mile he made a random right.

"Where are you going?" Tosh inquired.

"Don't really know," Crosby plainly responded.

"I guess that's the beauty of this trip. Don't really know. Don't really care. Doesn't really matter."

"Whatever happens, it's better than doing the same old thing back home."

"True, true." Tosh reached under the side bed to grab a cold beer. "Want a frosty pal?"

At that moment, the van lurched to the left and sent Tosh flying. "I guess that's a no," he said.

When he rose from the carpeted floor, Tosh opened his shaken Budweiser to find they were driving down a dirt road. Tall conifers closely lined the sides.

Tosh spotted a car and a pickup sitting in a small clearing off to the right. "Right over there," he pointed. "In the trees. It looks like a cool place to camp."

"How do you think they got there?" asked Crosby.

No visible path led to the autos as huge trees stood in their way.

"Keep driving. We'll see."

Soon, a less traveled dirt trail, barely wide enough for a car, appeared to their right.

"Bingo."

The guys followed the winding path slowly, evidently backtracking. A faded, hand-painted sign reading **MINE CREEK CAMP** dangled from a tree trunk as Crosby maneuvered the van into the small clearing with the pickup and the car. He parked opposite the river that ran rapidly alongside the campsite.

Darkness approached briskly as the clouds rolled in and, back in the woods, the guys had even less light because of the many tall trees filtering the day's final rays of the sun. They had to work quickly. Crosby pitched the tent as his partner went to search for firewood.

Tosh scrounged up a selection of dead wood, from thick logs to twigs. He piled it in his arms and dragging back more than he could handle, dropped his beer.

"Damn!" he cried.

Some had spilled out, but plenty of the cold brew remained. Leaning down to pluck the damp Bud from the earth, Tosh could not grasp the spilled beverage with the load of wood in his arms. He set his load down to grab the bottle, brushing off the pine needles and dirt that clung to its side and wiping them on his shorts.

Tosh drank down the last sips and was about to whip the bottle far into the woods when an image of the past entered his mind. Once again, he thought of his journey in Malaysia to visit the ancient tribe of headhunters, the Ibans.

Tosh and his companions, well prepared for the rain forest, carried bug repellent, Swiss Army knives, flashlights, lighters, cigarettes, granola bars, toilet paper, sunscreen, aspirin, Band-Aids, sewing kits, cameras, notepads, binoculars, deodorant and, most importantly, first-aid kits.

No warthogs, cobras or giant spiders could stop them.

If the anticipation of meeting the ancient tribe wasn't thrilling enough, traveling to their village was. To get there, Tosh and his friends had to travel by canoe deep into the jungle of Borneo. As their longboat crawled up the remote Skrang River, Tosh's eyes searched the overhead canopy of tree limbs and hanging vines for snakes. Every log that broke the surface of the murky, brown water took the appearance of a fearsome crocodile. The calls of tropical birds and insects sounded like the screeches of wild monkeys. Tosh's adrenaline bubbled as they paddled cautiously and quietly, wondering what lurked beyond every bend.

His excitement boiled over when their canoe came to a sudden halt alongside a dock. Wooden steps climbed up a steep bank.

What waited beyond?

Tosh pictured a band of fierce warriors with spears and face paint performing a loud, energetic welcome dance. He expected pounding drums and ritual sacrifice. He wanted to hunt with blowpipes and eat wild boar cooked over a large fire.

But as Tosh clambered out of the boat, he found something disturbing. A glass soda bottle glared at him from the muddy bank. On the other side of the world, Tosh had traveled for two days on three bus rides, three plane flights and a boat trip, far into isolation, only to find a goddamned Squirt bottle.

Tosh climbed the stairs with his buddies and, as the adventure continued, it got worse.

Anticlimactically, the few Ibans present at their arrival went about their humdrum business in Adidas shorts, Mickey Mouse T-shirts and flip-flops, a far cry from spears and face paint.

Disappointingly, a hello nod replaced the frenzied dance he had awaited.

Later, instead of hunting with blowpipes as their tour agent had promised, the group joined one Iban as he demonstrated the use of his primitive weapon on an innocent tree. What a hoot.

Tosh felt letdown. He wanted to visit with an ancient tribe of headhunters, not a modernized clan of hermits. Except for the creepy bats flying far overhead, Tosh had seen more engaging things at a flea market.

Later that evening, however, while watching the elder natives perform their traditional dances, Tosh's views had changed.

Skeptical, he sat back to watch the show. Soon, he began to feel woozy from the homemade rice wine. As the slow, rhythmic beating of the drums and gong lulled him into an intense state of relaxation, Tosh tuned out everything around him except for the tribal music and dancers.

The smooth brown skin of the elder tribesman stretched tightly over his rippled muscles, flickering in the light of the fire. The old man stepped and kicked suddenly but softly as his arms and hands swirled and waved gracefully. He turned his head around and then up toward the heavens, an unnatural expression on his face. Clenching his teeth, he turned his mouth up slightly at the corners. His eyes stared unblinking, fixed on nothing. This unnatural expression conveyed, at the same time, a sense of fear and of power. The paradoxical countenance showed no emotion but expressed all emotions.

At that moment, Tosh realized he was not watching a show, but a ritual. This dance had served, unchanging, as an integral part of the Iban existence for hundreds of years. It had great importance to these people, and his generous hosts shared it with him.

Tosh finally understood the purpose and virtue of his journey. It had nothing to do with fierce, headhunting warriors living primitively in a jungle. That no longer existed. Instead, Tosh visited the same tribe in their present-day situation and experienced a part of that culture preserved by their descendants.

In that light, Tosh looked at his journey as an incredible opportunity to visit an ancient tribe in the middle of an inevitable transformation. As the world continued to grow, technology reached out to every inhabited place on earth, changing them. Eventually, Tosh knew, there would be no more jungle tribes. The Iban culture and tradition itself might be forever gone within ten years.

But a little piece of it would always remain inside Tosh.

Tosh looked at the Budweiser bottle in his hands and then at the beautiful woods surrounding him. He decided littering would be a bad idea.

Carefully, he gripped one piece of firewood at a time. He tucked some under his arms. Some he stuck in his shorts, preparing to haul it all back to camp.

Tosh had always prided himself on his ability to make one trip. Whether it be lugging boxes full of Christmas decorations for his mother or transporting his entire load of laundry without the use of a sack or basket, Tosh always attempted to accomplish a burdensome task in one trip. He relished the challenge.

Underwear and socks he stuffed in his pockets and T-shirts hung by a pinkie.

He'd drag all the recycling containers out to the curb at once while pushing the garbage cans with his feet. On one occasion, he had dropped the "green glass" crate on the driveway. The empty wine bottles rattled, but did not break, as Tosh drew a dubious glance from his father.

The only casualty of his career was a broken ketchup bottle on the kitchen tile that had occurred while hauling an overload of grocery bags.

With virtually all the firewood he had gathered, Tosh walked back to camp, the empty beer bottle firmly in hand.

*   *   *   *

When Tosh returned to camp with the firewood, a light rain began to fall. Crosby stood knee-deep in the clear, cold rapids, fishing for trout. None of the other campers could be found. The storm clouds promised a heavy rain, so Tosh deposited the firewood under the van and ducked into the tent to catch a few zees.

Crosby ignored the drizzling rain, for this little river seemed to be a fisherman's paradise. On two of his first three casts, Crosby received hits from hungry trout. His enthusiasm increased with every cast and subsequent hit, culminating in one crazy crash.

Crosby snagged a trout and briskly reeled it in. Fighting for his life, the pesky fish pulled Crosby toward the river. While laboring to keep his footing, Crosby yanked the pole upward. At the moment he pulled the trout out of the water and made eye contact with his slippery prey, an explosive thunderbolt tore through the sky. A gust of wind ripped through camp and torrential rains rushed down.

Crosby slipped.

He found himself in a precarious position — one hand holding on to the pole with the frisky trout and the other gripping a rock. Crosby braced himself with his left foot against a large stone as the rain poured down and the river ran around him, trying to tear him away. He remained like this for a minute, figuring out his next move. He knew one thing — his next move did not include letting go of that pole.

"What are you doing?"

An unfamiliar voice. A stupid question.

Crosby turned to face the speaker. On the bank of the river, a few feet away, stood a man dressed in a bright yellow rain poncho. His lopsided hood covered most of his face. He was smiling.

A stupid question deserves a stupid answer, thought Crosby. "Fishing," he said.

Puzzled, the man accepted the answer. Then, after some more thought, he asked another obvious question. "Do you need a hand?"

Crosby wanted to say, "What do you *think*, you stupid fuck?" but considering his position, he realized that would not be a smart response. Instead, he nodded vigorously.

The helpful stranger took a step into the river and extended his hand for Crosby. Within a few seconds, Crosby stood on the bank of the river, soaked to the gills. He reeled his trout in the rest of the way and held it right up to his face, taunting the poor critter. "I got you. I got you. Ah-*ha-ha-ha.*"

"It's a nice fish."

"Uh, thanks." Crosby had forgotten about his rescuer looking on. "Thanks for the hand, too."

"Not a problem. The name's Steve."

Crosby, still miffed by Steve's questionable mentality, did not respond. He took a final look at the trout, too small to eat, and threw it back into its wet niche. "Grow up to make some fisherman a very happy fellow."

Despite the raging rain, Crosby continued to fish — he was already wet and the rain felt warmer than his river-soaked clothes. Besides, the trout were biting. This time, though, Crosby stayed on the bank, well out of reach of the aggressive river.

*   *   *   *

Tosh had quickly become relaxed, snuggled in his sleeping bag as the rain pelted down against the roof of the tent. The roaring thunder made him feel cozy but at the same time kept him from falling into a deep sleep.

After an hour or so, the downpour ceased and the clouds fled. Lingering daylight trickled into the damp campsite from above.

He might have dozed off for a few minutes because he didn't recall hearing the first three songs. Now, although his eyes remained shut, his ears became astute. Drifting through the thin walls of the tent came "Idiot Wind." He thought he was dreaming one of his favorite Dylan songs, but when his eyes opened, the tune continued. Tosh enjoyed the rest of the eight-minute song lying in the comfort of his bag.

As Bob went into the fifth song on *Blood on the Tracks,* Tosh ventured out to see who had the good taste in music. A campfire burned steadily where Crosby, drenched, moved closer for heat. Two guys joined him — one a clean-cut yuppie type and the other, a burned-out hippie. Over by the pickup truck, an older gentleman fiddled with his chainsaw.

"What's up?" asked Tosh to no one in particular.

"Hey Tosh. Nice nap? I caught *seven* trout! Seven!" Crosby spoke quickly, with an astonished look on his face.

"That's great, Cros. Maybe you should, uh, get changed? You look wet."

"Yeah, yeah. That's a good idea, good idea." Crosby scurried over to the van to get his backpack.

"What's with him?" Tosh asked his new acquaintances.

"I think the river got the best of him," said the hippie, his tangled hair hanging down a green tie-dye. Thick eyeglasses magnified his friendly face, which featured a small nose and chubby, rose-colored cheeks.

"So who's playing the poet?" asked Tosh.

The hippie jumped up and giggled, "That would be me, Willy." Performing an energetic little dance complete with a modest bow, his large, bare feet protruded from his short frame and gave him the appearance of a psychedelic gnome.

"Pleased to meet you, my good man Willy. My name is Tosh. Tosh Tyler."

"This is my cousin, Steve," said Willy, motioning to the guy next to him. "Steve's driving me to California for my sister's wedding."

Steve shook Tosh's hand and sat back down. As matted and unconventional as Willy looked, Steve was tidy and regular. Steve was as flat as Willy was bubbly.

"Driving your cousin all the way to Cali," remarked Tosh. "That's love."

"Well, I have a job lined up, so I was heading out west anyway."

Crosby rejoined the group, wearing some old jeans and a flannel. "Oh, please don't say the J-word."

"Crosby and I just graduated, but we have no idea what we want to do. We have to find *careers.*"

"Don't say the C-word either," added Crosby. "Not now."

Tosh did not want to hear about jobs, especially when this guy had a nice path to follow and Tosh had no clue what he was going to do. He did not want to think about careers. Tosh knew this trip wouldn't last forever and when he returned to Jersey, he would be aimless and unemployed.

That nagging anxiety had crept up a few times, but Tosh had always managed to suppress it. During the long stretches of driving, usually late at night, his mind tended to wander, sometimes digging up thoughts that had no place in his head during the journey.

This trip lived for the moment. Considering the future would defeat its purpose. Exploring the present should not be clouded by a preoccupation with what lies ahead. Carpe diem, goddammit.

"Who's the dude with the chainsaw?" asked Tosh. "I hope he's trustworthy."

"That's Chuck. He's a local. Got thrown out of the house by his old lady."

Chuck looked over and tipped his GMC Trucks cap.

"Chuck hooked us up with some firewood. Sliced up a fallen tree like a zucchini. He also made these nifty stools." With that, Willy jumped up on one of the round tree stumps sitting around the fire. "We got lucky. There was a nice pile of kindling sitting under that blue van."

Tosh looked over and noticed the wood he had gathered had been put to good use. "You like reggae?" he asked Steve, who donned a Bahamas T-shirt.

"Why do you ask?"

"Hey, Tosh," Crosby interrupted, "how about spaghetti and toast for dinner? I'll cook if you clean."

"Spaghetti? What about your seven trout?"

Crosby frowned. "Too small. Had to throw them back."

"O.K., deal — you cook, I'll clean."

Crosby got out a box of pasta, tomato sauce, six slices of wheat bread and the pot, which he filled with river water. He boiled the water on the Coleman while he stuck the bread on sticks to toast over the fire.

"The shirt. It's got a reggae flavor," Tosh continued.

"Not really," said Steve. "It kind of bores me."

"Bores you?"

"Yeah."

"What do you mean?"

"I don't know. It all sounds the same."

Oh shit, thought Crosby. *Here we go.* He'd seen this conversation before. Tosh got pretty intense when discussing his passion.

"Who have you listened to?"

"I don't know. I've listened to Bob Marley and stuff. He's O.K."

Tosh shot up from his seat. "O.K.? I can't believe you think Bob Marley is just O.K.!"

Steve sat motionless, unsure what to say.

"*Rastaman Vibration* takes me to Jamaica. When I listen to Marley, I can feel the sticky heat of the Caribbean. I can smell the salty sea air and the bush fires burning in the hills. I can see people sitting around on empty cases of Red Stripe, playing dominos, watching the lizards crawl."

Crosby looked over at Willy, who pushed up his thick glasses but otherwise sat still. He watched Tosh with delight, a silly smile on his face.

"You say all reggae sounds the same?" continued Tosh. "Not even Marley's music *itself* sounds the same. Listen to the difference from the suffering of *Rastaman Vibration* to the sweet, sweet love songs of *Legend.*"

Tosh spoke with distant eyes, as though picturing detailed images. His hands moved expressively with the ideas he vocalized.

"I don't think there is a collection of more uplifting songs in this universe. *Legend* puts me on a white, sandy beach. The sun is shining and I'm lying in a hammock under a palm, drinking a coconut, swaying in the mild ocean breeze. How could you feel anything but irie, anything but totally positive, after listening to 'Three Little Birds?'"

No one answered.

"You say all reggae sounds the same, but compare Bob Marley to Peter Tosh. As vulnerable and pained and soothing as Bob's voice was, Peter's boomed with authority. Whether the song was a celebratory hymn or a militant anthem, Peter's voice held a cosmic vibration. The man sang with unbridled passion, equally joyous and angry, a powerful, visceral voice."

Tosh leaned into Steve and asked intensely, "Have you ever listened to Peter Tosh?"

"Yeah, I heard him," Steve said, a little defensively.

"You might have *heard* him, but did you listen to him, man?"

Steve did not respond.

"Peter Tosh spoke through the universal spirit! His rugged voice demanded attention. His music captured the minds and hearts of people."

"Hoo!" squealed Willy, perched on a tree stump, kicking his feet back and forth.

"Peter Tosh was the Minister of Righteousness, defending the poor downtrodden people of the world, uplifting humankind. Nothing frightened him. He spoke his mind for the truth. Truth in God. Truth in humanity. Truth in spirituality. Truth in life and in death."

Tosh's intensity even transfixed Crosby, whose toast caught fire as Tosh continued with his sermon.

"When he sings 'I am an intelligent man, and I love intelligent people, I am a progressive man, and I love progressive people,' man, he's pouring out his soul! His soul comes right through the music. It's unbelievable!"

Tosh wiped the sweat off his forehead and lowered his voice. "If there is one concept that Peter Tosh stood for, that permeated his life and works, it is *dignity.*"

Tosh met everyone's stares. Sinking back into reality, he sat down, shocked by his own exuberance.

A moment of silence followed, no one really knowing what to say.

Steve broke the hush. "You really get all that out of reggae?"

Tosh nodded proudly.

"It just sounds like a bunch of bass to me," Steve nettled.

"What are you, an asshole?"

"Lighten up, Tosh!" chastised Crosby. "Everyone is entitled to his or her own opinion."

Tosh got up without saying anything and headed over to the van.

"Sorry about Tosh," Crosby apologized. "He just likes to be understood."

"I understand him," said Steve, a little agitated. "He's a wannabe Rastaman."

Crosby defended his friend. "That's not true. Tosh is not a poser." He wrapped spaghetti around his fork and brought the dangling noodles to his mouth. "He doesn't try to be anything that he's not."

"What's with the dreads?"

"He's just a huge reggae fan and he digs the hairstyle. Big deal," said Crosby through a mouthful of pasta. "Tosh feels very passionately about things. Especially his music."

"Stronger than most people."

Crosby watched his shaggy friend dig a beer out of the cooler. "Yeah, Tosh marches to the beat of a different drummer."

"And his drummer has a reggae beat," winked Willy.

CHAPTER 7

After dining on Crosby's spaghetti and toast, Tosh took the dirty pot and pan over to the river to rinse them out. Nightfall had set and Tosh lit his path with the lantern as he strayed away from the campfire's faint, flickering flame. While the rushing water dispersed the bits of tomato sauce from the pan and plates, two bright headlights suddenly illuminated the campsite.

Tosh made his way back to the campfire and joined Crosby, Chuck, Willy and the new guy, an older man with a kind, rotund face. Steve had already gone to bed.

"This here's Angelo," said Chuck.

"Nice to meet you, Angelo."

"Likewise."

The group sipped beers and Applejack, listening to the crickets and the river.

Angelo got up and vanished into the back of his camper truck for a minute. He reappeared with a crinkled, brown paper bag. "I'm a baker," he said. "As every day begins with the sunrise, I begin with the muffins. These are from this morning. Help yourself."

With that, he handed the bag to Crosby. Inside the bag, there sat muffins of all kinds — blueberry, banana, bran, chocolate-chip, corn, carrot. Crosby grabbed a chocolate-chip and passed the bag along. Soon, everyone munched Angelo's muffins with their beers as they bullshit about the earlier storm.

Out of the corner of his eye, Tosh could see Willy staring at him. He tried to ignore him but, becoming unnerved, he blurted, "What? What is it?"

"I've seen you before."

"Whaddaya mean?"

"I've seen you at a Dead show at the Meadowlands."

"Really?"

"Yeah."

"That's pretty weird," said Tosh. "Giants Stadium or the Arena?"

"Summer tour. The Stadium."

"Are you sure? I mean, Giants Stadium holds like 76,000 people."

"I think so. Have you ever seen a show at Giants Stadium?"

"More like, have I ever *missed* a show at Giants Stadium?"

"It rained at the show I saw you at," said Willy. "Poured. Lightning, the works."

Tosh thought for a second. He remembered a show like that a few years back. Massive thunderstorms hit in the middle of the first set, but the Dead played through it. "I was at that show."

"Then I saw you."

"Were you wasted?"

"Well, of course."

"Maybe it was someone that looked like me."

"No, it was you."

"How can you remember? Did I say anything to you?"

"No, but I was tripping my face off and I remember this shirt you were wearing."

"Really? What shirt?"

"I remember thinking that it was like the only shirt there that wasn't a tie-dye. It was white with a big green peace sign on the front. On the back it had this wicked cool saying. Let me think for a second."

Willy closed his eyes and put his fingers on his temples while everyone looked on with interest. "Damn," he said, opening his eyes again. "I can't remember what it said."

Tosh smiled. He knew the shirt. "Dream, you dream alone, is nothing but a dream. Dream, we dream together, is reality."

"That was it! It *was* you!"

Tosh laughed. He couldn't believe it.

"I knew you looked familiar. Where did you get that shirt?"

"Actually, I made it."

"Did you make that saying up?"

"No. I think John Lennon said it. Or Yoko."

"I remember reading it about a thousand times. Or reading it once and then repeating it a thousand times," Willy recalled. "I was trippin' out and I was thinking, like Jerry was infusing this idea into everyone at the show as he was playing 'China Doll.' I felt like everyone was on the same cosmic wavelength and we were all gonna make something happen to change the world."

"Like what?" Tosh asked eagerly.

Chuck, Crosby and Angelo watched and listened intently, eating their muffins slower and slower as the story progressed.

"I have no idea. But then, all of a sudden, lightning flashed and thunder crashed. The sky opened up and rain just poured down. I thought we had caused it. I thought we were talking to God."

"Man, that must have been some good acid."

"And then the Dead went into 'Tennessee Jed' and this girl started wiggin' out. She was dancing hysterically and she stepped on my foot. She fell down and was laughing, the rain falling on her face. She was lying at my feet, laughing, just laughing. Her mouth was wide open and the rain was falling in her mouth. I remember seeing her tonsils. They were really big."

Chuck and Angelo exchanged glances at this point, wondering what the fuck Willy was talking about.

"Her tonsils were kind of red, so I thought maybe she was sick. I thought that the rain in her mouth was making her sick, like it was acid rain or something. So I covered her mouth with my hand to save her."

"What happened?"

"She must have thought I was trying to strangle her or something and she freaked and kicked her foot straight up into my balls."

"Ouch."

"Bulls eye. Down I went. Then, she got up and started dancing again. She ran away laughing and dancing. I just lied on the ground, all curled up on the wet tarp. We were on the floor, you know? I remember lying on the tarp in pain as the rain poured down and the Dead played 'Tennessee Jed.'

"Then Jerry sang, 'He blacked my eye and he kicked my dog,' and I was thinking, like, I was the dog."

"Hmmm," said Tosh.

"It's a small world, huh?"

"Yeah, it sure is," said Tosh, finishing his beer.

"Actually, it's the opposite. It's not a small world at all." Chuck spoke for the first time all night. "The world is huge. It's just too damn crowded."

Noticing he had the other campers' attention, Chuck continued. "Y'all say it's a small world when two paths cross. Y'all chalk it up as coincidence, right? Lemme tell ya, if there's one thing I've learned in this life, it's that there ain't no such thing as coincidence."

"So you're saying," began Crosby, "if I wear green socks and Tosh just happens to wear green socks too, it's not a coincidence?"

"No, that's not what I'm saying," scoffed Chuck. He took a swig of the Applejack. "Let me rephrase my point here," he said in his best grammar. "Y'all can call wearing the same socks coincidence, because that's about the extent of coincidence. Coincidence merely deals with trivial, meaningless nonsense. But nuthin' in life of any importance is coincidence."

Chuck thought for a moment. "Face it fellas, it's highly unlikely that yer choice of socks will affect anything. But maybe a shirt."

Everyone looked at Chuck with confusion.

"Lemme tell you a story," he said.

"Let me get a beer first," said Tosh. "Anyone need one?"

"Hook me up, dude," said Crosby.

"Me too, please," said Willy.

Tosh fetched a couple of cold ones from the river and dished out the supplies. Everyone settled in for Chuck's story.

"One night, back in the day, I had a dance to attend. In the evenin', I got dressed in a pair of trousers and my finest shirt, which happened to be green. Now, they didn't serve much food at these dances, mainly beer and some biscuits or somethin', so I fixed up a little sandwich for dinner before I left.

"So I was sittin' out on the front porch, eatin' my sandwich, when this darn bee landed on my arm. Now I'm not all that fond of bees, so naturally, I flinched. Well, darn it, would you believe this dollop of mustard dripped from my sandwich right on to my nice green shirt. So I got up and dug out another shirt, which happened to be a light cream color, almost white.

"Later that night, I'm on my way to the dance, walkin' down this back road. Back then, I couldn't afford a car. Anyhow, over the knoll comes this car travelin' at a high speed. I see it only has one headlight. Well, that was almost the last thing I ever see, because the car barrels down the road and alla the sudden, I realize he's gonna hit me. I couldn't do anything; I just froze up, like a deer does in the light.

"Well, the car didn't hit me, otherwise I wouldn't be sittin' here today. At the last second, the car swerved out of the way. It flipped over and over and I thought the driver had to be killed. But back then, cars were built much stronger, you know, and when I run up to the car, I see Hap, this fellow from town, bloody but conscious. So I pull him from the car and we flag down the next car to go get us some help."

Chuck grabbed the bottle of Applejack from Crosby and took a swig. He looked around the campfire, surveying the audience that eagerly waited for him to continue.

"Hap made it to the hospital O.K. and the next day I didn't have to work, it was Sunday, so I hitched a ride over to the hospital to check on 'ole Hap. I visit with him a while, he had broken a few bones, but he was otherwise O.K.

"Then he says to me, 'Hey, Chuckie, it's a good thing you was wearin' that white shirt. I never woulda seen ya. The eyes are gettin' bad, ya know?'

"So all I'm thinkin' is, *bad eyes?* That's a loada crap. The only reason Ole Hap's eyes were so bad is 'cause a the fifth a whiskey the bastard had in him."

Angelo shook his head in disgust.

"A coupla days later it hit me, though," Chuck continued. "I had started out wearin' a green shirt that night and, you know, Hap woulda crushed me if I hadn't changed my shirt. And why did I change my shirt? 'Cause a that mustard stain. And that mustard stain woulda never happened had that bee not landed on my arm."

Chuck paused a moment to reflect, his expressionless face shimmering in the firelight as the campers silently mulled over his story.

"So, what are you saying?" asked Tosh. "That someone or something sent that bee? Like a guardian angel or something?"

"I ain't sayin' nothin' 'bout no angels. But you never know. The world works in mysterious ways."

"So, Tosh running into Willy on the other side of the country in some random little camp is not a coincidence," Crosby said.

Willy mimicked the theme from *The Twilight Zone*.

Chuck took a swig of beer, swishing it around in his mouth before swallowing. "All I'm sayin' is that everything in life happens for a reason."

"The whole bee thing is weird," said Tosh. "I'll admit that. But what about the fact that you chose a light-colored shirt. What if you chose a dark one? You might be dead now. That's pretty lucky."

"You can call it luck," said Chuck. "If you call it luck, then so's the bee. Luck's the same as coincidence. That argument goes that it's all chance, total chaos. Everythin' is a result of man's free will mixed with luck. That's a valid thought, I suppose, but I don't believe it.

"Based on my life, I gotta believe there's order in this here universe. I believe in *fate* and *destiny*. Destiny is yer final place and fate is how you get there.

"So you think everything is pre-planned?" Willy asked.

"Every last detail," Chuck answered. "Down to the bee landin' on my arm and the last scoop of pralines n' cream in that bucket."

"No one really knows which one it is, huh?"

"Hell no, Crosby! That one is tough to prove."

At that moment, a bug flew into Crosby's nose. No one but Crosby knew it, of course, and when he started blowing his snot into his hand, everyone winced.

"Bug in the nose," he gasped, losing his breath to a loud barrage of sneezes.

The group politely offered their blessings.

"Thank you," Crosby said, wiping his hand on his sock. "But what could be the reason for Tosh and Willy running into each other?"

"Ya don't always know right away why somethin' happens," said Chuck. "In fact, sometimes you never even find out, like if it affects someone else."

"What do you mean?"

"Well, when I say everythin' happens for a reason, you naturally think that reason has somethin' to do with you. But it don't have to. It could happen for a reason in someone else's life an' you might not even know it."

"Hmmm," said Crosby. He looked to Tosh, who nodded as though he understood Chuck, even though he probably didn't.

"Lemme tell you a little story."

"Hang on, Chuckie," said Willy, getting up to secure some beverages. "Anyone?"

"Bring 'em on, dude."

When Willy returned with the fresh suds, Chuck began the second feature. "One day, when I was livin' down in Arizona, I went to get some ice cream. No other way to beat that scorchin' desert heat than pralines n' cream slidin' down yer throat. So I get there an', darn it, they're outa pralines n' cream! So I curse my luck, and I'm lookin' at the other flavors to choose from, when this other guy orders some peanut-butter ice cream.

"He says, 'Boy, this is some good ice cream. You should try it.'

"'Peanut-butter ice cream?' I say. I'd never heard of such a thing. Well, I was already disappointed, so I had nothin' to lose. On the stranger's advice, I ordered the peanut-butter ice cream. And believe it or not, stuff was great.

"So it's a year later and now I'm livin' in Washington here. It's one a them sweaty days so I get in the mood again for some ice cream. 'Cept this time, when I go into the shop, I don't even think about pralines n' cream. The girl in there, well, she was very fair, an' I ask her right off the bat if by any chance she had some peanut-butter ice cream.

"'Why yes,' she said. 'In fact, it's my favorite.' It was her absolute favorite out of the 31 different flavors or whatever."

Chuck paused for effect, making eye contact with his listeners. "Well, I married that girl."

"All because she liked peanut-butter ice cream?"

"No, Crosby, for a lot of other reasons, too. But the point is, I probly never woulda had the guts to socialize with a pretty woman like that had we not started chattin' about the peanut-butter ice cream. That opened the door, an' the door led to 35 years of marriage."

"So you met your wife all because of that guy who told you about the peanut-butter ice cream. Some guy that you never saw again."

"Bingo, Tosh. That guy urgin' me to try the peanut-butter ice cream changed my life. An' he never even knew it."

"Actually," said Willy, "the person who came in and ate the last scoops of pralines n' cream changed your life, too. Because you probably never would have tried the peanut-butter ice cream had there been pralines n' cream."

"That's a point."

"And you never even *saw* that guy!"

"Ya see, all our lives are intertwined, like a giant web. Everythin' you do has an effect on the way things turn out. Not necessarily on your own life, but maybe someone else's. Of course, it doesn't always have to be as profound as saving a life or findin' a wife."

"So, basically we don't have any idea why Tosh and Willy ran into each other here?" Crosby asked, still seeking an answer.

"There's no way to know *now*," answered Chuck. "Maybe someday. For now, just know there's a reason."

Angelo spoke up. "Maybe the fact that we're having this conversation right now explains their encounter."

"Could be," said Chuck. "Could very well be."

Willy giggled. "Far out."

*   *   *   *

The group took a five-minute hiatus to urinate, gather new beverages and add wood to the fire. The air had become a bit chillier as the night grew older, so Tosh and Crosby threw on some warmer shirts. They settled in around the fire again, this time a little closer.

"Man, it's so beautiful out here," said Crosby. "The pine trees, the clean river. Beats the hell out of concrete and cars."

"Screw the city," said Chuck.

"I hate pollution.

A couple years ago, we had medical waste wash up on the beaches in Jersey."

"Medical waste?" asked Willy. "Like spleens and stuff?"

"No, no body parts, thank God. Hypodermic needles and crap like that."

Willy shuddered. "That's nasty."

"It's disgusting." Crosby spit a mouthful of tobacco juice into an empty Bud bottle. "They've really made an effort to keep the beaches clean since then, though."

"Once I was hiking in the mountains near my school," said Tosh. "And we found this river that was orange."

"Orange?"

"Yeah. We had the feeling that, you know, like, nothing lived in that river. It depressed us."

"How did it get orange?" asked Crosby. "What, did they spill paint in it?"

"Coal mining," said Chuck. "Had to be coal mining."

"Too much pollution. Too much ignorance," said Angelo.

"What about the whole Exxon thing? The Valdez," said Crosby. "It made me positively ill to see all those birds covered in oil, struggling to hang on to their lives, fighting for survival."

"People have no respect for the earth," said Angelo.

Chuck spit on the ground. "Look at that cocksucker in the Middle East. That miserable son-of-a-bitch set fire to the Eastern Hemisphere."

"All that damage from just one person," said Tosh.

"One mad fucker," said Willy.

"People have no respect for nature," Angelo lamented. He shook his head sadly. "You know why I'm here?"

No one answered.

"I came here today because a horrible thing happened to me today." Angelo looked around the campfire. With everyone's attention, he continued. "Every evening, on my way home from the bakery, I drive along a river. A group of about twenty geese live on the banks and I pull over and feed them bread. I usually have some loaves and rolls left over that I can't sell because they're not fresh, so I take a half hour and sit down among the geese and I feed them. They have grown accustomed to my presence now, and they let me get quite close."

Angelo paused for a moment, reflecting on his little friends. "Often, the geese cross the road that follows the river. Why they cross, I don't know. To get to the other side, sure, but what's over there, I don't know. Anyway, when the geese cross the road, they always do it as a group. Never does one goose decide to cross on his own. Always, they cross as a group, in twos, one pair after another, in a line. It is the most magnificent thing I have ever seen."

Angelo searched for the words to express his feelings. "I can sense the companionship among the little creatures. Precious, they are." He touched his chest, over his heart.

"Today, when I arrived at the spot where I feed the geese, the birds were on the other side of the road. Seeing me and knowing I had food, they lined up and began to cross. Now, the birds take a little time in crossing the road. They have little legs and they walk very slowly. Sometimes, they stop for no apparent reason. Maybe they're resting.

"The cars stopped as the geese walked across the road. The flock is quite large and it takes about five minutes for all of them to get across, so some traffic built up."

Angelo paused and took a look at the group around the campfire. "The car at the front of the line started beeping its horn. The geese became flustered by the loud noise and their orderly line scattered. They were squawking and milling about in the road, confused. 'Stop it!' I yelled to the man, but the bastard hit the gas. He ran through the geese on the road and kept on going."

The group around the campfire reacted with a hail of insults aimed at the perpetrator.

"Did he kill them?" asked Crosby.

"One goose had surely been killed. Another looked severely injured. The geese were hysterical. They were terrified! I could not believe my eyes."

"Man, what a dick," said Tosh.

"How can someone be so cruel?" asked Angelo. "So selfish?" He squinted and shook his head, obviously pained. "People have no respect."

*   *   *   *

Angelo's story was a buzz kill. It turned the once philosophical campfire conversation into an all-out bitch session. The group complained about everything wrong in the world including pollution, crime, abuse, disease, forest fires and the injustice of marijuana laws.

Everyone contributed to the griping forum except for Willy. He made a string bracelet. He picked his toenails. He tied tiny knots in his leg hairs. He drew a picture of Magilla Gorilla on his thumb.

Finally, he could take no more. "Shut up already! Man, you guys are depressing me to death. All this negative energy. Come on, cheer up! Life isn't that bad."

"What about the hole in the ozone layer?"

"Forget the hole in the ozone layer!"

"I can't forget about it," said Crosby, obviously rattled.

"If it bothers you so much, why don't you quit complaining and do something about it?"

"What the hell am I going to do about the ozone layer?"

"Do your part. Don't use aerosol cans. If you're very inspired, I suppose you could organize an awareness group or something."

The group remained silent.

"All I'm saying is don't dwell on all these crappy things going on. Do what you can and then let it be. Move on."

"It just seems endless, though," replied Crosby.

Tosh agreed. "Yeah, it seems as though our world is more fucked-up than it's ever been."

"Could be, but you never know. Times have always been tough. It's the nature of life.

"Problems have always existed. It's never been easy to live. Even the damn dinosaurs had problems. Their problems were so bad, in fact, they became extinct."

"Maybe that's where we're headed," Chuck chuckled.

Willy frowned at him. "If you're not part of the solution, you're part of the problem."

"That's a good point," said Tosh.

"I never thought I was part of the problem," said Chuck. "I don't litter, I recycle, I put the toilet seat down. What more can I do?"

"You can start by appreciating the good things in life," answered Willy. "There are just as many good things as bad things, and every negative has a positive side.

"For example, the other day I was walking down a hill. Coming up the hill, this dude was riding a ten-speed with a little kid strapped into a baby seat on the back of the bike. This guy pedaled up the hill with all his might – unsteady, legs churning, sweat pouring down his face.

"Now, some people will see this and say, 'That poor man. Look at him struggling.'

"Others will say 'What is that lunatic doing? He is endangering the life of his child, bringing him on a bike ride on this busy road!'

"Still, others will say 'God, that man looks exhausted. He is working his ass off, barely moving. The poor kid is scared to death. They are breathing in the fumes of the cars driving by and mosquitoes are eating both of them alive. What a miserable situation.'

"That's the way people think. But when I saw that guy with his kid, you know what I felt? Joy. I said to myself, 'Man, that's great. That dude is taking his son out for a cruise around the town. It's a beautiful evening and the guy wanted some exercise and instead of just taking off, he made the effort to take his son along. Now, the two of them are riding around, bonding. The kid is probably thrilled, hangin' with his dad, checking out the sights. It's probably the coolest thing in the world for that kid. Even better than a car ride, 'cause he got to strap on this little helmet with a chinstrap and everything.' The kid had to be stoked, wearin' that helmet, cruisin' with his father.

"I stared at them as they passed and I could just sense the love between the two of them. It made my night."

Willy summed up his hippie sermon. "Don't let the negative get the better of you. Be positive. Instead of focusing on the people starving in Africa, think about the generous relief efforts. Instead of dwelling on the harm of AIDS or cancer, look at the advances in medicine and the programs to help victims."

"Instead of focusing on the medical waste that has been washing up on our beaches," added Crosby, "focus on the group of people who volunteer to clean the beaches each spring. Think about the new environmental policies that aim to stop such pollution."

"Right on, dude."

"Tell me, son," interrupted Chuck, "what's good about what Hitler did? What good came out of the bombs we dropped on Hiroshima?"

Everyone instantly soured.

Willy thought hard for a minute in the silence. "The likelihood of another Hitler rising to power or a full-scale nuclear war taking place has been greatly reduced because of those events." With a stick, he crushed the last log in the fire into dying embers. "You have to admit — that's a positive."

*   *   *   *

The next morning Tosh woke to a slap on the head. He opened his groggy eyes and found Crosby leaning over him with a disgruntled look, clutching a whip made from a twisted T-shirt.

"What the hell are you doing?"

"There was a fly on your head."

Tosh sat up. "Well couldn't you have waited till he landed somewhere else? Did you have to nail him on my head?"

"Didn't you feel it? All morning long that little fucker has been walking on my face. I couldn't take it anymore!"

"I didn't feel a thing until you just whacked my head."

"Well, he was spreading germs on you."

"Thanks."

"No problem. It's time to get up anyway. Time to start the day."

As they climbed out of their tent, Chuck was packing his truck. He started the old Cherokee, waved a goodbye and pulled out. Angelo had already left, presumably to go make the donuts. Willy and Steve crawled out of their tent shortly after, awakened by the sound of Chuck's engine.

Crosby and Tosh headed over to the river for a shower. Crosby, already acquainted with the cold clear water, lowered himself into the natural bath. He stretched out and grabbed on to a rock, letting the water wash over him as his body floated in the docile rapids.

After a minute, he pulled himself out. "Damn, that felt great! What a way to start the day!"

Tosh stuck his hand in and quickly recoiled. It felt like the ice water in the beer cooler. "No thanks."

"Come on! It feels great! A real eye-opener!"

"No way. You're nuts, dude."

"Wimp."

"I may be a wimp. But I'm a dry, comfortable wimp."

"Whatever suits you, dude. I'm gonna go fix some breakfast."

Tosh decided he could deal with dipping his head in. He dunked his head into the freezing water for a few seconds. It felt so cold it hurt, but it did manage to knock the cobwebs out of his skull. Soon, with a towel twisted around his wet dreads like a turban, Tosh joined Crosby by the coals of the campfire.

Unfortunately, breakfast would have to be postponed due to the inclement weather. Rain started to fall, and rather than trying to light the fire and cook, they decided to pack up and hit the road. Steve and Willy did the same.

They had the packing routine down pat by now and within minutes, they were ready to roll. The two groups exchanged good-byes. "Safe travels," Tosh called as he climbed into the front of Josephine.

"Yeah," called Willy. "See you again somewhere weird down the road."

*   *   *   *

They drove through the rain on empty stomachs.

Tosh put in a Neil Young tape that he had made. On the first side he had included acoustic classics, such as "Old Man," "Long May You Run" and "Sugar Mountain." For the damp morning drive he put on side B — electric Neil Young — and cranked it to a steady volume. Neil's whining guitar in "Cowgirl in the Sand," "Down by the River" and "Like a Hurricane" mixed with the sound of the rain pounding the van's metal roof.

"Hello ruby in the dust..." Crosby sang along. Then, keeping the melody of the song, he alluded to his hunger, "Eat some food, I really must. Love some eggs, now, and some orange juice. With so much hunger, some waffles too..."

"Crosby, ya want to stop for breakfast?"

"Sounds like a plan."

A few miles down the road, the guys got off the highway. At the end of the exit ramp, they noticed a large sign made out of a painted plank nailed to a tree. It read **FOOD.** Underneath the lone word, a purple arrow pointed left.

"Details. That's what I like," said Crosby. They followed the advertisement along a back road into Cedar Falls, where they found an open restaurant.

Tosh and Crosby were the youngest people in The Sunnyside Coffee Shop. The tiny diner seated about twenty people, but at the moment contained about half that. Most of the folks, a mix of truckers and local farmers, sat around the small tables.

Tosh and Crosby positioned themselves at the counter for a hearty meal of eggs and hash browns and biscuits.

They ate quickly and silently, and afterwards relaxed with one more cup of coffee. As Tosh stared at the inside of his mug, stained brown from the thousands of gallons of coffee that had passed through it, someone entered the restaurant and sat on the stool next to him.

Tosh looked up at the gentleman seated next to him. A silver-lined beard hung from his rugged but gentle face. Dust kicked off his frayed, suede cowboy hat as he put it on the counter. Now freed from the confines of the aged sombrero, long, graying brown hair fell down his shoulders.

Sensing Tosh's eyes upon him, the man nodded a greeting. "Howdy."

"Good morning," Tosh replied.

"That's some hat you got there," he said, referring to Tosh's towel turban.

Tosh laughed, a little embarrassed. "Oh, yeah." He quickly returned his gaze to his own coffee mug, keeping the corner of his eye on his new neighbor.

The man waited patiently, almost unnaturally still, for the waitress. In a minute she came to his service, placing a table setting and an empty mug in front of him.

"Coffee?" she asked cheerily, a plump, middle-aged woman with dyed blonde hair.

"Thanks," he said, fumbling for something inside his jacket. "Three eggs over easy, hash browns and toast."

As the waitress returned with the pot of coffee, the rugged man brandished a half pint of Jack Daniels from his coat. He unscrewed the lid and held his spoon over his coffee mug.

"Sour mash in the morning?" asked the waitress, without judgment.

"Just a teaspoon," he remarked, filling the spoon and then letting another ounce of whiskey pour over the metal utensil into the cup. After dropping a healthy amount of booze into his coffee, the man held the bottle up to his face, measuring how much remained. He took a small swig from the bottle, swishing the whiskey around in his mouth like Listerine. After swallowing it and emitting a robust sigh, he finally tucked the half-pint back into his dusty brown jacket.

"A little bit of the dog that bit ya?" the waitress asked knowingly.

"Yeah. It's half my hangover cure."

The woman glanced up from wiping the counter. "What's the rest?"

"Cold Chinese food."

"Tosh, ya ready to roll, dude?"

The rain had ceased momentarily and Crosby wanted the opportunity to make a dry escape.

"Yah, mon." Tosh jumped off his stool and followed Crosby out of the Sunnyside, glancing back at the old timer at the counter. He looked familiar.

Outside the coffee shop, a beat-up, red pickup truck jarred Tosh's memory. He had passed the hippie cowboy on the highway back in Wyoming! What a coincidence!

Tosh remembered the cool sticker on the back of the truck — Never Die Wondering.

A clap of thunder shook through the gray morning sky and immediately rain began to fall again.

Tosh hustled around to the rear of the vehicle and found the sticker stuck on the truck. To his bewilderment, though, the sticker contained a different message. It looked identical to the last one with thick black lettering on a white background, but it read **QUESTION REALITY.**

"Oh, that is weird," Tosh said aloud. Did this guy buy a new sticker and place it over the other one, he wondered? Maybe it wasn't the same guy, just a similar-looking guy in a similar-looking truck with a similar-looking sticker.

No way.

To more closely inspect the sticker, Tosh dropped to his knees and reached for the bumper.

Crosby beeped the horn of the van, waiting for his dawdling friend. "Come on!" he shouted. "What are you doing?"

"Fuck it," said Tosh, jumping into the van. "He probably just put on a new sticker or something."

"What were you doing, praying to that truck?" Crosby asked him as he climbed into the van.

"Something weird happened, man. I'm all vexed."

Crosby pulled out on to the highway and they headed for Canada.

*　　*　　*　　*

As Crosby burped up his pork roll, Tosh explained the story.

Crosby offered a simple explanation. "So he changed the sticker. Big deal."

"Why would you change a sticker?"

"Maybe he changed his mind."

"Yeah, but what the hell does all that mean, anyway?"

Tosh and Crosby pondered the two messages. They conflicted. "Question Reality" seemed the opposite of "Never Die Wondering." The latter phrase suggested conviction, where the former hinted at skepticism.

"If you question reality, you will certainly die wondering," said Tosh. The truck was giving off mixed signals and it pissed him off.

"Who knows?" said Crosby. "Maybe he's just a confused man."

Tosh felt a wave of excitement. "Let's go back and ask him!"

"You're not serious, are you? Let it go, man."

He's right, thought Tosh.

108

"Too much philosophy, not enough drugs. Let's smoke up, Tosh."

Tosh dug the ganja out of his backpack and began to roll a very fat joint. After all, they were going to be crossing the Canadian border in a few hours — and they had a ton of weed.

*   *   *   *

Tosh put on the Wailing Souls for the smoking session. Because of the size of the joint, they had to roll down the windows and let the rain blow in just to clear some of the smoke out of the van. Even after the j had been reduced to ashes and the air in the van had been filtered, Tosh and Crosby's clouded vision did not clear. It fogged somewhere behind the retinas, causing them to focus more on the thoughts inside their heads than on the rain-slicked highway.

For a while, Tosh and Crosby were too high to speak. They drove along at a slow speed, staring out the windshield. The Wailing Souls' righteous melodies drowned out the drone of Josephine's overworked engine and set a mellow but upbeat tone.

An hour after bypassing Seattle because they were too stoned to stop, their marijuana stupor finally faded enough to enable Tosh and Crosby to vocalize their thoughts.

"Cros, you know that whole thing with me and Willy running into each other again?"

"Yeah?"

"Well, it's the same thing with that guy in the diner, you know? I saw him on the road and then in the diner. I mean, it was a lonesome stretch of rural highway and some rinky-dink diner in the middle of nowhere, not Grand Central Station and Newark Airport."

"You don't even know for sure if it was the same guy."

"It was."

"Don't get too excited. I'm not sure I buy into the whole 'Everything happens for a reason' plan. I might be leanin' towards the old 'Random shit happens' option."

"Never Die Wondering. What do you think it means?"

"You're not gonna start that again, are you?"

"I'm intrigued. Why not?"

"O.K., you win. Let me conjure up a theory here." Crosby put a wad of chewing tobacco in his cheek. "Grab me a spittoon, will ya, dude?"

Tosh foraged around the van for a suitable receptacle. In one of the coolers he found a half-empty Mountain Dew bottle. "Want some Mountain Don't?"

"I'll take a swig." Crosby guzzled half the green liquid, leaving some for Tosh. When Tosh polished it off, he gave it back to Crosby, who promptly deposited a gob of tobacco juice.

"O.K., here goes," said Crosby. "Obviously, we have no control over when we die — ruling out suicide, of course. So, maybe it means, like, throughout your life, attain as much knowledge as you can. You can never learn too much. Learn as much information as possible and, therefore, reduce the chances that you would die wondering. How's that?"

"Damn, that's good. That works for me. I was thinking that maybe it expressed conviction. You know, do not doubt yourself. Stay true to what you think."

"That's a good theory, too."

"I think I like yours better."

"You know what, Tosh? We're fucked."

"Why? Are we low on gas?"

"No. I mean, we're fucked because it says 'Never Die Wondering' but we'll spend our whole lives wondering what the hell that means! It's a trick!"

"We've been duped!"

"We're doomed to die wondering!"

Tosh and Crosby began to laugh, but Tosh abruptly stopped. "No, don't say that. It can't be a trick."

"Of course it is," said Crosby. "That's why that guy has the 'Question Reality' sticker, just to fuck with us."

"No. That's not it."

"Why not?"

"Because life isn't a joke. Something bigger is happening here. I can feel it."

Crosby glanced over at Tosh. He had an odd expression on his face. "Well, time will tell, old buddy."

On the stereo, the Wailing Souls sang "Things and Time Will Tell." Tosh jabbed Crosby in the shoulder and grinned. "See what I mean, Cros? Something bigger!"

The coincidence escaped Crosby. "Huh?"

"Listen to the song playing right now. They're saying, 'Things and time will tell.'"

Crosby smirked. "Doesn't Jimmy Cliff sing a song called, "Time Will Tell?"

Tosh turned to his friend, impressed. "Mi bwoy, him learnin', mon, him learnin'!"

"Yah, mon!" Crosby high-fived Tosh. "You know, we've grown up listening to the same music. I mean, I like reggae. But dude, you are really passionate about it!"

"I am. It's like the love of my life."

"You were ready to drop the gloves with that guy Steve last night! That's very un-Tosh-like."

Tosh smiled sheepishly. "What can I say? I lost my cool."

"The guy is entitled to his own opinion, after all."

"I wasn't trying to force him to like it. I just wanted him to know what reggae was all about. I wanted to show him how powerful reggae is, give him a new perspective."

"Right on."

"Well, he pissed me off because he made me feel like an idiot. I had practically poured out my heart and soul to him and he had the nerve to belittle reggae as 'just a bunch of bass.' I know when I'm gettin' dissed."

"Well, it's his loss."

"Damn straight it's his loss. He's missing out." Tosh gazed out the window. "You know, everywhere I've gone, I've found reggae fans. Japan, India, Africa, Brazil. And you know why? 'Cause of the message it carries. It's totally positive. Reggae chant down Babylon. It rebukes racism, prejudice and discrimination while it praises equality, brotherhood, love and God. Gotta love that."

"And ganja."

"Exactly, dude." Tosh sang, "Legalize it, don't criticize it." Then, fingering one of his dreads, he seemed to lose himself in thought for a moment. "The thing with reggae is, some people don't realize the meaning of the music. They like the way it sounds, and that's cool, but they don't get the full message, the whole impact. You know, they kinda miss the boat. I mean, when I realized the message that was in the music, that's what did it for me, man. That's what turned me into a Rasta Reggae Crusader."

"Tosh Tyler, Rasta Crusader!" shouted Crosby. "Listen to reggae or he'll call you an asshole!"

They laughed.

"Seriously, though," said Tosh. "Reggae artists sing about fighting down war and crime and loving one another as brothers and sisters. They call for unity, respect and love. That is serious business. They're not jabbering about trivial crap up there. They're not like Jim Morrison, singing cryptic, surreal lyrics that no one can relate to."

"Hey, I like Jim Morrison!"

"So do I, but I'm just comparing his style, you know?"

"Jim Morrison was a poet."

"Yeah, I know. But what the hell does, 'Blood is the rose of mysterious union' mean? Come on. That is some artsy-fartsy bullshit."

Crosby shrugged. "Well, it's good for what it is."

"True, true. But yuh see," Tosh continued with his Jamaican accent, "reggae come from a whole 'nother level. It come from deep wit'in de soul, and it come to enlighten mankind. De man Bob Marley sing, 'We free de people with music.' Reggae music free de people spiritually. Reggae is God's Music, *Jah* Music. Dat is heavy, heavy music, mon."

111

*   *   *   *

Tosh and Crosby found themselves headed north for British Columbia. Tosh rolled another monster joint but they couldn't finish smoking it.

"This is ridiculous, man. We can't finish all this pot."

"Well, what do you want to do?" asked Tosh, taking another hit. Then, holding the smoke in his lungs, he squealed, "Should we try to sneak de ganja in ta Canada, mon?"

"I don't know, dude. Somethin' tells me that ain't a great idea." Luckily, Crosby's reason prevailed through his marijuana high.

"Den we haffe smoke more."

"Your eyes are about as red as a dog's dick and my head feels like it's about to explode. I don't think we can smoke anymore."

"If we cyan't smoke no more, den wha fe we to do wi de ganja, mon? I not gonna t'row it away like garbage, mon. Dis herb is sacred."

Knowing Tosh was too baked to think, Crosby took charge. He mimicked Tosh's pseudo-Jamaican accent to obtain his buddy's sanction. "Yah, mon. But if we get caught wit de weed, mon, den we get beaten by de police, mon. We go to jail, mon!"

Tosh howled, "I nah go a jail, for ganja no more, I-man nah go a jail!"

"Tosh, we *can't* bring the weed over the border," Crosby said sternly. "Pack it up and wrap it up good. I have an idea."

Tosh followed his orders and Crosby pulled off the highway at the next exit. Right after the exit ramp, he stopped the van alongside the road. "OK, is the ganja wrapped up good?"

"Yah, mon. It's wrap in a plastic bag and den tin foil, too."

"OK, good. Now, go hide it under a rock or something."

"Under a rock?"

"Yeah. Where else are you gonna hide it?"

With that, Tosh left the van. He hopped over the steel guardrail and scoped the roadside brush. There were plenty of little nooks to hide the illegal substance.

"Hey Tosh!" called Crosby. "Don't forget which rock!"

CHAPTER 8

The Canadian border arrived before Tosh and Crosby's marijuana buzz left. There, a pleasant young woman dressed in a drab, polyester, magisterial uniform asked Crosby a few basic question. He answered her simple inquiries with straightforward ease. The uneventful interview lasted about thirty seconds and ended with the customs agent handing Crosby a yellow card and saying cheerily, "Pull over to the left and hand this card to someone in that building."

"What's this all about?" Crosby turned to Tosh.

"Beats me."

They followed the woman's instructions. An older gentleman quickly took their yellow card and handed it to a young man with a crew cut. "Follow me," he said, heading out toward the parking lot. "Which vehicle is yours?"

"The blue van."

"Give me your keys and wait over here."

Tosh and Crosby sat on a bench in front of Josephine and watched the customs agent open their hood.

"What the hell is he doing?" Crosby whispered to Tosh.

"I have no clue."

Soon the agent disappeared into the back of the van.

After he began taking things out of the van and placing them on the pavement, Crosby got up to find out what was going on. "Excuse me, but what are you doing?" he asked.

"Please be seated, sir. I am searching for illegal or controlled substances that cannot be brought into Canada."

"Why?"

"Why?" repeated the customs officer, a little surprised by Crosby's audacity.

"Why are you searching *us?*"

"Canadian Customs search random vehicles at the discretion of the screening agents. Please be seated."

Crosby nodded and sat back down. "That bitch at the drive-thru dicked us!" he whispered to Tosh. "Do you believe this shit?"

"Yea. It figures she would have our van searched. If anybody would be carrying drugs, it's the two dudes in the van with the surfboard and the Deadhead stickers."

"That's total bullshit."

"Don't worry about it, man. We have nothing to fear."

"Are you sure? Did you get rid of the bowl, too?"

"Yeah, the pipe, the ganja, everything. There's not a trace of anything."

"Good."

Crosby and Tosh sat back and watched with amused aloofness, covering the touch of anxiety that inherently accompanies statutory examinations. They heckled the aggressive jarhead under their breath, mocking the commonplace items he examined closely.

"That's a *radio*. Can you say radio? Ray-dee-o. It plays music."

Their sense of humor wore thin when the accumulation of stuff outside the van amounted to more than what remained inside. Exasperated, Crosby spoke loud enough for the agent to hear, "We don't have any drugs!"

"We just say no!" added Tosh.

The agent gave them a dirty look. A minute later, he approached, clutching something in his hands. "What are these?"

"Bracelets," said Tosh. "You wear them on your wrist. Or your ankle, if you want."

The agent tightened his lips and thought a moment. He threw the bracelets aside and continued his search for the ten pounds of heroin that he knew was hidden in the van.

Tosh had ordered the colorfully woven bracelets from an import company in California and over the past couple of summers, he and Crosby had been selling the string jewelry to help them earn some extra cash. Made in Guatemala, the bracelets cost them 20 cents each. They bought them by the thousand.

Selling the bracelets at concerts in the tri-State area made a great little business. Bringing only the bracelets and a few dollars change, Tosh and Crosby would go to the concerts a few hours before the show and parade through the parking lots, displaying their merchandise on cardboard planks. Each board held about thirty bracelets and could be folded and stuffed into their shirts in case of any trouble with concert security. (Vending was illegal without a permit.)

The system worked well. Tosh and Crosby made out like bandits. As the tailgating activities progressed, their customers got more and more bombed and became less thrifty and increasingly generous. Not only would they gladly drop a few bucks for bracelets, but they often got Tosh and Crosby high or gave them food and beers. By the time the concert began, Tosh and Crosby would have picked up tickets from people selling extras, gotten totally wasted for free, and made a profit to boot.

Tosh and Crosby used sagacity to determine which shows they would work. They speculated what type of crowd would attend the concerts depending on who was playing. The more relaxed the atmosphere, the better the sales. They refrained from the heavy rock concerts like AC/DC and Metallica, as their merchandise appealed more to a classic rock and neo-hippie type of market than to metal heads. James Taylor, Bob Dylan and Santana attracted some of their best customers.

Although it would have been their greatest market, Tosh and Crosby refused to work at the Grateful Dead shows. Everyone has something to sell at a Dead show, they reasoned, and many of the vendors are hardcore Deadheads that need the cash to keep touring. Tosh and Crosby did not want to compete, especially when it involved people's livelihood.

So, Tosh and Crosby refrained from working these concerts. Instead, the Dead shows served as a holiday, where they attended the shows with nothing in mind but amazing music and a great time. The bracelets stayed at home and in their place, Tosh and Crosby brought tailgating treats — coolers of cold beer, Frisbees and hackey sacks — to the Meadowlands parking lot.

Tosh had completely forgotten about the bracelets. At the last moment before they left, he had stuffed them into one of the van's storage areas, figuring if they ever needed some extra cash, they could try to sell a few somewhere along the line.

Finally, the disappointed agent acknowledged they had no illegal drugs and crudely returned their stuff, haphazardly piling the coolers, radio, stove, lantern, sleeping bags and Tosh and Crosby's ravaged backpacks back into the van. Everything except for the cardboard boards containing the colorful string bracelets.

The agent locked the van and grabbed the bracelets off the ground. "Your vehicle is being seized by Canadian Customs for failure to declare commercial goods."

*   *   *   *

Tosh and Crosby were ushered into an office of one of the superior custom agents and informed of the charges against them. Apparently, the screening agent had asked them if they were carrying commercial goods into the country and Crosby, not thinking of the bracelets, unknowingly answered negatively. In his search for possible drugs, the second agent found the bracelets and knew he could bust the two guys from New Jersey for some hard cash.

So Tosh and Crosby found themselves clear across the continent with all their belongings, save the clothes on their backs, seized by the Canadian border patrol. They were pissed.

Under the supervision of the Canadian forces, Tosh and Crosby counted the bracelets. They totaled nearly 900.

"You are supposed to pay taxes on items that you are going to sell in Canada," chastised the customs officer.

"We weren't gonna sell them," remarked Crosby.

"Well, what were you going to do with them? Why were some displayed on cardboard?"

"We were going to give them away to our friends," Tosh contended lamely through his thick ganja high.

"900 of them?" The officer frowned. "Those bracelets were to be sold. And you tried to sneak them into the country without paying taxes on them."

"That's not true!"

"Then why were the bracelets hidden?"

"Hidden? We didn't even know they were there," pleaded Crosby.

"I hardly think so."

115

Crosby knew that arguing was useless, especially since Tosh and he were completely baked. These guys were not going to cut them a break. The bureaucratic bullshit piled too high to climb over or around it. They had to cut through it.

He wanted to mock the power-hungry bastards. Say something riddled with sarcasm, like, "Yep, we're busted! We were trying to smuggle the bracelets in. We would have made it, too, if it wasn't for you meddlin' customs officials! You guys are good!" But he knew the men in cheesy uniforms would not take kindly to flippancy from a young perpetrator. Instead, wisely stifling his insolent urge, he minimized his jeer and concluded his defense with a single word muttered with attitude: "Whatever."

*   *   *   *

"That sucked my smelly ass," said Crosby.

"Not exactly the red fucking carpet, that's for sure," said Tosh. Then, leaning his head out the window as they pulled away from the border, he added, "A lot of good this will do for political relations!"

Without looking back, they drove toward Vancouver entrenched in bitter silence.

Integral to the amount of the charge levied against them was the value of the seized goods. The Customs officials refused to believe that Crosby and Tosh had paid twenty cents each for the bracelets. Instead, they declared the merchandise to be worth two dollars each, since, ironically, that was the "going rate" for string bracelets in the Vancouver area.

To get their van back, the guys had faced a two thousand dollar charge.

Tosh and Crosby were at the same time outraged and deeply concerned. They didn't have half that amount of cash. What could they do?

Their only hope had been to debate the decision. Like a major league manager appealing a bad call, Tosh and Crosby gave it their best effort. After fruitless arguing and then utter imploring, the officials finally broke down and gave in. The officers sent Tosh and Crosby out of the office so they could hold a private conversation to discuss their fate.

When the officers had reached a decision, they called Tosh and Crosby back in and said, "Just so you don't think we are totally heartless, we are willing to accept the fact that the bracelets are worth twenty cents each."

Totally heartless. Yeah, right.

So after losing a couple of hours to unpleasant, stressful negotiations and wasting a perfectly good buzz, Tosh and Crosby begrudgingly shelled out a couple of hundred bucks and recovered their ransacked van.

Driving towards Vancouver, Tosh broke their angry silence. "Well, I'm glad that's over with."

Crosby said nothing, still moping.

Tosh wanted the bad vibes to end. Like Willy had taught them, he decided to focus on the positive aspects of the situation. "Thank God in heaven above that we ditched that pot!"

"No doubt!"

"Man, if we decided to take a chance, we would have been royally fucked."

"We'd be behind bars, man. Jailbirds."

"Whatever you do, don't bend over for the soap."

They laughed, glad the incident was behind them.

"Oh well," summed up Crosby, "shit happens."

"Yeah. Let's just get completely lit and forget about this whole thing."

"Right on. Canada – here we come!"

*　　*　　*　　*

There should be a sign on Granville Avenue upon entering the city reading **WELCOME TO VANCOUVER: THE MOST IRIE CITY ON EARTH.** There isn't, probably because most people would not know what "irie" meant, or even know how to pronounce it.

It's a Jamaican slang term that basically means "perfect."

A Rastaman lounges on the soft sandy beach, the warm turquoise water lapping at his bare feet as the brilliant amber sun dips below the horizon. The sweet scent of ganja lingers in the air, comfortable and still. In the nearby coconut grove, birds merrily chirp little "yah-mons." The dread inhales deeply, his eyes barely open. This, is *irie.*

No other term can really capture the moment.

Terrific and *excellent* just aren't good enough.

Splendid is too pretentious.

Tremendous is too intense.

Fabulous is too effeminate.

Fantastic is apt to sarcasm.

Amazing questions.

Awesome intimidates.

Incredible and *unbelievable* doubt.

To perfectly describe such a situation, a native term must be used. Hence, irie.

"Irie, irie, irie, irie, irie," Tosh repeated as he and Crosby drove into the sparkling city of Vancouver.

Vancouver will do that to a person. Simply enchanting, it rests on the west coast of Canada, awaiting visitors like the castle at the end of the yellow brick road. Snow-capped mountains surround the clean, colorful port, a gateway to the Pacific Ocean.

Tosh and Crosby followed Granville Avenue into downtown Vancouver where they found a parking garage they could park in all night for a dollar.

"What a deal!" Crosby hollered as he jumped out to untie his windsurfing equipment off the roof of the van. The entrance hung low and the van could not fit through with the board and sails on top.

"New York City this is not," Tosh replied, opening the back doors for Crosby to throw the board in. "We'd have to get a mortgage to park overnight in Manhattan."

Once the equipment was off the roof, they drove around the garage, passing from level to level to find an empty spot. After a few minutes, Tosh pulled the van into an available space.

"Man, I need a shower."

"Yeah, it would be nice," agreed Tosh, scratching his balls.

"Shoulda stayed in Kansas."

"Screw that."

"Just kidding," said Crosby making his way into the back of the van. "If we can't shower, I'm gonna at least get changed. If I can find anything."

The van was a disaster area — the beds dismantled, the coolers pulled out, clothes and surfing equipment strewn about. "It looks like a bomb went off in here."

The guys hurriedly re-packed the van, jamming Burning Spear's *Live In Paris* on the boom box. Soon, the van regained its old order. Crosby finished things off by leaning the surfboard against the long bed. Tosh, invigorated by the sweet melodies of the roots reggae, shouted at top volume, "Jah Rastafari!!"

"Yeah, mon," replied a voice.

Tosh abruptly turned to find a young man and his girlfriend standing at the edge of the van. "Welcome to Vancouver," he said.

"Thanks," smiled Tosh.

"What're you guys doin' in here? Besides jamming reggae, of course."

Tosh liked this guy. "We had a little run-in at the border. We're just trying to get settled in again."

"Oh, yeah. Those guys can be pricks. They bust you?"

"Yeah. For bracelets."

"Bracelets?"

"Don't ask. We're trying to forget about it." Tosh glanced at Crosby, who rolled his eyes.

"No worries. Hey, why don't you join us for a beer? This is my girlfriend, Julie. I'm Greg."

"Sounds good, bud."

After introducing themselves to the friendly couple, Tosh and Crosby changed their clothes, got some beer funds together, and locked up Josephine.

"We're going to a little pub around the corner for Happy Hour. They've got killer nachos, too."

Tosh *really* liked this guy. A Mexican-food-eating reggae listener.

The Jolly Taxpayer reminded Tosh of the typical Irish pub he and Crosby and their friends would frequent back home in New York City — dimly lit with tasteful but not extravagant decor. Neon beer lights and maps of Ireland adorned the wood paneling. A sign behind the bar read:

**MAY YOUR PATH BE STREWN WITH FLOWERS,
MEMORIES, FRIENDS AND HAPPY HOURS.
MAY BLESSINGS COME FROM HEAVEN ABOVE
TO FILL YOUR LIFE WITH PEACE AND LOVE.**

Tosh pondered the message.

Did *happy* act as an adjective, describing the noun *hours*, or was *happy hours* the full noun? In other words, were the happy hours wished upon the fortunate reader the kind that offered reduced drink prices? Or were they just hours happily spent, alcohol consumption notwithstanding?

In any case, it was Happy Hour and time to drink.

"What'll it be?" asked Greg, his long, thick black hair pulled pack tightly in a ponytail.

"Bud's cool," commented Crosby.

"Bud? As in Budweiser?" teased Greg.

Crosby nodded, unsurely.

"Ahh, you don't want to drink that schwag. That stuff'll kill ya."

Crosby rubbed his thumb and forefinger together and frowned, indicating that they had no money to buy gourmet beers.

"No problem, I'm treating. I got a raise today. You guys ever have Black and Tans?"

"Nope. We pretty much drink cheap, American beer. Usually Bud, Busch, Miller, Old Milwaukee. You know, 'It doesn't get any better than this.'"

"Well, it does, my friend. It does get better." Greg turned to the waitress. "A pitcher of Bass and a pitcher of Guiness, my love."

Julie kiddingly slapped him and he kissed her.

"We reason, the cheaper the beer, the more we can drink," explained Crosby. "We sacrifice taste for a better buzz."

"Well, its a sacrifice no one should have to make," said Julie, taking the pitchers from the waitress.

"Work it, girl!" shouted Greg.

Julie instructed them on how to pour the black and tans. "Step one. Fill the glasses halfway with Bass Ale. Let it breathe." She licked her lips, staring into the dark amber brew. "Step two. Pour Guiness into the Bass slowly, letting the Stout slide down the side of the glass. Again, let it settle."

"Step three," interjected Greg. "Drink it with a friend."

The four raised their glasses and toasted.

Greg and Julie's friendly warmth and laid-back attitude single-handedly turned around the negative vibes that Canada had thrust upon Tosh and Crosby at the border. They felt as if they had known the two Canadians all their lives.

The group gabbed continuously as they downed pitchers, conversing about life in Vancouver, life on the road, ice hockey and the mating habits of the duck-billed platypus. (Julie was a Discovery Channel junkie.)

They talked so much they forgot to order food. The realization hit them when Tosh explained to Julie that he and Crosby were searching for the Ultimate Burrito.

"No problem," she said. "We'll take you to a great Mexican joint. But first, we've got to catch a band. It's almost time for the show. You guys wanna come along?"

*   *   *   *

The Town Pump filled steadily with the evening's partygoers. Already sufficiently intoxicated, Tosh and Crosby and their new friends smoked a joint on line for the show to top off their buzz.

"Who are we seeing tonight?" Crosby inquired.

"They're called Bliss Tex," said Greg. "They wail."

"They named themselves after a lip treatment?"

"Guess so."

"They're from Seattle," added Julie. "Lots of chapped lips."

"How much is cover?" asked Tosh.

"It's eight bucks. But not for you."

"Why is that?"

"'Cause we are on the list and you are our guests."

"All right!" said Crosby. "How did you swing that?"

"My friend Parker tends bar here. He's friends with the band and gets us on the list."

"Sweet. Thanks, dude."

"Not only does he get us high and bring us to see a band," said Tosh, "but he gets us into the bar for free as well!"

After getting the back of their hands stamped with a large black ink splotch, Greg bought a pitcher and they found a table near the back of the bar.

"What is this?" asked Crosby, referring to the hand-stamp.

"It's supposed to be a set of lips, like this." Julie puckered her kisser to model the distorted print.

People were still coming in when Bliss Tex began their act. The five-piece outfit jumped on stage and instantly launched into the first song without a word. The music pumped out of the sound system at thunderous levels, vibrating through the wooden floors and furniture.

Crosby could feel the energy flowing through his torso as he watched the beer ripple in the pitcher resting on their table.

The crowd rose to greet the band and never had a chance to sit down again. From the first song they flew right into the next. The two guitarists ripped a flaming riff and a hellish lead while the bassist and drummer pounded out a frantic beat. Yet amid this frenzy of downright grooving music, the singer stole the show.

Completely engrossed in the music, Marcus clutched the mic like it was his own heart as he spilled his guts out on the stage. Passion dripping from his brow, he would roar like an omnipotent warlock and in the same breath soften his voice to an ethereal whisper, consistently melodic from the powerful bellow to the tender hum. Although his eyes remained closed, his face held expression and his voice conveyed emotion.

The audience knew Marcus lived these songs and opened themselves up to his catharsis, their sentiments moved by the exhilarating music, so that the show realized its full potential and fulfilled its ideal purpose, becoming a communal experience, a celebration of human life; suffering and healing, believing and feeling. People danced and hugged and cried and screamed and jumped and fucked and fell. The glowing stage blared, the delirious music filling the Town Pump from the upper balcony to the back bar. It chewed its way through the rubber soles of Doc Martens and rattled the steel and glass and tile of the dimly lit men's room.

In the middle of the whirling audience, Crosby stood completely still, staring at Marcus. The music pulsated through the singer's lean, muscular body. People revolved around Crosby, individually responding to the thumping music, closing in on him.

Closer.

Closer.

Closer — until a pair of hands wrapped themselves around his body. Crosby felt breasts push against his back and a soft, warm cheek nuzzle his shoulder and jawbone.

At first he stiffened. But as the hands soothingly groped his chest and stomach, Crosby began to loosen up. The barrage of stimuli —a heavy buzz, an energizing concert atmosphere and close physical contact — exhilarated him. Crosby released his guard and let himself go. Closing his eyes, he ceased watching and started feeling the electrical sensations, the power, the rhythm, the human current running through him.

The hands slipped under his shirt and stroked his bare belly. Crosby completely lost himself as everything around him disappeared.

There was no bar.

No people.

Crosby could only sense the throbbing music surrounding him and the warm hands upon his stomach. He remained in this state as long as the hands touched him. When they left his body, they left too soon.

As the hands removed themselves from his flesh, Crosby felt the pressing body leave his back. Opening his eyes, he turned around in time to catch the rear view of a girl in dark, fishnet stockings and a tight black skirt, disappearing into the crowd. A mound of white dreadlocks cascaded down her back.

He impulsively reached out for the punky vision, grabbing a milky white hand. It pulled away, but in the brief moment that he had held it, Crosby caught a glimpse of a savage-looking, silver skull ring on the pinkie. He saw the letters **H-O-P-E** tattooed in olde English letters across the knuckles.

Fazed, Crosby stood motionless in the pack. Did he imagine that? He closed his eyes again, stoned and drunk and confused, and let the music take over again, hoping the hands would return.

They did not.

*   *   *   *

Bliss Tex played for a little over an hour and ended the show abruptly with Marcus, an exhausted bundle of sweat, mumbling "Thanks. Let's do it again sometime soon."

Tosh sat down, mesmerized by what had just gone down. Never had he seen such a fervent non-reggae show. "Damn," he exclaimed to Greg and Julie as they emerged from the men's room, adjusting their disheveled clothes. "All that entertainment for eight bucks!"

"Yeah, they're pretty intense," Greg said. He shot a sneaky smile over to Julie.

Tosh caught on. "What were you guys doing in that bathroom, anyway?"

"Greg and I like to fuck to Bliss Tex, but they don't have a c.d. out yet," Julie said unabashedly. "So now it's club bathrooms. Romantic, huh?"

"Did ya ever hear of a bootleg tape?" kidded Tosh.

"It's got to be loud. Actually, we really like the excitement now. The fear of getting caught. The live music. The energy all around us. I've never came this much before!"

Embarrassed, Tosh looked away, pretending that something else had caught his attention.

"She's very up front," said Greg, laughing.

Tosh nodded with a smile, but changed the subject. "Where's Crosby?"

*   *   *   *

The crowd filed out of the bar slowly, everyone gratified yet drained of energy, like after a huge Thanksgiving feast with all the fixings.

Crosby darted his way through the shuffling patrons, his eyes scanning the buzzed and bedraggled bunch for the girl that had molested him during the show.

He searched desperately for the punker with the magic hands, but he could not find her.

*   *   *   *

Ramone's Hottacosalsa burned like lava from Mt. St. Helen's spilling down Tosh's throat.

"Water, gimme water!" Tosh hissed. He gulped the liquid, trying to extinguish the blaze in his mouth.

"This stuff is great," muttered Crosby, sniffing in his runny nose. "Look at Greg!"

Greg ravaged his food, eating every last jalapeno that dropped from his Ramone's Flaming Burrito onto the table. He looked up from his plate and smiled with a mouthful of food, revealing a sweating face and bright red ears.

"I think I see smoke pouring from his ears."

"He loves that, Tosh!" marveled Julie. "The masochist. Why does he do it?"

"It tastes good!" said Crosby. "Peppers get the heart pumpin'."

"Just wait till tomorrow morning. He'll be screaming on the toilet bowl."

"Cries of agony coming from the bathroom. There's nothing like it."

Tosh finished two giant cups of water before the jalapeno sting in his mouth abated, whereupon he offered his judgment of the latest specimen in their search for the Ultimate Burrito.

"Hottacosalsa notwithstanding, because you can substitute Notsohottacosalsa and Nothotatalltacosalsa, I hereby declare Ramone's Flaming Burrito at Ramone's Cantina in Vancouver, Canada, the best burrito we have had yet. But still a far cry from the Ultimate Burrito."

Tosh took another swig of water before continuing. "My reasoning is as follows: It's a solid burrito. Pinto beans, cheddar cheese, jalapenos, beef, guacamole, sour cream. Very good. But not perfect. Why, you ask? It's this boiled, shredded beef. It reminds me of stew. Who knows where it came from or how it was cooked?"

Tosh waited for a response but no one spoke up. "Why do we find this kind of meat in so many burritos? Restaurants think that because a burrito has so many different elements, the individual ingredients lose their distinct flavor. They believe that if there's enough stuff in it, the quality of the stuff is not important. Not so."

Tosh stood up. "I want steak! High quality meat! I want to taste that flavor! Where's the beef, damnit?? Where's the beef??"

"It's in their stomachs," answered Julie, pointing to Crosby and Greg who sat back with queasy looks on their faces, holding their stomachs. "Probably not the best meal choice after all that beer. Lord help you both."

"Hey! Isn't that the dude from Bliss Tex?" exclaimed Tosh, pointing at a booth on the other side of the dimly lit room.

"It's Marcus all right."

"Looks like Marcus has to baby-sit tonight," said Greg.

"That's Rudi, the drummer, that he's with," Julie explained. "Rudi's kind of an asshole."

"Why is that?"

Greg shrugged. "He's just obnoxious and rude. Rock star attitude."

"He's a pig," blurted Julie. "All he cares about is getting laid."

Crosby excused himself to the bathroom while Greg and Julie served up the low-down on Marcus and Rudi.

While the rest of the band worked overtime shmoozing record company people, Marcus chose the lesser of two evils and baby-sat the band fuck-up, Rudi. The executives always wanted to speak with Marcus, the focus and core of the group, but Marcus absolutely hated the business and anything to do with it.

He hated the pretentiousness, the egos, the politics. He detested the empty, guileless groupies that incessantly flung themselves at the band members, especially himself. And he despised how the music industry constantly ruined good music and, with it, honest musicians.

Some of the cool independent label dudes were all right. They knew what was going down. They were part of the scene. But the execs with the money were merely posers, fake fucks who came to flaunt their power and position and take advantage of the groupies who were not lucky enough to bed a musician that night.

Marcus never hid his true feelings for the bullshit going on around them. He refused to kiss any type of ass with the exception of his long-time girlfriend's, who was presently studying in Chicago. After shows, Marcus would remain elusive and slip out the back door before he found himself trapped by people he did not want to be with — before he snapped and clocked some asshole and screwed things up for the band.

So while the other three musicians fed the execs drinks and compliments and introduced them to sexually permissive young women at The Town Pump, Marcus took the perpetually wasted Rudi out to get some grub before they took off for their next gig. (Rudi did not excel at public relations either.)

"Let's go over there and say hello," suggested Greg.

Marcus looked worn out as he half-heartedly perused the menu, his head resting in his hand while his elbow leaned on the table. Rudi paid no interest to the choices of cuisine but rather sipped a Dos Equis and scanned the room for babes.

"Hey Marcus," called Julie, "great show!"

"Best I've ever seen, dude. Intense," added Tosh.

"Thanks, man," said Marcus, looking up. "Have a seat."

"You don't mind?"

"Actually," said Rudi, "we was..."

Marcus cut him off. "Shut up. Drink your beer and just be quiet."

"Piss off," Rudi retorted.

Tosh, Julie and Greg slid in the booth among the two rockers.

"You guys get better every time I see you," said Greg.

"Me and Greg fuck in the bathroom to your music — the best sex I've ever had."

Greg put his hand over his face and shook his head, embarrassed by his girlfriend's unscrupulous candor. He spoke to Tosh and Marcus, pretending Julie wasn't there. "Her uninhibited reckless attitude attracts me, but sometimes it makes me wish I didn't even know her. Like a mosquito getting too close to that mysterious purple light and then *tzzzzt!*"

"I'll give you *'tzzzzt!'*" said Julie, grabbing his crotch.

Marcus smiled. Then, something dawned upon him. "That's *you* having sex in the bathrooms? You gotta stop that. That gets us in trouble. You're gonna cost us gigs."

"Really?"

Marcus laughed. "Naa. We catch shit but we bring in too much money to lose gigs. But I'll give you a demo if you'd like."

"It's not only the music. It's the energy," Julie beamed. "I don't think listening to a tape will have the same energy as the shows."

Marcus nodded. "That's why I do it, man. To affect people. To move them."

"So what's goin' on?" inquired Greg. "Are you guys any closer to a record deal?"

"Ahh, who knows, but the rest of the band is setting the groundwork right now. Rock n' roll negotiations."

"That's cool."

"To tell you the truth, I couldn't care less."

"Isn't that your goal, though? To make it big?" asked Tosh, bewildered. He couldn't understand Marcus' apathy when an hour earlier, the singer seemed so passionate.

"Not really. I don't want to make it big."

"Don't you want the money? The fame?" asked Julie.

"Fucking yah!" shouted Rudi.

"Fuck that," said Marcus.

"Yeah, but don't you want your music to reach as many people as possible?"

Marcus sighed deeply, like the most misunderstood person in the world. "Look, this is what I believe. Bands toil and struggle to make it. Whatever their motivation may be, whether it be money or girls or fame, everything they do is to attain exposure. They try to get their music played everywhere possible. Then they reach a certain level of success and the industry takes over. They merely have to produce something of any level of quality, however real or true or contrived it is, and the business will promote it till it's dead. They'll play it on MTV every half hour and every Top 40 station from Tuscaloosa to Tuscon if they can. When you reach that level, when you're about to become a household name, if you still care about your music, if you ever did, you strive to keep its integrity. At that point you are trying against all odds to keep your music from being overexposed. Like the woman who loses respect by sleeping with a lot of men, you don't want your music to become a cheap whore."

"Wow," muttered Tosh. "It's a fine line, huh? You want to succeed, but only to a point. You want to reach an audience, but only so big."

"Yeah. I mean I don't want housewives in Kentucky singing my songs. I cringe at that thought."

"But isn't that the ultimate snobbery?" questioned Julie. "The artist who discriminates against his audience?"

"Maybe," said Marcus, thinking for a second. "But these housewives in Kentucky have absolutely nothing in common with me. They don't understand where I'm coming from. When I'm making music that's so meaningful to me, I don't want them singing my words just because they like the melody. Then, they might actually think about the words and be like, *'This guy's a freak!'* I'll be scrutinized and misunderstood by all these people, the media. I'll have my hands full with bullshit and all this negative attention directed at me. Attention that I didn't want in the first place."

"How do you know you don't share anything with these housewives? Emotions are human. Maybe you can connect with a forty-year-old divorcee in Arizona and make her feel good through your music."

"It's a chance I don't want to take. What can I say? I'm selfish. I do not want to make my life hell."

A waitress came by and Rudi bought everyone a shot and a beer. "To sit at this table, you have to drink," he declared. "Or you can get under it and blow me."

They all drank.

"It's crazy," continued Marcus. "So all your time and energy and hopes are focused on this goal and then, when you obtain it, your focus changes to the complete opposite. That's my view anyway. That's my attitude. I realized this a long time ago. I took a step back and said 'OK, what am I trying to accomplish here?' I realized it was useless. A waste."

"So why are you still doing it?"

"Because right now, things are great. I love the shows, man, I live for them. The whole process is such a release. Also, you know, I love to affect people with art. I mean, you guys are doing it in the bathrooms. That's great. I love that. I'm flattered."

Julie smiled proudly. "If you made it big, though, you could affect even more people."

Marcus took a swig of his beer. "Too much of anything is bad. Like I said, when something gets too big, it loses its true core anyway. It becomes a filtered-down version. I mean, if we were playing the Pacific Coliseum or the Kingdome, people in section 353 would be talking about *Beverly Hills 90210* or some shit while

I'm pouring my heart out. Half the people will be there just to be there. For the scene. Not for the music. That just takes away from the experience for everyone around them. I need to know that everyone is involved. The show doesn't work with distractions."

"That's a bunch of shit," said Rudi. "Ole Marcus here is just 'fraid of fame. He doesn't want his mug plastered on every stinkin' corner." Then, to himself, he mumbled, "I shoulda been born a singer. Why the drums?"

"I'm happy the way I am," said Marcus. "I don't want money or girls, this so-called rock n' roll lifestyle. And I certainly don't want the fuckin' media following me everywhere. That shit is not for me. I just want to keep it the way it is now for as long as possible. When it's over, I'm just gonna live in the country with my girl and own a music store or something. Raise a family, read, fish. That's the life for me."

"What about the rest of the band?" asked Tosh. "Do they know what your plans are? They can't really continue without you."

"Well, that's another point," Marcus went on. "I owe it to them to go through with it. And I will until I can honestly take no more. At that point, hopefully we will have made a name for ourselves to the point where they can continue on without me. Or go their separate ways in the business. They are great musicians, I'll tell you. They don't need me. Besides, I'm sure they all have things they want to say. Like Rudi, here. Rudi has aspirations of his own."

"Fucking yah!" said Rudi, his drunkenness warping his Cockney accent. He became animated with an air of pomp. "I have ambition. I want my name in big fucking lights. I want people to know me when I walk down the street."

"Rudi, you're a drummer," Julie reminded him.

Rudi continued vocalizing his dreams, undaunted. "I want free tickets to choice events. I want to be on magazine covers and MTV. I want to drive around in limousines for the rest of my life and have accountants pay for it all. But most of all, I'll tell you what. Five reasons why I'm really in this business..."

Everyone remained silent.

"One — supermodels. Two — porn stars. Three — centerfold chicks. Four — go-go dancers. Five... Five... Damn! I forgot what five was."

"Groupies?" asked Julie.

"Prostitutes?" asked Greg.

"Yeah, they're easy," quipped Tosh.

"Oh yeah!" exclaimed Rudi, jumping up in his seat. "Five — I don't have to cut my hair!" He let out a big haughty laugh. "See? I have ambition! I don't want ta *fish!!*"

Speaking of fishing, Tosh thought, where the hell was Crosby? He had disappeared into the bathroom and never returned.

*　　*　　*　　*

In the third stall from the wall, Crosby sat limply on one of the toilet bowls. Precariously perched on the porcelain altar, his head leaned against the metal wall. It looked as though he went to take a dump and passed out.

Tosh feared the worst.

Upon closer inspection, Crosby showed vital signs. In addition, Tosh's nose told him that Crosby had even controlled all of his bodily functions. What a bonus.

Tosh jostled his buddy. "C'mon, Cros. Wake up. You can't sleep here!"

No response.

"Dude, wake up. We're gonna sleep at Greg and Julie's. Nice soft couch. Blankets. It's better than a ceramic sphere. Much more comfortable."

Crosby groaned without opening his eyes.

Tosh knew any kind of response showed hope. "Let's go, Cros! You can't sleep here, dude. The building is on fire."

Tosh shook Crosby until one eye gradually opened. "Remember me? We gotta go!" As he picked Crosby up, the other eye opened.

Crosby got to his feet and put his arm around the sturdy Tosh for support. They walked out into the cool Vancouver night.

CHAPTER 9

Greg and Julie shared a small house on the outskirts of the city. A bedroom and a kitchen adjoined the main living quarters, which featured an old couch, a color television and a fireplace. Quite cozy.

Crosby headed straight for one end of the large, mushy couch and instantly fell asleep before even making contact with it — fully clothed, face down, no pillow or blankets.

"That guy is all class," joked Tosh. "What manners."

"No worries. I'm just glad we got him out of Ramone's. The Mexicans would have stripped him clean."

"Like a stalled car in the South Bronx. They don't even wait for you to leave. They're just like, 'And I'll be taking *this,* thank you very much.' They'll steal your hubcaps while you're at a red light."

"Really?"

"No. At least, I don't think so."

"What the hell do you do in the Bronx?"

"Yankee games."

"Ohh." Greg shook his head. "Great place to take the whole family, huh?"

"It's not really so bad. In fact, it's educational. I learned half my vocabulary in the bleachers. Cocksucker, faggot, douche bag..."

"Mothafucka?"

"Nah. I already knew that one."

"Well," Greg said, kicking off his shoes and settling into the couch. "Looks like Julie crashed too. What do you want to do?"

Tosh snuggled into the enormous beanbag in front of the fireplace. "Anything that does not involve physical activity. I think I've found heaven. This chair is killer. I feel like I'm resting in God's scrotum."

"No balls, though."

"Are you saying God has no balls?"

"If there was a God, I certainly would not imply that he had no balls."

"You don't believe in God?"

"I don't know. Not really. Do you?"

"Yeah. I mean, I believe in something."

"I've lost all faith in organized religion. I'll take my chances."

"Believing in religion and believing in God are two different things."

"Yeah, well, I don't know. I think God just exists in people's minds."

"What's the difference?"

Greg pondered this abstract idea for a moment, but he could not sustain the appropriate concentration the conversation demanded. Coming down from a wicked buzz, he looked quite drained from the night's festivities, especially nailing Julie in the men's room. (God bless her.)

"Want to watch a movie? I got *Fritz the Cat* on video."

"Can we smoke a bowl first?"

"Indeed." Greg lifted himself off of the couch and secured the necessary provisions. He threw in the flick and packed a pipe full of ganja. After emptying it himself, he refilled it and tossed it over to Tosh, still sunk deep into the beanbag. "Incoming!" he shouted.

Tosh inhaled the sweet weed and with a perma-grin on his face, watched the impudent blue feline prance around the screen decrying the "system." Fritz was a cool cat, a smooth-talking prankster always after some pussy.

Soon, the thick ganja high pulled heavily on Tosh's eyelids as he seemed to sink deeper into the nucleus of the beanbag. The spirits of the night called him, and Tosh could no longer resist the temptation. He intended to shut his eyes for only a second, but when he opened them again, it was morning.

$$* \qquad * \qquad * \qquad *$$

"Go down into the garage, will you Tosh, and grab some eggs from the refrigerator. There should be a whole crate of them."

Tosh did as Julie asked, eager for a home-cooked breakfast. The first step in beating a bad hangover, besides smoking a bowl, was a big fat breakfast. Tosh felt pretty crappy and he assumed Crosby would feel even worse, considering his condition the previous night and the fact that he still hadn't made it off the couch since they set foot in Greg and Julie's house.

Descending the stairs into darkness, an unexpected but unmistakable odor greeted Tosh. *Dog.* The garage smelled like a pooch. No doubt about it.

Tosh grabbed the string that dangled in front of his face, illuminating the bare bulb that protruded from the spackled ceiling. He quickly spotted the fridge, but no Spot. Then the bulb flickered and blew.

Once again in the darkness, Tosh clicked his tongue and whistled for the dog that he could smell but not see. His call went unanswered, so he groped his way towards the fridge, stumbling over a rusty lawn mower, probably left out in the rain one afternoon while Greg retreated to the house to watch a hockey game.

Tosh opened the refrigerator door and grabbed as many eggs as he could manage. As he turned around, in a dark corner of the garage, he caught a glimpse of a dog's eyes reflected in the light of the refrigerator. Tosh opened the door all the way to shed more light on the timid, homely creature.

In a recess in the wall sat an old mutt. At one time playful and rambunctious, the aged canine stayed curled on a ratty cushion, looking at Tosh but not acknowledging his presence. His once gleaming eyes had abandoned their sparkle and had grown cloudy. The dog's fur was matted and falling out in some places. He was a sad, gruesome sight.

Not what a dog should look like, thought Tosh.

Distressed, Tosh closed the fridge and carefully retraced his steps, cradling the eggs close to his chest. He made it over the lawnmower without a problem, but stubbed his foot on a tire, causing him to juggle the nest of eggs. One nearly plummeted from safety, but Tosh's forearms protected it from the menacing force of gravity.

After climbing the stairs without incident, he carefully placed the bundle on the counter next to the stove, where Julie was making pancakes. "What's with the dog?" he asked.

"That's Jackson, Greg's dog. He's old."

"I don't think *old* is the word."

"Talk to Greg about it. He doesn't want to hear it."

"What's that?" said Greg, who had entered the room toweling his head dry. "I heard my name."

"What's with your dog, dude?"

"Oh, Jackson? He's a good dog."

"What's he doin' in that dark corner of the garage?"

"He's old. He can barely walk. Can't make it up the stairs — bad hips."

"What's with his fur?"

"He's got some kind of skin condition and his hair is falling out. He's goin' blind, too."

"Well I'm sure sitting in the dark garage doesn't help his vision."

Greg ignored Tosh's comment. "Sometimes he can't control himself. Wets the rug and shit. Besides, he likes it down there. He's got his little bed."

"How do you know he likes it?"

Greg could not answer that question. "What's your point, Tosh?"

"He didn't look too happy down there. I mean, that's not what being a dog is all about. Sittin' alone in the dark all the time. No offense, but I think that's cruel. Dogs are social creatures, you know? They're used to being around people or with other dogs. They need company."

"I visit him every day."

"Visit him? That's exactly what I mean. What do you spend, 15 minutes with him? An hour? One hour out of 24 every day. You shouldn't have to *visit* him. He should be living with you. Right now he's cooped up in a dungeon."

"I told you, he likes it down there. He's got a comfy bed, his food, water."

"Do you let him out?"

"Of course. I let him out to shit and everything. But I can't leave him out there unattended. He's practically blind." Greg ran a comb through his hair. "He probably doesn't even know the difference, anyway."

"He looks so unhappy down there. If you're just gonna keep him in the basement, maybe you should put him to sleep."

"You mean destroy him? Murder him? No way. The vet said he's only slightly uncomfortable and inconvenienced, not in bad pain or anything. He jst looks bad. Who am I to decide that his time is up?"

"I don't even think he knows he's alive anyway," added Julie.

Greg looked away, hurting. "Tosh, when I was a little kid, I won one of those goldfish at a carnival. I brought him home in a plastic bag, bought him a little tank and named him Goldy. They said he'd live a year or so. Well, he made it through the year and then two more.

"I got more goldfish. Bigger, faster fish with brighter colors, a bigger tank, treasure chest at the bottom, the works. He even survived the transfer to the new tank. Nothing could kill this fish.

"He aged and became ugly, the little runt of the tank. I guess the other fish respected him, or whatever, 'cause he always got enough food. He managed. But he looked like hell.

"One day I decided that he was too old to live. On a whim, I fished him out of the tank with the little net and flushed him down the toilet."

"He didn't stand a chance with the vicious current in the bowl," Julie cracked.

"Shut up, Jules. Who knows what fate he met after that? If I didn't know any better, I'd say he's still living somewhere in the Pacific.

"Anyway, a week later, it dawned on me that for absolutely no reason, I had taken that fish's life away. That fish had persevered and strived to live, and I had unnecessarily ended his life with the snap of my fingers.

"I felt so fuckin' bad, man. I cried. I was sad about Goldy and frightened by the power I had exercised. Frightened that I could disrespect life like that, no matter how insignificant it might have seemed.

"I just don't feel right putting Jackson to sleep. I shouldn't have the authority to decide when things should die. That is nature's job."

Tosh remained silent for a minute. Who could argue with that?

"I just think that maybe Jackson would enjoy getting out of the garage every now and then," said Tosh. "More than just long enough for him to take a dump. Even though he can't see, I'm sure he would like to sit out in the yard and feel the warm sun on his back and listen to the birds sing. I bet fresh air and a cool breeze would make him feel good."

Greg listened.

"If you're going to keep him alive, give him a reason to live. Give him something to enjoy," Tosh continued. "Freedom, companionship, affection. Whether he likes it in the garage or not, it's not good to keep him alone all day. Right now, you're basically storing him until he dies. Give him something to look forward to besides death. Down in that dusty garage, he's just waiting to die. That's not really living, is it?"

Greg draped his towel over his head like a hood and disappeared into the bedroom.

* * * *

The smell of fresh bacon finally got Crosby off the couch. He rubbed his eyes and licked his chops. "I can't thank you enough, Julie. Bacon, eggs, pancakes. This is too much."

"Just help with the dishes. That's thanks enough."

"No problem. Where's Tosh and Greg?"

"They took Jackson for a drag."

"Jackson?"

"Greg's dog."

"A *drag?*"

"Well, he's old and he can't walk too well. Tosh borrowed a wagon from the neighbor's lawn and they put Jackson in it. They seemed pretty enthused about the whole thing, Jackson included."

Crosby shoveled scrambled eggs down his throat. "I can't believe how generous you guys are."

"Generous?"

"Yeah. I mean, you just met us last night and you took us out, got us into the club and even put us up. Now you're making breakfast."

"It's no big deal, Crosby. Really. I just threw a few extra eggs in the pan."

"Well, we appreciate it."

After devouring the wonderful breakfast and helping with the dishes, Crosby hopped in the shower. Midway through shampooing his hair, Julie opened the bathroom door. "Comin' in?" Crosby asked.

"Don't you wish."

"I have some hard to reach places that haven't been cleaned in a long time."

"I bet. You're out of luck though, pal. Greg and Tosh are beeping outside. Greg's gonna take you guys back to your van. He's got to go to work."

"Shit," said Crosby.

"No, you don't have time," Julie razzed him, leaving a dry towel for his use.

Crosby quickly rinsed the suds out of his hair, ran the towel over his body and jumped right back into the clothes he had slept in. He hugged Julie goodbye and ran out into the bright sunlight, nearly stumbling over an old dog that was stretched out on the lawn in front of the porch. The dog looked old and sick, his eyes foggy and his coat falling out. His ears perked up when he heard Crosby, though, and he wagged his tail vigorously.

That is the sign of a happy dog, thought Crosby.

* * * *

133

Greg dropped the guys off at the parking lot where they had left their van and gave them some buds for the road. "You guys take care. Stay out of trouble, you hear?"

"Thanks for everything, dude." Tosh leaned in the window of the car. "Drop us a line if you're ever in New York City."

Tosh and Crosby searched three different levels in the garage before locating their van, finally spotting it next to a beat-up Saab with California plates.

Crosby fired up Josephine and they meandered through the garage, looking for the exit. Once outside the dim concrete building, they stopped at the first gas station they could find.

"Bonus," commented Crosby. "This one has a mini-mart,.."

Tosh and Crosby looked at each other and simultaneously burst into song, belting out Jimmy Buffet's "Peanut-butter Conspiracy": "Runnin' up and down the aisles of the mini-mart, stickin' food in our jeans..."

"Pay for *everything,*" interrupted Tosh. "We already dealt with the Canadian law. I don't wanna end up on a work farm in the Northwest Territories."

"Okay, Dad," quipped Crosby, giving him a what-do-you-think-I'm-stupid look.

While Tosh added fuel and oil and washed all the windows, including the oversized rearview mirrors, Crosby restored all of his windsurfing equipment to the roof rack. Twenty-four dollars covered all the petrol, Tosh's sunflower seeds and a pack of red pistachios for Crosby.

They hit the road again, looking for the auto ferry to Victoria on Vancouver Island.

"Man, I can't believe Greg and Julie," said Crosby. "They were so cool."

"I know. To open the doors of their home to two total strangers they met in a parking garage. People don't do that in New York, that's for sure."

"We could have robbed them blind."

"Or worse. You could have puked all over their den."

As it turned out, Crosby had merely drooled on their couch and left a stinker in the bathroom, but he and Tosh could have turned out to be complete assholes.

"They must have had confidence in their character judgment," said Crosby.

"Especially since they based it solely on a brief conversation in a public parking facility and a wasted night out at the bars."

Were Greg and Julie naive? Stupid? Crazy?

"They were trusting," continued Tosh. "They opened up. Took a chance."

Greg and Julie did not throw the dice just to help a broken gambler, however. They stood to gain from the experience as well, like a dog that rolls over on his back and bares his stomach in order to get a belly rub. Nothing ventured, nothing gained. That's part of life.

"You have to give to get," said Tosh.

"Gotta invest to collect."

"Exactly, Cros. Look at it this way. If they ever come to New York, they know they have a place to stay. My door will always be open."

"Mine, too."

Greg and Julie could have been exceptions rather than the norm for British Columbians, but their amicability reflected in everyone Tosh and Crosby encountered. Surely assholes existed in Vancouver just like everywhere else in the world, but Tosh and Crosby had the good fortune of continually avoiding them.

"Are you enjoying yourselves?" a middle-aged Chinese man asked them as they sat at a red light, their well-scrubbed but hung-over faces brooding in the bright morning sunlight.

"Huh?" said Tosh, snapping out of his fog.

"Are you enjoying Vancouver?" The man's wide smile practically closed his Asian eyes. He motioned to the van, recognizing that they were from out of town.

"Oh, yes, very much," Tosh offered, miffed by the man's concern. He looked at Crosby. "A total stranger at a stoplight asked if we were enjoying ourselves," he muttered, as if his friend did not witness the encounter — as if the whole episode occurred solely in Tosh's mind.

Crosby nodded, equally amazed.

"Do you hear the music?"

"What music?"

"The *Twilight Zone* music."

"I know," laughed Crosby. "I'm not used to people being this nice."

Behind them, someone beeped and Crosby realized the light had turned green. He promptly accelerated, noting that it seemed to be a kinder, gentler beep, not the usual aggressive blast of the horn filled with frustration and hatred.

"More of a 'Come on lads, move along now' beep," said Tosh.

They drove on, searching for the auto ferry to Vancouver Island.

"There," Crosby pointed out.

He followed the signs toward the ferry, at one point having to dangerously cross three lanes at once in order to stay on the correct path. Like a master, Crosby handled the big old van, sans power-steering, power-brakes, power, period. Unfortunately, falling in love with his Indy 500 driving techniques, Crosby became more concerned with dodging traffic than with following signs and ended up in the wrong lane as the highway split apart.

Suddenly, there were no more signs for the ferry.

"Great, Mario. Now what?"

"Hey man — I was doin' the best I can!"

"I thought you were gonna have us up on two wheels back there."

"Naa. Van's too heavy."

"Let's ask this guy here for directions," said Tosh, pointing to the fellow in the old station wagon next to them.

A heavyset fellow with a lot of hair and a beard hunched over the wheel and chewed on a Big Mac. The burly man looked like a Hell's Angels reject. He had everything except the Harley. The wagon just didn't cut it.

"You know how to get to the Vancouver Island Ferry?" Tosh asked over the din of the road .

"Sure," called the man through a mouthful of cholesterol and fat. "In fact, I'm headin' that way! Why don't you follow me?" (He didn't have the biker attitude, either.)

"All right!" shouted Tosh, slapping Crosby five. "Thanks, man!"

The man's car was packed tight with all kinds of stuff, right up to the back of his seat, pushing him up against the steering wheel. It looked as though he sat in the driver's seat while someone packed the car around him. His draggin' wagon also towed a U-Haul.

"Following this guy should be a piece of cake," said Crosby. "I should have no problem keeping up with him."

Tosh was thankful the man wasn't driving a sports car.

Crosby trailed the wagon for about ten minutes when the traffic suddenly slowed to a stop. The four-lane highway had been narrowed to one lane for vehicles coming from both directions. The traffic slowly merged into the single lane as a road worker wearing a reflective orange vest permitted them to pass for five minutes at a time. After exactly five minutes, the worker darted in front of the line of cars, wielding a red stop sign. After securing the traffic behind him, he radioed ahead to his partner at the other end of the construction zone who, in turn, opened the path for the vehicles stopped on his side.

Crosby trailed the wagon closely. As they approached the single lane, an old lady in a gold Omni attempted to merge between them.

"Don't let her in," urged Tosh.

"I know, I know. Our time's almost up," said Crosby. "Damn! She won't let up!"

In a shocking display of aggressive driving tendencies, the old lady forced her way in between them and the wagon.

"No — no fuckin' way! I don't believe it!"

The gold Omni was the last car allowed to pass, leaving Tosh and Crosby to eat her dust, the first in line for the next round.

"There goes our directions."

"He must have known we were following that guy," Tosh said about the human traffic light. "I don't believe it. He must have. He just wants to mess with us."

"Maybe he'll let us through," suggested Crosby. He pleaded with the man through the windshield.

Tosh even waved a dollar bill out the window but the apathetic worker wanted no part of it. He just frowned and turned away.

"Guess not."

Tosh and Crosby watched helplessly as their guide drove off into the construction zone. The ragged station wagon slowly shrunk into a small spot of light where the sun reflected off the chrome bumper before finally disappearing altogether.

"This really sucks," said Crosby. "I have no idea where we are and I haven't seen any signs for the ferry for a while."

"He was probably takin' a short cut."

"Yeah. He was goin' 'the back way.'"

Things brightened a little when Tosh found a Bob Marley song on the radio. "Lively Up Yourself" got them feeling all right.

Soon traffic began moving again and Tosh and Crosby passed through the single-lane construction zone. As they passed the orange diamond-shaped sign that read **END CONSTRUCTION** and the road opened up, Crosby could not believe his eyes.

The station wagon with the U-Haul sat on the shoulder of the highway with its hazard lights blinking. Out in front stood the driver, excitedly waving them down.

"He waited for us!"

"This dude's made friends for life. I love this guy."

They resumed following the wagon until the driver motioned for them to follow a sign for the ferry. The road split and he departed with a thumb up. Tosh climbed halfway out of the window and screamed a thank you at full volume.

The ferry cost fifteen dollars plus seven dollars per person. Since they tried to cut back on expenses whenever possible, Tosh naturally chose to hide himself. He hastily emptied the storage space under the side bed and climbed in.

Crosby maneuvered the van into a parking space on one of the lower decks. He then rolled a joint while Tosh put the storage bed back together. Once most of the people had left the surrounding cars, they sat on the floor and smoked it to a tape of the old Sixties folk singer, Donovan.

"'First there is a mountain, then there is no mountain, then there is?' What the fuck kinda lyrics are those?" asked Crosby.

"It's from the Sixties. I don't know. Obviously acid had something to do with it."

"'Caterpillar sheds its skin to find the butterfly within.' How profound."

"It's got a happy beat, though."

"Yeah. I feel like skipping through a field of daisies."

Tosh and Crosby finished the joint, getting completely baked. Tosh found his favorite Donovan song on the tape, "Hurdy Gurdy Man," and cranked it up.

"Check this song out. It's so psychedelic."

"I'm so high," said Crosby.

Tosh lay back with his head against the speaker of their portable tape deck. "I just want to get so blasted and listen to this song on headphones, man."

"It sounds like he's singing underwater."

"Not shitty little Walkman headphones but those big fuckin' stereo headphones that cover your ears. Leather. Hi-fi, man."

"Is that a guitar or a sitar?"

"Those babies just drown out everything. With headphones like that on, you become part of the music. On some cds you can actually hear the singer take breaths an' all. It's so trippy."

"What the hell is a hurdy-gurdy man, anyway?"

"You can hear every instrument so clearly," continued Tosh. "There is no musical experience more intense than being stoned out of your mind and listening to a cd through stereo headphones."

"Maybe making the music," said Crosby, giving up on his one-sided conversation and joining Tosh's line of thought.

Tosh leaned up off the floor. "Maybe. But that is *active*. I'm talking passive here."

"What do you mean?"

"No creativity. Just letting the music pass over you. Pass through you."

"Some concerts are pretty intense. Think about tripping at the Dead shows."

"Yeah. But there are a lot of distractions. I'm talking dim room, maybe a candle burning, incense. Headphones on and one hell of a mellow buzz. Acid is too hyper."

"Not all the time. Especially if you take the edge off with about forty joints and fifty beers."

"That'll calm you some, but your mind is still hyperactive on acid. This buzz has to tune out everything but the music. I want to do a drug that has a high like pot but is ten times stronger. Something that is so intense you can't even move. You can't think. You can only feel."

"Heroin."

"Yeah, but fuck that. I'd never do that trash – stickin' needles in my arms. I hate needles."

"It's probably the most intense high available," reasoned Crosby. "And did you ever see a junkie? They don't look like they're doin' much thinkin'."

"They don't look like they're doin' much feelin' either. Besides, it's too risky. Overdosing. No high is worth dying for."

"It is for some people."

"Not me. Life is too beautiful. I don't need drugs to enjoy life. I just use psychedelics because they open your mind. They give you a new way of seeing things."

"Getting high *is* fun, though."

"Hell, yeah, it's fun. But I don't depend on drugs for happiness. I can get high without them," said Tosh, becoming more theatrical. "The sun makes me high. A breeze of fresh air."

He stuck his head out the van's window to exemplify his point, forgetting they had parked on one of the lower levels of the ferry. The still, stale air around him offered only remnants of exhaust coughed from the hundreds of vehicles aboard.

Tosh quickly sat down again. Noting that he still had Crosby's attention, though, he continued on without missing another beat. "Give me the sweet scent of a rose. That's all I need."

Crosby listened but didn't say anything.

Tosh scratched his dreads. "That joint kicked?"

*   *   *   *

Tosh and Crosby made their way up onto the top deck of the auto ferry. Staking their claim in a sunny corner, they spread out a sleeping bag to kick back on for the three-hour ride to Vancouver Island.

"Hey Tosh," began Crosby, "remember what you were saying about not needing drugs to be happy?"

"Yep."

"Well, hell knows I smoke a lot of pot. But you know what? I honestly don't need it to be happy. Give me the smell of the ocean. That's all *I* need. You know how when we go down the shore and we start getting close, the air smells differently? It's got that salty squid smell? That smell makes me really happy."

"Yeah, I like that smell, too. Makes me ponder what lies on the other side of the ocean. Distant lands, adventure."

"Makes me think of fishing and windsurfing and sailing and diving."

"Makes me think of the beach."

"Yeah. Makes me think of beautiful girls in bikinis. God, I love girls."

"Me, too." Tosh thought of Sally. A truly sweet, gorgeous girl stuck in Kansas. What a shame. Maybe she'll make it to the ocean one day. "Girls are amazing," said Tosh.

"They have this smell..."

"That smell..."

"And they feel soft. Girls feel like..."

"Silk."

"Yeah. I love that. Nothin' in the world better than feeling a soft, warm girl against your skin. Oh, I'm gettin' chills."

"Easy does it, fella."

"I'm O.K."

"What's your most important quality in a girl, Cros?"

"A tight ass."

"That's not what I meant."

"Moaning. I like girls who moan."

Tosh breathed with a touch of exasperation. "No, no. I mean — don't get me wrong — I like a tight ass, too. Not too small, though. I like to have something to grab hold of. Something to squeeze. Meat on the bones. I hate those twiggy girls that feel like they're gonna break when you hold 'em."

"Are you telling me you like fat chicks?"

"No! I'm not saying *that*. It's not like I crave an ass of cellulite. I don't want an ass that's all over the place."

"I don't believe it," teased Crosby. "You like a corn-fed ass."

"No. I just mean I like a regular ass."

"A regular ass?"

"But that's *not* the point I was trying to make!"

Tosh did not know how he got sucked into this asinine conversation. He shook out the mental cobwebs Crosby had spun and tried again. "A girl's ass is hardly a priority for me. If she happens to have an ass that's compatible with my tastes, great. But the size or shape or tone of a woman's butt has nothing to do with my most important female quality."

"You're a tit man?"

"Crosby!"

"What?"

Tosh felt infuriated. Sometimes he found it difficult to converse with Crosby under the heavy influence of ganja. They thought on different levels and Crosby often misled Tosh.

"Yes, I do love tits. The bigger the better, if you must know. But you're getting me off track here."

"It's all you, bud."

"You mean to tell me that the most important thing to you in a girl is a tight ass? I didn't think you were that shallow, dude."

"Hey!"

"Well, you're disappointing me."

"I didn't know you were talking about a girlfriend. I thought you just meant my ideal sex partner."

"Whatever."

"What?"

"Does it make a difference? Shouldn't your girlfriend be your ideal sex partner?"

"It's an imperfect world, Tosh. No, man. I'm just talking about my fantasy here."

"O.K."

"My most important quality in a girl is a sense of humor. Someone who is not too uptight to laugh at themselves. Someone who can take a ribbing and give one out. I love girls who laugh a lot. Someone like that is fun to be around. Laughter is good for you."

"It is."

"Physically, I mean. I read somewhere that laughter actually is good for your body."

"Yeah, I heard something like that, too," said Tosh.

"What's yours? What's your most important quality in a female companion?"

"Affection."

"Affection is good."

"Affection is *key.*"

"Unless it's hardcore, primal sex. Flat-out fucking. Like dogs in heat."

"You have a way of putting things, Cros."

"You have to admit, affection seems out of place during animal-like sex."

"I guess during those lust-crazed, hormone-driven sessions, you can forego the affection."

"I mean, while you're panting and pumping and sweating and she's squirming and thrusting and moaning, you're gonna plant a little I-love-you-honey kiss on her cheek?"

"I guess not."

"No. You'll probably bite her."

Tosh took a deep breath. "The affection I'm talking about doesn't only occur during sex, Cros. I'm talking about snugglin', or when you're walking down the street, or just hanging out. Someone who likes to touch me and hold me and feel my energy."

"Even when you haven't showered in three days."

"Exactly," said Tosh, smiling.

He closed his eyes and reclined on the sleeping bag. Sensing the end of the discussion, Crosby did the same. The heat of the mid-day sun shining directly overhead caressed their faces as they drifted into a state of deep relaxation, purely contented.

CHAPTER 10

A three-hour nap on the Vancouver Island Auto Ferry had rid Tosh and Crosby of their marijuana high, yet their minds remained a bit cloudy. (It was good weed.) They debarked the boat at a crawl through the congested waterfront area, where tourists browsed leisurely in the midday sun. With stomachs growling, they eagerly found a parking lot for Josephine, put on some shoes and shorts and headed out to find some lunch.

The picturesque capital of British Columbia had many quaint shops and friendly pubs. Colorful flowers hung from street lamps, their vines almost reaching the concrete below. The clear blue sky invited them to settle down at one of the outdoor cafes that lined the streets.

Tosh and Crosby decided to split a plate of deluxe nachos.

"It's huge," the waitress assured them. "Would you like some beers with that?"

"No thanks," said Tosh. "It's too early to have a beer."

"I could use a water," said Crosby, feeling dehydrated and hung over from the night before.

"Me too. With a twist of lime."

When the waitress returned with their waters, on her tray sat a couple of frosted mugs for the table next to theirs.

"They have frosted mugs," whimpered Tosh.

"I haven't had a frosted mug in ages," Crosby added.

The temptation was too great. They promptly ordered beers.

While they ate, they flirted with the waitress. She went along with them, in keeping with the good nature of the British Columbians Tosh and Crosby had previously encountered. Before they knew it, their lunch of nachos washed down by a beer turned into a lunch of beer with some nachos to nibble. They left the table happy and buzzed, but kind of woozy.

"Where to?" asked Crosby.

"I don't know. Let's stroll."

"Stroll it is."

Victoria brimmed with life. Birds darted from street lamp to street lamp. Bicyclists dodged taxis stopping for tourists while rollerbladers weaved around vendors selling pretzels and soda. Wandering cheerfully, Tosh and Crosby heard the sound of live music in the distance. Tracking the source of the tunes, they shuffled into a park called Butchart Gardens.

The sweet scent of fresh flowers saturated the air, intoxicating them like honey wine. In full bloom, each bud proudly unfurled its precious petals for the parade of people pedaling by. A light breeze rippled through the old trees.

With such a soothing setting and the day's doses of ganja and beer lulling him, Crosby could not resist the desire to doze. "This would be the ultimate place for a nap," he announced, plopping down on the soft grass next to a patch of petunias. "It's so damn peaceful. I've got to give it a go."

He lay back, put his hands behind his head and shut his eyes.

"We slept on the ferry," Tosh complained. "How can you be tired?"

Crosby's silent response and the look of utter contentment on his face told Tosh there would be no argument. Defeated, he walked back to the van to grab his book.

Upon returning to the park, he sought a seat under a handsome tree with sweeping limbs. Leaning up against the chiseled trunk, Tosh flipped through the pages of his book searching for the place where he had left off. Soon, his eyes became heavy and he drifted off, joining Crosby in dreamland.

*   *   *   *

Something tickled Crosby's face, but it did not wake him. Rather, the bothersome sensation appropriately fit into his disjointed dream as the floating seedlings of a dandelion brushing against his cheek.

Crosby simply wiped the hindrance away with his three curved toes, toes that enabled him to climb to the top of magnificent trees and hang for great lengths of time, lounging in the dense, damp heat. For, in his dream, Crosby was a three-toed sloth, munching nutritious leaves in the canopy of the rain forest. (No telling what a dandelion was doing in the South American jungle, but dreams have a tendency to make little temporal sense.)

Then, a more startling sensation interrupted Crosby's sleep. Something soft and wet smeared his forehead.

Was it a smashed papaya?

A large drop of some sticky tropical dew?

Toucan shit?

No. It was the curious nose of a frisky German shepherd.

Laying down the Frisbee he had fetched nearby, the young dog inspected the dozing fellow lying in the grass. Wagging his tail briskly as he sniffed Crosby, the pup then tendered a wake-up call in the form of an old-fashioned face-licking. From brow to chin, his long, pink tongue blanketed Crosby's unsuspecting face.

This prompted Crosby to open his eyes and when he did, two black caverns filled his vision. The imposing nostrils miffed him at first, but he swiftly identified the strange vision as a canine nose. After distinguishing who the nose belonged to and assessing the possible danger of his situation, Crosby rolled over onto his stomach and shut his eyes again, confident the intruder would bring him no harm.

The persistent pup pawed his back like an over-zealous camp counselor.

"Five more minutes," Crosby groaned to the dog.

The shepherd responded with a playful growl, his tail wagging even more excitedly as he grabbed a hold of Crosby's sweatshirt in his teething jaws.

"Hey, cut it out, buddy!" Crosby sat up and gently pushed the pup away.

The shepherd advanced with another face licking.

"Easy, fella," laughed Crosby. "I don't kiss on the first date."

"Sure you don't."

Crosby turned around. There, with the orange sunlight shining horizontally on her pale face, stood a captivating conundrum.

Crosby had never seen a woman like this before. Possessing a strange blend of exotic beauty and pure punk, she masked her God-given gorgeous looks with self-made alterations, style choices more at home in the seedy underground clubs of New York's East Village than in Victoria, British Columbia.

Deep, sultry eyes peeked out from under thick, dark makeup, while heavy black lipstick gave her mouth the appearance of a ripe plum. A matted mess of white dreads fell from her scalp. The most shocking part of her semblance, though, was the oversized silver ring that pierced her septum.

Crosby unwittingly stared at the large hoop through her nose. "Hi," he began cautiously.

"Hi," she said.

White dreads, thought Crosby, *where have I seen that before? Last night, that's where! The girl at the concert!*

"Hey — I know you," he said.

"You *do?"* teased the girl.

"Are you that girl that was at the show last night?"

"What girl?"

"Last night. The girl at that show."

"What show?"

"That band."

"What band? Could you maybe be a little more specific?"

Crosby couldn't remember too much from the night before. He attempted to smile but felt really stupid. "Sorry. It's just that I was kind of drunk. I don't really remember."

She stared at him blankly.

At a loss for words, Crosby looked at the smiling pup to ease the awkward moment of silence. He thought this was the girl from the show but he didn't know for sure. Most of the night a blur, he tried to recall some more details about his molester.

Then, it hit him. She had a tattoo on her hand. **H-O-P-E** across the knuckles.

"My name is Crosby," he said to her, extending a hand to shake.

"I'm Melinda," she responded, shaking his hand.

As Melinda helped him up, Crosby noticed her tattooed knuckles — but they read **L-E-S-S**. Confused, he said to her, "I thought it said *hope.*"

Melinda clenched her fist and took a swing at Crosby.

Instinctively, he put up his forearm to block the hit, but her punch stopped right before his face.

Melinda grinned. "Wrong hand!" She held out both of her hands, palms down. Together, her knuckles spelled **H-O-P-E-L-E-S-S.**

*   *   *   *

Crosby wondered if the nose ring would get in the way.

He could foresee Melinda's nasal jewelry possibly hindering a passionate kiss. After all, it was not an elegant little diamond chip buried in her nostril flesh, but a hoop large enough for an obese Chihuahua to hula through.

Crosby sat across the table from Melinda in her favorite pub. An outrageous paisley piano covered in bright silicone flowers contradicted the classic hardwood floor and brick walls. Its high ceiling gave Ferris' Oyster Bar a roomy, cavernous feel, but Melinda and Crosby sat on the back patio under the stars. Moonlight illuminated a huge painted menu on one wall while jars of sun-brewed tea lined the base of the other.

The longer Crosby talked to Melinda, the more he wanted to kiss her. He closely watched her black lips form each word. Crosby imagined those luscious babies wrapping themselves around him. He could feel their velvet touch on his skin.

Melinda smiled demurely and slugged her Wild Turkey, exemplifying the conflicting traits that composed her.

Despite her shocking appearance, Crosby felt attracted to her. He saw natural beauty through all of her disguises. Makeup could not camouflage her facial structure or bury her bewitching eyes. The dreads did not bother him either, although they reminded him of Tosh.

Crosby peered inside and noticed that Tosh seemed to be hitting it off with an attractive lady over by the bar. It looked like the two of them were engaged in an intense conversation. They talked closely and excitedly, ignoring the rest of their surroundings.

It figures, thought Crosby. *Show her your soul, dude.*

Tosh rarely participated in small talk. Even at a bar, within minutes of an introduction, he was debating reincarnation or animal rights or literature. Tosh could discuss anything with anybody, and he always seemed to know at least a little bit about everything. People liked Tosh because, for the most part, he was an easy-going, laid-back dude. They felt comfortable around him and, therefore, opened up to him. It amazed Crosby how quickly Tosh got to know people.

The waitress put down a steaming heap of sweet potato French fries on the table. Sesame oil glistened on their browned sides. As she followed with another mug of brew, Crosby's second drinking session of the day officially commenced. (For Crosby, two beers were just a couple of beers. Three beers constituted a drinking session, for a third beer usually signified many more to come.)

He slid a fry through a puddle of ketchup and took a swig of beer. Feeling brave, he spoke. "Can I ask you a personal question?"

Melinda considered it for a moment and then said, "Since I just downed that shot of whiskey, sure."

Crosby tried to figure a way to phrase his query without insulting Melinda. He began, "I just want to tell you that I think you're really pretty."

If Melinda were blushing under her pale makeup, Crosby couldn't tell. After an obligatory smile, she asked, "Is that you're question?"

"Oh, yeah. Well, I was just wondering, you know, like why do you..." Crosby's sentence trailed off into silence.

"Why do I..." she prompted him.

"Why do you wear all that stuff?" he blurted.

"What *stuff?*"

"That black lipstick and the makeup on your face and eyes. Your hair."

"Do you not like it?"

"No. I think it's cool."

"Well, that's why I wear it." Melinda said with attitude. "'Cause it's cool."

"Sorry I asked," Crosby said half-sarcastically. He felt awkward now and kind of wished he hadn't inquired.

"Why do you have the haircut you have? Why do you dress like you do?" Melinda drilled.

"I don't know. It's just me."

"Well, it's the same for me. This is how I express myself," she said defensively.

"That's cool," Crosby said appeasingly.

It obviously wasn't a good idea to ask Melinda personal questions. It seemed that Crosby had better luck when he just scammed girls, anyway. Somehow, bullshit and small talk got him farther. For Crosby, sex always preceded meaningful conversation. Getting to know someone ended up as pillow talk.

Crosby shrugged, took a big gulp of brew and burped so long and loud it sounded like a chainsaw ripping through an air conditioner.

A small smile found its way to Melinda's face.

Crosby said, "It's just that I've never known anyone that dressed as weir— dressed like you do. I've never known any girls with tattoos across their knuckles."

Melinda shook her head. "I'm sorry. It's a legitimate question. You're just trying to get to know me. You deserve an answer."

Melinda's curt explanation had hardly explained the actual motivation for her outrageous image, so she proceeded to fill Crosby in on her life's story.

Words came pouring out of Melinda's mouth. Like opening an old, shook-up can of Budweiser stuck under the seat of a Land Rover, Melinda vented the corrosive resentment she had amassed over the years, spewing sentence after sentence, pausing only to take a breath.

All her life, Melinda Lewis had received special attention from the male gender. They sent her Valentine cards, candy and flowers. She was treated to the nicest meals, the raddest concerts and sporting events that no one could get tickets to. Once, she received an expensive necklace from an admirer she didn't even know.

From her high-school classmates to the army of eligible bachelors and ineligible bastards, every male wanted her.

They wanted to woo her.

They wanted to shmooze her.

Kiss her.

Feel her.

Suck her titties.

But no one ever wanted to know her.

Whether it was poor judgment or just bad luck, Melinda had never found a good boyfriend. All of her romantic relationships failed horribly, sometimes causing her bitter tears.

She dated financially secure older men who offered maturity and experience. They used her.

She became infatuated with a musician. He abused her.

A couple of other relationships seemed promising, but both ended prematurely due to infidelity.

"He didn't want to be tied down," she'd say to Lucky, her German shepherd, roommate and best friend. While devouring a pint of Ben and Jerry's Double Chocolate ice cream, she'd recount her sad stories. In times of joy, Melinda celebrated with chocolate. In times of stress, she wallowed in it.

Melinda went unhappy and unfulfilled for a long time. Her dissatisfaction ate away at her little by little. She became paranoid and calculating when it came to meeting men. The brunt of her buried anger, though, she took out on herself. She blamed herself for her misfortunes, accepting her good looks as a curse rather than a blessing.

"Maybe if men weren't attracted to me, they'd see me as something more than a sexual object," she said to Lucky. "Maybe they'd like me for who I am, not how I look."

It started with an ankle tattoo of a skull. Her affinity for body art quickly developed into a fever and spread. Next came tribal bands around her ankle and arm. The letters on her knuckles followed soon after.

In between tattoo sessions, while she saved money for her next addition, Melinda made other alterations — the nose ring, the dreadlocks, the different makeup styles.

Within a few months, Melinda had transformed herself from an olive beauty into a punk witch. With her shocking appearance disguising her good looks, she felt confident that the men pursuing her would have truer intentions.

So far, however, there were no men to put to the test. Not so much because she looked like a member of the Addams family, but because of her own actions. Unfortunately, Melinda hadn't taken into account *her* feelings for men. She hadn't forgiven the gender in general and she harbored an underlying venom toward them. She realized this now, she told Crosby, and didn't know how to deal with it.

"I'm just a freak," she said.

Crosby sipped his beer, digesting Melinda's hour-long diatribe. He could see how badly Melinda had needed to share her anxieties.

"Doesn't sound like you're a freak to me," he said.

*　　*　　*　　*

"Santa Claus rules, man." Tosh gulped another swig of beer to wash down the tequila shot lingering in his mouth. He had struck up a conversation with the woman sitting next to him at Ferris' Oyster Bar. After Tosh complimented her on her beaded necklace, Darla promptly bought him a shot of Cuervo.

"When I was a little kid, I used to want to be Santa when I grew up," he continued. "I figured he'd want to retire by the time I got out of college and he would need someone to take over. Flying, sliding down chimneys – it seemed like a blast. Plus, the reindeer. I've always loved animals."

"You can't really beat the hours — one day a year," Darla pointed out.

"Actually, he probably works more than that. There's got to be a lot of preparation. Supervising the elves and stuff."

"Don't you think he had foremen to do that?"

"Oh. You're probably right."

"Santa has 364 days of vacation," asserted Darla.

"What about checking his list?"

"That's not work."

Tosh pictured himself a couple of hundred pounds heavier, his silver dreads floating in the crisp December wind as he steered his noble reindeer over the rooftops. Gold and green trim would line his big red suit. *Rasta Claus,* he thought.

"Think of the travel benefits," Darla added.

"Yeah, well, you can imagine how devastated I was when I found out he didn't exist. Besides the usual disappointment, I had to find a new career."

Darla laughed. "Get this," she said. "My sister has a couple of kids but she won't observe the traditional Santa Claus myth."

"What do you mean?"

"She won't let her kids believe in Santa Claus."

"Why not?"

"She doesn't want to lie to them."

"Oh, come on."

"I'm serious." Darla put away the last of her vodka tonic. "Do you want another drink?"

"Let me get this one," said Tosh, digging in his pockets. From two different pockets he produced seven crumpled dollar bills. Dropping them on the bar one by one, he ironed each one with the side of his hand and placed them in a neat pile. "Another round, please."

Tosh handed Darla her drink and held out his own frosted mug. "Cheers," he said.

"To my drinking partner," said she.

They clicked their glasses together and sipped.

"Actually," said Darla, "when you toast, you're supposed to touch hands." She held out her glass again, gazing deep into Tosh's eyes.

Tosh felt Darla's look said more than her words. Was she sending sexual signals? Was she planting the seeds of seduction? He toasted her again, this time keeping his glass up for a few seconds as their fingers connected.

Darla had a few years on Tosh but she barely looked it. Her shoulder-length black hair, dark brown eyes and lean figure surely turned heads wherever she went. Tosh noticed the sexy woman as soon as he, Crosby and Melinda walked into the bar. After talking to her for a while, he found himself incredibly attracted to her.

Darla projected a very docile, confident energy. She spoke softly and displayed polished manners, yet she had no pretension.

Sensing Darla might be interested in him added fuel to Tosh's fire. He continued the conversation. "So, your sister doesn't want to lie to her kids, huh?"

"No. She wants to have a completely open and honest relationship."

Well, I'm all for that," commented Tosh, "but don't you think she's getting a little carried away?"

"She wants a clean slate." Darla leaned in closer to Tosh. "She's a little neurotic, I guess."

"I never thought of Santa as a lie. That's such a negative way to look at it." Tosh pondered the fable of St. Nick for a moment. "He's more like a legend than a lie."

"I know."

"Santa Claus brings so much joy, you know? Why would anyone want to deprive their children of that?"

"She says that she is their Santa Claus. *She* wants to be their source of happiness instead of Santa."

"Makes sense, I guess." Tosh grabbed a sesame stick from a bowl of snacks on the bar. "But it lacks all the mystery and imagination that Santa brings. Kids gotta have that. Adults sure don't."

"Yes, you're right. Adults live very linear, logical lives. It's quite boring and sad." Darla reached over the bar for another wedge of lime. "Sections of our mind are blocked off. Like someone slams the door on that childlike creativity and sticks a huge 'Do Not Disturb' sign on it."

"Yeah. 'No Trespassing.'"

"When you're a child, you can't rationalize what can and can't be. As a result, there are no limitations on your imagination."

"But to a child, it's not even imagination," reasoned Tosh. "It's just his or her regular thought process."

"Exactly! As an adult, we say 'wouldn't it be cool if...' but accompanying that inventive thought is the knowledge that it's not real," said Darla, squeezing the lime into her cocktail. "But a child doesn't have reality whispering in his ear, hindering his imagination. When a child says 'wouldn't it be cool if...' he thinks it could happen. Nothing separates his imagination from his reality. The monster in the closet really exists until Mom says there's no such thing, and she puts the light on and he's not there."

"And even then," said Tosh, "the child is not entirely sure that the monster doesn't exist. He could still be there, hiding or something."

"Of course." Darla smiled. "Or maybe he went under the bed."

Tosh picked a honey-roasted peanut out of the mix. "So although that monster may never physically exist, he's real to the children."

"Precisely. So when people say there's no such thing as Santa, they're wrong. He lives in the minds of children."

"But people say that is imaginary."

"Reality is subjective," said Darla. "Kids *believe* in Santa and monsters so they exist in *their* reality. In an adult's reality, they're imaginary."

"Damn, that's cool." Tosh scratched his goatee. "I wish I could get that childhood innocence back. Where I could imagine without the adult-world skeptic modifier."

Darla placed her hand on Tosh's thigh, leaned in even closer to him and spoke just above a whisper. "They say children are telepathic."

Tosh's heartbeat quickened, but he tried to play it cool, pretending he didn't notice the hand on his leg. "Yeah?"

"Supposedly, everyone is born with psychic powers. But society conditions people to shut off these extra-sensory powers."

"Why?"

"It's just the way our society has evolved. You see, children often use their sixth sense without trying. It's unlearned, part of their basic nature. But their psychic power is rejected and ignored in the same way that mothers open the closet doors on the monsters."

"How are children psychic?" asked Tosh.

"Well, they may have moments of psychic activity. Let me give you an example. My niece — she's three — let's say while she's playing in the yard by herself, her mother kept a constant eye on her. When she comes in, she tells her mother that she talked to another little girl outside, but her mother knew there was no one else out there."

"The imaginary friend."

"Yes, the imaginary friend. How do we know that she didn't really see someone there? Maybe a spirit, or a guardian angel."

"Most people don't believe in that sort of thing."

"Well, exactly. They don't believe in it, but does that mean that they're not there? So the girl's mom tells her that she must be wrong. She *couldn't* have seen anyone there. Naturally, the girl believes what her mother tells her. Maybe next time she sees that vision, she tells herself that it can't be. Or she ignores it. Pretty soon, she stops seeing the angel altogether. That sort of thing is what I'm talking about. So the psychic powers of most people sit unused for the rest of their lives in the corners of the mind."

"Is that what you meant when you said earlier that there are sections of our minds that are blocked off?"

"Yes. We only use a small percentage of our brains."

"What a waste."

"Indeed," said Darla, gulping the last of her drink. "Excuse me, honey." Darla got up and headed for the ladies' room.

Tosh took a deep breath and a sip of his brew. Darla had got him excited. Her physical nature made the engaging conversation even more stimulating. Tosh couldn't help but feel that their discussion might lead to something else.

But Darla did not return. *What the hell happened to her?* Tosh wondered. He got up to look around and his buzz really kicked in, leaving him kind of dizzy. After scanning Ferris' to no avail, Tosh asked the bartender if he saw her leave, but the bartender just responded with a puzzled look and a mutter.

And suddenly Crosby was nowhere to be found. He and Melinda must have slipped out without saying anything. *What a dick.*

Tosh shook his head, shocked and disappointed. In one minute, his entire situation had collapsed, abandoning him in some strange bar in some strange city on the other side of the continent.

Tosh lumbered out past the paisley piano into the lonely Victorian night, wondering what happened to Darla.

*   *   *   *

Crosby hoped the nose ring would not get in the way. Sandalwood incense burned slowly and *Led Zeppelin III* hummed from the small but powerful speakers. A large candle illuminated Melinda's one-room apartment as the two lovers reclined on the soft couch.

151

Nose ring or not, Crosby moved in for the kiss. Melinda opened her black lips, eagerly awaiting him. It had been a long time since she'd been with a guy, and Melinda had all systems working.

They kissed long and sloppy, sucking each other's tongues. Sparks flew, spit dripped and lipstick smeared. Melinda almost melted when Crosby put his hand on her breast, letting out a quiet groan.

Crosby had never been so turned on by a kiss. He had wanted to taste those blackberry lips from the first time he laid eyes on them. The way Melinda responded to his every move drove him crazy.

Suddenly, Melinda sprang up. "Wait."

"What's wrong? What did I do?" said Crosby, alarmed.

"It's not you. It's *him.*"

"Who?"

"Lucky." Melinda pointed to her German shepherd sitting beside the couch.

"The dog?"

"Yeah."

"What's wrong with him?"

"He's watching."

"Aw, forget it. He's not watching."

"He's staring right at us."

"Yeah, but he doesn't understand what's going on."

"Oh, yes he does. He knows. Dogs can smell it."

Crosby sighed. "So?"

"I feel weird having sex in front of him."

"What makes you so modest all of the sudden? Miss Giant-Nose-Ring who molested me on the dance floor last night."

"That was different. That was dancing."

"It seemed pretty suggestive to me."

Melinda placed her mouth on Crosby's. She poked her tongue in his mouth. "There are similarities," she whispered, her lips brushing against his. "Intense energy."

She kissed him. "Heavy breathing."

She kissed him again. "Sweating."

And again. "Release."

She placed her hand on his crotch. "But they are not the same thing. You can't equate anything to life's greatest pleasure."

"That's true," Crosby snickered.

"Nothing beats dancing."

"Dancing?"

"Yes, dancing. You can't beat it! It's the greatest high in the world. All that fun. No commitment, no guilt."

Commitment and guilt had never been part of Crosby's sex life. "Well, what do you want to do?"

"I'll put him in the bathroom." Melinda straightened her clothes and got off the couch. She crossed over to the bathroom and called Lucky. He did not budge. "Lucky, come! Come here, boy!"

Lucky laid down.

"Just let him stay there. He's going to sleep."

"He can't watch me have sex. I can't let him see me in that way."

"In what way?"

"As a sexual being. Lucky and I have a platonic relationship. I don't want him to get any ideas."

"What do you mean?"

"I don't want him to try and hump me when I'm cuddling with him. I'll be settling down for a little affection and he'll be trying to put the moves on me."

"Get him fixed."

"That's cruel."

"Cruel is making this dog live without sex."

"I'll find him a girlfriend. Lucky get over here now!!"

Melinda's dog begrudgingly rose to his feet and ambled over to the where she stood.

"Go in there," Melinda pointed into the bathroom.

Lucky followed instructions and Melinda closed the door behind him. "There," she said, skipping back to Crosby on the couch. "Now, where were we?"

As the Led Zeppelin and the sandalwood filled the room, the two lovers continued on.

Meanwhile, from under the bathroom door, poked a moist, black nose.

*   *   *   *

Lucky did not live up to his name. As if the moniker had ironically cursed him, the hapless canine never caught a break. Starting with his miserable birth as the runt of the litter, a streak of ugly misfortunes had befallen the poor pup.

At three months of age, Lucky ate discarded sauerkraut and was struck with a severe case of diarrhea. It ravaged his tiny digestive tract and liquefied his bowels for a day. Melinda awoke that bright morning to a bewildering wheezing sound — like that of an empty hand-lotion bottle being squeezed vigorously. Acute curiosity got her out of bed to discover the horrifying scenario — the wheezing came from Lucky's ass. Tracked across the floor were little puddles of puppy poo. Melinda vomited immediately and both she and Lucky nearly became dehydrated.

At the age of five-and-a-half months Lucky smelled something oh so sweet. A yummy, half-empty cup of grape soda stood in his path. Lucky stuck his face whole-heartedly into the large plastic cup and inhaled deeply. It smelled good enough to eat, but just as Lucky dropped his tongue into the sticky purple liquid, he realized the drink was not his alone.

No, Lucky shared the soda with a bee. And that bee was selfish. He did not take kindly to Lucky's intrusion and he let Lucky know at once.

Lucky could sense something was amiss and he sprang back. Unfortunately, Lucky had exercised his better judgment a bit too late. The sticky cup lodged itself around Lucky's snout. No matter how far backwards Lucky retreated, the cup followed.

The bee became angrier. And angrier. Finally the bee erupted in a furious rage and sunk his fierce stinger into Lucky's sensitive nose. It swelled up like an avocado and, for three days, Lucky sulked around the house, humiliated and hurting.

At the of age of seven months, Lucky got worms.

At the age of nine-and-a-half months, Lucky accompanied Melinda on a road trip up Vancouver Island. Six hours in the car and a couple of nights camping in the woods went off without a hitch. No troublesome encounters with wildlife. No poison ivy. No carsickness.

Lucky slept peacefully the entire ride home. He let out not even a silent deadly doggie fart. He kept so quiet, in fact, that Melinda had forgotten about him.

As she pulled up to her home, Melinda had one thing on her mind — the bathroom. Lucky awoke and stretched in the back seat, but Melinda didn't notice. He disembarked the car behind her. Sadly, though, he did not clear the swinging metal door as Melinda obliviously slammed it closed.

The door pulverized Lucky's tail. He passed out. A severe sprain caused Lucky much pain for a few weeks.

At the age of eleven months, Lucky looked like an adult shepherd. His body had finally grown into his large head and paws and, quite frankly, he looked intimidating. But Lucky was a friendly dog.

Sven, the timid mail carrier, did not know this.

They say timing is everything, and one morning an ill-fated introduction between the young dog and the nervous mailman proved this.

Sven was walking up the path as Melinda opened the front door. Lucky burst out ahead of Melinda, eager to get out of the apartment. When Sven saw the savage wolf-like beast heading straight for him, his eyes bugged out of his government-employed head and he instinctively reached for his mace.

Lucky got it in the face. His eyes burned horribly and he could not catch his breath. Never in his whole puppy life had he been so scared. He coughed and cried and ran in a circle until he fell down.

Seeing this, Melinda shrieked and punched Sven in the nose. She is up for an assault-and-battery charge.

Now, at almost a year and a half old, Lucky's love life suffered immensely. Unlike most un-neutered dogs his age, he still hadn't been laid.

CHAPTER 11

A skunk encounter is not necessarily a bad thing.

On the obvious hand, a noxious attack from the anal glands of a Pepe LePeu wannabe could be a traumatic experience. The appalling stench left by a hideous rectal mist binds itself to every fiber of one's being for an extended period of time and may sever some interpersonal relationships.

But on the other, more obscure, hand, some positives can be ascertained from the unlikely occurrence of a confrontation with a skunk.

For starters, it is the opportunity to see some North American wildlife. Skunks are nocturnal and live in the trunks of trees. The timid creatures usually go to great lengths to avoid contact with humans, so many people go their entire lives without seeing a skunk. (And are quite pleased.)

Secondly, when dealing with a skunk, it is recommended to remain calm and not make any sudden moves. Panic brings trouble. In this way, a skunk-encounter can provide useful experience that may come in handy when dealing with even rarer, more dangerous North American wildlife — such as a bear.

Finally, if the skunk-encounter unfolds into a worst-case scenario, it is recommended that the sprayed victim use tomato juice to aid in washing away the fetid vapor. So, at the very least, when else would someone have reason to bathe their entire clothed body in crushed tomatoes?

It's too bad Tosh hadn't considered these points the night he stumbled out of Ferris' Oyster Bar onto the midnight streets of Victoria.

Tosh had ambled around the nearly vacant city for an indefinite period of time before he realized he had no idea where he was or where he was going. Blindly and drunkenly he had trodden until his path led him alongside some shrubs at the edge of a small park.

There, his Converses skidded to a halt.

Tosh Tyler found himself face to face with a skunk.

Instinctively, Tosh put up his hands, as though the skunk had brandished a .45 and asked him for his wallet. Luckily, adrenaline quickly cleared the way for what remained of his logic, and he reasoned the small mammal probably did not interpret his raised hands as a defenseless position. On the contrary, Tosh probably looked more intimidating.

This could be bad, he thought.

As Tosh slowly brought his arms down, the skunk seemed to tense up a bit. He paid less attention to the tasty grasses and more to the wobbling dude with the weird, ropy hair.

The skunk raised his tail ever so slightly and kept his beady black eyes riveted on Tosh.

155

Tosh stared at the skunk, giving his best imitation of a mannequin. Realizing that the skunk, which probably had the patience of an eggplant, could make him stand like that all night, Tosh became uneasy. Normally, Tosh would accept this challenge, perhaps even enjoy it. But at this time he had another concern — relieving himself. Those damn beers had caught up to him.

The skunk returned his attention to the grass.

Thank God, thought Tosh. He took a step backward and the skunk eyed him again.

Damn.

The skunk munched grass cautiously, keeping an eye on Tosh like a stoned babysitter watches a toddler.

The pain in Tosh's groin worsened. He considered whipping it out right there, but figured that the skunk probably would not appreciate the gesture. Instead, Tosh painstakingly circumambulated the little critter with baby steps, even crossing to the other side of the street to insure against a sudden, slingshot sphincter squirt.

As soon as Tosh felt he had put a safe distance between himself and the skunk, he regained his normal stride and focused his thoughts on the other pressing matter. Quickly finding a good spot to relieve himself, he unzipped his shorts and let it flow.

Ahhh.

Suddenly, the rodent appeared at his feet. Milky foam frothed from his fanged, alligator jaws. The skunk glared at Tosh and spoke, *"I have an ass like a fire hose and I've come to take you down!"*

Immediately, Tosh put the clamps on, zipped and hit the afterburners. He ran for a few blocks before collapsing. Wiping the sweat from his brow, still panting, he said to himself, "I've got to stop smoking pot."

$$*\qquad*\qquad*\qquad*$$

Tosh learned a valuable lesson that night. When leaving his car in a strange city, he should be sure to remember some type of landmark, such as a street name, to help him recall the location of his vehicle.

After the confrontation with the bionic skunk, Tosh continued to wander the empty city streets aimlessly, hoping for a glimpse of a vague familiarity. Where had they left the van? His feet aching, he sat down on a curb, fed up with the futile search.

The silky night offered a pleasant, gentle breeze coming off the water. Tosh leaned back and gazed at the stars. Contemplating his run-in with the skunk, he spoke aloud to himself. "One second he was quietly munching some grass, the next he was chasing me — fangs hanging out..."

"Who?"

Tosh looked up. He hadn't heard footsteps, but before him stood a heavenly apparition, a beautiful red-haired girl.

"The skunk," said Tosh.

"A skunk was chasing you?"

"I think he had rabies."

"Are you feeling all right?"

The girl who appeared out of the shadows spoke softly. Her auburn curls hung over her pale, cherubic face. Though she possessed an extremely well-developed body, she looked no older than sixteen. A sleek scarlet dress, just a shade lighter than her hair, revealed a touch of her bounteous cleavage and the majority of her firm thighs. Yet despite her sexy, almost slutty, evening wear, she came off fresh and pure.

Tosh became aroused sitting beside her. He felt guilty, feeling this way toward a girl barely out of her training bra. In that dress, she could have been on her way to the prom.

Tosh wanted to ask her out. He wanted to fall in love with and take her home to his family and marry her.

She's probably a virgin, he thought.

"I lost my friend. I lost my van," Tosh said. "I guess you could say I'm lost."

The girl squatted next to Tosh and leaned toward his face. "Are you lonely?" she asked pityingly, her long eyelashes fluttering like the wings of a butterfly.

"Alone, but not lonely," Tosh replied. "What brings you here?"

"Work."

"Work?"

"Yes, work," she said with a scowl as she sat down next to Tosh.

"What do you do?"

"I ho," she said matter-of-factly.

"In that?" Tosh asked, puzzled. "What are you, some type of fancy gardener?"

A sneer now tarnished the girl's attractive face. "I suck latex," she said.

Tosh was confused. "Come again?"

"Very funny. You're just a comedian, aren't you?"

The girl had obviously become very angry with Tosh but he didn't know why.

"I don't think I understand you..." he delicately began again.

"I'm a whore!" she screamed. "I'm a hooker. I suck cock."

That's it — the wedding plans are off, thought Tosh.

This lovely little lady was a hooker? Tosh couldn't believe it. What a shame.

"I'm sorry," said Tosh. "I didn't know."

"It's O.K.," she sniffled, "I just hate to say it." Wiping away a teardrop, she sucked up her emotions and gave her customary pitch. "So, do you want a date?"

Tosh had been propositioned by prostitutes all over the world. In New York City, the women disgusted him — strung-out, wretched drug addicts, some grotesquely fat and others just incredibly ugly. When offered blowjobs, Tosh unhesitatingly declined. "No thanks, I'll pass," he'd say.

However, many of the prostitutes Tosh encountered while traveling through some of the foreign countries such as Kenya and Brazil were very attractive. Dark, exotic women who projected a sensual, sexual energy certainly enticed him. Even though they were hookers, his young male hormones clouded whatever moral hang-ups he had.

He had considered it, but Tosh's good sense prevailed. He knew these women could be very dangerous. If they didn't knife or shoot him as soon as they were in private, he'd probably get AIDS or some scuzzy virus. When propositioned, he would just pretend he didn't understand what they were saying and coyly slink away.

Tosh had never been seriously tempted to go with a prostitute. Until now.

He'd never been in a situation like this. Besides the fact that this girl was a complete gem, she didn't seem like the rest of the whores he had seen who came on like sex machines, bragging about the incredible orgasms they could give him. No, this prostitute practically romanced him. She had an unpretentious innocence about her that drove Tosh wild.

On the other hand, Tosh figured she must have sucked 100 dicks in the past week. Would he want to kiss those lips? Yuck! No way.

However she seemed, the bottom line was that she was still a hooker, a worthless urchin cast away and spit upon by society, no more respectable than the scum on 11th Avenue.

Or was she?

Tosh wondered how such a girl ended up selling herself on the street. He wanted to hear her story. He wanted to see if this girl had more to offer besides getting a guy off.

Most hookers, though, were not much for talking.

"Do you want a blowjob? I give the best head," she said, licking her lips.

So much for romance. Instantly, she had transformed herself into the apple of sinful temptation.

"I'm sure you do," Tosh said, shocked by the explicitness embodied by her sudden change, yet excited by the thought of her doing it. Really excited. More excited than he had ever been.

What should he do?

He stalled. "What's your name?"

"Bisbee."

"That's an interesting name."

"It's a nickname."

"How did you get it?"

Bisbee sighed. "I was a very hyper kid. My mother always said I was 'busy as a bee.' It kind of evolved into Bisbee. So, what do you say?"

"Do you take credit cards?"

"No," answered Bisbee, becoming tired of this dilly-dallying. "But for fifteen dollars cash I'll make you come like never before."

This sounded cliché, an X-rated commercial on late-night TV. The reality of the situation finally hit Tosh and it turned him off. "No thanks. I'll have to pass. No money."

"Good. I didn't really feel like doing it anyway."

"Whaddaya mean?" asked Tosh, offended. That's pretty lousy — rejected by a whore.

"I just don't feel like working tonight," complained Bisbee. "I'm tired."

"I know the feeling," sighed Tosh. "I just want to go to sleep. If only I could find my van."

"Where did you park it?"

Tosh frowned and shrugged. "I don't remember."

Bisbee looked at Tosh with sympathy. "You could stay with me tonight."

"Are you serious?"

"Yes."

"How much?"

"You don't have any money, remember?"

"Oh. Yeah."

*   *   *   *

Bisbee lived in a cramped one-room apartment above a bowling alley with a herd of Harleys parked out front. She had a cat named Binky who meowed constantly and a healthy fern in her one window. Above all other possessions, she prized her Nintendo.

Throughout the night they played — a Nintendo marathon.

Although Tosh had sworn off video games in college, he rescinded his edict. As Bisbee played, she talked, and he liked the conversation.

Bisbee's dad left when she was young. Her mother, an alcoholic, was never much of a mom. She got remarried to a real son of a bitch. He sexually assaulted Bisbee on occasion and told her that if she ever told anyone, he would beat her mother so badly no one would recognize her. Bisbee put up with his advances for as long as she could. Finally, at the age of fifteen, she left a note for her mother that she hated her stepfather and ran away.

Now, she maintained minimal communication by sending an occasional letter to let her mother.

She came to Victoria because of the temperate climate and the relatively unhostile environment. She lived on the streets with other runaways, begging from tourists and running from the cops. That lifestyle quickly wore her down and she became ill.

159

One kind woman took her in and nursed her back to health. But she wanted to call Bisbee's mother, so Bisbee gave her a fake number and bailed out.

Bisbee couldn't get a job due to her ragged appearance caused by living on the street. She didn't want to go back home, but she knew she would end up sick again if she didn't change her lifestyle.

After an unsuccessful stretch of begging, she decided to try prostitution. She knew some girls who did it and they said it wasn't that bad. Within a few weeks, she had herself a roof over her head, rent paid in cash, no questions asked.

Whoring took some getting used to. She still cried sometimes, but at least she was healthy. She used protection always and could charge more money for her services now because she could doll herself up real good and approach the rich tourists off the cruise ships.

"Do you, uh, *sleep* with these guys?" Tosh asked.

Bisbee put down her joystick and took a deep breath. Her face suddenly wore a sullen expression.

Tosh stared at a stain on the green shag carpeting, wishing he hadn't asked that question. Bisbee sat silent and motionless. "Not usually," she finally bemoaned, barely over a whisper. "I never used to. That's where I drew the line."

Why did you cross the line? Tosh wanted to ask. But he didn't dare prod any further, for fear of upsetting her more.

"I don't do it often. But I have done it a couple of times."

Tosh remained silent, but he looked at Bisbee and with his eyes, he asked, *Why?*

Bisbee burst out. "I just wanted stuff! I needed more money! There was some cool clothes I wanted. I wanted Nintendo!"

That's it? You sacrificed your principles for an outfit? You gave it up for a toy?

Tosh's fledgling respect for Bisbee sank like a brick. What a crappy reason. What an answer. This girl had no morals, no values.

Bisbee began to cry hard. Tears gushed from her eyes as she let it out. The pain flooding Bisbee smeared her black eyeliner as it washed down her reddened cheeks. Like a little girl who runs whimpering for her mother when she has fallen off her bike, Bisbee reached out and hugged Tosh. Wrapping her arms around him like a grizzly bear, she held Tosh tight to her chest. Bisbee's soaked face rested over Tosh's shoulder, dampening his cheek as she embraced him with all her might.

Tosh no longer felt disgusted by Bisbee.

How was she any different than others her age? She wasn't fucking men because she was an unruly slut. Bisbee just wanted the same things other teenagers wanted, and she didn't want to be deprived any longer. It might not have been the most ethical decision, but he understood. After all, she was just a kid.

Tosh squeezed Bisbee hard.

* * * *

The nose ring did not get in the way.

* * * *

Tosh and Bisbee's hug lasted a long time, long enough for a cartoon owl to lick a lollipop down to the Tootsie in its core. When they finally separated, Bisbee smiled meekly. "You get used to it pretty fast," she began. "It's a routine. I put a rubber on them and just do my job. I never look at their faces once I begin. I don't want to know who they are or anything about them. It's like they're just a dick with no body attached."

"Would you, like, give anyone a blowjob?" Tosh asked.

"Well, not everyone. If the guy is really disgusting, I send him over to one of the junkies. They're too fucked up to care. Or if a guy gives me weird vibes, I'll probably bag it."

"How can you tell?"

Bisbee paused. "I don't know exactly. After a while, you can just sense these things." She thought for a moment and then smiled. "Maybe it's woman's intuition. If you get a funny feeling about a guy then you just stay away."

"Man, it must be so dangerous," said Tosh. It really bothered him to picture the youthful Bisbee working the corner.

"I carry mace. And I pretend I have a pimp watching over me. That usually discourages any tricky business."

"Still..."

"But I have a place to live. Being a prostitute is safer than living on the street. The threat of a nasty pimp with a big gun can go a long way. I know more girls that were raped while living on the street."

"Well, you do what you have to."

The digital clock on Bisbee's bed stand read 4:46 am in large red numbers. The night had slinked away quickly and, as the sunrise crept upon them, a gentle sleepiness filled their eyes.

Bisbee brushed her teeth and got into her bed.

"Are you coming to sleep, Tosh?"

"In bed with you?"

"Yeah! I'm not gonna make you sleep on the floor. It's hard."

The day's first light trickled through the window as Tosh crawled into the twin bed next to her. The two of them laid side by side, staring up at the cracked paint on the ceiling.

Tosh could not stop picturing Bisbee in the cars of strange, dirty men. Men of all shapes and sizes, ages and races.

Bisbee rested her hand not-so-innocently on Tosh's boxers. "Do you want a free-bee, Tosh?"

This caught him by surprise. "Uh, I have a girlfriend."

"Right." After a moment, Bisbee removed her hand.

*   *   *   *

The sound of Cocoa Puffs hitting a ceramic bowl reverberated through Crosby's aching skull. He pulled Melinda's pillow over his head to hush the distant rumbling and stretched out on the side of the bed she had just vacated. Clearly, he was not ready to start another day.

Melinda vigorously shook the giant brown box with a demented looking rabbit on it, filling her bowl high with the sugary cereal. Last night Melinda got laid, and today she celebrated. For breakfast, Melinda completely indulged in chocolate. Instead of milk, she poured Yoo Hoo over her Cocoa Puffs and even added a couple of shots of Bosco. She topped it off with a healthy sprinkling of jimmies. "That should do it," Melinda said to Lucky with a sense of satisfaction. "Go wake up our friend Crosby. I'll be all worked up from this sugar and I'm gonna wanna work this off."

A short while later, Crosby woke up to the queer sensation of Bosco Chocolate Syrup drizzled on his belly.

*   *   *   *

In the middle of the night (or morning, considering they went to bed at sunrise) Tosh woke to find Binky, Bisbee's pussy, on his head.

He tried to sleep through the distraction, but Binky's incessant purring pounded like a jackhammer on the pavement of his ear. He turned away from the fishy feline breath only to feel wet sandpaper chafe his cheek.

Tosh did not have the energy to coax the cat from the master bedroom of his face. Unable to lift his anvil eyelids, he mentally willed Binky to scuttle down the hall to the guest suite at his feet. When this tactic proved futile, in one disgruntled swoop he hurled Binky to the floor. The purring ceased and the cat did not return. Binky knew when she was not appreciated.

*   *   *   *

The higher the sun rose in the sky, the more it shined into Tosh's eyes. Sleep became more difficult as the bright light made him restless.

Tosh pondered Crosby's whereabouts. He hadn't seen him since he slipped out of the Oyster bar without a word. At this point, probably more than twelve hours later, Crosby could be anywhere.

He could be in a hospital, stabbed and stitched, his wallet floating down a river already emptied of its cash by a drug fiend. Worse, he could be dying a slow death, lying unconscious, bloodied and bruised in some fetid roadside ditch outside of town.

Then again, Tosh wouldn't put it past Cros to be on the back of Melinda's motorcycle (if she had a motorcycle, who knew?) racing toward Alaska on some bizarre gothic sexual escapade.

Or he could be in Banff, wherever that was.

If things worked according to plan, though, Crosby would be waiting at the van. Earlier in the trip, the guys had made a pact that if they ever got separated overnight, they would return to the van by noon the next day. That way, one guy didn't get stuck in the dark for a couple of days, worrying and waiting while the other gallivanted like a careless hedon. Despite the unspoken understanding and intrinsic informality of their relationship, the best friends were traveling partners, and a certain degree of respect and consideration were due.

Based on the height of the sun in the sky, Tosh figured noon had to be right around the corner. With the pact in mind, so as not to disturb Bisbee, he smoothly slipped out of bed like the Grinch fingering candy canes from under the noses of snoozing Whos on the night before Christmas.

He crept into the bathroom, picked the crusties out of his eyes and splashed some cold water on his face. Wanting to thank Bisbee for letting him crash at her place before he skidaddled, he scurried about for a pen and scribbled a note on a paper plate, along with his address and phone number:

Bisbee darlin' (The Biz),
> *I have crossed this entire country, and you are one of the most beautiful*
> *girls I have ever met.*
> *I'm lucky that I had the chance to get to know you.*
> *You are sweet, kind and generous. Thanks a zillion*
> *for letting me shack up. You're a tough cookie.*
> *Keep surviving. Best of luck, my good sister.*

Jah Guide,
Tosh

As Tosh put down the pen, Binky rubbed against his calf. He leaned down and scratched her behind the ears. After a moment of thought, he picked up the pen again.

P.S. I really do have a girlfriend.

*   *   *   *

"How can you order a salad at McDonald's, Tosh?" Crosby barked.

"I don't want to eat that shit," replied Tosh, wrestling with a foil packet of honey mustard dressing.

"A salad at Mickey D's. Man, that's like going to Jamaica and not smoking the herb."

"Greasy hamburgers are bad for you. I don't want to put that crap into my body. If I'm gonna have a burger, I want a *real* one."

"You work it off. That's what exercise is for."

"I don't get as much exercise as you, Cros. You windsurf. You ski. You're just a more active person than I am. Reading may exercise the mind, but it doesn't do much for my cholesterol level."

"You have to admit that they taste good though," Crosby mumbled as he chewed his Big Mac.

"Oh, yeah. I love burgers. I mean, cheeseburgers are my weakness. I could be a vegetarian if it wasn't for them. They're one of my favorite foods."

"Yeah. And pizza."

"In fact, cheeseburgers might be my absolute favorite food in the universe."

"Taylor Ham."

"Ben and Jerry's."

"Garlic bread," said Crosby. "Just soaked in butter."

"Yeah, with melted cheese!"

"I love those French toast sticks."

"And of course, burritos!"

"The Ultimate Burrito, baby! We'll find it some day."

"Search and ye shall find," said Tosh, grabbing one of Crosby's fries. "Damn, these are good."

"Yep. Nothing like eating shoe-string potatoes soaked in oil and then dipped in salt."

"Why is it that everything that tastes good is bad for you?" questioned Tosh.

"Yeah, really."

"No, I'm serious. Think about it. Everything that we love to eat is bad for us. Almost all the best foods have tons of fat or sugar."

Crosby looked at Tosh blankly. Nutrition had never mattered to Crosby. He had always been healthy.

He never missed many days of school, though his grades did not reflect that. He had never broken any bones. Even though he lived an active lifestyle, the worst injury Crosby had ever suffered was a splinter.

Crosby ate for taste. Nutritional value played no role in his diet.

"What's wrong with sugar?" he asked Tosh. "Besides being bad for your teeth?"

"Sugar has a lot of calories and if you don't burn 'em off, they turn to fat. Fat makes you fat and clogs your arteries with cholesterol, you know? Gives people high blood pressure and heart attacks and strokes."

"Steak is good for you. It has protein," Crosby pointed out.

"Steak may have some positives, some necessary nutrients. It does have protein, true, but overall, with all the fat and cholesterol, steak is definitely bad for you. Besides, the protein that steak gives you can be obtained in healthier ways. Like eating beans."

"Well, there you go. Burritos are good for you. They got beans."

"Not really."

"What do you mean, not really? I know burritos, and burritos definitely have beans."

"What I mean is that most burritos have refried beans and refried beans are cooked with lard."

"Lard is definitely bad for us," said Crosby. "I can tell just by the way it sounds."

"Besides, all burritos have cheese. Cheese has loads of fat and cholesterol."

"So does that mean pizza is bad for us?" Crosby asked disappointedly.

"Well, it's not the best thing in the world, but I love it so much, I try to justify eating it by saying that it's a well-rounded meal. You know, that all of the food groups are represented."

Crosby remembered this from grade school. The Four Major Food Groups were about as far as his nutritional knowledge went. "Well, you got your bread group," he began.

"The crust," said Tosh, stealing another one of Crosby's French fries.

"Fruit and vegetable group."

"The sauce."

"Dairy group is the cheese, right?"

Tosh nodded.

"What about the meat group?"

"Add some pepperoni or sausage to that slice."

"Of course. So pizza is a well-rounded meal."

"I'd like to believe that, Cros, but sausage and pepperoni just drip with fat and so does the mozzarella. I kind of think all that fat outweighs the benefits of the other aspects of pizza."

"Damn. You're telling me all my favorite things are bad for me. Well then, how come I'm not a porker?"

"You're young. You have a good metabolism. Give it time, it will catch up with you."

Crosby peered at Tosh in disbelief. "Now I'm getting depressed," he sighed. He put the remains of his Big Mac on the wrapper on the table and stared at it.

"Tell me about it. I mean, it makes no sense. You would think that the foods we like to eat would be better for us."

"I like *broccoli!* Broccoli is good for you."

"You're right. Broccoli is good for you. But Cros, that's not my point. I'm not saying that all the food we like to eat is bad for us or that we don't like the taste of anything that is good for us. It's just that, in general, the food we like the most is the worst for us."

"I like zucchini! In fact, I love zucchini!"

"Yeah, but what would you rather have, a zucchini or a big piece of chocolate cake?"

Crosby didn't need to answer the question. They both knew the answer. He slumped back in the red Formica booth of the McDonald's. "Lots of sugar, right?"

"Sugar, eggs, butter. Calories, fat and more fat."

Crosby buried his face in his hands.

"That's all right. Once in a while it's O.K.," said Tosh. "I'm going to get some fries."

*   *   *   *

With their fast-food meal, Crosby and Tosh celebrated their last moments in civilization.

After an uneventful reunion at the van, the guys had departed Victoria and headed north on Vancouver Island, searching for Lake Nitinat, a little-known refuge for hardcore windsurfers buried in the wilderness. Crosby had brought his windsurfing equipment along with the hopes he might get the opportunity to test some new locales and, while perusing the road atlas that morning, planning their next move, the words "Lake Nitinat" jumped off the page and sparked his memory; someone had told him about the place a couple of years earlier. Crosby excitedly requested that the lake be their next destination.

Tosh had voiced some protest. "What the hell am I gonna do in the woods for three days?" He had said. "There's nothing to do in the woods. You're going to be surfing the whole time."

"You can watch me," responded Crosby.

"Oh joy."

"Remember what you said about Kansas? We're exploring and how will we know what adventure awaits us if we don't go and check it out. I thought Kansas was gonna suck and we had fun there."

Crosby had called him on his own reasoning.

So they headed for the wilderness. On the way, they stopped at McDonald's. If Tosh and Crosby were going to abandon civilization for a few days, they might as well wallow in it.

"It would just make life more pleasant," Tosh continued, "if cheeseburgers and chocolate cake were healthy — if pizza gave you strength and knowledge." He dumped his newly acquired French fries on Crosby's Big Mac wrapper spread out on the table. "Or, why not make our taste buds crave spinach and peas and tofu instead of a bacon double cheeseburger?"

"I crave burgers 'cause they smell so good."

"That's true. Smell has a lot to do with taste. It's the fat that makes things smell good. That's why you don't crave a heaping plate of lettuce." Tosh slid a French fry through some honey mustard dressing left over from his salad. "Why do we hunger for fat? I wonder why God planned it out that way? Wouldn't it make more sense, in terms of human survival, to hunger for healthier foods?"

It seems they had uncovered a flaw in God's plan. "Maybe God screwed up," Crosby said.

"I don't think God makes mistakes," said Tosh. "There has to be a reason."

Crosby fingered a fry and thought about it.

He rarely considered such odd concepts unless Tosh prodded him, sucking him into one of these damn philosophical conversations. Normally, he was content to just exist and enjoy life without questioning everything. He could admit, however, that once Tosh got him going, he kind of enjoyed the debating, and he especially savored those occasional moments when he had a good point to make.

Belching, Crosby realized he felt satiated. He had really pigged out at the McDonald's, with the excuse that he needed to store up energy for the next few days. *Windsurfing is physically demanding,* he had told himself as he polished off a nine-pack of McNuggets and unwrapped his Big Mac. Deep down, though, Crosby knew he had stuffed his face not to store energy, but because he loved that greasy food taste. Three upcoming days of camping promised them no culinary delights, only bland canned food.

Wait a second, thought Crosby. He had an idea. "I think I know why we like fat," he said.

"Why's that?"

"O.K. Fat has the most calories, right?"

"Right," Tosh confirmed.

"And calories equal energy. Man is drawn to fat because it gives us the most energy. And back in early times, people had more active lifestyles and less food too eat. Fat gave us our best chance to survive when food was hard to come by."

"So our fancy for fattening food is a survival instinct," said Tosh.

"Totally. Do you think mankind evolved as well as it did because of rhubarb?"

"I don't know if mankind has really evolved that well. Just look in the papers," quipped Tosh.

"You know what I mean. Do you think mankind would have flourished like it did if our taste buds craved Brussels sprouts over steak and butter? Do you think man would have had the energy to build railroads and fight wars?"

"Probably not. Maybe that's it. If we were built as herbivores, maybe the world wouldn't be such a ballistic place."

"Oh, cut the hippie crap. Do you think Lawrence Taylor is a vegetarian? Do you think Mark Messier could have won all those Cups eating salads? No way. Their ferocious instincts come from eating animals. It's the fat. The fat gives them the necessary energy to excel in professional sports."

"O.K., so our desire for fat stems from our human need for energy."

"Yeah, but now, that design is backfiring because we live in a society of surplus. Nowadays, we don't have to store up energy for indefinite periods of time. We eat three meals a day."

"Plus, most people burn less energy these days. They don't have fields to plow. Hell, they don't even have to get up to change the channel."

"Yep. So, most people don't burn off enough of the calories that they consume. So our attraction to fat, which at one time was helpful, is now bad for us."

"That makes sense. Damn, Cros, very impressive. Good thinkin'!"

Cros crunched an ice cube from the bottom of his empty soda cup. "Any more questions I can help you with?"

*　　*　　*　　*

Tosh and Crosby stopped in Duncan, which they figured to be the last large town on Vancouver Island before they reached Lake Nitinat. They refueled and stopped in a supermarket to pick up a few necessities — beer, ice, water, milk, barbecue potato chips, bananas, bread, beer, eggs, V-8's, beer, batteries and beer. Tosh wheeled their goods into the express line, *Ten Items or Less,* as Crosby jogged over and deposited a package of Fig Newtons in the shopping cart.

"Aw, Cros. We can't get those."

"How come?"

"Express line. Those are our eleventh item," Tosh said with a touch of sarcasm.

"So, I'll pay for them separately. They'll be my only item."

"Don't worry about it, fellas," said the crinkly old lady at the register. "Just give me i.d. for the beer."

Tosh handed over his driver's license.

"Joshua Tyler."

"That's me."

"New Jersey, huh?"

"Yep."

"What are you doing here?"

"Is this part of the identification process for purchasing alcohol?" Crosby asked. The lady shot him a scornful glance.

"We're driving around the country," said Tosh. "We're heading up to Nitinat."

"Nitinat? What in God's name for?"

"Windsurfing."

"And fishing," Crosby added.

168

"Don't they have wind and fish in New Jersey?" The lady directed her inquiry to Crosby with a sneer.

Crosby nodded his head and smiled. "Touché."

The lady rang them up and Crosby bagged their essentials. Putting the Fig Newtons into a brown paper bag, he said, "I've been eating these all my life, and I don't even know what a fig is. What the hell is a fig?"

"For that matter, what's a Newton?" asked Tosh.

"Yeah, really."

They made their way through the automatic doors out into the parking lot. "A fig is a type of fruit, I think," said Tosh.

"What does it look like?"

"Oh, it's kinda small and brown. Like a giant raisin, I guess."

"So it's in the grape family?" asked Crosby, putting a bag of groceries into the van.

"Maybe. Like a distant cousin to the grape."

"A raisin is a dried grape, right?"

"Yeah." Tosh left the cart in an empty parking space nearby. He jumped in the back of the van to ice the beer in the cooler and organize the cupboard. "Actually, I think figs are green. *Dates* are brown."

Crosby started the van. "A prune is a dried plum."

"I don't eat prunes."

"Neither do I."

*   *   *   *

Pavement ended in Youbou.

The sleepy country town offered Tosh and Crosby a final glimpse of civilization before their journey to Lake Nitinat took them into the forest.

The rest of the way required them to bump along 40 miles of gravel logging roads on which, nearly every day, giant trucks hauled massive loads of timber wrenched from the mountains of British Columbia. The menacing machines had chewed up the rural routes, leaving huge ruts. As a result, Tosh and Crosby had to maneuver their van with great care. Josephine, though dubbed the Dodge *Sportsman* van, did not excel off the highway.

The ditch-ridden trails needed a steady rainfall to quench their thirst. Even though Tosh and Crosby rambled along at a slow pace, Josephine kicked up a load of dry dust, forming a constant gray cloud that seemed to follow them. Even with the headlights on, Tosh and Crosby could not see more than ten feet ahead of them. Soon, the dusty haze moved into the van as well.

Tosh rose to close the windows. Earlier, the Pacific afternoon had blown through the van with gusto, a salty breeze keeping them cool and comfortable. Now, only stale, sallow air filled the van.

169

Josephine suddenly shook violently and threw Tosh to the floor.

"What the hell, dude?" Tosh groped one of the carpeted benches.

"What?"

"Whaddaya tryin' to do, kill me?"

"It's not my fault, Tosh! This road sucks!"

Tosh pulled himself up and made his way around the van, closing the windows, this time grasping the walls for support. His task accomplished, he plopped back into the shotgun seat next to Crosby. "Sorry, man. Just keep your eye on the road."

"I can't even see the road, dude."

"Then just keep your eyes on the fog."

The air in the van cleared a little, but dust still managed to find its way in.

"Where is this shit coming from?" asked Tosh.

"It must be coming through the floor or the engine."

"Yeah, I'm sure Josephine isn't airtight."

"Hey, you know, this road isn't very wide," Crosby noted.

"So stay in the middle."

"Yeah, but what about those big-mama logging trucks that we saw before."

"They were on the highway."

"But they were probably coming from here."

"Well, take it real slow and let's hope that since they were on the highway, that means they're not here." Tosh leaned forward and ran his finger through the layer of dust that had settled on the blue metal dashboard. He scrawled the phrase, Never Die Wondering.

"What day is it?" asked Crosby.

"I don't know. Why?"

"'Cause I don't think the loggers work on Sundays."

"Then let's hope it's Sunday."

*   *   *   *

It felt like an hour had passed while Crosby and Tosh continued to maneuver over the rough dusty roads. No signs helped direct them to the lake, so when the road forked, they didn't know which direction to take.

"Heads to the right, tails to the left," prompted Tosh. "Call it in the air." He threw the coin in the air.

"Tails," said Crosby, rubbing dust and sweat from his eyes. "I wish I could shower, man. I feel gross."

When they entered the forest after Youbou, the air had become still and more humid. With the windows closed, the van heated up quickly and became very stuffy.

Tosh located the coin, which had fallen off his arm and bounced under the seat. "Tails it is. Head leftward, bro."

Crosby followed Tosh's directions, letting a tossed coin map their route. "Tosh, if heads were to the right and tails were to the left, why did I have to call it in the air? What difference did it make what I chose?"

Tosh thought about this. Crosby was right. It didn't matter. "Duh," he said. "Habit, I guess."

The road bent sharply towards the right. Immediately after, a left turn appeared through the brush.

"Go there!" exclaimed Tosh. "I've got a good feeling about this one."

The trail to the left took them through an *S* shaped curve. As the road straightened out, they caught a glimpse of something red. It was a cooler.

"Ah, we must be close. Motor on, Cros."

A minute later, the guys knew they had found the campsite. First they spotted an old Subaru wagon. Next came a V.W. camper and then, a Toyota pickup. All of the autos were rigged to carry windsurfing equipment.

After passing about six vehicles, they pulled into a little clearing of their own. The underbrush had been cleared away leaving a cozy little niche amid the towering conifers. Conveniently, and somewhat by design, this patch of ground was cushioned by a thick layer of fallen pine needles, much softer than the rocky trail that led them to the secluded campsite.

Tosh and Crosby swiftly pitched their tent. Then, they arranged some huge round tree stumps, cut from the trunks of giant redwoods, to serve as tables and chairs — wooden furniture in its least ornate form. Finally, before the daylight faded completely, they scoured the area for enough firewood to last the night. They returned to their temporary dwelling amid the trees with armloads of branches, and plopped down on a couple of stumps.

"Should we cook dinner?" asked Tosh.

"Yes," said Crosby. "But first let's have a beer."

And so began their adventure on the banks of Lake Nitinat.

CHAPTER 12

"So what shall it be?" asked Crosby. "Baked beans? Spaghettios? Ravioli?"

"Ugh, I hate ravioli," shuddered Tosh. "It has to be the worst pasta known to mankind — especially in a can. Puke tastes better."

"Unless that puke is half-digested ravioli."

"I'm sick of canned food, man," Tosh lamented. "You should go fish, Cros. We could have a seafood dinner."

"It's too late. I'll catch us some trout tomorrow."

"Cool." Tosh sighed, trying to decide which would be the least painful dinner option. "I don't know. I guess beans. We've been eating a lot of beans, Cros."

"I like beans."

"I do, too, but I'm getting a little sick of them. I don't know, I guess they're better for us than that Spaghettio crap. Who bought that stuff anyway? You?"

"My mom. She was trying to help. Making sure we had enough food."

"You probably lived on Spaghettios, didn't you?"

"Yeah. My mom can't cook." Crosby searched the van's cupboard under the side bed. "I think we might be out of beans, dude."

"Uh-oh."

"Spa-ghet-ti-os," Crosby sang, mimicking the legendary TV commercial.

"Hey, what's that smell?" Tosh jumped off the stump he had been lounging on and thrust his nose up to the sky. "You smell that? It smells like..."

"Meat!"

"Yeah, mon! Someone's barbecuing! Oh, I could go for a burger right now!"

"Let's go meet the neighbors," Crosby suggested.

They threw some beers in a knapsack and grabbed a bag of salt and vinegar potato chips they had been saving for a special occasion. Darkness had set upon them completely, and the thick canopy of branches overhead blocked any trace of moonlight. Only a lantern lit the path that their noses followed in search of a flame-grilled dinner.

"Man, it's dark in here," Tosh said, holding the lantern toward the bushes alongside the trail.

"We're outdoors, dude. You make it seem like we're inside or something."

"I feel like we are. These woods are so dense, it's like we entered a huge dome that's separate from the rest of the world."

"Yeah. It's very quiet. Very still," Crosby noted, taking a gulp of beer.

"Very dark."

The first campfire they came upon was not the root of their watering mouths. Four old-timers sat around a smoldering fire. One man packed a pipe while a small Yorkshire terrier curled itself in the lap of one of the ladies.

"No burger action here," Tosh whispered as they passed.

"No action at all," added Crosby.

They walked on a little further and spotted a mound of empty Budweiser cans next to an old Bronco. A skinny guy with long stringy hair and work boots poked the fire with a big stick while some fat girl massaged the shoulders of a burly biker dude wearing shades. Black Sabbath rang out from a tape deck.

"These guys should get together with their neighbors back there. They could bond," cracked Tosh. "They have so much in common."

"I want to know where the hell all the windsurfers are," Crosby remarked. "Maybe we're at the wrong lake."

"Probably locals from Youbou."

"Maybe. The first cars we passed when we drove into camp had surfing gear, right?"

"Yeah. Don't worry about it." After walking for about another minute, the burger smell became more intense. "I think we're getting closer, Cros."

Finally, the next camp proved to be the pot at the end of their culinary rainbow. Beyond a jeep, a cumulus cloud of smoke billowed from a towering inferno. Propped on two stumps over the fire was a piece of steel grating. On the grating, mounds of meat sizzled and sparked, spitting grease, shooting little flares of beef fat onto the forest floor which would undoubtedly attract every wild animal and insect within the vicinity.

"Oh baby," groaned Tosh, quickening his gait.

A young guy in surfing shorts and a torn white T-shirt oversaw the whole operation. He held a giant spatula in one hand while he fanned the smoke away from his face with the other. "Beeer! I need beer!" he shouted out absently.

Tosh waltzed up to the Burger King and held out an opened beer.

Taking a step back, the Burger King looked at Tosh and then at Crosby, who approached humbly, presenting the salt and vinegar potato chips like a magi with myrrh, extending his arms forward with one hand below the bag and one above.

The Burger King looked them over and momentarily considered their offerings. Without wasting another second, he snatched the beer and doused the burgers with it.

"Name's Jack," he began. "Beer is the key to grillin' a good burger. I don't know where my helpers are."

"You should've had a beer ready," Crosby recommended, drawing a disapproving look from Tosh.

"Kicked it over," Jack replied.

"We've got extras," said Tosh, opening the knapsack and showing Jack the contents.

"And some chips, I see."

"If you can't have fries, chips are the next best thing," asserted Tosh. "Especially Salt n' Vinegar."

Jack reached into a cooler and dug out a handful of chop meat. "I got my sister and her boyfriend. We should have some extra food. Burgers might be kinda small, though."

"That's all right. We just want some of that *flavor.*"

"Where's your gang?" Crosby asked.

"They must be in the tent," Jack said, forming patties with the chop meat. "Hey Lizzie! Brad! Get your asses out here! We got visitors!"

Lizzie emerged from the tent, tying back her frizzy brown hair. Brad followed, rubbing his eyes. Lizzie grabbed the baseball cap off of his head and placed it on her own, pulling her long hair through the back of it.

"Can't you two go a day without it?" Jack asked.

"Shut up," Lizzie snapped. "We weren't doing anything."

"Yeah, right," said Jack, winking at Brad, who looked at him as if to say *I have no comment.*

Lizzie had green eyes that stood out from her tanned face. Her little nose and rounded cheeks were a little burnt from the sun. "Who's this?" she asked Jack.

"Dinner guests," he said.

"We smelled the burgers and came running. I'm Tosh. That's Crosby."

Everyone introduced themselves and then, following the Burger King's instruction, prepped their plates for dinner. Crosby wasted no time grilling Jack and Brad on the wind conditions at Nitinat.

Lizzie was more interested in mixing a precise blend of condiments on her hamburger bun. After spreading ketchup over the entire surface of both the bottom and top buns, she took great pleasure in applying the mustard, squirting globules in the form of a detailed face. Tosh watched over her shoulder as she added some final wisps of hair. Lizzie admired her work for a moment and then laid a piece of crisp green lettuce over the creation, smearing the bread canvas.

"John Lennon?" inquired Tosh.

"Why, yes!"

"That's incredible."

"Thank you," Lizzie tittered.

"Do you make your burger the same way all the time?" Tosh asked, grabbing the edible paints to decorate his own meal.

"Yep. It's a science. I like to have two parts ketchup to one part mustard."

"What do you like better, ketchup or mustard?"

"Ohh, that's a tough question," said Lizzie, biting into her dinner. "The two go together like peanut-butter and jelly."

"Yeah, they do." Tosh drew his bun-face with mustard dreadlocks. "Don't you think they should have invented a ketchup-mustard mixture by now?"

"But then I couldn't adjust the ketchup-mustard ratio," Lizzie reminded him.

"True, true, but I still think it would be cool. I guess it would be orange."

"And then if you added relish," Lizzie pointed out, "it would probably turn brown and look like puke."

"Especially with all those chunks," grimaced Tosh. "Well, anyway, if you *had* to choose one. If, for the rest of your life, you could only have *one* condiment, which would it be?"

Lizzie stopped chewing her food and thought about the inquiry. "Mustard, I guess."

"That's weird," said Tosh, "'cause you put more ketchup than mustard on your burger."

"Yeah, but I put more mustard than ketchup on my hot dogs."

"Oh."

"I wish we had French fries."

"We brought chips. Would you like some?" Tosh handed Lizzie the foil bag.

"Oh, no thanks. I don't like flavored chips."

"No?"

"Not really."

"Why not? Most people love 'em."

"I got sick once after eating sour cream and onion potato chips, so now I kind of associate flavored chips with throwing up."

"Oh."

"Same thing with fried fish sandwiches."

"That's too bad," Tosh mumbled through a mouthful of meat.

"It's O.K. I don't really like tartar sauce anyway."

"I guess we should have brought popcorn or something."

"Pretzels," said Lizzie. "I like pretzels better than popcorn."

"The soft kind or the hard kind?"

"Oh, the soft kind. The warm ones that you get from the street vendors. Those are the best."

"One time my friend bought one of those from a vendor in New York City and when he bit into it, he found a clump of hair."

Lizzie frowned. "I really wish you hadn't told me that. That's disgusting."

"Sorry. I wasn't thinking." Tosh changed the subject. "What type of salad dressing do you prefer, Thousand Island or Honey Mustard?"

"Honey Mustard."

"I should have known. O.K., Honey Mustard or..." Tosh thought for a second. "Raspberry Vinaigrette?"

"Ohh," Lizzie moaned, "Raspberry Vinaigrette."

"Raspberry Vinaigrette or Ranch?"

"Raspberry Vinaigrette."

"Raspberry Vinaigrette or Blue Cheese?"

"Blue Cheese."

"Blue Cheese?"

175

"Yeah, Blue Cheese."

"Hmmm. O.K., Blue Cheese or Honey Mustard?"

Lizzie pondered the decision for a moment. "Honey Mustard."

"So," said Tosh, "you like Raspberry Vinaigrette better than Honey Mustard and you like Blue Cheese better than Raspberry Vinaigrette but you like Honey Mustard better than Blue Cheese. How can that be?"

Lizzie remained silent for a minute.

Tosh regretted that he might have stumped her.

Then, she said, "Blue cheese is tasty for a little while, but then it gets gross."

"I know what you mean," Tosh said. "May I continue?"

"Please do," Lizzie smiled. They had finished eating their dinners at this point and had reclined by the fire while Jack and Brad showed Crosby their windsurfing equipment.

"What do you like better, sunflower seeds or pumpkin seeds?"

"I don't know," Lizzie said. "I'm not really a seed person."

"O.K. What would you rather have, trail mix or mixed nuts?"

"Trail mix."

"Almonds or walnuts?"

"Almonds."

"Almonds or peanuts?"

"Peanuts."

"Pistachios or macadamias?"

"Damn. That's a tough one," said Lizzie. "I'd have to go with pistachios."

"I thought so. Red or plain?"

"Red."

"Really? You'd rather have *red* pistachios than the natural ones?"

"Yeah. I think they look more attractive."

"Doesn't that red stuff get all over your hands?"

"Yeah, but it's cool. I like eating red things."

"So you're the reason why they paint those damn things red."

Lizzie laughed.

"I've been trying to figure out that one for years. And another thing — why do they only paint pistachios red? What about the other nuts?"

"That's a good question," said Lizzie.

"O.K. You ready for this one?"

Lizzie nodded.

"Peanuts or pistachios?"

Lizzie smiled and stared into Tosh's eyes. Then, confidently, almost defiantly, she said, "Peanuts."

"No way!"

"Yes way!"

"I can't believe, if you were stranded on a desert island and you could only have one nut for the rest of your life, you would choose peanuts over pistachios."

"I would. I don't know, I just feel that peanuts are like the ultimate nut. Maybe because they have the word *nut* in their name."

"I'm searching for the Ultimate Burrito," Tosh stated.

"What's in the Ultimate Burrito?"

"I'll tell you," said Tosh, adjusting the logs in the fire. "First and foremost, guacamole. Guacamole with the correct amounts of garlic and lemon juice is the cornerstone of the Ultimate Burrito. That understood, I'll continue."

"Guacamole. Understood."

"O.K. Next, the meat department — sliced pieces of flank or skirt steak and chicken breast marinated in olive oil and red wine vinegar. Do you want to write this down?"

Lizzie smiled and rolled her eyes. "Go on."

"Black and red beans, mostly black. Rice, brown or yellow, but not too much. You don't want it to be too ricey. Lots of melted cheese, cheddar and jack. Spinach, raw, instead of lettuce. In a common burrito, lettuce would be used."

"But this is the *Ultimate* Burrito."

"Exactly, so we use spinach. More vitamins, better taste. Vine-ripened tomatoes, onions –"

"Raw or fried?"

"Both."

"Ah…"

"A dab of sour cream and — very important — salsa. The degree of spiciness is optional, but it's got to be a quality salsa. A thick, chunky salsa with chipotles would be ideal, but know that lame salsa will sink a burrito in a heartbeat."

"Must have quality salsa," said Lizzie, scribbling down the critical information on her palm with an invisible pen.

What about the other nuts?" "Furthermore, note that the tortilla must be soft and chewy. A worthy tortilla can't be dry and flaky. You don't want it breaking when you roll it up."

"It seems that you've done a bit of thinking on this subject."

"I do a lot of thinking on every subject."

"Well," said Lizzie, throwing a log onto the fire, "what makes *you* the authority on burritos?"

"Uh, I don't know. I guess 'cause I've eaten a lot of burritos and I know what is good and what is not."

"Yeah, but who says that is the Ultimate Burrito? What if someone hates onions? What if someone is a vegetarian? Vegetarians wouldn't like meat in their burritos."

"Obviously not," said Tosh. He tried not to be agitated by Lizzie's argument because he knew she had a point. Diplomatically modifying his aim, he clarified, "I am searching for my own Ultimate Burrito. The Ultimate Burrito according to *my* taste buds. Eating is a subjective experience, dependent on personal preferences. How can I say what tastes better or worse to someone else?"

"You know, it's the same thing with religion," said Lizzie. "On the way up here, when we stopped to get gas, some freak was wandering around preaching. Like I'm going to convert based on what this guy tells me at the gas station. It burns me up. People think that they have found God and you should listen to them and believe their views are right. But religion is supposed to be spiritual, and spirituality is a personal thing. What makes sense to them may not make sense to others."

"You're exactly right," said Tosh.

"Why do people force their religion upon others?" Lizzie asked. "How can people today worship one religion devoutly when there are so many other religions out there? I mean, how can they believe that just one is right and all the others are wrong?"

"I tend to think all religions have certain elements of truth to them."

"That would make sense," Lizzie agreed.

"But most people don't know that," said Tosh. "they believe that their views are correct and all the others are complete fallacies. And what's even more ridiculous is that many people have never even *thought* about religion or spirituality — their religious beliefs were handed down to them. They learned things as children and they accepted this as fact without ever questioning it or looking into other beliefs."

"Don't you think this is ignorance?" questioned Lizzie.

"Well, at least they have faith in something," said Tosh. "Everyone should have their own Ultimate Burrito."

He picked up an empty beer can and threw it into the fire, watching the fire turn its white paint to brown. "There is no harm in believing in a certain religion, unless those beliefs provoke a person to do something destructive. And, like you said before, I don't think it's right to force a religion on someone else. You have to let every individual make up his or her own mind. Like I can tell people what I believe is the ultimate in burritoness, and I can possibly direct them to the places where they might have a better shot at finding their own Ultimate Burrito, but in the end, only they can decide which is their favorite. Likewise, you can suggest paths for people to follow in their search for God – by suggest I mean just that, gentle encouragement, an invitation — not threatening people with eternal damnation if they don't choose it. That's almost as bad as physical coercion. It's really useless unless people make their own decisions. And hopefully, people will give much thought to their decisions."

Lizzie stabbed at the fire with a branch and broke up the burnt logs, causing the flames to die down a bit. "Before I choose my faith," Lizzie stated, "I want to make sure that I've researched all the possibilities. I want to make an educated choice."

"Me, too," said Tosh.

"I'm tired."

"Me, too."

As the campfire went from a flicker to a glow, Tosh bid Lizzie goodnight.

Crosby made a date with Brad and Jack to surf the next morning and joined Tosh for the walk back.

As they trod along, the lantern's kerosene flame fought to cut through the thick darkness around Lake Nitinat.

*   *   *   *

Jealousy, among other things, kept Tosh awake. He rolled onto his side, making sure to accidentally elbow the snoring Crosby. "Shut up," Tosh mumbled under his breath. "Dick."

Nothing woke Crosby. Moments after they had entered the two-man tent and slid into their sleeping bags, Crosby drifted off. His deep, clamorous breathing made it more difficult for Tosh to fall asleep. It taunted him, rubbing in the fact that Crosby rested easily while Tosh continued to toss and turn.

"Ass wipe," said Tosh. "Momo. Buttlick. Monkey dick." His voice grew louder. "Cornhole. Dipshit. Nimrod. Fuckhead."

Crosby, buried in his sleeping bag up to his neck, did not flinch.

"A fucking pea," Tosh announced with enough volume to wake Sleeping Beauty. "A pea in a fucking pod."

Crosby's snoring head poked out of his top-notch sleeping bag, his soft pillowy cocoon the apex of portable bedding technology.

How, Tosh wondered, could Crosby's big puffy sleeping bag be stored in a lunch-box size canvas sack? In seconds, Crosby would just stuff the bag effortlessly into the sack, pull the drawstring and strap the little ultra-light package to his backpack. On the other hand, Tosh, with his ancient napkin of a sleeping bag that offered only a fraction of the cushioning comfort, had to endure a complex sequence of zipping, folding, rolling and tying to condense his sleeping bag to something resembling a half keg of beer.

The ground felt hard under Tosh's body. A rock poked his butt.

"Guess I got shorted on the pine needles," he snapped. He rolled in his sleeping bag over to the edge of the tent. Pulling his arm out of the sack, he ran his hand along the bottom of the tent, searching the thin nylon for the problem pebble. Tosh used the side of his hand to sweep the culprit aside, ushering it to the edge of the tent as if it were a wasp stuck in his car. "And stay out!"

What seemed like hours passed, but Tosh couldn't get comfortable. *I need to be stoned to fall asleep,* he finally determined. *What was I thinking, trying to camp without getting stoned? This whole mess is my own damn fault.*

Pulling himself out of his sleeping rag, Tosh molested the inside of the tent, looking for the zipper. "My own damn fault," he said out loud, which propelled him

179

into a mosquito-bit rendition of Buffet's "Margaritaville." With Jimmy Buffet in his head and the prospect of smoking a little herb on the horizon, Tosh's spirits picked up for a moment. He found the zipper without much of a struggle, but the damn thing got caught on a piece of fabric. He yanked it down. He pulled it up.

Down.

Up.

Down.

Up.

Down.

Up.

Tosh huffed furiously. Looking toward the heavens, he said, "I'll claw my way out if I have to."

*   *   *   *

While Crosby confronted nature with his forearms, fighting the infallible wind to maneuver him back and forth across Lake Nitinat, Tosh decided to try and outsmart it. Strength would not pave the road to success when it came to fishing. The fish clearly had the physical advantage — they could out-swim him any day. To triumph, he would have to use man's greatest resource — intelligence.

Though a glance through any newspaper would tell Tosh that most people do not take advantage of this asset, there is no denying that intelligence has led to incredible advances in technology. And, fortunately for Tosh, he had access to that technology. Armed with Crosby's fishing rod and some miniature decoys that resembled fish meals, Tosh set out to beguile some trout.

Inspecting the lures he had taken from Crosby's tackle box, he hoped they would do the job. Crosby kept a substantial collection and Tosh had no clue which ones to use. Since he did not know the specific purpose, pros and cons or casting technique of each lure, Tosh used his own criteria in selecting two for his fishing expedition: the ugliest one and the one with the funkiest name. (Crosby had scrawled the names of the lures on the compartments in which they resided.)

Judging them on their appearance was no easy task; they all looked pretty unattractive. Imagining which one he would least like to see on his bedroom wall, he finally settled on the aptly named Creepy Crawly Critter, a particularly ghastly, rubbery purple thing that looked like a worm crossed with a ten-legged spider.

The Creepy Crawly Critter had edged out the Guido Bug, a tiny black lobster with hideously long antennae and claws. Tosh felt the two lures were equally ugly, so he resorted to second criteria for the tiebreaker. The Creepy Crawly Critter earned a trip to the lake because of the alliteration of its name, which made Tosh smile. On the other hand, he disliked the name Guido Bug because it reminded him of the knuckleheads he had left behind in New Jersey.

However, neither of those came close to the name of the other lure that Tosh chose. It was an unassuming little gray and white fish with a yellow eye, but it was called Rattlin' Flat Wart Bleeding Tennessee Shad.

"Anything with the words 'bleeding wart' has to be a winner," Tosh declared as he tied the lure to Crosby's line.

He headed down a dirt path away from Lake Nitinat, where Jack had advised him not to fish. He had said Tosh would be wasting his time without a boat. "There are other lakes around good for trout," Jack said. "Just follow one of those dirt paths out of camp."

Tosh walked for a while, thinking of his conversation with Lizzie the night before. Why would some religions try to coerce people into following them? Why would religions go out and actively seek members? It can't be out of a philanthropic desire to deliver people to salvation. On the surface, maybe, but greed was a more likely motivator. Protecting their own interests. Strength in numbers.

That's another cool thing about Rasta, thought Tosh. You don't see bredren standing on the corner passing out brochures. To learn about Rasta, you must research it on your own.

Tosh read a lot about the religion of Rastafari and he had a basic understanding of it. Although he did not fully agree with all the Rasta doctrines, he respected their spiritual way of life and embraced the elements of Rasta that he identified with, such as their call for unity among humankind.

Rasta, like most religions, prescribed the way a person should live. It was this controlling nature that turned Tosh away from organized religions. He did not want to be told how to live. He wanted to remain a free thinker, a free spirit. Why the hell should anyone tell him what to eat and how to dress?

Tosh didn't need rules of conduct. He was an ethical person and he would always conform to society's general morals. It's common sense, anyway, he figured, based on the only necessary guide — The Golden Rule: Do unto others as you would have them do unto you.

Tosh figured he would keep his eyes and ears and heart and soul open, and as life went on and he gathered more information and insight, he would form his own beliefs about God and the Universe. *With a desire to know, the answers will come*, he thought.

Tosh noticed the trail had become thinner and thinner as he got further away from the campsite. It became more overgrown with shrubs, which made it increasingly difficult to pass without getting scraped by branches or stuck with thorns. Many weeds grew along the narrow path and Tosh knew some could be poisonous. He spotted a plant that resembled poison ivy and wished he had put on socks — long socks with horizontal colored stripes that he could pull up to his knees and look like a dork — to protect him from the evil rash.

Tosh envisioned the itchy red bubbles spreading up his legs and settling around his crotch. Poison ivy on the privates would be living hell, he imagined. One step below leprosy.

Suddenly, he felt something tickle his calf and his stomach leapt into his mouth. Tosh whirled around and grabbed the back of his leg, expecting to find something resembling one of Crosby's lures imbedded in his muscle.

To his surprise, however, a young dog stood behind him. The dog looked like he had mixed breeds in his genes, probably some collie. Covered in shaggy orange and white fur, he stood as high as Tosh's knee. His wagging tail matched the cheerful, alert look on his face.

Where did that dog come from?, Tosh wondered. *Maybe he's one of the campers.* "What are you doing here?"

He noticed the pooch did not have a collar on. Most likely, the dog followed him out of camp. "Are you lost?"

The dog scuttled about ten yards ahead of Tosh and then turned around and looked at him. "What? What is it?" Tosh asked. "Do you want me to follow you?"

The dog pranced a little farther and turned around again, so Tosh walked on, trailing the dog. "Hell, I'm the one who's lost," he said. "You seem to know where you're going!"

The two partners continued on this way for another ten minutes.

How far is this lake? Tosh wondered.

With his four legs to Tosh's two, the dog moved quickly and Tosh had to work to keep up. Once in a while the dog would get too far ahead and Tosh would lose sight of him until he'd round a bend and find the dog waiting for him impatiently.

Tosh was traveling faster than he would have liked. He'd rather have surveyed his surroundings more and made note of where he was going, but he enjoyed the dog's company. The dog gave him someone to talk to, something to take his mind away from the anxieties that went with walking alone in the wilderness with no idea about the territory, mild anxieties that swam around the perimeter of his consciousness like invisible jellyfish, briefly stinging his peace of mind.

Another plus to his new-found company, Tosh realized, was that if any type of trouble were in the area, the dog would most likely warn him. As the pooch disappeared up around another curve, he thought to himself half-jokingly that if the dog should come running back toward him, it would probably mean that danger lurked ahead. No sooner did he finish chuckling at the thought, did Tosh look up to see the dog galloping toward him, backtracking hastily.

The dog sped past him and did not look back.

The irony stunned him for a moment until the reality of the situation pushed it aside. As he watched the dog's tail vanish in the other direction, Tosh couldn't help but wonder, *What did that dog see?*

He did not wait around for an answer.

With a boost of adrenaline, Tosh took off after the dog to escape possible peril.

What lurked behind?

It had to be a bear. A giant fucking grizzly with teeth the size of corn-on-the-cob holders. The bear had tasted human blood and it had a craving. It would gash Tosh's stomach open with one swipe of its lethal claws and chew him from the inside out. Tosh would die an agonizing death watching Gentle Ben digest his limbs.

Holding Crosby's fishing rod like a lance, he leapt over fallen tree trunks and puddles, his sandaled feet pounding the soft earth. With his free hand, Tosh shielded his face from the web of twigs and vines strewn across the path. They smacked against the fishing pole, snagging it and tugging his arm backward. Without stopping, Tosh tore the pole free.

Tosh kept running but, a moment later, the fishing rod got caught on a branch again. This time it wrenched the pole right out of Tosh's hand. Less scared of the invisible danger than what Crosby would do to him if he lost his pole, Tosh halted, grabbed the pole dangling in the air and yanked with all his might. A loud snap sent the Rattlin' Flat Wart Bleedin' Tennessee Shad catapulting through the air.

For a helpless moment, Tosh watched it fly.

He took his eyes off the airborne lure to find the dog sprinting toward him again. Again, the canine scrambled past without acknowledging him.

What are we, surrounded?

Perplexed, Tosh froze. He did not know what to do.

Tosh screamed to the dog, who, without answering, veered off the path into a rougher, less defined trail beyond a grove of smaller deciduous trees.

Making a split-second decision, Tosh followed the running dog into the trees, barely keeping him in view and eventually losing sight of him altogether. The trail descended a steep but short incline and then disintegrated into terrain that would make a Green Beret weep.

Fueled by fear, Tosh turbo-hiked solo until he finally caught up with the dog again, who was resting. "Where are you taking me?" Tosh panted, reaching out to the dog.

The dog blinked, sniffed Tosh's hand and walked on.

So much for fishing, thought Tosh.

*   *   *   *

Following his new canine companion got Tosh lost. Getting lost got him pissed, and then spooked. His feet hurt, his clothes stuck to his skin, and the bugs started to pester him. What was he going to do — stuck, miserable and clueless, deep in the woods with nothing more than Crosby's fishing pole to protect him?

To start off, he would sing Jimmy Buffet. This would appease his discomforting feelings. A few bars of "Margaritaville" would turn his undesirable, slightly scary situation into nothing more than a nature hike, an opportunity to enjoy the outdoors and spy on some wildlife.

The words of Jimmy Buffet filled his head, but unlike the night before when he found himself trapped in the tent, they did not come from his consciousness alone. This time they floated lazily through the air, bouncing off of branches, sliding down tree trunks, weaving their merry way through Tosh's dreads into his ears.

Stepped on a pop-top, blew out a flip-flop, cut my heel, had to cruise on back home...

Jimmy Buffet's voice echoed distantly through the forest, but Tosh did not realize it. He sang along absentmindedly, picturing a lime wedge on the rim of a wide, frosty glass.

It took an insect flying up his nose to jar his awareness.

"Uggh!" Tosh cringed, and blew the little bugger out in a batch of booger.

Inspecting the corpse of the mercenary gnat, it dawned on him that the sound of Jimmy Buffet continued, even though he had stopped singing. "I'm losing it," he said to himself. Confused, he sat down on a rock and listened closely to the still of the forest.

But the forest was not silent.

Tosh's ears told the truth. His mind had not betrayed him. His sanity remained intact, despite the discovery of this baffling phenomenon. Deep in the middle of nowhere, a mile or two from even their remote campsite along Lake Nitinat, Tosh could hear the jubilant ode to frozen cocktails.

And, straining to listen, Tosh swore he could make out the whir of a blender.

*   *   *   *

The dog barked, urging Tosh to follow. "Might as well," he said. "You're the one who got me into this mess. Maybe you can get me out." Tosh had a feeling the dog would lead him toward the source of the music. Where else could he be going with such a purpose?

As they made their way through the bushes and trees, the music gradually became louder, confirming Tosh's hunch.

After climbing an embankment, Tosh could hear Jimmy Buffet clearly. The soft humming sound that Tosh mistook as a blender revealed itself as the buzz of a gas generator, undoubtedly powering the good tunes.

They were close.

Then, through the leaves, Tosh saw a flash of bright blue. He froze. Nylon. The side of a tent. His heart quickened.

He had found a campsite. Was he intruding on someone's vacation? Someone who obviously wanted privacy very badly and might not be too sociable?

Tosh saw a man. His short grayish hair peeked out from under a black bandanna. A camouflage Stetson hung down his back from a strap around his neck.

Of medium build, he wore a soiled long underwear top and boxer shorts. The man leaned over and fiddled with something, but Tosh couldn't see what it was.

Something caught the man's attention, and he turned around and bent down. Losing sight of him, Tosh ducked below a branch to see better. It was the dog, who had left his side and greeted the man with a wagging tail. The man, crouching in his worn leather sandals, gave the dog a good pat without saying a word.

From his perch, Tosh inspected the campsite. The tent looked extremely weathered. Next to it, suspended high in a tree, hung a wide rope hammock. Under the hammock, Tosh spotted a nifty little shed with a door cut out of one wall.

The dog crawled into the shed, walked in a circle and laid down with his head in the door.

Cool doghouse, thought Tosh, dropping to his knees.

Wait a second, Tosh thought, *why would this guy bring a doghouse with him?* Then, it hit him. *Holy cow!* This guy wasn't camping. He was living there!

The man looked up sharply in Tosh's direction. His eyes peered for a second, then slinked away carelessly. Did he see Tosh?

This is stupid, thought Tosh. *I should just go introduce myself. Why am I spying on this guy?*

Because the wacko is living out in the middle of nowhere, that's why. He obviously doesn't enjoy people, so unexpectedly waltzing into his den probably wouldn't be a favorable move.

But the guy's listening to Jimmy Buffet, Tosh reasoned further. *How bad can he be?*

With the whimsical confidence afforded by his last consideration, Tosh stepped forward, clumsily emerging from the brush.

The man briskly turned around to face him.

"Hi, I don't mean to intrude," bumbled Tosh. "But could you possible tell me how to get to Lake Nitinat?"

The man looked Tosh over with a discerning eye.

For a few anxious moments, Tosh waited for his next reaction. Thankfully, it was a chuckle. The man asked, "Care for a margarita?"

*   *   *   *

The wind ripped across Lake Nitinat with as much constancy as in Vantage, where Tosh and Crosby had stopped to clean the van. Not a cloud littered the sky and the water chilled Crosby just enough to refresh him. His forearms burned, not from sunburn, but from the strain of his muscles. Gripping the boom, Crosby pulled the sail tightly toward him and hoisted himself onto his board. Immediately, the board jetted forward. Crosby dug his feet in, looking forward to another speedy ride.

*   *   *   *

"I could have sworn I heard a blender, but then I saw the generator and I realized that is what I had heard," Tosh explained. "But you do have a blender. That's so weird."

"Not really," said the man. "Your *intuition* told you about the blender."

Tosh scrunched his face, attempting to thwart the sharp ache in his cranium brought on by the frozen drink.

"Ice headache," said the man. "I hate it when that happens."

"Intuition?" Tosh questioned.

"People should learn to trust their intuition more. It's usually quite accurate."

Tosh nodded and tried to make sense out of the strange situation.

He had stumbled upon a guy living in the woods. That was surely out of the ordinary.

The guy made him a frozen margarita complete with salt and a twist of lime. Weirder still.

But something else was awry.

Tosh's eyes searched the campsite for a clue, but he could not find anything. There was nothing else to see besides the tent, the hammock, the doghouse, the generator, a lantern, a record player, a box full of Jimmy Buffet records, the table with the blender, and a cooler.

"It's not what is here, it's what *isn't*," said the man.

"What do you mean?"

"You feel like something is amiss, don't you? Something doesn't feel quite right."

"You mean besides the fact that I'm sitting here with a total stranger in the middle of the forest drinking margaritas and listening to Jimmy Buffet?"

"Yes, besides that fact."

"Yeah, you're right. Something else is bothering me."

"Well, what you see here didn't help you, so maybe it's what you can't see."

"What I can't see?"

"Yes. What is not there says as much about a situation as what *is* there."

Inspecting the campsite to see what it lacked, Tosh started with the basics. What were the requirements of camping?

Shelter. First off, the camper pitches a tent.

Food. That's it! Tosh didn't see any food! Then, he remembered the cooler. *Probably in the cooler,* he thought.

"You're getting warmer," hinted the man.

Warmer, thought Tosh Fire! Every campsite has a fire for warmth and cooking. Where was the fire? No flames, no wood, no ashes, no sign of a fire whatsoever.

That's what had bothered him. Tosh felt stupid. How could he not realize it?

"Bingo," said the man.

"Where's the fire?" Tosh asked.

"I don't have one."

"You don't have a fire? How do you cook, gas stove?"

"I don't cook."

"You don't *cook?*"

The man shook his head.

"What do you eat?"

"I don't."

"Don't?"

The man said quietly, "I don't eat."

"You don't eat," Tosh repeated.

"No."

"Ever?"

"Never."

"But you drink," Tosh said, holding up his margarita.

"Fridays."

"Well," said Tosh, nervously gulping at his cocktail, "at least you have your priorities."

*   *   *   *

Crosby skimmed across the whitecaps like a water bug on a puddle, happy as a pussy in a patch of catnip. Thoroughly enthused, he let out a high-pitched "yahoo" to express his pleasure. While his vocal chords strained, in a bit of timing that couldn't have been orchestrated better by God Herself, a huge gust whipped through Crosby's gear and yanked the boom from his hands. The nylon sail smacked the water violently, pulling Crosby, in his harness, down with equal force. Crosby's face planted itself in Lake Nitinat quicker than he could stop his bellow, turning his joyful scream into a vigorous gargle.

*   *   *   *

"Name's Tim," said the man, placing a Buffett record on the turntable. "I've been living here for some time now. Very peaceful."

"Nice to meet you, Tim. I'm Tosh. Love the Buffett."

"Yeah, he's the best."

"So, what brought you out here?"

Tim reached into the cooler and dug up two hands full of ice. He held the ice in his palms for a minute, staring at the melting droplets in the mid-day heat. "Used to be a lawyer in L.A., where I made a killing winning loot for grieving divorcees. When a Beverly Hills businessman got caught in bed with a bikini model, his soon-to-be ex-wife came to my firm for the best possible settlement."

Packing the blender, Tim whipped up another batch of cocktails. "My business partner and I had worked up quite a reputation. A woman who secured our representation had essentially hit the jackpot. Our careers were booming. We had plenty of money, a great pad in Huntington, lots of women."

Tim filled his glass with the frozen drink. "I had accomplished what I had set out to do. Since high school, my life had revolved around having a successful career. That's what I had been taught to want. That was the goal set for me, the goal that I had unquestioningly accepted. I took S.A.T. courses, joined all the extra-curricular activities so I could get into Stanford. Then, at Stanford, I focused all my attention on getting into a good law school. Everything I did, I did to achieve success, both professional and financial."

Tosh, beginning to feel like an aimless loser, held out his glass for a refill. "So, I had achieved my success," said Tim, topping off Tosh's drink. "And for a while, I was happy. Or at least I thought I was. But I began to realize something was missing. Something important."

"Spirituality?" asked Tosh.

"Well, at the time, I wanted love, a wife. I had gotten to the point in my life where the one night stands and shallow, physical relationships didn't satisfy me anymore. Random erotic encounters are exciting for a while, but they don't top true love. Trust me, the scene gets old. Eventually, you want more than just hot sex. You want something deeper. Something stable."

"I can understand that."

"I had everything else set in place, but I couldn't complete the picture without a mate. I wanted someone to share it all with, someone that I could connect with and care for. I would have given up everything for someone special."

Tim shuffled over to a board he had propped between split tree trunks and cut a few more wedges from a lime. "Care for more salt?" he asked.

"No thanks."

"So, my longing for love made me approach relationships much more seriously," Tim continued. "Sex stopped being my prerogative. I stopped dating women who I only wanted to sleep with. Instead of putting up with shallow or boring or even annoying women — and in L.A. there are quite a few, I can tell you — just so I could get them in bed, I started to look deeper into people."

The man squeezed a lime wedge into Tosh's drink and then his own. "And most of the time, I didn't like what I saw. It was very frustrating. I felt like I would never find her. And the few times I found a woman that had wife potential, it didn't work out."

The dog stood up, groaned and stretched. He lumbered over and rubbed up against Tim's leg. "They say you won't find love if you're searching for it. You can't force it. It's got to happen by itself."

"Why's that?" asked Tosh.

"It seems that if you want love too badly, you often try to force it and you end up coming on too strong, not being yourself. Plus, you run the risk of finding yourself in a relationship where you are more in love with being in love than with the person you're supposedly so in love with. Does that make sense?"

"I think," said Tosh.

"Whatever the darn reason, from my own experience, the maxim is true. The moment I ended my search, the day I said to hell with it, I've got to be happy by myself, I met my soul mate." Tim patted his pooch on the side of his belly. "Like an angel sent from heaven, Jody was smart, funny, sexy, outgoing, witty, independent — she could even cook. We hit it off from day one and my life had never felt so complete."

"What happened?" Tosh asked, sensing tragedy.

"A week after we got married, I found out that the girl of my dreams was in love with my best friend."

"What? Oh, shit."

"My best friend and business partner." The man climbed into the hammock and kicked off his sandals. He spoke with no hint of emotion, like he had gone over the situation in his mind hundreds of times and now his wound had turned to painless scar tissue.

"Have you ever been in love?" Tim asked.

"No," said Tosh. He had been in *like* many times before, but he always seemed to pull the plug when things got too close. At this point in his life, love had always taken a back seat to maintaining his independence.

"Well, love is the treasure of life. No other sensation can compare to it. Nothing fulfills the human spirit like love does. It runs deeper than any other emotion, into the core of our being."

Tosh looked at Tim and listened. "That's pretty heavy, man."

"I'm serious. You'll know some day."

"I suppose."

"But know this. Just as love brings all that joy, its loss devastates. Love fulfills, but when it leaves, it takes a piece away. It leaves you feeling empty."

"I bet."

"Her betrayal ruined me. I felt worthless. I felt like I couldn't go on. My every thought was with pain. I couldn't even bury myself in work, because my partner screwed me, too."

Tim shooed away a horsefly that buzzed his ear. "I decided to get away for a while. Take some time to be by myself and get out of the city. I came to Vancouver Island because it held good memories for me from when I visited here as a kid with my family."

He took a long sip from his margarita, sighed and smiled. "Nothing beats the stars up here."

Does the taste of lime make him happy, Tosh wondered, or the loco Mexican spirit lacing the crushed ice? Was alcohol this man's panacea?

"You know, it took me a long time," said Tim, "but after all those years, I finally realized that being successful did not make you happy. *Being happy made you successful.*"

Tim looked at Tosh to emphasize his point. "And since I've come to live in the woods, I've learned that you shouldn't depend on anything to bring you happiness, whether it be material possessions, status, love or acceptance. I've learned that happiness can be found within yourself — in life, in the creations of the universe."

*   *   *   *

His confidence somewhat diluted, Crosby once again traversed the windy, finger-shaped lake. He exchanged his reckless abandon for a more cautious and alert approach, his sore face a constant reminder of the awesome and unpredictable power of Mother Nature.

This time, when another mighty gale struck, he was prepared. Gripping the boom even tighter than his previous runs, Crosby refused to surrender his sail to the pull of the wind.

Then, he hit a wave, propelling him into orbit. Crosby had never left the water before and vaulting over the lake like a kangaroo sent a wave of electricity through him. In one dazzling instant, Crosby was jolted by shock, a rush of adrenaline, fear and a narcissistic *I must look so fuckin' cool right now.*

Unfortunately, this brief ego massage did nothing to ease the pain of his back, when, seconds later, his frame smacked the surface of the water. To further his discomfort, before his face became submerged, it met the falling surfboard.

*   *   *   *

"Lime makes me happy," said Tosh.

Tim stirred his margarita with his finger. "Oh. Me, too. That's why I love these things so much," he said, lifting his drink.

"It's not because of the alcohol?"

"Naah. I just use a touch of tequila for flavor. I'm not a big drinker."

"Where do you get all of your supplies?" Tosh asked.

"There's some Indians that live on the other side of the lake. They run into town every so often." Tim gave an abrupt, loud whistle. "Gotta keep the dog fed." The dog returned from the surrounding brush and cozied up to Tim.

"What's his name?"

"Yogi," said Tim, scratching the dog behind the ears. "Thata boy."

"After Yogi Berra?"

"Nope."

"Yogi the Bear?"

"Nope."

Tosh leaned over and pet the frisky fellow who had led him to the strange oasis of sorts. "Just Yogi for the sake of Yogi?"

"A yogi is one who practices yoga."

"Yoga," Tosh repeated. "I've heard of that. I always picture that little E.T.-looking dude from *Star Wars*. The guy who sounded like a chain smoker on helium."

"That was *Yoda.*"

"Right. Yoda."

"Yoga is a discipline that involves certain postures and specific methods of breathing to achieve a state of meditation."

"You meditate?"

"Quite a bit," said Tim, getting up from a blanket.

Tosh had heard a little about meditation. He knew that Rastas smoked marijuana religiously because it aided them in meditation. One dread Tosh had met in Africa told him meditation was the key to a new understanding of the self, the universe and God. He explained that God dwells within each and every human being, and that every person was capable of being or realizing God by searching for Him within the wisdom of his or her own soul.

Or something like that. The dread had mystic vibes and this Rasta concept sounded intriguing, but Tosh couldn't really understand what he was talking about.

Still, this encounter sparked an interest in Tosh, so, when he returned from his travels for his final year of college, he took an extra-curricular meditation class. Tosh had trouble grasping it, though, and quit half way through.

Tim walked over to the doghouse and pulled out a couple of foot-long sticks.

"What are those?"

"Knitting needles — another way I pass the time."

"Oh," said Tosh. "I thought they were like, high-falutin' chopsticks or something."

"I don't eat, remember?" Tim said it with neither a trace of sarcasm, humor nor confrontation.

Tosh had written that off as a ruse. He hadn't wanted to contradict Tim, despite the outrageousness of his statement. Now, Tim had just said it again — earnestly.

"You're serious?"

"Of course."

"No offense," said Tosh, "but I find that hard to believe."

"I don't blame you. Most people would."

"Most people? Who wouldn't?"

"People who practice yoga."

*   *   *   *

191

Crosby dragged his gear on to shore. A few good hours worth of windsurfing still remained in the day, but not in him. Battered and worn, he laid down on top of his board and let the sun dry him off. He hurt, but it was a good hurt.

*   *   *   *

"You don't need to live like a hermit to practice yoga," Tim said, threading his needles with orange yarn. "I just got sick of city life, so after I had my so-called partner buy me out, I came out here to escape the rat race."

"Don't you get bored out here?"

"Never. You may not realize it, but there is so much drama unfolding around me every day. I've got ant colonies in battle, beavers building dams, finches warding off bluejays and spiders preying on everything that gets caught in their intricately constructed webs. And that is nothing compared to the discoveries on the inside."

"The inside?"

"Inside myself. The yoga. The meditation."

"I don't get it."

Tim began to knit. "By using yogic techniques, you can look inward and see your true self."

"What's that?"

"Your spirit. Your soul. Your inner light."

"What does it look like?"

"It's difficult to put into words, Tosh."

"Well, please try." Tosh didn't want to be disrespectful, but he yearned to understand what Tim spoke of.

"It's super-consciousness. Essentially, it allows you to transcend this world. You can shed your body, the vessel that holds your spirit on this plane of existence."

Tosh couldn't believe someone who looked so regular could be so far out. Tim would never draw a second glance walking down a city street — average build, short hair, no tattoos, body piercings or facial hair except for a little scruff — yet, he lived in the wilderness, drank margaritas and knitted. And what the hell was this stuff about "transcending this world?"

"Have you ever done acid, Tim?"

Tim chuckled and said that he had never tried it. "Smoked a little reefer from time to time, but not in years."

"Just checking."

"That's all right. The concept of yoga is very hard to grasp for someone who hasn't studied it."

"So what does all this have to do with not eating?" asked Tosh.

"Yes, not eating. Let me try to explain." Tim took a deep breath. "Do you know what chlorophyll is?"

"It's the stuff in plants that makes them green and allows them to conduct photosynthesis," Tosh said proudly.

"Right. Chlorophyll allows plants to more or less trap the solar energy and use it for photosynthesis. Photosynthesis is the process by which plants take water and carbon dioxide and produce carbohydrates by using the sun's energy.

"When we eat, we gain our energy from the solar energy that is stored inside plants, or the energy that is stored in the flesh of animals that eat the plants."

"The food chain."

"Yes. By certain advanced yogic techniques, I can take in this energy in its simplest form. Basically, I do not need to eat because I recharge my body from the cosmic energy of the sun and air."

"Are you telling me you are a plant?"

"No. But I have plant-like abilities."

"This is heavy," said Tosh. He felt slightly confused, somewhat strange and a little drunk.

"Of course."

"How did you learn all this energy-soaking business?"

"My guru taught me this special yogic technique during my meditations."

"Your guru?"

"My teacher."

"Where is he?"

"He's here."

Tosh looked around. All he could see amid the forest was Tim and Yogi, his dog. Tosh pointed to the dog and looked at Tim with questioning eyes.

"No. That's my dog."

*   *   *   *

Crosby made his way back to camp. He was surprised Tosh hadn't returned from fishing yet and hoped that meant that his buddy would return with a handful of trout for dinner. With his last ounces of energy, he shed his wet suit and cracked a beer, but dozed off before the can was even half-emptied.

*   *   *   *

Tosh didn't know whether Tim was bullshitting him or not, and he began to feel slightly awkward. Tim seemed sincere, but Tosh found it extremely difficult to believe all of the things he was saying, especially the part about not eating. Tosh downed the last of his frozen margarita and asked Tim if he could fix him another.

Tim took his glass and headed over toward the blender.

"So, your guru taught you how to live without food," Tosh posited, "but you drink margaritas and listen to Jimmy Buffett? What's with that?"

"Earthly existence fosters earthly pleasures. As long as I'm here, I might as well enjoy the good things, no?"

"Can you see your guru right now?" Tosh asked.

"No. I can only see him in a meditative state," Tim explained as he loaded up the blender. "But I know he's here, because the slightest thought of him invokes his presence."

"Can *he* see ud?" Tosh disliked this notion, feeling like his privacy had been infringed upon.

"As only gurus can," Tim laughed. "He told me you were coming."

"He did?" Now Tosh felt downright spooked. "Hey Tim, would you make it a double?"

*   *   *   *

Tosh awoke to the sound of thunder. Nursing a fierce headache, he kept his eyes closed momentarily, unsure of his whereabouts. The patter of the rain on the tent refreshed his memory — Lake Nitinat — but he couldn't recall all the details from the previous evening. He remembered the gist of his conversation with Tim, but his recollection of his trek back to camp was hazy. Too much tequila.

Tosh sat up. He had no idea where Crosby was.

About the only thing he knew for sure at that moment was that he had to take a shit real bad.

Damn the luck of it all, he thought. He squirmed out of his sleeping bag, adjusted his boxers and threw on a T-shirt that sat crumbled in the corner of the tent. He unzipped the door and poked his head out into the light but steady rain.

That solved the Crosby mystery, for Cros knelt alongside the van, wrestling with his windsurfing equipment with a disgruntled look on his face.

"Hey."

Cros looked up. "Morning!"

Tosh scampered out of the tent and into his pair of sandals getting soaked by the nearly extinguished fire. "What's up?"

"I feel like strangers."

"I gotta drop the kids off at the pool."

"No pool, pal." Crosby reached into the van and pulled out a roll of toilet paper. "Nice way to start the day," he said, tossing it over to Tosh.

"Shut up."

Tosh was not happy about the situation at hand. He had hoped to avoid shitting in the woods, definitely the low-point of the camping experience. Nobody likes mosquito bites on the ass.

"Where do you think I should go?" he asked Cros.

"Wherever."

Wherever? This was a big decision, finding the right place to go. Tosh had many issues to consider, such as, first and foremost, avoiding getting caught in the act, and secondly, not wanting to make a deposit too close to someone's camp. He should have known better than to ask Crosby, who obviously didn't give two shits about it. Crosby gave as much thought to his bodily excretions as a N.Y.P.D. horse dropping a load of manure while he trots down the middle of Broadway.

"Should I just pinch a loaf right here?" Tosh asked.

"Just walk into the woods over there," Crosby answered without looking up. "As far away as possible."

"This sucks."

"Don't worry about it. Bears do it all the time."

As Tosh turned to leave, Crosby added some further advice: "You might want to stick that t.p. up your shirt. It doesn't hold up too well when it gets damp."

Clutching the roll of toilet paper underneath his T-shirt, Tosh crossed the dirt road that led into camp. The rain picked up a little, prompting him to hurry through the woods.

No wonder Tim doesn't mind living out here, Tosh thought to himself. *The guy doesn't eat, so he doesn't have to shit in the woods.* "Bears do it all the time," he said out loud, mimicking Crosby.

Without the luxury of a ceramic pot to rest on and a plumbing system to carry away his unwanted waste, Tosh would have to squat down, rest his elbows on his thighs and let it fly. He looked for an appropriate place but he couldn't find even a small clearing in the thick underbrush. With his t.p. growing damper by the second, despite the cotton shield of his shirt, he hastily decided to drop his boxers right where he stood.

Luckily, he had performed this action previously. His experiences in the Far East, where they don't believe in toilet bowls, primed him. Tosh would never forget the first Oriental bathroom he walked into — a public restroom in Shanghai.

Inside the dim shanty, Tosh skipped around the puddles on the mud floor and approached the cement platform. There, to his horror, instead of bowl to sit on, he found a ceramic basin and a trench. That disappointment he dealt with easily enough, but the small hose supplanting a roll of toilet paper troubled him deeply. *Millions of Chinamen do this every day,* he had consoled himself. And by the looks of the restroom, they did it right there.

Tosh learned a valuable lesson in China: Never enter a public restroom with your shoes untied.

Now, Tosh crouched in the woods like Johnny Bench setting up for an inside pitch. In seconds, insects pounced upon his exposed butt flesh with the voracity of a homeless man snatching up a book of McDonald's gift certificates.

Normally, Tosh took his time on the john. Instead of just writing it off as unproductive down time, he wisely utilized his bathroom sessions for more than just waste removal. He exercised his mind as he exercised his bowels, informing himself with a *National Geographic* or a good book while his intestines performed their daily (hopefully) duty (pun intended). Essentially, Tosh had converted shitting into an enlightening experience.

Not this time. In the woods, Tosh drastically curtailed his extra-defecative activities. He took care of business, finished the paperwork and left the office without looking back.

When he got back to camp, Crosby had tied his gear to the roof of the van and begun to collapse the tent. "Come on!" he urged.

"We're splitting?" Tosh asked, removing the collapsible metal rods from the sleeves in the tent. "No more windsurfing?"

"Not in this weather. I'm not gonna make us wait around all day in the rain."

That's pretty generous of him, thought Tosh, not knowing that even if it were the clearest day on God's green earth, Crosby would still be packing up his board. In one long day, the lake had gotten the better of him.

"Let's hit a city! A *big* city," said Tosh. "San Francisco!"

"You drive," said Crosby, massaging himself.

CHAPTER 13

Tosh and Crosby bounced their way along the logging roads out of the Nitinat wilderness.

"So how was the fishin'?" Crosby asked.

"Didn't."

"Didn't? You didn't fish?"

"Nope."

"I don't believe it. How could you lose the Flat Wart without even dropping a line in?"

Tosh hit the gas when they hit pavement again and Josephine chugged into gear. "Don't ask."

"Well, what the hell did you do all day?"

"Went for a hike."

"See any bears?"

"No." Tosh scowled at his friend, remembering his snotty attitude during his bowel-movement crisis. "Met some guy, though."

"Where? By the lake?"

"No. Way back. He was living in the woods."

"Living there?" asked Crosby. "Windsurfer?"

"Nope. Just a hermit."

"Weird. He try an' rape you?"

Tosh didn't even bother answering that one. He decided to not tell Crosby the whole scoop. He'd never believe it anyway.

"Pull in here," said Crosby, pointing to a convenience store.

Inside, Crosby picked up a pouch of Red Man, a bottle of Mountain Dew and a *N.Y. Times* for Tosh, knowing his friend would probably appreciate an update on the global happenings.

"You got a paper? I can't believe they have the *Times* up here."

"It's a few days old."

"Like it matters," said Tosh, pulling back on to the highway to begin the very first leg of their long trip to San Francisco. "Read me some, will ya, dude?"

"Can't you just wait until we get to the ferry? You'll have three hours to read the whole thing."

"Just read me some headlines. Give me a preview."

"You want headlines? I'll give you headlines," said Crosby, leafing through the paper. "You're just gonna get depressed."

After a minute, Crosby shook his head and groaned.

"'Young Girl's Body Found.' She was stabbed 40 times, Tosh."

"Jesus."

Tosh drove silently while Crosby read on, listening to the tap of the rain and the hum of Josephine's engine.

"'Woman Raped by Gang of Youths in Park.' They beat her over the head with a fuckin' rock, for cryin' out loud." Crosby turned the page. "Here's a carjacking. What the hell?"

Crosby crumpled the newspaper and tossed it in the back of the van disgustedly.

"Wow," murmured Tosh. He took a sip of Crosby's Mountain Dew.

"That's why I only read the sports section." Crosby grabbed a big wad of chewing tobacco and tucked it between his cheek and gum. "It's so depressing."

"Fe real, man."

"Why do they always focus on all the bad shit? Same thing with the news on TV — do we really need to know all that? Why don't they tell us more of the good things? Like Willy said, why can't they focus on the positives?"

"I guess it won't sell papers."

"There's so much damn hostility in our society. People have no respect for life."

Rarely did Tosh see Crosby so heavy-hearted. Maybe things were getting to Crosby, after all. Maybe, deep down, he felt tormented by all the wickedness out there.

"What's happening to our country?" Crosby asked.

"Too many guns," said Tosh.

"Well that's part of it. But it goes beyond that. I mean, the first two things I read to you didn't even involve guns."

"That's true."

"It's television, dude. And the movies. There's so much violence. That's all everyone sees."

Tosh thought about how much impact TV had on society. "You're right. It starts early, with cartoons even. Kids are weaned on brutality and it continues as they grow up. That's all they know."

Crosby went into the back of the van, looking for something. "I think it's the parents' faults. You and I saw all the same crap on TV when we were kids, all those cartoons — Daffy and Bugs dukin' it out, Tom beating on Jerry—"

"That redneck moron Elmer Fudd blasting his damn gun all the time," interjected Tosh.

"But we're not out killing people."

"Because we were raised properly. We know it's morally wrong to kill and rape."

Crosby returned to his seat with an empty soda bottle. "The problem is that too many people in this country are not good parents. I guess because so many of them are fucked-up themselves."

"Well, if society can't rely on parents to do what they have to, the government has to step in and teach basic human values in school and within the community."

"And they should ban violence from TV and the movies."

"Oh yeah, right."

"I'm serious. Something drastic has to be done. Look at the paper, dude." Crosby pointed behind him to the crumbled ball.

"Violence has always been a part of the entertainment business," Tosh reasoned. "Look at Shakespeare. *MacBeth, Hamlet, Julius Caesar.* There is murder in every one of those plays. Conflict is central to drama. And what conflict packs more emotional punch than murder?"

"Yeah, but back then, people had morals."

"I don't know if they had morals or not, but they feared God. Religion dominated the culture. Society revolved around it. So you didn't have to worry about the violence in theatre influencing the actions of people."

"Ban all the violence on television, that's what I say. At least the movies have a rating system."

"But you're talking about the First Amendment, man. We can't just do away with free speech.
We'd be living in a fascist society!"

"I'm not saying completely eliminate free speech. I'm just saying we have to limit the violence. The First Amendment was based on people's right to express their beliefs, anyway. I don't think it was meant to be exploited by a handful of people so that they can get rich at the expense of our society."

"It's based on the same premise."

"Well, it's not even worth talking about, because it will never happen. There's too much money to be made in violence and the entertainment industry has too much power."

Tosh took another sip of Crosby's soda. "I'll say. In fact, our society basically revolves around the entertainment industry. Actors and television celebrities, athletes and musicians, get all the press. Everyone worships entertainers, no one of real importance, no one with any real value to society. Big fucking deal, a guy can throw a ball. A guy can play guitar. How does that further humanity? It's like the entertainment industry has taken the place of religion. Nowadays, God is second string to the quarterback."

"Unfortunately, money runs the show," Crosby said, taking back his Mountain Dew. "The entertainment industry lets cash dictate its actions. And violence makes money. Do you think *The Red Balloon* would have drawn millions to the theaters? I doubt it."

"So then, the problem actually goes beyond the violence in television and film. Violence is so prevalent because it sells. That's why the news and newspapers cover all that crap. The true root of the problem is money."

"So what are we supposed to do, eliminate money?"

Tosh tucked a stray dread behind his ear. After some thought, he answered Crosby's question. "If we eliminated money, it would be communism. We're talking about bagging the whole capitalistic economy. We're talking about completely overhauling the structure of society."

"Maybe that's the answer," said Crosby, knowing that it couldn't be. "But the Soviet Union hasn't made communism look too enticing."

"We can't change our economy. That's impossible. But capitalism is not the evil anyway. Capitalism creates the need for money, but it does not create greed. It doesn't take a lot of money to survive. You can get by with very little. The problem is, people are obsessed with material goods. They always want more stuff. Their goals revolve around the accumulation of goods, so they need more money."

"He who dies with the most toys, wins."

"Exactly. Things would be better if less emphasis was placed on material wealth and more on the importance of spirituality. Spirituality can fulfill you more than a BMW, but nobody knows that. I bet our country would be a more harmonious place if people changed their thinking, from 'He who dies with the most toys wins' to 'Everything you gather, is just more that you can lose.'"

"Words of wisdom from the Grateful Dead," said Crosby, depositing another gob of tobacco juice into his spit bin.

*   *   *   *

Aboard the Vancouver Island Ferry, Tosh and Crosby gorged themselves on salmon like grizzlies in spring. Their meals in Nitinat, neither hearty nor wholesome, provided far less sustenance than the heaping bins of Chinook offered by the cafeteria as part of the all-you-can-eat buffet.

"Good stuff," Crosby mumbled through a mouthful.

Tosh nodded in agreement, although he was thinking about his meal beyond its taste. As he chewed the meaty fish, Tosh pondered the Pisces on his plate.

At a certain point in the salmons' lives, they begin to spawn, which involves the arduous task of swimming upstream to eventually lay their eggs in the place where they had once hatched. From that moment on, the salmon dedicate their lives to fulfilling this inborn yearning, tenaciously fighting against the current. An incessant battle, the feisty fish repeatedly catapult themselves out of the raging river and through the air, flapping like a desperate duck.

And then they die.

One generation after the next, the salmon continue this exhausting effort. Day after day, hour after hour, minute after minute, the salmon finish their lives with constant labor.

And for what?

No one knows this except for the salmon.

It transcends tradition.

Legacy has nothing to do with it.

Something deep within drives the salmon to climb against the torrents. Maybe the impetus comes from a higher force. Perhaps the supernatural beckons them.

Whatever the case, the salmon never get weary in their quest to attain their goal.

How admirable, thought Tosh. Despite the struggle, they stay focused. Their resolve remains untattered.

Imagine if humans knew their cosmic purpose and concentrated on achieving it.

If only humans had the faith and fortitude of salmon and applied it to fulfilling themselves spiritually.

If people sought God, whatever God is, rather than seeking money to buy toys, society could regain direction. There would be less time for violence and no room for hatred — just people living out their destiny and allowing others to do the same, everyone working together to reverse the destruction done to the planet.

Pollution would disappear and in its place plants and animals would thrive. Harmony would rule.

Sounds like a John Lennon song, he thought.

Tosh swallowed his last bite of salmon and sighed. Whatever happened to *Brady Bunch* reruns? Life used to be so simple.

*   *   *   *

After their meal, Crosby met Tosh at the same sunny spot where they had snoozed on the trip out to Victoria. Tosh looked troubled, so Crosby offered his buddy a cookie he had grabbed from the van. "Want a Fig Newton, dude?"

"How can you be hungry? We just ate like 50 pounds of fish."

"It's dessert."

"No thanks."

Crosby threw down his sleeping bag next to Tosh's. He sat down and took off his shirt.

"Crosby, what do you think happens to you when you die?"

"Well, first they do an autopsy."

"No, dude. What do you think happens to your soul?"

Crosby stopped eating his dessert and gave the idea some serious consideration. "I have no idea, Tosh," he finally said.

"Doesn't it bother you that you don't know?"

"Not really."

"Why not?"

"Well, I figured since there's no way to find out, why drive myself crazy thinking about it."

"Well, I want some answers," Tosh demanded.

"But Tosh, if there's no way to find out until you die, maybe that is knowledge that we are not meant to have yet."

201

"But I want it now," Tosh whined, like a little kid in Toys R Us. He jumped up from his sitting position. "There are so many questions I have that I can't get answers to. It's so frustrating."

"It probably wouldn't do any good at this point. I mean what difference does it make?" Crosby laid back on his sleeping bag and kicked off his sneakers.

"Infinity."

"What?"

"Doesn't that concept blow you away? Something that just keeps going."

"Like the Energizer bunny?"

"Space is infinite. Infinite, I mean, what is that? It never ends? Ever? I just can't conceive that. The whole thought is so…overwhelming. I think it scares me."

"Why does it scare you?"

"Because it makes me feel really, really small."

"Insignificant."

"Yeah, it makes me wonder why I am here. It makes me wonder if there is a reason for my life. Why are any of us here? What is this whole thing about? How did it all begin? Was it just a random phenomenon? I mean, is this a cruel joke or what?"

"Maybe space doesn't go on forever," said Crosby, shutting his eyes from the bright sun. "Maybe it just goes really far, so far that we can't find the end, and then it stops. Maybe all of space, the whole universe and all the planets and all the stars and all that shit out there, is in a cardboard box in God's garage. Maybe God created this whole thing as a hobby and then he got occupied with something else and just put it in an old beer case and threw it in the garage and forgot about it, and now the world is going to hell because God is letting the universe collect dust."

*   *   *   *

The guys put Canada in their rearview mirror with Crosby at the wheel. After they found the ganja they had hid somewhere near the border, Tosh and Crosby planned to drive straight through to San Francisco, stopping only for gas, snacks and stretch breaks.

The voice of Joseph Hill, lead singer of the Jamaican roots reggae band, Culture, filled the van with good vibes: "Jah alone can give I satisfaction, fill I heart with love."

Tosh stuck his head out of the van window and shouted, "Jah — Rastafari!!"

Crosby looked at his best friend, sitting in the shotgun seat with a smile on his face and a matted mop on top of his head. "Cut your hair, you hippie."

"Come on, say it," Tosh goaded. "It mek yuh feel good when yuh seh it."

"That's your thing, dude. I don't even know what 'Jah Rastafari' means. Explain to me what all those reggae dudes mean when they yell that."

"No problem, mon. Mek we reason." Tosh dropped the pseudo-patois for the Rasta lesson. "Basically, when the Rastas say 'Jah Rastafari,' they're praising God, because 'Jah' is the Rasta word for God. I think it was derived from the ancient Hebrew word, 'Jah-weh.'"

"O.K."

"And 'Rastafari' refers to His Imperial Majesty, Haile Selassie I, Divine Light of the World, King of Kings, Lord of Lords, Conquering Lion of the Tribe of Judah."

"What?"

"Haile Selassie — King of Kings, Lord of Lords."

"Who?"

"Haile Selassie, the Emperor of Ethiopia."

"The Emperor of Ethiopia? What are you talking about?"

"Haile Selassie was the emperor of Ethiopia."

"I didn't even know Ethiopia had an emperor."

"Well, they did," said Tosh, turning down the music, "and he was a highly respected international figure and powerful black leader. And based on certain biblical passages which could be interpreted to mean that God was black and a prophecy made by Marcus Garvey, the Rastas believe Haile Selassie was the Messiah."

Crosby put the wipers on momentarily to scrape away a good-sized insect that had plastered itself in the center of his line of vision. "Who's Marcus Garvey?"

"Marcus Garvey was this radical Jamaican thinker who strove for the elevation and equality of the black race, but he did so without hatred for whites, sort of like a Jamaican Martin Luther King. He said that he had no time to hate anyone because all of his time was devoted to the up-building of the Negro race. He denounced violence and that sort of thing."

Crosby listened intently, keeping his eyes on the highway.

"You kind of need to consider things from the perspective of black Jamaicans at that time. Things were not good. They were living in poverty, and after centuries of oppression at the hands of the white race, they found it difficult to embrace the white man's God. People started to believe that the doctrines of Christianity were modified to suit the aims of white imperialism and were no longer sufficient to fulfill the spiritual needs of the black people. Marcus Garvey, who was hailed as a black savior and prophet, gave a cryptic prophecy during a speech in Kingston in 1927. He said, 'Look to Africa, where a black king shall be crowned, for the day of deliverance is here.'"

"What does *that* mean?"

"Garvey was more or less predicting that a black African king would redeem the black people of the world." Tosh took off his T-shirt and threw it into the back of the van. "Shortly after his prediction, in 1930, Haile Selassie was crowned the Emperor of Ethiopia. Then, after a couple of years studying scriptures in the Bible, four Jamaican ministers deduced that Haile Selassie was the king that Garvey had spoken of and agreed that he was divine. They were the first Rastafarians, the founding fathers of the Rastafarian movement."

"O.K., but I still don't understand where the word 'Rastafari' comes from."

"Haile Selassie *is* Rastafari."

Crosby shot Tosh a confused glance.

"I'll explain. Haile Selassie's birth name was actually 'Tafari,' O.K.?"

Crosby nodded.

"In Ethiopia, they use the word 'Ras' as the title for a nobleman — kind of like 'Lord' in Britain — so Tafari was called 'Ras Tafari.'"

"Ah-hah."

"Yeah, so 'Rastafarian' comes from Ras Tafari. He took the name Haile Selassie when he became emperor. It means 'Power of the Trinity.' Now, when Rastas say, 'Jah Rastafari,' they mean 'God,' or 'Haile Selassie as God,' or 'God within Haile Selassie.'"

"Did *Selassie* think he was God?"

"Selassie believed that his position as emperor was divinely sanctioned, but he did not believe he was the Messiah. The funny thing is, the early Rastafarians believed that the Christian doctrines had been adapted by whites to suit their imperialism, but, ironically, Selassie himself was a devout Christian."

"Wow. How do you know all this, dude?"

"College."

"You learned this in college?"

"Well, I didn't learn it *in* college. I learned it while I was there."

"What do you mean?"

"You know that massive library we had at my school? We had endless books, books on everything. They had their whole card catalog computerized, full-out Dewey decimal. So I cruised up there, punched 'Rasta' into the computer and checked out some books."

"Well," said Crosby, turning the reggae back up, "at least your parents got their money's worth."

*   *   *   *

"Which rock is it, damnit?" Tosh searched the roadside where less than a week ago he had stashed their stash. Unfortunately, due to his extremely stoned frame of mind at the time, he forgot exactly where he had put it.

Then, Tosh spotted a groundhog, or the ass of a groundhog, actually. The critter had his head in a crevice, enthralled by something inside the hole.

Tosh snuck right up on him. "Hold it right there, buddy," he called. The groundhog did not budge, so Tosh picked up a small rock and tossed it near him. No response.

I don't believe this, thought Tosh, looking for a bigger stone. *What a dumb animal.* He found one slightly larger than a golf ball and threw it, trying to graze the laborious land pig.

It did not connect. Instead, the projectile landed just above the hefty target and then rolled down and landed on its back.

Still no response.

At that moment, Crosby called out for Tosh, urging him on from the van, "Hurry up, you momo!"

"That's it," said Tosh, clutching a heavy stone half the size of a cinder block. "Prepare to meet your maker, little man!"

Tosh dumped the aspiring boulder next to the soil swine. It crashed down with great impact, causing a rumbling of the surrounding stones.

At once, the earth boar made a hasty retreat, backpedaling its stubby little rodent legs on the gravelly turf. As its head emerged from underground, the dazed dirt dweller whirled around and coughed, *Man, that's some good shit.* The furry fiend stumbled away like a barfly in 4am fog.

"Get out of here, you beast!" cried Tosh. He reached into the recently vacated crevice and pulled out their pipe and the paltry remains of their weed, which sat among shards of tin foil. *Damn groundhogs.*

*   *   *   *

The sun sank as sluggishly as Crosby motored on toward the Oregon border. "Don't worry, brah," he said, "We'll score some buds in Frisco, for sure."

Tosh salvaged every last grain of pot from the crinkled aluminum. He dabbed his finger on the foil and carefully transferred the sparse supply into their pipe, which had just returned from a brief furlough under a rock in Northern Washington. "Looks like this is it, man. One last buzz. Should we burn it?"

"Smoke 'em if ya got 'em."

And that they did. To the Stones' *Sticky Fingers,* mainly "Sway."

"It's just that evil life, got you in its way," sang Crosby in the strained groan familiar to pot-smokers who attempt to speak while holding their breath. "Or something like that."

His chest loaded with the kind herbal smoke, Crosby nearly coughed up a lung and then passed the bowl over to Tosh.

"A little harsh, huh?"

Crosby nodded, keeping his watery eyes on the graying highway.

It did not take long to kick the bowl and by the end of "Wild Horses," the buzz had fully kicked in.

Tosh scraped the bowl, bouncing along to "Can't You Hear Me Knocking."

"Dat some good ganja, seen?" he said, slipping into the counterfeit Jamaican vernacular.

205

"Sure was. Where did it come from?"

"I don't know, mon."

"Didja ever wonder about the weed you smoke?" asked Crosby.

"Whaddaya mean?"

"I'd love to know where it grew. Who planted it. Who cultivated it. Who harvested it." Crosby let go of the wheel to take off his T-shirt. "Like the stuff we just had. Did it come from Jamaica? Mexico? Iceland?"

"Iceland?"

"Just keeping you on your toes, brah." Crosby kicked off his old Vans to let his bare feet feel the evening. "But you never know. I mean, I don't know diddly about Iceland. Maybe they grow some killer herb."

"I doubt it. I'm gonna catch some zees, mon." Tosh climbed on to Crosby's sleeping bag spread out on the back bed and pulled a sheet over him. It felt good to stretch his legs and rest his eyes from the road. "Doesn't matter where it came from. It's the same sun shining all over."

Crosby continued to speak as if Tosh had never left his side. "Get this — I heard that Iceland is actually leafy and lush, and Greenland is covered with snow. Isn't that weird? The settlers named them opposite to trick unwanted visitors. You know, to steer away any possible invaders."

"No kidding, that's wild." The words barely trickled out of Tosh as the ganja put him in a state of heavy relaxation.

In the rearview mirror, Crosby could see that his best friend's interest in the conversation had waned in lieu of a well-timed nap. It looked like it would be just him and the road for a while.

Crosby's stoned mind wondered about the origin of the marijuana they had just smoked.

Where did it come from? Did it grow naturally, outdoors, reggae floating lazily on a Caribbean breeze, or under high-powered lamps in a basement in Connecticut?

Who brought the cannabis its drinks, Mother Nature or Mothafucka?

Who picked it — Juan? Cecil? Mbuzukibatswami?

Which borders had it illegally crossed? Did it drop from a Tequila Airlines flight, a Glad garbage bag hoisted from an old Cessna, falling through the night sky like a lone dark star into the barren Texas desert? Or was it pressed into a brick and smuggled inside a smelly shoe, between a thin layer of sweaty cotton and a worn leather sole?

From its cultivation to its final fate as smoke in Crosby's lungs, how much money had that weed made? Through how many hands did that grass pass? Were they kind, caring hands or the cold-blooded grip of a murderer, claws that would slash and stab, fingers that would steadily pull a trigger? *If that marijuana had the gift of gab,* Crosby thought, *think of the stories it could tell.*

*   *   *   *

The inevitable happened.

After three years of constant wear, Crosby's tattered, once white, University of South Carolina Cocks baseball cap finally gave out. The plastic strap in the back of the hat used to adjust the size lost its last remaining notch. The other six partners, disloyal to the cause, had already jumped ship at different times in various places. This final plastic knob, about the size of an erect nipple on a voluptuous Barbie Doll, abandoned its station somewhere in northern Oregon, retiring to live out its days as a purposeless particle amid the gum wrappers and lint of life.

Though filthy, the hat had retained good shape — especially the brim, which arched perfectly. Without the critical plastic band to hold it in place, however, Crosby could no longer keep the cap on his head. The hat was history.

A rookie might try to thwart such a finality, but a seasoned veteran like Crosby knew better. He had attempted to rescue previous hats with the same problem, using everything from staples to paper clips to the household panacea, duct tape — all to no avail. Once, he even started a small structure fire in his garage when he tried to melt the stripped plastic strap together with a blowtorch.

Now, the cap had become several sizes too large and only one person Crosby knew could make use of such an item.

Conveniently, that person happened to be sleeping in the back of the van. His head covered with a nest of matted hair, Tosh would fill the Cocks cap with no room to spare.

"Time to move on to another melon," Crosby said to the hat, placing it gingerly on the engine cover. "You have served me well."

He didn't know how long he had been driving, but Crosby started to feel very drained. A face full of fresh air could not thwart the lashes of his eyes from mingling with each other. Soon, he pulled the van over to the side of the empty highway. Nudging Tosh, he said "Your turn, dude."

Tosh opened his eyes a sliver and then closed them.

"I *tried* to be nice," Crosby said, raising his voice with a sinister tone.

"All right, all right." Tosh sat up and rubbed his eyes. "What time is it?"

"I dunno."

"Where are we?"

"Dunno. Oregon."

"You gonna sleep?"

"Yep. So get outa the bed, dude."

Tosh lugubriously climbed off of the back bed.

"Here, this is yours," said Crosby. "Wear it well — what's left of it." He placed his favorite hat upon the head of his friend.

*   *   *   *

207

Tosh finished off the night and drove through the morning, blowing through what remained of Oregon and passing into the dry hills of Northern California. As the A.M. dwindled, he pulled into a truck stop outside some pasture of a town to stretch his legs and let the van take a break.

The mid-day sun beat down on Tosh as he fed Josephine a drink of petrol. He topped off the tank and placed the fuel nozzle back in its place, scarcely aware of the eyes upon him, eyes that belonged to an oversized youth in baggy overalls leaning up against an old Ram pickup. Taking off his newly acquired Cocks hat to let his dreads breathe for a moment, Tosh wiped the sweat off of his brow.

The giant approached. "Howdy," he said, clasping his powerful hands together in front of the massive belly that oozed from behind the bib of his Oshkoshes. He nodded toward Tosh's cap. "Cocks, I like that." Keeping his palms together, he flexed the biceps of his steel girders, obviously for Tosh's benefit.

"Thanks," Tosh replied.

"That's a real nice hat ya got there."

Pretending not to notice the tree-trunk limbs swaying before him, Tosh inspected the object of consideration and then placed it back on his head. "Yeah. It's broken, though."

"Ya don't want it?"

I didn't say that, lard ass, Tosh wanted to snap. What he really said was, "Actually, I just got it."

The behemoth took a step closer and glowered at Tosh. "I don't think ya really want it."

I don't believe this, Tosh thought. *Crosby gives me this hat and it gets me battered by Bart Simpson on steroids.*

The woolly mammoth came closer, putting his fat face in front of Tosh's. He smelled of festering body odor and when he suggested "Ya should gimme that hat," his breath reeked of pickled pig's feet.

"But it's broken," stammered Tosh. He wished he could grab a handful of the bully's fleshy cheek and shake it like a bowl of Jell-O.

The walnut-brained defensive lineman (or, considering the guy's stench, *offensive* lineman) looked at him like a cat eyes a sparrow. "I don't care if it's broken. I want that hat."

"But my best friend gave it to me."

The meathead sort of rolled his head around slowly and pouted his lips. "Well then, whaddaya say I kick yer ass for that hat?"

Tosh had the feeling the guy wanted to kick his ass more than he actually wanted the hat.

"I'd prefer it if you didn't," he said. The honest response came to his lips before he could censor it. If Crosby had said the same line, it would have sounded brazen and gotten his ass kicked, but Tosh's matter-of-fact delivery pulled a bunny from the hat. It made the goon laugh — not a sinister, *You're dead meat* cackle, but a genuine chuckle.

"I like ya," he snorted, smacking his bare knee that protruded through the large holes in his pants. "Ya can keep yer hat."

Tosh felt so elated and relieved at the fortuitous turn of events, he wanted to buy the big lug a beer. "Let's get a cold one," he said. "It's on me, big guy."

The two new acquaintances entered the mini-mart. There, they found Crosby paying for the gas and some beef jerky. Tosh pulled out a couple of cans of Budweiser from the refrigerator and placed them down on the counter with Crosby's aged meat. "Hey Cros, could you finance these beers for my friend and me?"

"Sure." Crosby glanced back at Tosh and did a double take when he spotted the human dump truck.

"Baxter Hulligan," said the truck, extending an enormous gearshift to shake. Crosby's entire arm quaked when he placed his own mortal hand in the grasp of their new associate's.

Back outside, Crosby and Tosh pulled the van over to a shady area at the end of the lot where Baxter joined them along with a girl he seized as she exited the gas station bathroom.

Baxter introduced the freckled girl to them as his "old lady."

"That's your mom?" asked Crosby in astonishment.

A look of bewilderment crossed Baxter's face for a moment. Then he burst into his obnoxious laugh, a combination of a snort and a cackle. "Y'all are funny," he said. "Both of yas. I like y'all."

"That's his girlfriend," said Tosh to Crosby, lifting his face from his hands.

"Wife," Baxter corrected. "Yes sir. Me and the Mrs. was just married in Vegas."

"Congratulations," Tosh and Crosby recited simultaneously.

The girl looked young enough to be in high school.

"Me an' Daisy been on the road since we left Tennessee a few weeks ago. Had to get outa there due to some unlucky circumstances," Baxter explained. "Went to Vegas to get us a high class weddin'. Now we're lookin' for a place to live. Daisy always wanted to come to California, so here we are."

"But there's no beaches here," whined the thin, pasty girl. "I wanted to get a real California sun tan. And where's all the surfers and movie stars? There's nothin' 'round here but mountains an' desert an' bikers an' critters. We got all that back home in Tennessee. 'Cept for the desert, of course."

The paint chipped on her bright pink toenails as Daisy ran her bare foot through the loose dry dirt. Her firm legs stretched up to her high-cut shorts, while her flat white belly peeked from under a half-shirt.

She'd be pretty hot, thought Tosh, *if she washed that greasy hair and scrubbed off some of that grime.* Someone get that girl a shower. And she could definitely use that Hawaiian Tropic tan she sought.

At least she kept her pits shaved, Crosby noted.

"I think the beaches are a little south of here," Tosh explained gently. "Actually, they're a lot south of here. They're in southern California. You're in northern California now."

As soon as he said it, he wished he hadn't. Tosh waited for Daisy to snap, "We *know* that. What do you think, we're stupid?" and for Baxter to suddenly revert back to a mean-spirited brute and sock him in the nose.

Luckily, they just remained silent for a moment, pondering the situation, until Daisy said, "Well then, Bubba, let's head south!"

"She calls me Bubba," Baxter said to them before addressing his wife.

Tosh and Crosby watched the young couple converse.

"Darlin', I don't think the truck is gonna make it much further."

"But Bubba, you promised."

"I said we'd make it to California, darlin', and we did. I can't help it if there's no beaches here."

Her face reddening, Daisy began to pout. "Bubba you said we were gonna teach our baby to swim!"

"We'll teach him to swim in a lake, honey. I'm sure there's got to be a lake around here." Baxter nervously looked to Tosh and Crosby for assurance.

Tosh and Crosby glanced at each other absently. "Yeah, sure, there's a lake around here," Tosh confirmed, thinking of the scorched hills they had just driven through. He definitely had not seen a lake.

"Lots of lakes. Beautiful lakes," Crosby added.

"Do they have sandy beaches?" asked Daisy.

"Did you say *baby?*" Tosh asked, changing the subject.

Daisy's hands touched her as-of-yet bulgeless belly and she unscrunched her face, transforming her querulous frown into a tittering smirk. "I'm pregnant. That's part of the reason why we left home."

"Your parents don't know?" Crosby asked, popping a piece of beef jerky into his mouth. He held out his stash, offering the couple some.

Daisy grabbed a chunk for her hubby and one for herself and continued with her story. "Oh, they know! They know, all right!"

Daisy released the rear gate of the pickup and sat down on top of it. "See, this is how it happened. Bubba had a crush on me."

"I was in love with her!" Baxter interjected.

"Bubba would ask me out on dates. Continuously."

"But she would always make excuses. She'd blow me off!"

"I didn't want to go out with Bubba. He was a big jock who bullied people. He was always gettin' into trouble an' stuff."

"Aw, I was just havin' fun."

"So he hounded me an' hounded me until finally I couldn't take it no more, so I went out with him. To my surprise, Bubba was funny. An' he was sweet. So I went out with him a couple more times an' then the bastard got me drunk on cheap wine an' seduced me."

Baxter opened his mouth to defend himself but nothing came out.

Daisy went on. "An' wouldn't you know, during that night of passion, Bubba's lil' seed went ahead an' pitched camp in my uterus." Daisy pronounced the word "you-*tour*-us," like she had just learned the term out of a book. She looked to her belly, as if she could see the creation budding inside her.

"Guess I'm pretty, uh, what's the word — fertile!" Baxter said proudly. "Runs in my family."

"Now I wasn't ready for all this. I was scared. Scared shitless to have a baby and even more scared to tell my parents. I didn't know what to do. So in a panic, I was gonna have an abortion, but they ended up calling my parents.

"I told them about Bubba an' they was pissed off. See, my daddy's the preacher. It don't look so good when his little girl gets knocked up. But I think they were even more angry that I tried to have an abortion."

Baxter, chewing on a long piece of wild grass, sat quietly next to his wife as she spoke.

She continued, "Now, my uncle is the sheriff, so my daddy had him come an' haul Bubba off to the county jail."

"Jail?" Tosh asked.

"Yep. Locked him right up. Then they told me that I was gonna have the baby, an' I was grounded for the rest of my life."

"Whew," said Crosby. "The rest of your life?"

"Yep. So I was feelin' pretty bad. Jus' miserable. An' lonely. So I took to goin' down to the jail to see Bubba whenever I could get outa the house."

"How long was Baxter in jail for?"

"Well, Bubba's mom is gone and his daddy's always drunk, so he didn't have anyone to come and get him out. And Bubba didn't have the best reputation around town, so they weren't in any hurry to let him out. I don't know how long they were gonna keep him there. My parents weren't sayin' much to me. Just barkin' orders.

"Anyhow, Bubba told me that he wanted to marry me. He told me that he would take care of me an' the baby, no matter what, an' that we could get a house together an' everything. So I told my parents all this an' they did not like the idea of me settlin' down with this, 'unsavory character,' as they put it. They said I couldn't marry him 'cause he was in jail. So one night I stole my uncle's keys an' let Bubba outa jail. But the next day, my daddy was furious an' he an' my uncle grabbed Bubba again while he was workin' underneath the truck an' threw him back in the slammer."

"I had to change the oil," said Bubba, finishing his beer. He crumpled the can in his paw and tossed the little wad of aluminum over his shoulder into the back of the truck.

"They said that if I tried anything like that again, Bubba'd stay in jail for a eternity. At this point, I was gettin' real pissed myself. I figured, if I'm big enough to have a baby, then I'm big enough to make my own rules. First of all, I did not want to be grounded for the rest of my life. Second, I wanted to marry Bubba. So I packed a bag for myself an' got some a Bubba's stuff together an' I grabbed my daddy's shotgun an' I busted my Bubba right outa jail!"

Daisy howled and high-fived Baxter.

"You busted him out of jail?" Crosby asked in disbelief.

"Uh-huh!! My uncle was readin' some girly magazine an' I raised that shotgun right up to his face. He didn't think I was for real till I blew his cup a coffee offa his desk!"

"What did he do?" asked Tosh.

"Nothin'. What could he do? He ain't stupid. He just screamed to me as we were gettin' in the truck, 'This is the thanks I get fer teachin' you how to shoot??'"

Daisy and Baxter both cracked up and Tosh and Crosby laughed a little too.

"Damn," Crosby said. "It's kind of like a shotgun wedding in reverse."

*   *   *   *

It was too hot to drive. Not really, but Tosh and Crosby chose that excuse for killing the whole afternoon talking to the eloping teenagers from Tennessee.

"They're just young and misguided," Tosh explained to Crosby as they ventured into the mini-mart for a third time to buy more cervezas. "They're not white trash."

"But they survive by ripping-off mini-marts! If they didn't meet us here today, they probably would have raked this place clean."

"That's just it. They *survive.* They have to steal food so they can *eat.* At least they don't hold anyone up — just a casual slip up the shirt or down the pants. Or in Baxter's case, into the overalls."

"Jimmy Buffet style," Crosby said, grabbing more cheap beer from the fridge. Holding the door open, he let the cold air rush over him until he drew an evil glance from the old man behind the counter, at which point he thrust his head fully into the refrigerator as if searching for the last case of some rare imported lager.

The agitated clerk locked his register and hastily made his way from behind the counter, giving Crosby his cue to remove his cranium from the brew igloo and slam the door shut. "Why should *we* buy the beer again? We don't have much cash either, dude. We should make *them* get a round."

Tosh twisted one of his thick dreads in his sweaty hand. "Aw, screw it," he said. "They barely have gas money. I think that's the real reason Baxter doesn't want to go any further. His truck looks like it runs O.K. Besides, he's a mechanic."

Crosby handed him a twelve-pack while he dug into their collective wallet — the brown paper bag filled with their supply of cash referred to as "the pot."

"Hey man, we've made new friends," Tosh continued. "Maybe we've broadened their horizons. Maybe now Baxter won't be so quick to beat on hippies and clean-cut guys like you."

"Clean-cut? Yeah, right. I wish I was clean. I'd drink raw sewage for a shower. It's been so long."

"Tell me about it."

They paid for the brews and headed back outside into the bright, hot sun.

Baxter and Daisy waited for them on a sleeping bag in a grassy field behind the truck stop. A little earlier, the crabby clerk had firmly requested that the group take their activities elsewhere. He had pointed to a sign that read **NO LOITERING** and stated emphatically, "That means you can't sit in the parking lot and drink beer!"

Tosh and Crosby found Baxter and Daisy playing cards. "Whatcha playin'?" Crosby asked.

Daisy answered his question by telling Baxter, "Go Fish."

"Intense," said Crosby with a touch of sarcasm.

"D'yall wanna play?"

"Go Fish?"

"Yeah."

"Are you kidding?" Crosby asked.

"No, why?" Daisy looked up at him.

"Crosby doesn't know how to play," said Tosh.

"Yeah," said Crosby, popping a beer open, "Isn't that really complicated?"

"A little. But we'll show you how to play."

Daisy collected the deck and shuffled it. As she dealt, she laid out the rules. When she finished, she left the stack of remaining cards in the middle of the sleeping bag. "This is Bubba's favorite part," she said. "Ga'head Bubba."

"What should I use?" he asked. "Head or butt?"

"Use your face, Bubba!"

Bubba leaned down and planted his nose on top of the stack. Twisting his head in a circular motion, he spread the cards out over the sleeping bag.

I'm glad she didn't say butt, Crosby thought to himself.

*   *   *   *

"Do you have a six?" Daisy asked Crosby.

"Aw, shit. I don't believe it!"

"Fork it over, honey."

Crosby slammed the card down in disgust. Daisy laid down a pair of sixes.

"So, what are you guys gonna do?" Tosh asked Baxter.

"I dunno. Guess head down to southern California."

"I think you should stay up here."

Daisy took a loud slurp of her beer to call Baxter's attention to her frown.

"Why's that, Tosh?"

"'Cause southern Cal is wickedly expensive. You could get a lot more for your money up here."

"Yeah?"

"Hell, yeah," chimed Crosby. "You guys'll probably end up in a barrio in east L.A. How's your Spanish?"

Tosh wouldn't have put it so bluntly, but he knew Crosby was right. "Yeah, up here is a better place to raise a kid. You could probably get a job as a mechanic."

"You think?" asked Baxter.

"And you could live in one of those terrific trailer homes." Crosby's sarcasm was obvious to Tosh, but Baxter didn't pick up on it.

Daisy listened silently with her head down, pouting.

Tosh continued with his advice. "And then when you save a little money, you could go down south for vacation. That will give you something to look forward to."

Crosby burped and added his cynical opinion. "Yeah, you could look forward to the smog and traffic and gang shootings and earthquakes. It would be an excellent vacation."

Tosh expected they would see through Crosby this time and tell him to shut up, but Baxter just nodded in agreement and looked hopefully over to his wife. Baxter must have only heard Crosby's excited tone, reasoned Tosh, and not what he had said. Maybe he wasn't listening to Crosby at all, lost in his own thoughts, silently communicating with his wife.

"Do you have a two?" Baxter asked Daisy.

"Go fuckin' fish," she snapped, "In that *lake* of yours."

*　　　*　　　*　　　*

By the time the sun dipped below the horizon, the four of them (three of them, really — Daisy only had two beers since she was pregnant,) had finished a case of beer. Drinking all day in the sun did a number on them. They felt sluggish and dopey, wanting only to eat and sleep.

Boozing helps cut through distractions and places emphasis on life's true priorities — nutrients and rest. We'll find the diamond ring later, just give me a chilidog, extra onions. Forget about the deadline, I need a nap.

Daisy and Baxter returned with a loaf of Wonder, lifted from the mini-mart. She had won decisively at Go Fish and it seemed to cheer her up. "We got the bread," she called, digging her hand into Baxter's overalls and yanking it out of his crotch.

Tosh gave the pot of Spaghettios on the portable stove one more stir and then scooped out four servings. "Pasta and bread, a real Italian meal!"

"How did you guys get this?" Crosby asked, taking a piece of bread from its polka-dotted plastic bag.

"Same way we get everything," said Baxter. "We stole it."

"I know, but how? How do you guys steal everything?"

Baxter swallowed a mouthful of Spaghettios. "You mean what's our technique? I can't tell you our secrets."

"Come on. Enlighten us."

"O.K. Since ya put it that way." Baxter smacked a mosquito on his arm and flicked it off. "Ya see, Daisy distracts the clerk by flirtin' with him up front. She acts drunk and easy, maybe shows him somethin', bends over to tie her shoes, plays with his hair. She really gets him goin'."

Daisy proudly gave a little example of her show as Baxter spoke.

She could definitely play the part of a slut, thought Crosby. *How could a preacher's daughter learn to do those things?*

"While Daisy has the clerk goin' for the bait," Baxter continued, "I walk in, grab whatever goods we need and stuff 'em right into my overalls. I leave as quietly as I come in."

Crosby never took his eyes off of Daisy. He felt somewhat aroused, so he knew that redneck clerks nationwide would surely get off by her little act. She probably brought every 24-hour mini-mart cashier's fantasy to life.

"Hey, Daisy," Crosby asked, "where did you learn how to do that, uh, sexy *stuff?*"

"Oh, that?" she cooed. "H.B.O."

*　　*　　*　　*

Seven cold Spaghettios lingered in the pot, like groupies waiting to meet the band, long after the encore ended and everyone else had left.

"Wait!" Baxter called to Tosh, who took the pot to the men's room to wash. He grabbed the pot from Tosh and sopped up the remaining Spaghettios with a slice of Wonder. "Makes your job just a little bit easier."

"Hey, Baxter?"

"Yeah?"

"What are you and Daisy gonna do when she gets, you know, *really* pregnant?"

Baxter wiped the dark brown sauce from the corners of his mouth with the back of his hand. "You mean fat?"

"Well, yeah."

215

"We talked about that. I dunno. Guess we'll have to switch roles."

Tosh gave him a puzzled look.

"I can cause one hell of a ruckus, Tosh. And think of all the goods Daisy could fit in one of those pregnant-lady dresses!"

*   *   *   *

Tosh and Crosby passed out early that evening after wasting the entire day drinking and playing Go Fish.

They woke up the following morning at the crack of dawn. Tosh plodded into the mini-mart for some coffees as Crosby straightened up the van for their trip to San Francisco.

When Tosh returned, Crosby had his head buried in the engine block between the two front seats. "Uh-oh," he said. "What's up?"

"I don't know. I just got it open. Took me fifteen minutes just to get all the crap off of the engine cover."

"It won't start?"

"Won't turn over. Doesn't even come close."

"What do you think it is?"

"I have no idea, dude."

"Let's wake up Baxter. He's a mechanic."

They walked over to Baxter's pickup where he and Daisy slept peacefully in the back, sandwiched between quilts and blankets.

They look comfortable enough, thought Tosh, *weather permitting.* "I wonder what they do when it rains?" he asked Crosby.

Baxter woke up.

"Mornin', pardner!" Crosby exclaimed.

Baxter rubbed his eyes and sat up. "What time is it?"

"Too early. Unless you're a milkman."

"What do you guys do when it rains?" Tosh asked.

"We got a tent."

"You do?"

"Stole it," said Baxter.

Tosh shook his head affirmatively. "We need your help, big guy. Van won't start."

Baxter lifted his massive body out of the truck and lumbered over to the van, barely keeping his eyes open. The sun had not quite come up, making it difficult to see inside the van.

Baxter poked his head around the engine block, feeling a few wires. He tried to start the van, but had the same results as Crosby. "I don't know what it is. Could be anything."

"What should we do?"

"I got some stuff that might help." Baxter walked back to his truck and returned with a spray can.

"What do you want us to do, paint the engine?" cracked Crosby.

Jokingly, Baxter put Crosby in a headlock and then released him. "This is starter fluid, ya hear?"

Tosh and Crosby, rubbing his neck, nodded.

Baxter handed the can to Tosh and said, "Spray this into the carb while I start the engine."

"The carb?" asked Tosh.

Baxter smiled. "The carburetor."

"Where's that?"

"I'll do it," said Crosby, snatching the can from Tosh.

Baxter turned the ignition and Crosby sprayed the starter fluid and the engine turned over.

"Yee-hah!" said Tosh, holding his palm up. "Thanks, bud!"

"No problem," said Baxter, slapping Tosh five. "You guys keep the stuff. You might need it again."

CHAPTER 14

Twenty thousand half-nude revelers mingled like a colony of ants on a rotten papaya.

Perched on a ridge in the dry northern California countryside, Tosh wiped a drop of perspiration from his eye and peered into the valley below. "Looks like a festival of some sort."

After two hours of winding through the steep, scrubby hills without seeing another human being, Tosh and Crosby had unexpectedly stumbled upon a massive gathering of people and cars scattered around a river that curled like a long black snake along the valley floor. At the core of the gathering was an oval-shaped field with a crescent of colorful stands lining three-quarters of its perimeter. Opposite stood what appeared to be a large box.

"Wow," said Crosby. "What's going on?"

The guys hiked down a little ways to get a better view. Walking along the hillside allowed them a different angle, and Tosh assessed the box to be a stage. He took note of the red, gold and green banners festooning the platform and the bouncy bass rhythm reverberating up the mountainside. "I think," he gasped, "we need to go there."

*   *   *   *

With the help of a generous tailwind, Josephine effortlessly coasted into the canyon. Just as her momentum waned, Tosh and Crosby neared a cluster of California State Troopers.

"Yikes!" Crosby gulped. "Didn't expect this."

"Where's the weed?" asked Tosh.

"In the glove compartment."

"Good place for it."

"Shut up and hide your head," said Crosby. "Those locks are just screaming to be busted."

"This is a reggae festival, dude. There's probably a thousand dreads here."

Tosh and Crosby's anxiety was uncalled for. To their delight, the Troopers leisurely waved the boys through to the gate where a sunny teenage girl greeted them. She wore a green T-shirt with the word **SECURITY** across the chest in white capital letters.

"Hi," said the girl. "Welcome to Reggae on the River."

"Reggae on the River?" asked Tosh. He looked up to the sky. "Thank you, thank you, thank you."

"May I see your tickets?"

"Tickets?"

"You need tickets to get in," she said matter-of-factly.

Tosh pounded his head on the steering wheel.

"Are you Security?" asked Crosby, tantalized by the thought of her frisking him. He would have paid good money to have the lithe teenager pat him down.

"No, Event Staff," she smiled. "They ran out of shirts. This was all they had left."

"Listen," whispered Tosh. "We don't have tickets. But we've come all the way from New Jersey, and we were hoping maybe we could get in."

"New Jersey?" The girl glanced inside the van and then looked at Tosh and Crosby, who pleaded with their eyes like hungry dogs at the kitchen table. "That's a tough one, guys. I don't know if I can swing it."

"Do you know how *far* New Jersey is?" Tosh's voice quivered with desperation.

"I'll tell you what," she said, glancing over her shoulder. "Come back in an hour. My supervisor will be on lunch break."

"You rule," said Tosh.

"I agree with him," Crosby added.

She smiled and stepped back from the van.

"Hey, in the meantime, do you know of a place where we can grab some supplies?"

"Sure. Just keep on heading down that road there. You'll hit a market in a couple of miles. It'll be on your left side."

"Thank you much, sistah. We'll catch you in an hour." Tosh put the van in reverse and did a three-point turnaround. As they pulled away, he caught the girl's eye and saluted her.

"Toodeloo," she said.

*   *   *   *

Crosby sang with his own version of a Caribbean accent, "Come on Mister tolly mon, tolly mi banana."

The silver-haired woman ringing up their bundle of young green bananas shot him an annoyed glance.

"Twenty dollars and six cents."

Tosh handed her a twenty and a dime and told her to keep the change.

"The ice is outside to the left," she grumbled. "You only get two bags."

"We can do math," assured Crosby.

"I'm not so sure."

They decided to let the comment slide, holding their tongues while they bagged their groceries. Besides the bananas and ice, Tosh and Crosby had picked up granola bars, grapes, green peas and a case of the Beast, Milwaukee's Best.

219

Outside the store, Crosby lifted a couple of bags of ice out of the cooler and dropped them on to the pavement, attempting to break up the cubes that had bonded together to form a frozen, ten-pound boulder. He gently molested the bags with his bare feet, enjoying the cool sensation. Satisfied with his job, he added the ice to the cans that Tosh had deposited into the cooler. "Don't they look cozy?" he said.

"Hey, Cros, we forgot suntan lotion."

"Nope," said Crosby, pulling a bottle of Hawaiian Tropic out of his shorts. He flaunted the lotion with a big grin. "Baxter style."

"Dude, that's not cool."

"Gotta cut corners somewhere."

"I can't support that, man."

"What's the big deal? It was just one bottle of suntan lotion." Crosby put the cooler in the back of the van and took a seat behind the wheel. "Don't give me the high and mighty morality speech."

"It's not the morality," said Tosh. "It's the karma I'm afraid of."

"What?"

"What comes around, goes around. I don't want the bad karma coming our way."

"Well, it's too late," said Crosby, starting the van.

Tosh pulled the door shut and hopped up front next to Crosby. "Don't worry about it. I just won't use it."

"Fine." Crosby pulled the van onto the highway, heading back toward the reggae festival. "You'll avoid the bad karma but get skin cancer instead."

*   *   *   *

The cheerful teenager at the gate said her name was Meg, but Peter would have been more appropriate. For Saint Peter, the gatekeeper of Heaven — where Tosh thought he was.

Not only was it a full weekend of live reggae.

Not only was the sky clear, the air clement and the river refreshing.

Not only was there an endless supply of fine Humboldt County herb.

Not only were there thousands of people partying like there was no tomorrow.

To top it all off, a generous percentage of them were topless women. (And some bottomless as well.)

This made Tosh and Crosby very, very happy.

They entered the festival along a gravel road. Sport utility vehicles, campers, vans, pick-up trucks and Volkswagen Busses crammed the area, all packed to the brim with camping equipment and party supplies. Scattered among the field of steel and chrome, tents popped up like dandelions, while multi-colored tarps stretched between cars formed little havens of shade for sun-baked festival-goers.

The guys set up camp in a snug niche between a blue Toyota 4Runner and a Subaru Brat with Arizona plates. Eager to join the festivities, they hastily pitched their tent and locked up the van, leaving the windows open a crack for ventilation.

"You have cash?" asked Tosh.

"Yep-po," said Crosby, stuffing a cold can of beer into his shorts pocket. He cracked open the one in his hand and took a sip. "Let's boogie."

*   *   *   *

Tosh knew he had found paradise before even setting foot in the concert area. With every step he and Crosby took, reggae filled the air, pumping out of automobile sound systems as they walked along the line of vehicles. Marley, Tosh, Toots, Bunny Wailer, Burning Spear, Alpha Blondy, Lucky Dube and Culture, among other fine artists, blared from car after car, their hallowed music the perfect soundtrack to such a mirthful scene. People frolicked in the rivers and sun-bathed on the banks. They drank and ate, smoked and smiled, and laughed and danced.

"This," said Tosh, "is irie."

*   *   *   *

"May I have a squirt?"

"Sure, but this is only six," said an earthy blonde girl, rubbing suntan lotion into her slender, tanned arms. "Would you like something stronger?"

"Six works for me," said Tosh, attempting to pry his eyes off her sprightly nipples. He tried to seem nonchalant about the alluring presence of her bare breasts, but his distraction became quite evident when the girl tossed him the lotion and it hit him in the throat.

"Oh, sorry," she giggled.

"Don't be. Don't be sorry one bit."

As Tosh stood on the riverbank and applied the lotion to his face and upper body, he heard splashing. He looked to the river and saw Crosby approaching him with great hurdling strides. "Hey Tosh," Crosby called, "I've never seen so many titties in my life!"

Barely recovered from the embarrassment of getting caught gawking at the girl's breasts, Crosby's comment blew Tosh's cool cover completely. He nodded and tried to hide his chagrin by attempting a casual "Yeah," but his voice quivered with self-consciousness. He wanted to make like an ostrich and plant his skull in the sand.

"You like mine?" laughed the girl, turning around toward Crosby and wiggling her boobs playfully.

As she waded into the river, Tosh could see that her bikini bottom verged on a thong. *She doesn't have a modest bone in her body,* he thought.

*   *   *   *

Tosh and Crosby introduced themselves to the topless blonde.

Her name was Missy, she grew up in Utah and had studied literature at the University of Colorado at Boulder. After graduating, she moved to Aspen and had been "ski-bumming" — teaching snowboarding to kids and waitressing at a downtown tavern.

Missy stood about five-foot-six and had a toned body that befit her avid snowboarding. Sun streaks saturated her sandy, shoulder-length hair, and a few faint freckles powdered her high cheekbones and dainty nose. Her eyes were as green as a patch of virgin Bermuda real estate. The only flaw in her striking features was a slight snaggletooth, which, combined with the freckles, kind of gave her the look of a pubescent teenager. Her breasts were certainly beyond pubescence, however.

Crosby squeezed a generous dab of spf6 into his palm and, at Missy's request, began to rub it into her back.

"Make sure you don't miss anywhere. I don't want to burn," she said.

"Believe me, I won't," said Crosby. "I won't miss a single spot."

"So where are you guys from?"

"New Jersey."

"You came all the way from New Jersey for this?"

"That's what we told the girl at the gate," said Tosh. "She let us in without tickets, bless her sweet soul."

"Actually, we've been driving cross-country," Crosby added. "Searching for the Ultimate Burrito."

"The Ultimate Burrito?"

"Yep," Tosh and Crosby answered simultaneously.

"That's pretty cool. What have you found?"

"We've found a lot," said Tosh.

"But not it," said Crosby, massaging lotion into Missy's neck.

"That feels good," Missy groaned. "Have you tried the burrito stand up by the concert area?"

"No, we just got here a little while ago."

"You should check it out. They look pretty good."

Tosh nodded. "So, how's life in Aspen?"

"It doesn't get much better than there," said Missy. "I love Aspen."

"Except maybe for here, huh?"

"Definitely. This place is amazing. This is my third Reggae on the River. I don't plan on missing it, ever."

"Nice life," Tosh said with a trace of jealousy. "Living in the Rockies, skiing for a living, skipping out to northern Cal for reggae festivals..."

Playfully rubbing it in, Missy responded, "I usually hit Mardis Gras too."

"Really?"

"Yeah. It's a trip."

"What a life."

"You could have it, too," she said.

Crosby added a second coat of suntan lotion to the spots he had already hit, not wanting to remove his hands from Missy's body. She did not object. (Or didn't notice.)

"I wish," said Tosh.

"Why can't you?"

"Career. I gotta find a career."

"Why?"

"I don't know," said Tosh, cracking open his second beer. "To make money, I guess."

"I pay the rent," Missy pointed out.

"Yeah, but, I mean, do you plan on doing that for the rest of your life?"

"I don't know. Maybe. If I feel like it."

"Then why did you bother going to school?" joked Crosby. "You could have taught snowboarding and waitressed without a sixty thousand dollar education."

Missy turned around and frowned at him. "Just because I don't aspire to a long-term career, doesn't mean my education was a waste of money. Its value is not measured by the job I have."

"Sorry," said Crosby, "I didn't mean to sound cynical. It's just that I worked my ass off to pay my way through school and for a moment, there, it just seemed kind of ironic. It was a stupid thing to say."

"It's O.K.," said Missy. "You can make up for it by giving me another massage. I think my neck needs more lotion."

Crosby was glad Missy didn't hold grudges.

"I don't know what I want to do," said Tosh, picking up where he had left off, "but I don't think I'd be happy doing what you do, waiting tables and all. I hate coins."

Missy laughed. "Well, that's your choice. But don't say that you can't have this life, because you can. All you have to do is choose it."

"What about your chest?" asked Crosby with a fresh palm-full of Coppertone.

"What about it?" asked Missy.

"Do you want me to put suntan lotion on it?"

Missy grabbed the lotion from Crosby's hand. "No thanks. I can reach those," she said.

Tosh raised an eyebrow at his friend.

"What?" asked Crosby. "It was worth a shot."

*   *   *   *

The guy selling Ganja Goo-Balls along the gravel road looked like he had sampled a few too many. He wore ripped denim cut-offs and a pair of dingy two-dollar flip-flops. His long stringy hair looked as if he had just stuck his tongue in an electrical socket.

"Two dollars each, three for five," he droned to no one in particular.

"Three for five, is that the family plan?" said Crosby, gently elbowing Tosh in the ribs — a nod to their bracelet-selling slogan.

"Huh?" said the man.

Crosby repeated himself. "Three for five, is that the family plan?"

The man answered with a bland, "I guess."

"What's in them?" asked Tosh.

"It's a secret recipe, man."

"Just tell us," prompted Crosby. "I promise we won't tell anyone else."

The man looked unconvinced.

"Just tell us the basic ingredients," reasoned Tosh. "So we'll know if we'll like them."

The guy rolled his head slowly and said, "Nuts, granola, honey, molasses." He riveted his eyes on Tosh and Crosby and said, "And a healthy amount of Humboldt County's finest."

"Anything else in there?" asked Tosh. "I mean, are they dusted or anything? 'Cause I-man naw sniff de cocaine. I-man only smoke de sensimilla."

The guy looked offended by this question. "No, man, strictly cannabis. Strictly cannabis, man."

"You've got a deal. Give us three," said Crosby.

"How strong are they?" asked Tosh.

The guy smiled and croaked, "They're pretty strong, man."

"How much should we eat?"

"One per person should set you right for the day, man."

Crosby handed the guy a five-spot. "And we can split the third one for a little night-cap, right?"

"Dessert," said the man, taking three Goo-Balls out of his cardboard box with his sweaty hands. He placed them in a baggie and said, "If you want more, I'll be here tomorrow."

*   *   *   *

Tosh and Crosby strolled further down the gravel road, on their way toward the concert area to get the burritos Missy had mentioned.

"We must be insane," said Crosby. "Because I can't believe we bought something from that freak."

"He was O.K.," said Tosh.

"Better judgment would have been to *not* buy anything from that guy, especially food."

"Here's to." Tosh bit into a sticky Ganja Goo-Ball. "Na ba," he said, chewing like he had stuffed his mouth to the teeth with peanut-butter and Rice Krispies.

Crosby passed him a fresh beer. "What do they taste like?"

After swallowing and washing down the mixture with the suds, Tosh said, "Kind of earthy."

"Earthy? What do you mean, they taste like dirt?"

"They taste kind of healthy, actually."

"I can live with that," said Crosby, eyeing up the psychedelic treat. "I don't know what looks more repulsive, though, these Goo-Balls or the dude that sold us 'em. If I saw that dude in New York City and he tried to sell me a gnarly —"

"Will you eat it?"

"— greenish-brown —"

"Just eat it!"

"— with things stickin' out of it—"

"Eat it Crosby!"

Crosby ate it.

*   *   *   *

Bouncing to the calypso band on stage, Tosh and Crosby surveyed the concert area's dining options. What a smorgasbord! The exciting array of ethnic eateries was a welcome alternative to Tosh and Crosby's repetitive and often bland road meals.

A Thai stand offered heaping plates of Pad Thai — stir-fried rice noodles with broccoli, bean sprouts, tofu, snow peas and crushed peanuts.

Wo's Chinee Foo had vegetarian spring rolls — cabbage, carrots and string beans wrapped in a thin dough and wokked until crispy.

Kovalum, a booth cooking Indian cuisine, offered Dal Makhni — lentils fried in butter with onions, tomatoes, ginger and garlic.

Rocky's Jamaican Hut served jerked chicken and goat — seasoned with scallions, hot pepper, garlic and cane vinegar, roasted slowly in a giant metal grill — and Calaloo patties, a baked pastry filled with the West Indian equivalent of spinach.

Suddenly, the thought of another burrito didn't seem so enticing.

Every quest needs focus and commitment, because distractions always abound. Tosh and Crosby's search for the Ultimate Burrito was no different. In order to stay true to their pursuit, they would have to overcome procrastination and shun digression. That meant walking straight up to the burrito booth despite the wide variety of food to choose from.

Tosh felt irrevocably drawn to the jerk hut, knowing the meat would be as spicy as the music he was listening to. He acknowledged the notion of abandoning their mission and eyed the burrito booth with a twinge of guilt. "Should we get the burritos?"

Crosby did not answer. A portly Latin woman cooking arepas held his attention. He practically drooled while watching her melt mozzarella between two grilled corn pancakes, dripping with butter. "I'm all over that," he groaned.

"What about the burritos?"

"Screw the burritos,*"* said Crosby as he handed the woman two dollars.

She scooped up an arepa with her spatula and served it to Crosby in a sheet of wax paper. "Napkin?" she asked.

"Please."

"I'm not really in the mood for a burrito right now either," said Tosh, "but we owe it to ourselves to try one. It might be the one."

"We owe it to ourselves to try some of this good food. We'll try the burritos tomorrow."

"Tomorrow sounds good to me." Tosh clapped his hands and left to get some jerked chicken.

Crosby held his newly purchased arepa up to his mouth and giddily whispered to it, "Mamacita, variety is the spice of life."

The Latin woman looked at him strangely, shook her head and muttered, "Ay de mi."

*   *   *   *

Crosby sat Indian style on the grass and wrapped his lips around the arepa. He felt its warmth and sucked a little grease onto his tongue. His stomach growled. Sinking his teeth into the sinful treat, he found the corn patties to be crispy on the outside and moist and buttery on the inside. The flavor of mozzarella immediately filled his palate, but Crosby's incisors couldn't bite through it. He pulled the arepa a good distance away from him, hoping the melted cheese might break off, but it wouldn't snap. He sucked in the elastic band of mozzarella like a piece of spaghetti and tried another pull. No luck.

Enough of this, he thought. His stomach begged him to swallow.

He broke the string of cheese with his fingers and stuffed it into his mouth. Crosby chewed diligently, savoring the taste, and washed down each bite with a sip of his beer.

"This is so good," he moaned.

After ingesting the last of his dish, Crosby licked his lips and wiped his mouth on the back of his hand. He leaned back on the ground and burped, concluding that the arepa might have been the most delectable treat in his entire life, better than even a marijuana munchie-binge.

And his Ganja Goo-Ball buzz hadn't even kicked in yet.

*   *   *   *

Tosh's Ganja Goo-Ball buzz had kicked in. He felt lightheaded and flighty, yet more relaxed than lethargic. Bobbing and weaving his way through the dancing crowd, he inched closer to the stage, settling in a spot where the music was loud but not overbearing.

Tosh liked the sound. It was definitely roots reggae — a steady, deliberate skank of the keyboards, a lively brass section and a fat bass melody that bounced along like a jellyfish in a hurricane.

Tosh stared at the three Rastas with long nappy dreads standing behind microphones at the front of the stage. Squinting in the bright sunlight, he could barely make out the expressions on their faces. The musicians sang passionately, harmonizing like experts over the tight reggae beat. The blend of voices seemed familiar and so did the song they were singing.

Who was this band?

A glint of sunlight reflected off of something — something shiny and metallic. A microphone stand?

Fixing his stoned gaze on the stand, Tosh saw the glimmer again, but it came from somewhere else, something moving; the microphone stand had remained stationary.

Was it some type of jewelry? A gold bracelet or maybe a watch?

The band wrapped up the song they had been singing and Tosh clapped along with the applause. One of the singers saluted the crowd by waving a steel pole of some sort, most likely the cause of the shimmering sunlight.

As the band launched into their next number, Tosh instantly recognized it. Suddenly, the identity of the band and the mystery of the reflections all came together for him. The band was Israel Vibration, one of Tosh's favorite reggae groups, and the metal pole shining in the sun was a crutch.

In the late 1950s, a polio epidemic hit Jamaica. As youths, the members of Israel Vibration had all been stricken by the disabling virus. They met in a rehabilitation center, where they shared a love of music. Their paths traversed now and then as they grew up, switching from one institution to another. The trio reunited as young men, finding a common bond in the faith of Rastafari. They would pass the time smoking herb, reading the Bible and singing. When they sang, passersby became bystanders, riveted by the magical blend of their distinct voices, urging them to record their music. Over the years, Israel Vibration spread Jah Word from the yards of Jamaica to every corner of the world, not despite their affliction, but because of it.

Tosh couldn't believe his luck. For years, he had wanted to see "I-Vibes" in concert. Now, beside a crystalline river in the middle of the sultry Humboldt countryside, he found them performing, as if led to the resplendent oasis by Jah himself.

The sun felt warm on Tosh's cheeks, hot on his bare back as he danced jubilantly, swinging his arms, swaying his shoulders and stepping in place to the bubbly beat. The crowd around him moved similarly, yet each and every person had their own unique moves, their own style, thousands of people expressing themselves individually while enjoying a common love, sharing an exhilarating experience. The vibes of freedom, happiness and harmony were as tangible as the odors of incense and marijuana that, despite the wide-open sky above, saturated the air and filled Tosh's nose with every breath.

Adding to the merriment, Israel Vibration hopped and whirled and dipped and twirled as they sang, completely uninhibited by the steel crutches that braced their forearms, no less agile than a disco biscuit from *Saturday Night Fever.*

After a carousing hour or so, Israel Vibration announced they would play one final song. The audience's momentary disappointment dissipated as soon as the band began "Live In Jah Love," a definite crowd favorite. People lit thick spliffs, high-fived each other and boogied extra-fervently during the seven-minute paean to peace and unity.

When the song ended, I-Vibes took a humble bow and trod off the stage triumphantly. Through the keen perception of his potent marijuana high, Tosh scanned the pack of people. Most were smiling or laughing, all radiated kindness. Tosh couldn't stop grinning himself, filled with joy from his toes up to his dreadlocks.

This, he thought, *is what Bob Marley meant when he sang, "Positive Vibration."*

*   *   *   *

Lying on his stomach in cool, clear, knee-deep water, Crosby watched the red triangle rise from the river. He kept his sunglasses on. Being extremely high, Crosby knew his heavy eyes must have been bloodshot. The tributary seemed stoned too, its lackadaisical current exerting no force as it flowed gently around him.

Crosby kept a keen eye on the red triangle, floating there, inches above the river.

Slightly submerged like a crocodile, he moved toward it slowly. His mouth rested below the surface of the water, his nose and eyes just above it. Buoyant, he balanced his horizontal self on the palms of his hands. Digging his fingers into the rounded pebbles of the riverbed, he stepped forward with his arms.

The red triangle jiggled daintily, beckoning him.

Crosby approached cautiously, scheming to strike decisively at the last moment with his greatest weapon — his ravenous jaws. In one swift motion, he would clutch the red triangle and tear it to shreds.

That moment came closer.

And closer.

He was there.

The red triangle clung to the crescents of the woman's behind like plastic wrap on a cantaloupe. Crosby ducked under the water and poised himself to spring from the river. Bending his arms, he lifted off and...

... hit his head against something soft and rubbery? Stuck under the water beneath a large, heavy object, Crosby momentarily panicked. After the initial shock wore off, however, he regained his wits. The river was only three feet deep, so the vessel above him could not have been the Titanic.

Crosby tried to push the rubber thing off of him but it would not budge. *Now,* he thought, *I know what it feels like to be a sperm.* He swam out from under the object and shot out of the water. As he surfaced beside it, two streams of water pelted him in the head and chest.

"Got him!"

Crosby ducked back under the water instinctively. Somebody was shooting water guns at him — not wimpy pistols but big guns, heavy-duty artillery.

He came up the next time better prepared for an assault. Bracing himself to get hit by more ammo, Crosby stood still and flexed his arms in a Herculean gesture. He took hits in the chin and right nipple.

"We got the shark!"

He recognized the voice as Tosh's. "I'm an *alligator!*" Crosby called, "Sharks are *salt* water!"

Tosh sat in an inflatable round raft with some dude in Day-Glo orange surfer shorts. His conservative short brown hair, beer belly and lack of tattoos or body piercings seemed out of place at the hippie festival. "Rest assured, lady," he said to the girl in the red bikini bottom that Crosby had been scoping, "we got the alligator!"

The girl exchanged an amused glance with her friend, who wore a green bikini bottom. "You saved my life," she gasped in jest.

"Just another day at work for the Spliff Patrol."

"The Spliff Patrol?" asked Crosby.

"Hop in, bro."

As Crosby clambered aboard, the dude held out a joint to the girl in the red bikini. "Spliff?"

The girl thanked him and took a puff.

"Can I get some of that?" asked her friend.

"That's why we're here," said the dude, reaching out to place the joint on her lips.

"You girls look like two-thirds of the Rasta Bikini Team, said Tosh. "All you need is a yellow one."

"Got her," said the green-bikini girl. "She's around."

"Are you serious?"

"Of course."

"Take me home with you," Tosh begged.

"We'll think about it."

When the girls finished smoking, the dude introduced himself to Crosby. "Name's Santilli. Welcome to the Spliff Patrol."

"Thanks, man."

Santilli handed Crosby his paddle. "Onward, men," he instructed as he popped open a Heineken.

"Hey Santilli," asked Crosby, "why do I get the feeling you've been to Reggae on the River before?"

*   *   *   *

Tosh and Crosby maneuvered the inflatable raft down the river at a leisurely pace, steered by Santilli's hand commands as he briefed Crosby on the mission of the Spliff Patrol.

"We do not discriminate. The Spliff Patrol spares no one. We are here to uplift the attitude of everyone — men, women, young, old, fat, skinny, ugly, pretty, black, white, yellow, green, purple." Santilli held his Heineken up to the sun and took a hefty gulp.

"Do you really think people here need their attitudes uplifted?" asked Crosby.

"You can always get higher," Santilli remarked. He pointed to a couple sitting on a cooler on the bank. "That-a-way."

"What if they don't want it?"

"That's what these are for," Santilli said, patting his trusty water-Uzi. "If they refuse the spliff, we hit 'em with the Super Soakers. No exceptions."

The couple on the cooler both took big hits and the boys left them coughing up clouds of white smoke. "You don't cough, you don't get off," Santilli yelled.

The Spliff Patrol drifted down the river, pausing for every person within reach, whether partying on the banks or lounging in the river. Along the way, they burned two tampon-sized joints, subjecting only a few people to the barrage of the Super Soakers. The greetings they received were as colorful and diverse and wacky as the people they encountered.

"Cool," said a librarian-looking woman in a tie-dyed sundress. "Thanks, guys."

"Lay it on me," said a buff, crew-cut dude.

"I'd love to," exclaimed a woman old enough to be their grandmother.

"Hemp it up! Hemp it up!"

"Feed me."

"Bring it on."

"Gimme the herb!"

"What is that, weed?"

"I need a miracle."

"I just say no." (He just got soaked.)

"Oh baby," moaned a middle-aged lady bulging out of a string bikini.

"One love."

"You guys are the greatest!"

"Irie," said a Rastaman with wraparound shades.

"Peace."

"Love."

"Want a beer?"

"Kiss me, Santilli." (Santilli's girlfriend.)

"No doubt."

"Lick it up."

"Mawi-wanna?" asked a skinny, balding, Japanese guy. "Oh, vedy good. Tank you, tank you."

"I'm on the cakes, man."

"Step lively."

"Yes-I!"

"Have you seen my ferret?"

"Smoke 'em if ya got 'em!"

"Positive!"

"And it stoned me," sang a chubby guy with a bottle of rum, sitting on a submerged lawn chair.

"Wonder Twin powers, activate!"

"Level vibes, man. The *I* thanks you."

"Time to get loopy."

A ten-year old with a Mohawk sang, "Eat, bite, fuck, suck, gobble nibble chew, nipple bosom hair-pie, finger-fuck, screw." (He got spanked and was excused from further punishment from the Spliff Patrol.)

"One toke over the line."

"Jah provide."

"Jah guide.

"It's all too beautiful."

"We're kicked," said Santilli, flinging the microscopic remains of the last joint into the air. "All gone."

As if on cue, Kelly, Santilli's girlfriend, appeared on the banks of the river, waving another joint.

"All right. Just in time."

Tosh jumped out to take a dip in the river and pushed the raft over toward Kelly.

Santilli gave his girlfriend a kiss and took the joint from her. "Excuse me while I light my spliff," Santilli sang as he held the lighter up to it — a line from "Easy Skanking," Bob Marley's homage to reggae and ganja.

Tosh responded with the next line: "Oh God I got to take a lift..."
Back to Santilli: "From reality I just can't drift..."
"That's why I'm staying with this riff!"
"The Spliff Patrol's theme song," declared Crosby.
Santilli breathed the bone deep into his lungs. "Fe real."
Tosh hopped back into the raft and said, "I like you, Santilli. I like you a lot, mi breddah."
Santilli passed him the joint.
The guys floated by a couple who looked to be in their mid-fifties or so. They sat at a folding table in the middle of the river, sipping cocktails and playing cards.
"What're you playing?"
"Gin Rummy," said the man, without looking up.
"I could go for some gin," Crosby remarked.
"I could go for some rum," added Tosh.
Santilli held the spliff out to the couple and then turned back to Tosh and Crosby. "Seek, and ye shall find."

*   *   *   *

The "Spliff Patrol" ran out of river before they ran out of ganja. Rather than double back upstream, the boys elected to finish the fatty themselves.
Tosh, Crosby and Santilli tucked their Super Soakers under their arms and lugged the inflatable raft back to Santilli's van, where Santilli announced he needed to sleep. Tosh and Crosby bid him happy napping and intended to return to their van to do the same, but when they got back, Peter Tosh rang out of a nearby sound system, so Tosh opted for a fresh beer instead. Naturally, Crosby decided to join him.
Two thirds of the way through their next round of beers, a near comatose hippie in soiled shorts and a ripped Jerry Garcia tee shirt strolled by holding a large mushroom over his head.
"C'mere!" Tosh called. "Whatcha got there, dude?"
The hippie didn't speak, but instead placed the mushroom under Tosh's chin for further inspection.
"Let me see that," said Crosby.
The hippie turned and showed his product to Crosby.
"These good?"
The hippie nodded.
"How much for an eighth?" Tosh asked.
"Thirty."
"Can we see a bag?"
The hippie unzipped his Guatemalan fanny pack and carefully removed a plastic sandwich bag. He unrolled it and held it out for Tosh to examine.

"Looks pretty good," Tosh said. "Cros, what do you th—"
Crosby held out a hand full of money.

*   *   *   *

Once the mushrooms kicked in, it didn't matter that Tosh and Crosby had heads full of booze and marijuana. Psilocybin packs a powerful punch. Like a lead dog, it takes charge of the mind, relegating vast quantities of alcohol and THC to the back of the pack to merely help with the ride.

It hits in waves. As the psilocybin begins to take effect, periods of what seems like normality are interrupted by fleeting visual aberrations, a rash of giggles and difficulty with reasoning. During the peak effects of the drug, this evolves into full-fledged hallucinations, a fascination with light, hysterical laughter and no cognitive powers whatsoever. As the mushrooms begin to wear off, the experience likens itself to the first phase.

Tosh and Crosby were peaking. One moment, they would be strolling through the concert area engaged in a barely coherent conversation, the next they would be laughing hysterically at nothing they would remember the following day.

The intensity of every little thing they experienced grew exponentially, and at Reggae on the River, there was a lot to experience. People played devil sticks, drums and didgeridoos. Giant soap bubbles floated through the air while dreadlocked puppets, twenty feet tall, maneuvered through the crowd. And just overhead, reflective kites with long dangling tails danced without the aid of wind.

Tosh and Crosby found themselves completely enthralled by anything illuminated. A woman dancing with torches gave them a real charge, and a man juggling glow-in-the-dark balls mesmerized them for a half hour.

But nothing made them laugh as much as the Stick Man. Some clever soul donned himself in black clothing and attached green plastic glow-in-the-dark necklaces down his torso, legs and arms and around his face, giving him the appearance of a living, breathing stick figure. He scurried throughout the grounds, performing little jigs for the entertainment of all the stoned people.

To Tosh and Crosby, the Stick Man was nothing less than a phenomenon. They could not get enough of him. Like a couple of fanatic groupies, they followed him, giggling and snorting all the way, until he became unnerved or annoyed by the two freaks tracking him and, with moves that would make a secret agent jealous, ditched them.

After the Stick Man deserted them, Tosh and Crosby wandered up to a drum circle. On bongos of varying sizes, nine people methodically pounded the skins while a horde of tripping hippies danced around them. Tosh and Crosby began by merely observing from the outskirts of the gathering, but as the drummers gradually worked up to a frenzied tribal rhythm, it grew, and Tosh and Crosby found themselves sucked into the center of the surrounding scene. The energy was contagious and soon they began moving as well, feeding off the collective electricity, gyrating in all sorts of weird and wild ways without shame or modesty.

Ahh, mushrooms.

*   *   *   *

Crosby had to take a leak. Though he was grooving on the music and a hippie chick with a man-in-the-moon tattoo on her lower back dancing in front of him, he could not ignore a day's worth of beer trying to make an exit.

He looked at Tosh, jamming to the music with his eyes closed and his head tilted back. He shouted in his ear that he was going to the bathroom, and Tosh acknowledged him by opening his eyes a slit and nodding slightly.

Crosby had trouble making his way through the crowd in a timely manner. People were packed in tightly and not paying much attention to anything besides the carnivals inside their heads. He prayed there would not be a line waiting for him at the pisser.

His prayers were answered, but Crosby noted something strange about the port-a-potty situation. People waited two and three deep at some toilets, while others had no line at all. It was as if they were like express aisles at the supermarket, 10 items or less, reserved only for those that had an emergency situation unfolding in their groins.

Crosby had an urgent situation, so he went right in. When he entered the port-o-potty, he knew why it had no line. It was full.

And I'm wearing sandals, he thought.

There was no time to turn back, however, so Crosby just let it rip, hoping it could hold another liter or two.

Thankfully, Crosby kept his flip-flopped feet clean.

*   *   *   *

The headline act had begun. Direct from The Ivory Coast, African superstar Alpha Blondy, one of the world's most beloved reggae musicians, took the stage amid hoots and hoorays of total adoration from the audience.

Alpha Blondy had never come to New York as long as Tosh had been a fan, and it had been years since he had even toured the United States. Tosh often wondered if he would ever get to see him perform, but now, thanks to a kind turn of fate, his favorite living reggae artist stood before him.

*   *   *   *

Crosby got glittered.

As if extremely loud, hypnotic reggae, a throng of freaky hippies and psilocybin seizing control of his senses weren't enough, Crosby had to contend with smears of silver sparkles under his eyes.

A pubescent girl had appeared in front of him holding up a finger laden with body glitter. Wide-eyed, she smiled. Crosby smiled back, which apparently gave permission for the girl to glitter him up.

Gazing into his shining eyes, she whispered, "Welcome to my Glitter World."

"Glitter World?" he asked. "What's that?"

She moved on without answering him.

Crosby soon understood. He wandered aimlessly, bewitched by the lights flashing before his eyes.

Crosby looked up. He saw shooting stars.

Crosby looked out. On the highway that ran along the ridge, the headlights of eighteen-wheelers streaked through the trees.

Crosby looked down. Lights from the stage reflected off the glitter around his eyes.

Crosby shut his eyes. He saw swirls of color shifting shapes in the blackness of his eyelids.

Much of the time, he didn't know where the flashes were coming from. They could have been from the heavens or from his face, in the night or in his mind, but while the music of Alpha Blondy shook the earth beneath his feet, Crosby enjoyed his mushroom-enhanced Glitter World, a personal fireworks display without the booms.

*   *   *   *

English, Hebrew, French, Dioula and Arabic. Alpha Blondy sang in five different tongues, sometimes using multiple languages within the same song. Since Tosh only knew English and a little bit of Spanish, which was not in the singer's repertoire, he could not understand much of what Alpha sang.

It didn't matter.

From the first tap of a drum until the last stroke of a guitar string, with every push of a key, Alpha Blondy's band generated a spellbinding groove. From walls of amplifiers piled forty feet high on both sides of the stage, an ocean of sublime sound washed over the audience and up the surrounding hills to touch the sky, where, infused with celestial energy, it crested and rolled back down to gently envelop the people with fuzzy warmth.

Tosh swam through the music with no regrets, no fears, no concerns and no thoughts of the past or future whatsoever. He could feel every cell of his body filling with love, white heat spreading from the tips of his toes to the frayed fibers at the end of every tangled hair in his near shoulder-length dreadlocks. It was genuine rapture, unexaggerated by his psyche yet not completely pure, fueled by the drugs in his system, helping him to reach a crescendo of happiness so high it bordered on bliss, a state unattainable in normal consciousness.

Don't fear, my child, for though you may often be filled with questions and doubt, know that I am real. I have been here from the beginning and I will be here always.

Tosh did not hear the words. He felt them. They seemed to come not from the outside, but from within him, his chest and abdomen, his core, as if the energy flowing through his body had become the message.

A huge, puffy, white-gloved hand, like that of a giant Pillsbury Doughboy, reached down from the sky and gently patted him on the rear end.

Go now, my child, live your life without fear. Go anywhere, do anything, be anyone. Keep peace in your heart, for no matter how you may drift or waiver, I will remain.

Oh...oh....oh... wow, he thought. *What was that?* Tosh felt supported, as though he could recline in mid-air, and he wondered if he was floating. He opened his eyes to make sure his feet were indeed planted on the ground. People milled about in varying states of inebriation, happily doing their own thing, oblivious to what he had just felt. It seemed no one else had sensed the cosmic energy flowing through him or seen God's hand pat him on the behind.

"Mushrooms?" asked a voice. It came from a hippie-chick standing next to him.

Holy shit, Tosh thought. *She knows.*

"Yeah," he sighed. "Mushrooms, man. Whew. Damn."

"How much do you want?"

Want?

Tosh realized the hippie-chick had no idea he was tripping his face off. She had not perceived what he had just experienced. She was only selling mushrooms.

Tosh definitely did not need any more mushrooms. "No thanks, man," he gasped. "I'm perfect."

*   *   *   *

Though his mental jigsaw puzzle lay in a thousand scattered pieces, Crosby remained horny, a true tribute to his hyperactive hormones. He thought of a topless Missy and got a hard-on. Since his mind was of no use to him at the moment, he decided to follow his dick, both figuratively and literally. Crosby headed whichever way his erect penis pointed and, somehow, whether due to some psychic sexual intuition, a shred of logic or just sheer luck, he found Missy on the verge of retiring to her tent.

According to the norm, people wore clothes during the daytime hours and slept in the nude. (Or in some state of semi-nakedness, depending on the person.) Reggae on the River was not the norm.

The California heat and immodest, hippie vibe made for a lot more bare skin than usual and a definite scarcity of tan lines. Yet, even in the middle of summer, when the sun dipped below the mountains, the air got chilly. So, with the sun tucked in for the night, much to Crosby's disappointment, Missy had traded in her skimpy bikini bottom for some more substantial clothing. But if things went as he had hoped, she'd be naked again before the sun made its next appearance.

*   *   *   *

Tosh meandered along the road like a cow. Spending the day in the hot California sun, compounded with the synergistic effect of the weed and beers, not to mention the Goo-ball buzz, made Tosh feel woozy and sluggish. The mushrooms had pretty much worn off along with the thrill of his cosmic experience, which he had pretty much written off to the mushrooms. Fighting both the fog in his head and the darkness around him, he scanned the small city of tents, trying, with much difficulty, to recall where he and Crosby had parked their van earlier that day.

After an entire day and night on his feet, Tosh's legs hurt. He ached to shed his sweaty clothes from his body, curl up in his sleeping bag and shut his eyes.

Plus, he was hungry.

Tosh wandered for an indefinite period of time, weaving around cars and comforters, trucks and tarps. Nothing looked familiar. With his frustration developing into despair, he caught the sound of Ziggy Marley coming from a nearby stereo. *Forget your troubles and dance,* he thought, a quote from a Bob Marley song. Putting his predicament out of his mind for a few moments, Tosh leaned up against a Nissan pickup to rest and enjoy the song.

Tosh gazed at the moon, perched in the sky like a giant golf ball. "Jah," he said under his breath, "if yuh listenin', please guide I home. I-man tired and mi wan get some rest so tomorrow, mi have energy fe dance to Jah reggae music."

Despite his languor and lousy circumstances, Tosh smiled. For some reason, speaking in the Jamaican cadence always made him feel good.

When the Ziggy song ended, Tosh took a deep breath and set out again in search of their tent. He walked two car-lengths and stopped in his tracks, astonished. There, in the silver-blue light of the moon, sat Josephine.

Tosh stumbled up to the van and kissed her as if she were a coddling mother. After letting himself in, he kicked off his shorts and slipped into a pair of boxers. Before passing out, in a fervent, marijuana-induced bacchanalia, Tosh devoured their entire stash of granola bars and eighty-three percent of their grapes.

*   *   *   *

Crosby got his wish. He did not have to wait until the next day for Missy to shed her clothing again.

Naturally, this time, Crosby joined her in nudity, and after what he deemed an adequate amount of foreplay (Missy probably would have enjoyed a little more), he pulled a condom out of his pocket. In the lantern light inside Missy's tent, he held the contraceptive up to see which side to tear open.

Missy gasped. "No way. You're not going to use that thing on me."

Crosby looked down at his manhood and frowned. A twinge of fear shot through his head. "What's wrong with it? Is it too small?"

Missy giggled. "Not *that!*"

"Then what? Do you think it's diseased or something?"

"No, I'm not talking about your *penis,* Crosby. I mean the rubber."

Crosby felt relieved. "Oh."

"You're not using that thing on me."

Crosby tore the package and pulled the condom out of its wrapper. "What's the matter, you don't like rubbers?"

"No, rubbers are fine."

"Then what? What's wrong with it?"

"It's a Trojan."

"Trojan makes a good condom," said Crosby. "They're supposed to be the best."

"I don't care. I don't trust them."

"Why?"

"Because of their name. Trojan does not instill a sense of being protected in me. In fact, I can not think of a less suitable name for a condom."

Crosby unraveled the rubber and inspected it, feeling blue that he would not get the chance to use it. "What's so bad about Trojan?"

"Don't you know the story of the Trojan Horse?"

Aware of the dwindling of his erection, Crosby dejectedly climbed off of Missy. "Tell me the story," he sighed, snuggling up beside her.

"I can't believe you don't know the story of the Trojan Horse."

"Look, I wasn't a Lit major like you, all right?"

Missy put her hand on Crosby's stomach and rubbed him gently. "Sorry."

"It's all right. Tell me the story of the Trojan Horse."

"O.K. The Greeks were at war with the Romans, right?"

"Uh-huh."

"Well, the Greeks built this giant horse and hid a whole bunch of soldiers inside it. Then, they left it outside the gates of Rome as a gift, and sailed just out of sight of the city. The Romans brought the Horse into their city and, in the middle of the night, the Greek soldiers came out of the Horse and opened up the gates of Rome for their countrymen who had returned, allowing them to infiltrate the city."

"Cool," said Crosby, running his hand over Missy's soft skin.

"So, do you see the connection? How could I trust a condom named Trojan? Do you think I want to let all those Greek soldiers into my Rome?"

Crosby felt an ache in his groin. *Damn Lit majors,* he thought.

*   *   *   *

Tosh's feeding frenzy, consisting of a healthy amount of roughage, had chewed its way through his digestive tract throughout the course of the night. Now, as the sun poked up above the horizon, the grapes and granola bars sat at the base of his large intestine, pushing on his rectum with the force of an avalanche.

"Damn it," said Tosh, pushing the turtle back into its shell.

He got up hastily and clambered out of the tent, noticing that Crosby hadn't returned. *What luck,* he thought, *Crosby gets to wake up with a girl, and I get to wake up with a shit.*

Trying to restrain his bowel movement, Tosh hurried awkwardly down the gravel road toward the toilets. He tried to avoid communication with the early birds he passed along the way and tersely acknowledged the ones he couldn't. After an uncomfortable walk, he finally arrived at the "restroom."

A dozen port-o-johns beckoned him. Randomly selecting the third one from the left, Tosh opened the door and stepped in. He had expected something nasty, but nothing could have prepared him for the utter horror he encountered.

The port-o-johns made shitting in the woods seem like a stroll on the beach. The stench made him gag. Cringing at the load of refuse, he could sense the bacteria crawling throughout. Despite the pressure in his gut, Tosh questioned whether he wanted to squat over the wad of waste festering below. He opted to try a different john.

Filling his lungs with the misty morning mountain air slightly spoiled by a septic stench, Tosh held his breath and entered the next one.

No improvement.

He tried another.

Tosh didn't think it could be possible, but this john was even worse, loaded with revolting filth to the brim. A dirty, bloodstained tampon sat atop the heap, mere inches below the toilet seat, like a maraschino cherry on top of an ice cream sundae. Tosh winced and exited the john.

No way, he thought.

As the excrement in the port-o-johns piled higher and higher, using them sank lower and lower into the depths of human experience. Tosh did not want to spend another second inside one of those chambers of wretchedness.

But what other options did he have?

He could try to find a secluded spot in the nearby redwoods, but with twenty thousand people roaming around, the likelihood of someone stumbling upon him at his most vulnerable would be too great.

Despite the discomfort, Tosh would rather tough it out. He'd force the turtle to stay in its shell until after the festival, when he would release it into a private, sanitary pond in the nearest Denny's restroom.

*   *   *   *

Crosby woke up needing food badly. He exited the tent without waking Missy, grabbing one more glimpse of her bare ass and cursing himself for buying Trojans. Why didn't he buy Ramses? Lifestyles? Durex?

Crosby felt a pang of hunger. What would he eat? It was still fairly early in the morning, and none of the food stands at the concert area served breakfast-type foods, with the exception of maybe the fruit-smoothie stand.

He decided to head back to the van and chow-down on some of the snacks they had picked up before the festival. Granola bars and bananas would start him off the right way, especially after the previous day of decadence. Ganja Goo-Balls and arepas did not provide much sustenance.

Propelled by his cavernous stomach, Crosby walked back to Josephine at a New York City pace, much quicker than the hippies lolling off their highs from the night before.

Upon entering the van, instead of granola bars, he found a few honey-glazed oat flakes amidst a pile of foil wrappers. This did not please him. Knowing full well what fate had befallen his breakfast, he plucked a chocolate chip off the carpeting and grumbled, "Damn munchies."

Crosby's stomach rumbled, as if adding snide commentary on the grim discovery. "I don't need your input," he said to his gut as he made a move for the bananas.

The banana situation piqued him even more. The entire cluster had turned an unsavory brown. "Son of a bitch," said Crosby. "What the hell happened? What am I gonna do now?"

He got an idea. Crosby grabbed the mushy bananas and set out for the concert area. Maybe the fruit-smoothie stand would trade him some new bananas for the over-ripe ones.

As he suspected, Juicy Lucy's had opened early to serve fruit shakes as a morning meal for the health-conscious. Behind the counter, a tall, slender man with a handlebar mustache wiped a blender clean. "What can I do for you?" he asked over the whir of a juicer.

Crosby held up his batch of brown bananas. "These were green when I bought them yesterday. What do you think happened to 'em?"

"Did you buy them here?"

"No. We got 'em at a market outside the festival."

"Did you have them in a hot car?"

"Yep."

"That's your problem right there. Too much heat in the car — accelerates the ripening process. Did you hang them?"

"Hang them?"

"Yeah," said the man, stopping the juicer. "You've got to hang bananas up. Keeps them fresh longer."

"Really?"

"Yes, sir."

"I never knew that." Crosby looked at his bananas with a new sense of awe.

"Use a paper clip or a shoelace or something. Keep them from making contact with anything."

"And they won't turn brown?"

The man placed a carrot into the juicer. "It will keep them yellow for a little longer."

That's wild, thought Crosby. "What, are you fooling the bananas into thinking that they're still hanging in the tree?" he joked.

"That's right."

"Really? I was just kidding."

"Well, that's essentially what you're doing. When the bananas feel contact, they think they've fallen from the tree."

Crosby thought about this for a moment. "But bananas don't have brains," he said. "How can they think?"

"They don't actually think," said the fruit guru, digging the core out of a red delicious. "Let me explain what happens. When the bananas grow to a certain weight, they drop to the ground. This contact with the ground triggers a reaction inside the bananas where the carbohydrates begin to turn into sugars. Basically, they rot. The banana gets sweeter, making it more appetizing to an animal who might pass by. That way, the animal is more likely to eat it and disperse the seeds through his feces. The rotting of the bananas is called a seed dispersal mechanism."

"Damn, that's cool."

"Of course, keeping them in the hot car would defeat the purpose of hanging them."

"Right."

"Can I help you with anything else?"

"Actually, I was wondering if maybe you would trade me some fresh bananas for these rotten ones. They're too brown for eating, but I thought maybe you could use them in a shake."

"You want to swap bananas?"

Crosby nodded.

The man inspected the brown bananas. "Tell you what," he said, pouring himself a glass of some bright orange carrot concoction. "I'll throw these in the blender and doctor them up for you. I'll fix you an energy drink that will get your motor running."

"That would be great, man," said Crosby. "I appreciate it."

As the man prepared his special drink, Crosby took note of Juicy Lucy's inventory. Behind the counter, both lined on tables and piled in boxes, he saw apples, blackberries, beets, carrots, cantaloupes, dandelions, eggs, figs, grapes, guavas, honeydew, ice, jacarandas, kiwis, kumquats, lemons, limes, mangoes, nectarines, oranges, pineapples, peaches, pears, papayas, rhubarb, raspberries, strawberries, tamarinds, uva-ursi, watermelons, yogurt, zucchini and, of course, a load of bananas.

"Here you go," said the man, sliding a frothy fruit shake along the counter.

Crosby took a sip on the straw.

"Did we salvage the bananas?"

Crosby smiled and gave the man the thumbs up sign.

*   *   *   *

Tosh and Crosby stood outside the concert area, admiring a wooden bust of Bob Marley. Meticulously carved by a devout Rasta craftsman, the effigy depicted the reggae prophet, dreads billowing out from under his tam, smoking a pipe. The neck of his guitar rested against his chest and rose above his shoulder.

"That is the coolest thing I have ever seen," gasped Tosh.

"Looks just like him," Crosby noted.

"Give t'anks." The Rasta craftsman smiled broadly, revealing a gold front tooth. "It fe takin' de ganja," he pointed out. The sculpture had been fashioned into a bong, with Bob's pipe the receptacle for the weed.

"I've got to have that," said Tosh. "How much?"

"Hundred dollars, mon. Mi do a lotta work 'pon dat piece a wood."

"Damn. A hundred bucks?"

"Yah, mon," the Rastaman enthusiastically replied. "Mek I show yuh how it work."

To demonstrate the operation of the water pipe, the Rastaman pulled a fat green bud from his pocket and placed it in Bob's pipe. Leaning his head down next to Bob's, he placed his lips over a hole on the top of Bob's guitar and, with his right hand, covered Bob's nostrils.

"Selassie I," he said, and lit the ganja. Inhaling deeply on Bob's guitar, the water in the bottom of the bust bubbled. The ganja in the pipe glowed orange as the bong filled with smoke.

After most of the weed had burned, the Rastaman took his hand away from Bob's nose and sucked in a final massive breath of ganja. He held it in his chest for a minute and then exhaled through his nostrils, producing two separate streams of white smoke. Then, he smiled again. "Yuh see? De chalice burn wi Jah Blessing, ev'ry time, mon. What do yuh t'ink, mi breddah?"

"I think it's the greatest thing I've ever seen," said Tosh, "but I don't have a hundred bucks."

"Well," said the Rastaman, looking at the ground in thought, "what do yuh have, mi friend?"

"Nothing even close to that."

The Rastaman stood silent, pondering something.

"Listen, breddah, I love the piece, but I just can't afford to buy something like that now," Tosh explained. "We're on the road, you know, we're from New Jersey, and we need to conserve our funds, seen?"

The Rastaman nodded. "Respect."

"I think a hundred bucks is a fair price. You worked hard on that sculpture, and you deserve to be rewarded."

"I-man seek no reward fe Jah Work, mon. Mi jus' haffe eat, mon."

"I hear you, man."

Crosby nodded in agreement.

"Tell you what. How about this," Tosh proposed. "How about we give you five bucks just to take a pull on it. We gotta smoke at least one outa that gem."

The Rastaman flashed his gold tooth again through a wide grin. "Mek it ten, an' I-man pack de chalice fe yuh wi mi Lamb's Bread."

"Deal," said Tosh. He shook his hand.

"Bartering for bong hits," commented Crosby.

The Rastaman packed the pipe full of his stash and handed it over to Tosh and Crosby.

The first to try, Tosh tried to imitate the Rastaman. However, despite broken-in lungs, he didn't have the capacity to clear the pipe. Half the ganja still remained when Tosh's chest seemingly burst, sputtering clouds of smoke out in a deluge of coughs. "Whoah," he wheezed.

Without missing a beat, an eager Crosby took Bob before any weed could be wasted. He polished off the pipe and managed to hold the Lamb's Bread in his chest for a moment before succumbing to the same fate as Tosh.

"How yuh feel, mon?" posited the Rastaman.

"Irie," said Crosby.

Tosh smiled. "Wicked. Thanks, mon."

"Respect."

With Lamb's Bread in their blood and the warm sunshine on their faces, Tosh and Crosby ambled merrily into the concert area. Primed for another day of hot music and happy vibes, they joined the crowd of cheerful people for some easy skanking at the oasis of Reggae on the River.

CHAPTER 15

Most of the crowd filed out of the festival grounds in the few hours following the show's final chords. Drained from the day's activities, Tosh and Crosby declined to do the same, not wanting to get on the dark highway in a drowsy state. Instead, they chose to crash for one more night in their tent and planned on setting out for San Francisco first thing in the morning.

The next day, they rose with the sun. After dips in the river, they packed up their belongings, straightened up the van and split. The splitting only occurred, however, after some uneasy moments. The van would not start again. After a few futile attempts to fire her up naturally, they had to rely on the can of starter fluid that Baxter had given them.

"Induced ignition," Crosby called it.

Once they had finally gotten the van started, it seemed to run smoothly. Tosh felt like driving, so Crosby took advantage, lounging in the back bed, doing crosswords and doodling in his sketchbook.

*   *   *   *

Crosby stuck his neck out the window of the van to get a face full of air. He ran his fingers through the sweat-soaked hair sticking to his forehead, allowing the wind to blow it back. "Little things like that sometimes just blow my mind," he said as he brought his head back inside.

"Yeah," Tosh responded half-heartedly.

Crosby seemed to be deeply affected by the newfound fact that he could bluff bananas or something, but Tosh could not mirror his enthusiasm. Something strange along the side of the road had diverted his attention.

"What the hell is that?"

"I don't know," said Tosh, slowing the van down to get a better look.

On the shoulder of the lonesome stretch of northern California highway rested a rusted Pontiac station wagon, straight out of the 70s with faux wood panels running down the sides. A medium-sized guitar amp sat on its roof while a man and a woman dressed in sequined jump suits leaned side-by-side against the vehicle. In front of the car, a portable sign read, **ELVIS SHOW (PSYCHIC READINGS AVAILABLE.)**

Tosh pulled the van onto the opposite shoulder and stopped. Across the two-lane highway, he could see that the man, holding a guitar, had long bushy sideburns and a greasy mound of black hair. "Elvis lives," he breathed.

"Apparently," Crosby agreed.

The woman waved to them.

Tosh returned the gesture and killed the engine.

"What are you doing?"

"I've got to see this."

"Are you kidding? It's an Elvis impersonator, big deal. Let's go."

"Hang on," said Tosh, opening the door.

Tosh jumped out of the van and Crosby reluctantly followed.

"Hello there," called the woman. "Great day, huh?"

"Sure is," said Tosh.

"I'm Agnes and this is my husband Elv…Edgar," the woman said.

Elvis/Edgar nodded a hello.

"What can we do for ya?"

"What's going on?" Tosh asked.

"Well, Eddie can sing some numbers for you — it's five bucks for three songs of your choice — or I can give you a reading."

"Only in California," Crosby muttered, shaking his head.

"I want a reading," Tosh said. "No offense, Elvis."

"O.K., hon, it's fifteen dollars for a ten-minute reading."

"I'm down," said Tosh. "Let's do it."

"Dude," complained Crosby. "What are you doing?"

"What?"

Crosby's expression showed displeasure.

"Hold on a second," Tosh told Agnes. "Let me discuss this with my partner."

Tosh and Crosby walked about ten yards away from the car and huddled together.

"What's wrong?" Tosh asked.

"What are you, an idiot?"

"What's your problem?"

"They're ripping you off. This psychic crap is a total hoax."

"How do you know?"

"Please."

"Even if it is, so what?"

"It's fifteen bucks. That's almost a tank of gas."

"When did you become so concerned about our budget?"

"I'm just saying that our money is not going to last forever."

"We'll be O.K."

"Yeah, but why throw fifteen bucks away? You might as well just burn it."

"I'm curious."

"It's a waste."

"You'd plop down a twenty spot in a heartbeat at a Go-Go to see some titties. Tell me that's not a waste."

"It's entertainment."

"Well, so is this. No difference."

Crosby sighed. "You have a warped sense of entertainment, Tosh."

Tosh smiled. "Tell you what. I'll see if I can talk them down."

The guys approached the couple again.

"All set?" asked Agnes.

Tosh thought for a moment and then posited, "Do you have a special deal for young people?"

"No, we don't."

"What about for poor people?"

Agnes looked at Eddie. "I suppose we could swing that. How about two for the price of one?"

"Oh, no." Crosby rolled his head back.

"I don't think my friend is interested in prophecy."

"Do it for ten," said Edgar. "Not exactly busy."

"We'll do it for ten," said Agnes.

"Deal."

Receiving no argument from Crosby, Tosh stepped up to the plate. Agnes grabbed his hands in hers and closed her eyes. "Just relax, honey. Give me a moment to get focused." While Agnes concentrated on mystical matters, Edgar tuned his guitar and Crosby went back to the van to get a beer.

"Oh my, hon," said Agnes, keeping her eyes closed. "You are backed up."

"What do you mean?" Tosh asked.

"You know — have you had trouble moving your bowels recently?"

Tosh felt the blood rush to his face. "Uh, kind of. I haven't gone in like three days."

"There's nothing wrong with you, I don't think. Is this by choice?"

Tosh explained his whole bathroom dilemma at the reggae festival.

"Oh, hon, you've got to let it out. It's not good to keep all those toxins in the body."

I paid ten bucks to have this woman tell me I have to take a shit, thought Tosh. "Can we please change the subject?"

"Sure, hon."

Keeping her eyes closed, Agnes squeezed Tosh's hands. She moved her head back and forth slightly and silently mouthed words, as if she were reading to herself.

"You have a guardian angel, you know that?"

"I do?"

"Yeah. I can see him."

This news was exciting to Tosh. "What's he look like?"

"Let's see," said Agnes. "Sort of like an old hippie cowboy."

"An old hippie cowboy," Tosh repeated.

"He's helping you."

"He is? How?"

"On your journey."

"What do you mean?"

"He's guiding you."

"How?"

"Oh my," said Agnes, "has your van been giving you trouble?"

"Actually, yeah. Sometimes it won't turn over, you know? We can't get it to start."

"I think you've picked something up."

"What do you mean? Like a dead animal or something?"

"I'm sensing that you've picked up an entity."

Tosh had never heard of such a thing. "An entity?"

"For some reason it has taken a liking to your van."

"What's an entity? What are you talking about?"

"It's some sort of spiritual entity — most likely a lost soul. And this one seems to have a bit of an attitude. He's a prankster."

"Are you saying our van is possessed?"

"More like it's haunted."

"Our van is haunted," Tosh repeated, letting the concept sink in. "How did we swing this?"

"These things happen."

"Is the entity dangerous?" Tosh asked nervously.

"Oh, no. Just a nuisance."

"Great," Tosh quipped. "What should we do about it?"

"There's not much you can do. Unless you can find a psychic trained in entity removal."

Tosh buried his face in his palms.

"Don't fret. He might not stick around too long. These things are drifters. They tend to keep moving." Agnes glanced at her watch. "Looks like your ten minutes is up, hon."

After a bonus rendition of "Hunk of Burning Love," courtesy of Edgar/Elvis, Tosh and Crosby bid the roadside carnival farewell and hit the road again.

Tosh had mixed feelings. He felt somewhat freaked and slightly concerned about this entity business, but excited about the possibility of having a guardian angel.

"So, what did she say?" Crosby asked, crushing his empty beer can.

Tosh felt like driving barefoot, so he kicked off his sandals. "Well, I know what's wrong with our van."

"You do?"

"Yeah. It's haunted."

Crosby stared at his friend, trying to figure out if he was joking, but Tosh held a straight face. "Our van is haunted," Crosby repeated.

"That's what she said. She said we must've picked up a 'spiritual entity.'"

"What's an 'entity?'"

"Like a ghost, I guess."

Crosby digested the thought for a moment. "Good," he snapped. "Maybe the ghost won't mind doing some driving."

"It'll be like supernatural cruise control," said Tosh.

They both laughed.

"I told you not to spend ten bucks on that shit," said Crosby. "She took you for a ride, dude."

"I don't know, man. You never know."

"Oh please, Tosh."

"She knew we were having car troubles."

Crosby couldn't believe his friend. Sometimes he could be so gullible. "Gee, Tosh, we're driving a '73 Dodge van across the country. I mean, who wouldn't guess that?"

"She knew I hadn't taken a shit in three days."

"She knew that?"

"Yep."

"You haven't taken a shit in three days?"

"Nope."

"What are you waiting for, an invitation?"

"I'm waiting for a clean toilet," said Tosh. "Hell, it doesn't even have to be clean. As long as it flushes."

"Man, I could never go three days without dropping the kids off at the pool. You must feel like shit," said Crosby. "No pun intended." Crosby started giggling, but Tosh did not find his *shituation* very funny.

"Let's just say I'm looking forward to it very much."

"So, she thinks our van is haunted."

"That's what she said."

Crosby pondered the particulars. "And I bet she just happened to be a special supernatural mechanic who could perform an auto-exorcism."

"No such luck," said Tosh.

"So what are we supposed to do?"

"She said we could find a psychic who specializes in entity removal, or we could just let him be and he might leave on his own."

Crosby put a pinch of Copenhagen in his mouth. "I think I'll just take my chances with the starter fluid."

*　　*　　*　　*

Although the numerical identifications of the highways in America seem to be insignificant and completely arbitrary except for the fact that odd numbered routes head north/south and even ones head east/west, at least one road has a perfect match – Route 1, The Pacific Coast Highway. Overlooking the Pacific Ocean as it winds through craggy coastal mountains, Route 1 is aptly numbered because its continual breathtaking vistas undoubtedly make it the most scenic drive in the United States.

"El Numero Uno," Tosh said reverently.

It sounded like slow and sensual sex as Tosh and Crosby maneuvered carefully along the harsh curves, oohing and ahhing from every new vantage point. A salty breeze rippled through the open windows, blowing cool air over their shirtless chests.

The circuitous route down the coast certainly lengthened their trip, but Tosh and Crosby were in no hurry. They had no place to be. Their only concern was finding an ideal place to pull the van over and watch the sun set.

"Right there. That's the place," said Crosby.

Tosh gently pulled the van onto a dirt crescent along the edge of a turn and killed the engine.

"Oops," he said. "What if she doesn't start?"

"We'll worry about that when the time comes," replied Crosby, hopping out of the van. "Let's get out on that rock."

Tosh went into the back and pried open the bench that ran along the length of the van. He reached in and blindly dipped his hand into one of the coolers. Like little penguins, his fingers swam through the melted ice searching for beers. To his surprise, a few stragglers remained, so he pulled a couple out.

Crosby sat out on a rocky precipice, gazing at the Pacific.

"Here," Tosh offered.

"Thanks, dude," Crosby said, taking the beer and, in return, handing Tosh the camera. Tosh snapped some pics of the sinking sun, and then a few of Crosby, one with an easy smile, one with a silly pensive expression, and one with a ridiculous attempt at a sexy stare.

"What is that, your Tom Cruise impression?"

Crosby didn't answer, but took the camera and switched positions with Tosh.

After Tosh's photo session, they sat quietly and watched the sun slip below the horizon. They listened to the crashes of the waves on the rocks below and the moos of cows grazing on the other side of the road.

"This is incredible," Crosby whispered. "There's nothing like this in New Jersey."

"That's fe true," chirped Tosh. "And if there was, you can bet there'd be a hotel there too."

"Yeah, with a swimming pool, overpriced restaurant and cheesy gift shop."

Minutes passed. The sun sank. The surf splashed.

Tosh glanced back in the direction of the highway and the cattle on the hillside pasture, shooing flies away with lazy swings of their tails as they fed on the wild grasses. "You know land developers must drive by here and lick their chops, saying, 'What a waste. A million-dollar view wasted on a bunch of damn cows.'"

"Sad," said Crosby. "Real estate moguls. Should call 'em real estate mongers."

*　　*　　*　　*

When the oranges and reds in the sky started fading to gray, Tosh and Crosby pulled out the stove and set up for dinner. Crosby poured what was left of their drinking water into a pot and topped it off with some cooler water. He put it on the stove to boil and went scavenging in the door cupboards for a couple of packs of ramen noodles.

Using one of the coolers as a counter top, Tosh opened a box of graham crackers and placed six of them on a plate. He used Crosby's scuba knife to spread peanut-butter and jelly on them. "Hey, Cros," he said.

"Yeah?"

"Think about how you feel when you sit up here on this mountain and look out at the sunset."

"It's awesome."

"Literally," said Tosh. "Awe-some. Aren't you in awe of how beautiful it is?"

Crosby took his nose out of the cupboard long enough to say, "Yep." He placed the ramen noodles on the floor of the van and began to return the items he had removed back to the door compartment.

"Are you with me here?"

"Yeah, I'm with you. It takes your breath away."

"It does. Now, think about how you feel when you look at things that man has constructed. Like the mall, for instance."

"Well," said Crosby, "I don't sit in the parking lot with goose bumps on my arms, if that's what you mean."

Tosh balanced a glob of grape jelly on Crosby's scuba knife. "Exactly. In fact, you think, 'That's damn ugly.' You drive through the city and think, 'What a mess.'"

"Yeah, so?"

"So, what do you think that says about our existence on this planet?"

*　　*　　*　　*

Preferring not to navigate Route One in the darkness with tired reflexes, Tosh and Crosby decided to spend the night on the ledge. They also chose to take the night off from getting drunk or high, not wanting to wake up in the middle of the night to take a leak, only to stumble disoriented over the cliff down seventy feet to the rocky ocean below.

250

With the small size of the ledge not allowing much room for the tent, Tosh and Crosby had to sleep in the van, but they kept the side doors open so they could gaze out at the moonlight on the Pacific as they drifted off to sleep.

The northern California night, thanks to the ocean and the mountains, had grown downright chilly. Tosh and Crosby zipped their sleeping bags and divided up the blankets.

"The mall is a bad example," said Crosby. "You can't compare that to a sunset. It's not fair."

"Why not?" asked Tosh, propping up his pillow against the inside wall of the van.

"A sunset is like the most sublime thing in nature and you're comparing it to a mundane human creation. Nature's equivalent might be, like, a swamp or something."

"A swamp is a very rich ecosystem."

"Maybe so," said Crosby, "but you don't look at a mosquito-ridden bog and get chills up your spine."

"It still beats urban."

"I'm not so sure. I'd rather look at the skyline of New York on any clear night."

Tosh pictured the majestic view of Manhattan from New Jersey. The silky glow of the sky silhouetted the buildings as their lights reflected off of the Hudson River like iridescent jellyfish.

"If you're trying to draw some conclusion about our existence on this planet from our creations, at least take into account some of our better ones. What about the pyramids? The Sistine Chapel? The Taj Mahal? You can't look at those babies and diss humanity, can you?"

Tosh considered Crosby's point. "I agree that humans are capable of producing some magnificent things," Tosh said. "And we can look at them and admire the imagination and the craftsmanship of them and they may even take our breath away, but they still can't compare to the view of the sun setting over the Pacific Ocean. There's an intangible there…"

"That's because we *can't* build something like that. It's beyond our capabilities."

"Exactly. That's the work of God."

"Okay," said Crosby. "But you can't compare the work of God to the work of man. Just because our creations don't measure up to His, doesn't mean we don't belong here."

"But it's not that we don't measure up to Him. The fact that we can't build a mountain or manufacture a sunset is part of it, but there's more to it. There's something special about all of nature's wonders, even the less spectacular. It's that there's no sign of humanity. It's pristine, undisturbed. We haven't fucked with it yet."

Crosby nodded. "I know what you mean."

"That leads me to think that we're nothing but a nuisance here, a parasite of the earth."

Crosby mulled the idea over for a minute. "You know what it is? A result of the times. There is too much civilization. Nature has been diminished, so, nowadays, we have higher regard for landscapes and nature. But two hundred years ago, there was nothing but trees and mountains and plains and rabbits and squirrels and I bet the settlers would be damn glad to see the skyline of a city. They'd probably jump for joy with a view of Manhattan."

"I don't think the squirrels and rabbits would be jumping for joy."

"Well, we have as much right to be here as they do. Look, we didn't ask to be here. We just...appeared. *God* put us here, or whatever, and I guess, for a reason. So I don't want to hear we don't belong here or we are just a parasite of the earth. I love the outdoors as much as anyone, so don't give me that hippie bullshit. That's tree-hugging to the extreme, dude."

Tosh thought of the orange river he had seen at school, a result of coal mining in the area. "But, Cros, think about how much damage we've done to the earth. I mean we have practically stripped and gutted the thing."

"That was the past. Now, we conserve. More and more people are becoming environmentally conscious. We've learned. We've evolved. Now we know about the web of life, the importance of biodiversity."

"But people are still dumping waste in the rivers, ransacking the oceans..."

"There's always gonna be a few assholes in the bunch," said Crosby. "But as a whole, humans have learned to respect the earth. Now, we take efforts to restore and protect. It's not like any ol' guy can tear down a forest and throw up a bowling alley."

"Yeah, that's true," Tosh yawned. A cold Pacific breeze ruffled through the van, so he slid deeper into his sleeping bag. "It's too bad people can't learn to respect *each other*."

Crosby listened to the crash and fizz of the surf on the rocks below. "Maybe," he said, "that's further along in our evolution."

*   *   *   *

Tosh and Crosby snoozed late into the next morning, giving them the longest night of sleep they had had since they left New Jersey. It was much needed, coming on the heels of their two-day binge at the reggae festival, where they got a minimum of rest thanks to the residual effects of psychedelic drugs and the scorching 96-degrees-in-the-shade sun that heated up the tent well before the hour most people began their work days. Tosh and Crosby did not plan on sleeping late, but with the van parked facing south, the bamboo blinds blocked the early Eastern light while the ocean wind coming through the opened side doors kept the interior of the van from heating up.

The alarm clock read 9:40 when they awoke, but Crosby realized the clock had stopped running, so he figured it had to have been later than that. Then, Tosh further reasoned that they had not looked at the clock in a good long while, so they didn't really know if the clock had stopped running at 9:40 that morning or at 9:40 the night before, or at 9:40 during any of the days and nights since they had last noticed that the clock was running. Whatever the case, by the position of the sun in the sky, Tosh and Crosby knew it was closer to noon than to dawn, and time to get back on the road to San Francisco.

Tosh and Crosby smoked a roach to start the day, just a bit of a buzz to get them rolling since they had no caffeine and there were no mini-marts along Route One where they could find some to jump-start their hearts. They planned on driving straight through to San Francisco — not stopping until the Golden Gate reflected in their oversized rearview mirrors — much like they had planned upon leaving the Canadian wilderness of Lake Nitinat almost a week earlier, before they became distracted by Baxter and Daisy and the reggae festival and the roadside psychic and the glory of Route One.

But San Francisco would have to wait again.

*   *   *   *

While Crosby took his turn winding along Route One, Tosh studied the road atlas. He traced their circuitous course down from Canada, putting the territory they had recently explored into geographic perspective. As his eyes followed the thin red line of their chosen path toward the Bay area, something jumped out at him and he declared they needed to make a slight detour.

"Why, is the road closed?" Crosby asked.

"No, nothing like that," said Tosh. "Muir Woods."

"Muir Woods? What's that?"

"Muir Woods, named after the famous John Muir. The dude like trekked across the country."

"Didn't he have a car?" asked Crosby. "Some loser without a car walks across the country and he gets a park named after him? He should have hitched."

"I don't think cars were invented yet," said Tosh. "Anyhow, he didn't just *walk*, he took notes."

"What do you mean, he took notes?"

"You know, he kept a journal. He was a writer. He wrote a book about his observations."

"Oh, that's cool," said Crosby. "So what's in the Muir Woods that we should see?"

253

"Big cool trees," said Tosh. "It's right before San Francisco. Let's just check it out before we hit the city."

"No prob, I'm down," Crosby agreed.

Not long after stopping for egg sandwiches in some whisker of a seaside village, Tosh and Crosby parked the van at the entrance to Muir Woods. They chose a three-mile scenic loop from the trail map and set out up the trail. As soon as they found themselves alone, Tosh pulled a joint from his pocket that he had rolled with extremely powerful Humboldt County buds purchased at the reggae festival.

"Here," he said, sticking it in Crosby's mouth. "Let's spark this and make like Thoreau."

Crosby shot him an inquisitive glance.

"Let's get completely torched and, you know, just groove on nature. Chill with the birds and bees and the chipmunks in the trees."

Crosby lit the joint and they continued on up the path. Rounding the next turn, they came upon a bench that someone had carved out of a fallen tree trunk. Tosh and Crosby planted their butts on the nifty wooden seat. Sunlight drizzled down through the towering redwoods. Leaves rustled. Trees creaked. Birds chattered. An acorn fell to the ground. When the joint had been reduced to ash and the scent of the burning weed had dissipated, the air smelled fresh and nutty.

After a speechless minute or so, Tosh and Crosby both concluded they could observe nature just as easily from the wooden bench as they could trudging up the scenic loop.

*   *   *   *

Tosh had dozed off. He didn't know how long he had been asleep, but he was reasonably sure he had been awoken by a crunching sound. Through sleepy eyes he caught a glimpse of Crosby, who appeared to be kissing a Barbie doll. Tosh felt groggy and content and was on the verge of allowing himself to fall back to sleep, but at that moment, two things occurred to him.

First, the crunching noise came from Crosby.

Second, Crosby did not have any Barbie dolls. (He hoped.)

"What is that?"

Crosby pulled the Barbie-thing away from his mouth. "Pez."

"Pez?"

"Yeah. Mr. Magoo," said Crosby, holding the candy dispenser out to Tosh for his inspection. "Pretty good likeness, huh?"

"Why are you eating that here?"

"Why?"

"How can you eat that out here?"

"Uh, with my mouth?"

Tosh sighed, exasperated. "We are pulling a Thoreau in the middle of Muir Woods, paying homage to two great naturalists, acquainting ourselves with the glory of nature, and you choose to eat *Pez?*"

"The only thing you're acquainting yourself with is the glory of sleep," asserted Crosby.

"Wouldn't a granola bar be more appropriate?" asked Tosh. "A piece of fruit?"

"Some trail mix?"

"Exactly. Trail mix, yes."

"Go back to sleep, Tosh."

*   *   *   *

The traffic in San Francisco did not compare to the frequent, hideous gridlocks in New York City, but the congestion certainly slowed travel a bit.

"Hey, Cros?"

Crosby put on the blinker and brought the van to a halt, waiting for a break in the line of oncoming cars to make a left turn.

"I've got a question for ya."

"Shoot."

"It's bad luck if a black cat crosses your path, right?"

"Seven years, baby."

"Well, what happens if you cross the black cat's path? Does that mean the cat is going to have seven years of bad luck?"

"Why are you asking me this?"

"Because we just crossed a black cat's path."

Crosby inched the van forward, figuring he'd probably have to wait it out until the light turned red and then make a mad dash across the intersection. "I never really thought about it."

"And if so, is it seven years in cat time or in human time?"

"I don't know about these technicalities, Tosh."

"Because seven years is a long time to a cat."

"Yeah, but cats have nine lives."

"True, true." Tosh went to the back of the van and peered out the rear windows.

"What are you doing?"

"I'm trying to see where that cat went. If he tried to cross the street and got hit, that would pretty much answer my question."

"That wouldn't be bad luck," said Crosby as the light turned red. "That would be stupidity."

Crosby gunned the engine and swung the van around to the left, causing Tosh to tumble into the wall.

"Easy, mon!" cried Tosh. "I feel like I just got hip-checked into the boards."

"Sorry, dude. Had to do it. Some coke-head in a Cadillac was layin' rubber straight for us. We almost got hammered."

Tosh got to his feet and took a step toward the front seat just as the van began a steep ascent up one of San Francisco's legendary hills, causing him to stumble backwards. "What de bumboclaat a gwan up dere? You trying to kill me?"

"This is San Fran, man," Crosby reasoned, flooring the gas pedal. "No place for you to be surfing in the back there. Get strapped in, for cryin' out loud!" The pitch of the hill caused a half-empty Snapple bottle on the engine cover to slide, but Crosby deftly snatched it just before it toppled over the edge and spilled onto the beige carpeting of the van.

Tosh crawled on his hands and knees to the shotgun seat as the old van, using every last muscle of its lame horsepower, chugged inch by inch up the hill toward the Haight district.

"These hills are wacked."

"Oh, shit, stop sign. I don't wanna stop. We might lose our momentum." As they approached the intersection, Crosby swiftly scanned the area for approaching vehicles, old ladies in wheelchairs and kids on bicycles. Seeing nothing, he blew right through the stop sign without slowing down.

Tosh hoisted himself up into the seat beside his friend. Sticking his head out the window, he looked down at the vista behind them. Because the road descended so sharply, he could only see down to the street they had just crossed. Beyond that, the road disappeared from view completely, like a cliff. "Far out," he said.

"I hope we make it. Seems like this hill's takin' all she's got," said Crosby, patting the dashboard affectionately.

"What were they thinking when they built this city?"

Crosby took a sip of the iced tea he had rescued moments earlier before it flew off the engine cover. "They weren't thinking of rollerbladers, that's for sure."

*   *   *   *

Luck provided the guys with a parking space without too much of a search, but it took some anxious maneuvering to get the van into the tricky spot. Crosby had to squeeze between a Mercedes and a Volvo that inconveniently hugged both sides of the space, while contending with the steep grade of the hill without the luxury of power steering or power brakes.

"No wonder this spot is open," Crosby croaked, "no one wanted to deal with it." He put the van into park and breathed a sigh of relief.

"Make sure your wheels are turned to the left," Tosh reminded him.

"No problem. It's all taken care of."

Tosh strapped on his Birks while Crosby grabbed his sketch pad, a tin of Copenhagen and the empty Snapple bottle to use as a spittoon.

"All set?"

"Yah, mon."

Tosh and Crosby spent the afternoon excitedly cruising the Haight/Ashbury district, the bohemian area of San Francisco where all the psychedelic business went down in the late sixties and early seventies. Exploring the Haight gave them a sense of fulfillment and closure, for they finally got to see for themselves the area they had heard so much about, as they, growing up, had gradually wandered into the world of smoking herb and experimentation with mind-altering drugs. This was the stomping grounds of Ken Kesey and the Merry Pranksters, home of the Grateful Dead and Jefferson Airplane, the scene of huge be-ins with garbage cans full of acid-laced orange drink and marathon musical jams — the heart of psychedelia.

By the looks of it, the Haight had not changed too much since the sixties. Some chic cafes and stylish boutiques had popped up, yet with its plethora of used book and clothing stores, coffee houses, head shops, tattoo parlors and bearded, burnt-out relics lingering on the sidewalk, the area still retained its hippie vibe.

Catching a glimpse of a pink and yellow Volkswagen bus scurrying by, Tosh abruptly experienced a time warp. He suddenly heard Clapton's "Badge" — specifically, the moment just after the silent pause following the words "married to Mable" — a loop of cascading guitar repeating itself in his consciousness, over and over, as the neighborhood's mix of yuppies on long lunches and spare-changing grunge-punks transformed into a roving crowd of flower children and Mod Squadders, with long hair, bushy sideburns, painted faces, sheepskin jackets, polyester and long colorful dresses.

"This is it, Crosby," Tosh whispered, a distant look in his eyes. "This is where it all began."

*   *   *   *

"The Needle and the Image Done," said Crosby, reading a sign above the door of a tattoo shop.

"Neil Young," Tosh noted, referring to the song title from which the shop derived its name. "Cros! What do you say we get tattoos?"

Crosby looked at his friend with surprise. "Seriously?"

"Totally."

Crosby considered Tosh's proposal for a moment.

"Do you remember that tribe of headhunters I visited in Malaysia, how they were all covered with tattoos?"

"Yeah."

"Each of their tattoos represented a journey that they had taken," said Tosh. "This one dude had a 747 etched across his entire chest. It looked pretty ridiculous, actually, but considering what it meant to him, you know, it was cool. I mean, that guy felt so proud of that tattoo. He felt like a total bad-ass because he was the only one in the tribe who had traveled on a plane."

Crosby stared at Tosh. "So, what's your drift?"

"So, I dug that custom of theirs, you know, so I got that tattoo of the earth. I was feeling global and all."

Tosh designed an earth with green landforms and red oceans over a golden burning sun, which he had tattooed on his thigh during his international travels. The tattoo represented a realization that had occurred to him during his trip – that reggae was loved worldwide.

"Well," Tosh continued, "we're on a journey now. What do you say we commemorate it with tattoos like the headhunters?"

"Dude, this is so weird."

"It would be perfect to get tattooed here – in Frisco and everything."

"You're not gonna believe this."

"What?"

"See this?" asked Crosby, holding out his sketchbook.

"Yeah?"

"While you were driving down here today, I was sittin' in the back sketchin', right? I didn't even know what I was drawing — I was just messin' around. I wasn't really concentrating on it, to be honest. The next thing I know, I look down at the paper and I'm like, 'Holy shit! This looks awesome!'"

Crosby opened his sketchbook and showed Tosh his eye-catching design. Broad black lines zigzagged and cris-crossed, forming a pattern of disparate diamonds, with other strokes slashing through.

"Nice."

"Then — get this — I thought to myself, 'This would make a great tattoo!'"

"We must be on the same wavelength or something, brutha, 'cause yesterday at the reggae fest, I saw this Rasta wearing a T-shirt with a dancing dread on it. I was all baked at the time from tokin' out of that Bob Marley head, and I was thinking that it would make a great tattoo. So I started really getting into the whole idea, picturing a whole sequence of them, forming a band around my ankle or something."

"That's where I was picturing *my* design! Around the ankle!"

"The Needle and the Image Done?" asked Tosh.

"Let's do it!"

When Crosby tried the door, it wouldn't open. Then, he noticed the sign. "Closed for siesta. What does 'siesta' mean? I forget."

"Nap?" Tosh suggested.

"Nap?"

"I think."

"Well," said Crosby, "I guess that's good. I don't want my tattooist to be sleepy."

*　　*　　*　　*

Crosby sat in the shade of an old tree in Buena Vista Park and sketched Tosh's tattoo, as Tosh, alternately pacing back and forth and looking over Crosby's shoulder, described what he wanted. It was a high-intensity creative brainstorm — two minds, one vision.

"That's it," said Tosh. "Right on, perfect."

They headed back the tattoo shop.

*　　*　　*　　*

The tattoo studio seemed like a cross between a fraternity room and a doctor's office. The brutal glow of fluorescent lights sterilized the cozy character created by the colorful artwork and random knick-knacks adorning the walls.

Similarly paradoxical, the tattooist could have passed for both a surgeon and a member of Motley Crue. Apparently healthy and fit, he put in a clean-cut appearance except for the tattoos covering every inch of his exposed skin, including his hands and neck, but not his face.

"What can I do for you guys?" he asked in a friendly tone.

"We want to get tattooed," said Crosby. "But I guess that's obvious."

"Do you accept walk-ins?" asked Tosh.

"Sure do," said the tattooist, lighting a cone of incense. "Except for when I've got an appointment."

"Do you have an appointment?"

"Sure do. In about fifteen minutes."

"Damn. How long will it last?"

"Well, it's my last one of the day. Gotta cut out early tonight."

"That sucks."

"Not for me."

"I mean, we were just stoked to get the tats now. Spur of the moment kind of thing."

"Did you have anything specific in mind?"

"We have the artwork right here," said Crosby, holding up his sketchpad. He leafed through the pages until he found the band of skanking dreads he had drawn for Tosh and his own tribal design.

"Very nice," said the tattooist. "You do these?"

"Yeah," Crosby answered. "We were thinking around the ankles."

The tattooist put his hand on his chin and thought for a moment. "O.K. fellas, here's the deal. I don't really do this type of stuff, anyway. I work on the more intricate projects." The tattooist pointed to a framed photograph on the wall.

Tosh and Crosby moved to take a closer look at it. The photograph was a picture of a rain forest vignette with leafy green trees, snakes, monkeys, birds, butterflies, a waterfall and a jaguar.

"That's a tattoo?" said Tosh.

"It's someone's back. Took me fourteen months."

"Incredible."

"Anyhow, I have another artist who would be the one to do your tats. His name's Kris. He'll be in in about a half hour."

"Is he good?" asked Crosby.

"We'll see. You two will be his first customers."

Tosh and Crosby looked at each other with anxiety. "Uh..."

The tattooist laughed heartily. "I'm just kidding. He's very good. Crisp lines, very gentle. Take a look at his book over there."

Tosh and Crosby carefully inspected about fifty snapshots of freshly tattooed skin. The proprietor was right. Kris' work showed precision and a nice eye for color.

"I say it's a go," said Crosby.

"I'm down," agreed Tosh.

"I'll make the stencils now so you'll be ready to go when he's all set," said the tattooist. "I'll make a couple different sizes."

"Beautiful," said Tosh. "We'll be back in twenty." Then, subtly, he whispered to Crosby, "Gives us time to score some beers."

*   *   *   *

Kris had pork chops — not for lunch, but black sideburns that grew down to his jaw and jutted out across the middle of his cheek. He dyed his hair as black as the tattoos he was installing on Tosh and Crosby's ankles and spiked it up in matted clumps with goopy gel. "You're both getting tattoos?" he asked, pulling on plastic gloves.

Tosh and Crosby nodded, both too stoned to speak at the moment. While they were waiting for Kris, they had smoked some potent Cali kali and washed it down with a couple of 40 ouncers.

Kris opened a drawer and took out a small paper pouch. Ripping off one end, he took out a long, fine needle and held it up. "O.K. Who goes first?"

Tosh looked at Crosby and knew he had similar feelings. Maybe the marijuana in their blood had something to do with it, but reservations started to swim around their heads like sharks circling a bleeding marlin.

Tosh looked at Kris with the needle in his hand and suddenly paranoia set in.

This guy looks like a smack head, he thought.

How did he know those snapshots were really Kris' work? What if he and Crosby really were his first customers?

What if Kris drank too much caffeine today and had a shaky hand? Did he trust this guy to draw a permanent picture on his ankle? Permanent. It lasts forever.

And there was no eraser on his pencil.

"Tosh will," said Crosby.

"Whaddaya mean?"

"You've already got one," Crosby reasoned.

"So?"

"So, what's another?"

Kris crinkled his brow, like he didn't understand. "It's just a tattoo. I'm not removing your spleen or something."

Tosh ignored him and continued his rap with Crosby. "Every tattoo is a big thing. It's a life-long commitment, man. Besides, this time is different. It's on my ankle, not my thigh."

"So?"

"So, less muscle, more bone. It's gonna kill."

Tosh looked at the needle in Kris' hand. Was it really unused?

Maybe he just reused them and put them in those envelopes, so they appeared new. That thing could be dripping with AIDS or Ebola.

Did he really want to have that piece of steel piercing his flesh hundreds of times a minute, chewing away all the layers of skin, straight through his vein and even into his bone, just whaling on his ankle bone like a jackhammer?

"I'm gentle," said Kris. He raised his eyebrows and grinned maniacally.

Tosh looked at Crosby. "Ro-sham-bo."

"On three," said Crosby.

Tosh threw down a flat palm, signifying paper, and Crosby came with the scissors.

Without a word, Tosh kicked off his sandal and hopped up on the table.

"You sure you want this?" Kris asked.

Tosh looked into Kris's eyes. "Bring it, brutha."

*   *   *   *

Tosh admired his new tattoo for one last moment before Kris wrapped it in plastic. It looked so fucking cool.

"Satisfied?"

"Totally." The skanking Rastas had come out so good that Tosh had Kris add the words, "One God, One Aim, One Destiny" above them. The phrase was a Rasta doctrine, and words that Tosh firmly believed in.

One God: The idea that all of mankind was under the mercy of an omnipotent force — a force that linked everyone together. Some called this force Jesus. Some called it Allah. Tosh liked to refer to it as Jah, in keeping with his Rasta leaning, but he understood that all of these were simply different names for the same thing.

One Aim: The idea that all of mankind shared a common goal - to be closer to the truth when they departed this existence than when they came in.

One Destiny: Each and every person's destinies were intertwined. Everyone was in it together.

The underlying concept of the statement that Tosh had just permanently etched around his leg was unity; the essential message was brotherhood. Solidarity.

Tosh had his questions regarding the nature of God, but he had no doubts about the importance of unity. He held this notion in the highest esteem, along with love and respect. Love and respect made unity possible, and he knew in his heart and soul only unity could save mankind.

"I fucking love it, man." Tosh high-fived Kris. "Give thanks, bruddah mon."

"De nada," said Kris. "Another satisfied customer." He smeared Bag Balm all over the tattoo and covered it with Saran Wrap. Then, he turned to Crosby. "Your turn."

Crosby and Tosh switched places while Kris installed a new needle. He squirted lubricating surgical lotion on Crosby's lower leg and shaved off the hair. "Right above the ankle bone, right?"

"Same place as Tosh's," Crosby affirmed.

Kris took the stencil of Crosby's design and pressed it to his skin. After a moment, he removed it, revealing a bright purple outline. "Perfect on the first try. That's a first."

"Really?"

"Well, maybe a second. Ready?"

"Ready as I'll ever be."

Whatever remained of Crosby's buzz disappeared the moment the needle hit his skin. After the initial sting, Crosby felt a burning sensation coupled with pure pain. It was sharp yet precise, hurting only where the needle met the flesh, which, thankfully, was a tiny area.

Plus, it only hurt while the needle made contact. Whenever Kris removed the needle to wipe away the droplets of blood that had accumulated, the pain would cease. Those two factors made the experience more tolerable than Crosby had expected it to be, and he started to feel stoked.

"How do you feel?"

"Alive," said Crosby.

"Barely?" laughed Kris.

"No, *totally*. I feel so alive, man. It's like the pain just makes you more aware of your body or something."

"I know what you mean. It's a rush. I got off like that on my piercings."

"Your piercings?" asked Tosh. "I don't see any."

"At one point, I had seventeen of them."

"Seventeen?" repeated Crosby.

"Yeah, but I took them out," Kris explained. "For business relations. Most customers wouldn't put their trust in a tattooist who has thirteen piercings in his face."

"I really wish you hadn't told me that," Crosby joked.

"You had thirteen piercings in your face?"

Kris dipped the tattoo needle into the black ink. "I had one in my septum, three in my eyebrow, one in my lip, one below my mouth here and three in each ear."

"And you took them all out?"

"Except for this," said Kris. He stuck his tongue out and wiggled it playfully, showing off the silver ball imbedded in the middle.

Tosh cringed. "That looks nasty."

"Why?" asked Crosby. "Why would anyone do that?"

"Because you can."

Crosby looked at Kris and shook his head in amazement.

Kris continued. "Seriously. I just love that you can shove a piece of metal through your flesh and your body accepts it and grows around it."

"Healing is a beautiful thing," said Tosh.

"Absolutely. It's an incredible function of the human body. I'm perpetually amazed by the healing process. That's why I can appreciate self-mutilation."

Tosh cringed again. "That *sounds* nasty."

"Dude," said Crosby, "no offense, but you are a sick bastard."

"It's not as bad as it sounds. Just a little scarring. But you have to be careful where you do it." Kris stopped tattooing Crosby for a second and lifted his leg to show them a scar that had been carved on his calf.

"Some people would consider that a massive sin," Tosh posited. "You know what I mean? They consider the body a temple and all. I kind of like the whole temple analogy myself, but I don't know about the sin part. I mean, it's not like you're harming somebody. You're not even really harming yourself."

"I don't know," said Kris, wiping away some blood from Crosby's ankle. "To me, all the really important stuff is up *here*, you know?" He pointed to his head. "The rest is just flesh. It means nothing. As long as you're not doing anything to harm what's in your head, it's O.K. by me."

"True, true."

"No more for me, though. I don't find scars particularly attractive. I'd rather have a tattoo — much more pleasing to the eye."

"So," said Tosh, "I assume that you think body piercings have aesthetic value?"

"Yeah. I think they look pretty cool."

Kris asked Crosby to turn over on his stomach, so he could get a better angle on the back of his ankle.

"You can't even see that one on your tongue, though."

"It's not obvious, but you can kind of see it. Besides, that one has another purpose as well. It's a sexual aid, you know?"

263

"Ahh," Tosh nodded in understanding.

"The man is dedicated to his craft," Crosby commented. "Very admirable."

"Hardcore," added Tosh.

Kris grinned. "Chicks dig it, man."

Crosby swung his neck around. "Really?"

"Oh, yeah."

Tosh smiled. "Are you considering it, Cros?"

"Maybe. Does it hurt real bad?"

"Not too bad. It heals real fast, too. You know, things heal really fast in the mouth."

"It's gotta be a bitch to eat with," said Tosh.

"Oh yeah," said Crosby. "I forgot about that."

"Not at all," Kris assured. "Only while it's healing. You've just got to stick to liquids for a couple days. Ice cream, pudding, that sort of thing."

"Jell-O."

"Yeah, Jell-O. If you *really* want to please the ladies, though, you take it downstairs."

Tosh pointed to his crotch. "To the basement?"

"That's right."

Crosby craned his neck around again. "You pierced *that?*"

Kris smiled and nodded.

Tosh winced and said, "I think I'd just keep it on the first floor, thank you very much."

"That has got to hurt."

"I won't lie. It does," said Kris. He put the tattoo needle in its holder and pulled a cigarette from the pack in his shirt pocket. "But that's the best thing about pain, man. It's temporary."

CHAPTER 16

Kris cut Tosh and Crosby a much-appreciated break. Taking into consideration their financial constraints, the tattooist noted his appreciation for their walk-in business by charging them 25 percent less than his usual rate. To show their gratitude, Tosh and Crosby offered to get Kris drunk when he got off of work. They made plans to meet up with him at his favorite watering hole later that evening.

In the meantime, Tosh and Crosby went to get a burrito.

There were three Mexican restaurants in the Haight/Ashbury, but Kris had mentioned that one, Zona Mona, clearly stood above the rest.

Ambiance-wise, it was nothing special — cafeteria-style, Formica tables, bright lighting — but upon ordering their food, Tosh and Crosby's began to get excited. For starters, Zona Mona allowed the opportunity to custom design one's own burrito.

"Freedom of choice is *huge,*" stated Tosh.

"Very important," Crosby concurred. "And rare."

To their further satisfaction, Zona Mona had a wide variety of ingredients to choose from. Aside from the usual grilled chicken and beef, lettuce and tomatoes, the restaurant offered the option of shredded beef, shredded pork, grilled shrimp; ceviche (fish cured in lime juice), roasted vegetables, tofu; black, red and refried beans; yellow and brown rice, a mixture of cheddar and jack cheeses, two types of hot sauce, raw onions, fresh cilantro and, of course, guacamole. They even had two types of tortillas, corn and flour.

It was by far the best selection of fillings and toppings Tosh and Crosby had ever seen. They exchanged glances, as if to say, do you believe this place?

The tantalizing memory of his fraternity pig roast prompted Tosh to go with shredded pork. He chose black beans, a flour tortilla and all the toppings, instructing the man behind the counter to "go easy on the brown rice."

Crosby also selected brown rice, citing he was "not into the whole Saffron thing," to add to his roasted vegetables, pinto beans and corn tortilla. He ordered all the toppings, asking for extra guacamole as well.

Tosh and Crosby anxiously toted their burritos and a couple of Coronas to a chest-high, narrow table that ran along a plate-glass window. Hopping up on a couple of stools, they clinked the necks of their beers together and dug in.

They ate voraciously, grunting with enjoyment as they looked out on the Haight Street evening.

"This is awesome," moaned Tosh.

"Dee-lish," Crosby agreed.

Tosh forked some pork that had fallen from his burrito, not wanting to waste a bite. When he returned his gaze to the street outside the window, he met the stare of two dark, wistful eyes. They belonged to a filthy, disheveled man who looked to be of Mexican descent. Strands of saliva and mucus covered much of his craggy face and wiry beard. Seeing that he had Tosh's attention, the man broke into a disturbing grin, which revealed both of his rotting teeth and allowed more spit to drool out of his mouth.

"Oh God," mumbled Tosh. He could feel the bile rising in his throat.

The man leaned in closer, placing his hands on the plate-glass window. He had a hospital bracelet around his wrist.

"San Francisco General," groaned Crosby.

The man pointed to his head and made a circular motion with his hand, indicating he was crazy.

"No kidding." Tosh tried to ignore the man by focusing his attention back on the food, but the man's grisly image had been ingrained on his brain. He could feel the cretin's eyes upon him.

Tosh looked up in time to see the man's face plastered against the plate-glass window, smearing spit in all directions. "Oh, lovely."

The man pulled back and smiled like a little kid who had just played a prank on his teacher.

"What? What??" Tosh shrugged. "Why me? Why do you have to look at *me?*"

The man dropped the smile and stared questioningly.

"Look at *him,*" Tosh ordered, pointing to Crosby.

Instantly, the man turned his attention to Crosby.

"Oh, thanks."

The man began to make the "I'm crazy" motion again.

"No, no, no," Crosby shook him off. Putting a demented expression on his face, Crosby pointed to himself and in an exaggerated manner, mouthed the words, "Yo estoy loco. Yo!!"

This cracked the man up. He bent over and slapped his knee. He was really enjoying himself.

Tosh looked at the spit and snot spread all over the window. "I think I'm done eating," he brooded.

"Me, too," said Crosby, throwing down the rest of his roasted vegetable burrito. "Let's book."

Tosh and Crosby slid the remains of their burritos off the table. "Don't throw it out," Tosh instructed Crosby, who was heading for the garbage. "Gimme that."

Outside, the man approached them, smiling devilishly. Crosby immediately hailed a cab as Tosh placed the leftovers at the man's feet. The man stopped in his tracks and looked down at the food, allowing Tosh to get to the cab without a hassle.

Tosh and Crosby watched the man lean down and pick up the food as the cab pulled away.

"Where to?"

"Huh?"

"Where you boys goin' to?" asked the cab driver.

"Oh," said Crosby. "Just take us around the corner."

"Around the corner?"

"Yeah. We're not really going anywhere."

The cabbie turned around and sneered at them. "Fuckin' hippies."

*   *   *   *

The Haight night air held a chill, so after the shortest cab ride ever, Tosh and Crosby headed back to the van to throw on another layer of clothing. The sounds of Lynyrd Skynyrd filtered down from the open window of a second floor apartment as they brushed their teeth in the street, using a jug of spring water they had bought at a bodega.

Crosby spit out a mouthful of water and toothpaste. "Crap!"

"What's wrong?"

"I can't believe we left the wind surfing gear up on the roof. We're smoking too much weed, man."

Since they'd be leaving the van in the street, Tosh and Crosby decided to bolster security before locking up. They unfurled the window blinds and positioned the cardboard sun block in the windshield, concealing the interior from nosy passers-by and would-be thieves.

"You know," said Crosby, climbing up on a tire, "I think that was the best burrito I've ever had."

Tosh looked up at his buddy. "It was damn good. All the ingredients were fresh. Crisp lettuce, ripe tomatoes. The food was prepared perfectly."

Crosby grappled with a bungee cord. "And what a selection they had. I've never seen a place like that before."

"Me neither," said Tosh.

"I really think that was the greatest burrito I've ever had," Crosby reiterated. He undid the last hook and dropped the bungee cords to the ground. "Have we found the Ultimate?"

Tosh pulled an old sweatshirt over his head. "Tough call," he said. "It might have been the best burrito that we've found, but is it the Ultimate? I mean, can we find better? I'd venture to say that we could."

"You think?"

"Just because this is the best burrito that we've found, doesn't mean that it's the best a burrito can be."

Crosby took his roll of sails and leaned them up against the side of the van. "So what you're saying is, we still have to test more before we can pick an Ultimate Burrito?"

"Well, yeah, that's sort of what I'm saying."

"Well, what if we tasted every burrito in this country and then we went down to Mexico and sampled all of theirs and then we made our way over to, uh, Lithuania

267

or some place, Transylvania, and tasted all of the burritos there? Then, could we name an Ultimate Burrito?"

"Perhaps."

"Perhaps?" Crosby handed Tosh the surfboard. "What the hell kind of answer is that?"

"It depends on what we find. Remember, we are not searching for the best burrito. We are searching for the Ultimate Burrito."

This stumped Crosby. He jumped down from the tire. "Refresh my memory, old buddy, on the difference between the best burrito and the Ultimate Burrito."

"You see, Cros, the way I see it, the best burrito is simply that, the best burrito. But the Ultimate Burrito, the Ultimate Burrito is a burrito that has reached its full potential."

"Its full potential for what?"

"For burritoness."

"Burritoness? Oh come on. You are really *out there,* man, you know that?"

"I'm just talking about the being the best a burrito can be, that's all. The Ultimate Burrito is the best burrito that can possibly exist."

"I thought we were searching for the best burrito we could find. When did this whole potential thing enter the picture?"

"I just kind of realized it."

"So, what you're saying is that not only would we need to taste all the burritos that exist, but we'd need to test all the possible ingredients that could be put into a burrito to find the full potential for a burrito."

"Precisely. How do we know if Zona Mona's is the Ultimate Burrito if we've never had a burrito with, say, cucumber, or maybe mango, a mango salsa, before? Maybe mango salsa would enhance the burrito. Get it?"

"Mango salsa, enhance the burrito, la-di-da," said Crosby. He placed his board into the van. "Only you can take the fun out of this, Tosh."

"Why? How am I taking the fun out of it?"

"Suddenly this is a quest on a whole 'nother level. We're talking a lifetime commitment here, sampling a zillion different burritos — all of the sudden this is becoming an impossible task."

"We'll do it within reason," Tosh asserted.

"Still," said Crosby, "what if we were to sample a huge amount of burritos, burritos with figs and nuts and seaweed and rattlesnake or whatever, whatever is out there — how can we decide what the Ultimate Burrito is when there may be an ingredient that we haven't tried? Like maybe there's some kind of new vegetable that grows in the rain forest, and that ingredient can actually enhance the burrito?"

Tosh listened to Crosby's point.

"It just seems like an infinite search. We could go on forever and never find an Ultimate Burrito."

Tosh frowned. He didn't want to have anything to do with infinity.

"And that really sucks. I want closure. I want to find an Ultimate Burrito," Crosby whined.

"Well, I think it's a matter of faith, in a way," said Tosh. "It's a matter of making a decision. Deciding that it won't get any better. At some point, we will say this is our favorite burrito, this is as good as a burrito can get, and it won't get any better."

"When do we decide that?" asked Crosby. "How will we know?"

"When we don't feel like searching any more."

*　　*　　*　　*

Wilma's Tavern did not look inviting, but knowing that Kris went there regularly, Tosh and Crosby strode right in. Faded beer signs cast a pale, dim hue over the place as "LaGrange", an old ZZtop song, blared from the jukebox.

Patrons filled all of the stools at the bar, so after buying a couple of beers, Tosh and Crosby waited for their friend up against the opposite wall of the narrow room. They figured Kris must have liked Wilma's for the prices, which were low, rather than the clientele, which was also low, looking like a gang of opprobrious outcasts capable of committing unspeakably lurid acts.

Then again, who could tell?

If the untidy appearance of the crowd did not tell Wilma's story, the sign tacked to the wall behind the bar did. Written in red magic marker on the bottom of a cardboard beer case, it read:

IF YOU ENTER THE PREMISES, YOU MUST BUY A DRINK
WE DO NOT SERVE DRUNKS
NO GAMBLING
NO DRUGS
NO PROSTITUTION
NO SLEEPING - GET A ROOM
THIS IS NOT A BAGGAGE ROOM
ONE AT A TIME IN THE BATHROOM
WE DO NOT BUY STOLEN GOODS

"What a dump," said Crosby under his breath.

"Total dive," Tosh agreed, darting his eyes about, trying to avoid making eye contact with anyone.

Soon, Kris walked in, accompanied by a friend he introduced as "Raz."

Above average in height and build, Raz wore winter camouflage pants and a gray wool shirt. He had dyed his razor-short hair a shade of red. Fuchsia, maybe.

Kris nodded a hello to the evil-witch-of-the-west-like bartender, presumably Wilma. Grabbing two chairs that had just been abandoned, he ordered two whiskeys.

Tosh forced him to put his cash back in his pocket. "It's on us, remember?"

"No, it's on *me*," said Raz. "Welcome to San Francisco, boys."

Midway through their first round of drinks, a couple of old smelly guys stumbled off their stools and out the door, freeing up two more seats.

"So, Kris," said Crosby, hopping up on one of the vacated stools, "how did you get into tattooing?"

Kris explained how he had attended three different art schools over five years. After finally graduating from one with a degree in illustration, he landed a job as an animator for Disney, but quickly became bored and quit. "Mouseshwitz," he called it, due to their rigid policies and excruciatingly demanding workload. "I wanted to draw for a living," he said, "but animation was too redundant. It was like the movie *Groundhog Day.*"

Unsure where to go next, Kris took a job in a body-piercing place to hold him over until he figured it out what he was going to do with his life. "That's where I got all the piercings that I told you about," he said to Crosby. "When business was slow, we did each other."

Kris ended up really enjoying his job as a body-piercer, especially the interaction with the vast variety of people that came through the door. "Tattooing was really just the next logical step," he related. "It was a fusion of the drawing and the piercing. It came so naturally to me."

"There's got to be a certain amount of pressure," said Crosby. "No room for mistakes."

"Oh sure," Kris agreed. "But you get used to it. It makes you concentrate more." He added, "And actually, there is a little room for mistakes. It's minimal, but it helps."

Crosby was intrigued. Could it possibly be a path for him to pursue as well? "What do you like most about tattooing?"

"The flesh," Kris said emphatically. "There's nothing like it. It's a living canvas."

Midway through their second round of drinks, Carole King came on the jukebox. A heavyset woman wearing large hoop earrings and stretch pants cavorted around the bar singing, "I feel the earth move under my feet." In the course of her unsolicited karaoke, she scoffed at Tosh's dreads and grabbed Crosby's crotch.

"Not a pretty sight," said Raz.

"Not at all," agreed Tosh, turning away from the woman, who, at that point, had grabbed a pool cue and begun singing into it, as if it were a stand-up microphone. "So, what do you do, man?"

Raz took a swig of his Wild Turkey, rolling it around in his mouth before swallowing it. "I'm a sculptor."

"Really? What type?"

"I work with metals."

"That's excellent. Do you sell a lot of pieces?"

"I own a metal-working company," said Raz. "That's pretty much how I pay the bills. I work on my own art when I can get some free time, but lately things have been so busy with work."

Tosh asked, "What kinds of things does your company make?"

Raz lit a cigarette. "You want one?"

"No thanks."

"Just smoke the ganja?"

"Yah, mon."

"Let's see," said Raz. "We just made a spiral staircase for someone. We make custom furniture, that kind of thing. Displays for stores and stuff."

Tosh nodded.

"And we just booked a job to make this steel room for a music video. I'm looking forward to that. Should be pretty cool."

"What band?"

"I don't remember. Some rap group or something."

"Cool." Tosh ordered another beer and a Wild Turkey for Raz. "What does the furniture look like? Is it wrought iron?"

"That's really the old way of doing things."

"The old way?"

"Yeah. That stuff is all done by hand, and that takes a lot of time. See, the problem is, labor is so expensive these days, things need to be done more efficiently. So, we use tools. There's more machines involved now. So the stuff we do is more industrial-looking, more modern. It's bolted and screwed and cut, you know, rather than forged into a flower or something."

Midway through their third round of drinks, Wilma asked Kris to escort a gentleman out of the bar who had fallen asleep on his stool.

Midway through their fourth round, a skinny guy in a motorbike racing shirt, agitated over a disagreement at the pool table, threw a mug of beer at a big bald dude. The glass missed, hit the wall and smashed into hundreds of little pieces. The bald dude responded by grabbing the maroon ball and whipping it at the motorbike-racing-shirt guy. It nailed him right between the eyes. Wilma threw them both out, but let the bald dude back in after the ambulance left.

Crosby motioned to the sign behind the bar and said to her, "Better add 'No Throwing Things.'"

Wilma did not find it funny.

Midway through their fifth round, some guy in a fur coat and sweat pants bought everyone a drink.

Midway through their sixth round, Crosby got the munchies. "Do you serve any food here?" he asked Wilma.

271

She pointed behind her to another handwritten sign tacked to the wall, this one scrawled in pencil on a paper plate. It read:

BAR FLIES $3.50

"Bar flies?" asked Crosby.

Wilma looked at him like he was an idiot. She glanced at the sign and said, "Bar *pies*. Some nitwit erased part of my P."

"Does anything come on them?"

"Cheese."

Crosby ordered two pies. By the time Wilma brought them out, all four of them were pretty hungry. They dug right in.

"Is that your real name?" Tosh asked Raz.

"Nah. My real name is Dennis. Raz is short for Razor, a nickname my brother gave to me."

"You've got to meet his brother," Kris said to Tosh. "He's a dread. Sings in a reggae band and all."

"Really?"

"Yeah. That's pretty much how the nickname came about," said Raz, sipping his whiskey. "We grew up in Appalachia, in the mountains in North Carolina, and my mother used to keep our hair really short, 'cause of the dirt and ticks and things like that. You know, we were always outside playing in the woods and stuff. So she had the razor out every week.

"Then, when we were older, Daniel, my brother, started growing dreads. Partly out of rebellion, I guess, because it was the absolute opposite of what we were used to, but also because he was getting into reggae and everything. I still kept my hair really short. I was used to it that way, you know, it just felt right. So, Daniel, like most big brothers, used to tease me about my short hair, calling me Razor. And Razor evolved into Raz."

"Gotcha," said Tosh. "So, is your brother a Rastaman?"

"Sort of. I mean, I'd call him a Rastaman, but I'm not really sure of the intricacies of his spiritual beliefs. How about you? You a Rasta?"

"I don't know how to answer that," said Tosh. "I mean, I feel wrong saying that I am a Rasta, but at the same time I feel wrong saying that I'm not."

Raz nodded like he understood.

"Rasta is a steadfast commitment to a spiritual way of life," Tosh continued, "and I don't feel like I'm all that spiritually advanced yet. I am searching, though, that's for sure."

"What are you searching for?"

"For some answers, man."

"You should definitely meet my brother," said Raz. "He's coming into town, actually. His band's got a gig tomorrow night."

"We're there," said Tosh. Then, checking with his buddy, he asked, "That O.K. with you, Cros? I don't wanna o.d. you with reggae."

Crosby swallowed his last bite of pizza. "No complaints here, dreadlocks."

* * * *

At noon the next day, Tosh and Crosby woke up and smoked a bowl. Passing through Chinatown, they got hungry and decided to stop for lunch. They found a simple yet clean-looking restaurant where Crosby somewhat haughtily requested "the real thing, not the counterfeit American version of Chinese food." However, upon realizing that authentic meant chicken feet and duck blood soup, he quickly changed his mind and settled for egg foo young, which he ordered theatrically, using high-pitched, nasal shrieks while performing pseudo-karate moves — sort of a poor impersonation of Bruce Lee on a cafeteria line.

The Chinese workers did not see the humor in this, nor did Tosh, who quietly ordered vegetable lo mein and slinked off to the bathroom, embarrassed.

With fluorescent lighting, pale paneled walls and a worn, gray cement floor, the Chinese restaurant lacked in the ambiance department. The only color in the place came from a few scattered plants, but they were plastic.

Tosh emerged from the restroom with his dreads tucked up under a red, yellow and green tam. He had removed his long-sleeved shirt and tied it around the waist of his baggy jeans, revealing a shabby T-shirt with the Jamaican flag printed on the chest. Sliding into the booth, he nodded a thank-you to the waiter, who had placed their waters and a bowl of fried noodles on the table.

"Dude, let me ask you something," said Crosby.

"Shoot."

"Remember last night at the bar, when Raz asked you if you were Rasta? What did you mean when you said that you felt wrong saying you were a Rasta, but at the same time, you felt wrong saying you weren't?"

Tosh took a sip of his water. "Well, because in some ways I am Rasta, but in a lot of ways I'm not. I mean, for one, I'm not exactly convinced that Selassie was the Messiah, you know?"

"Do all Rastas believe that Selassie was the Messiah?" Crosby asked, dipping a noodle in the dish of duck sauce.

"To my understanding, in the beginning, that's what being Rasta was all about. Rasta started out as a very Afro-centric movement. It revolved around the belief in Selassie as the Messiah and the expectation that Selassie would deliver blacks back to their native Africa, where they would live in this, like, Utopia.

"But nowadays, thanks in part to the music of Bob and Peter, Rasta has spread to the far reaches of the planet and evolved into something different, something broader."

"What do you mean?"

"Well, Selassie didn't deliver blacks back to Africa, so you would think that the movement would have died out by now, right? But it hasn't. In fact, Rasta is still around and thriving more than ever. That's because there are other elements involved in the Rasta belief system."

Tosh poured himself a cup of green tea. "Rastas believe that Selassie was God, but at the same time, they don't deny the existence or divinity of other Supreme Beings, such as Jesus, or Allah. I think they believe that all of these Supreme Beings were incarnations of the same Creator. They have a saying, 'One God, Many Names.'

"In the same sense of their belief that God is one, they believe that people are essentially the same – one people, no matter what race they come from — one blood. These concepts are intertwined or tied together by the Rasta credo, 'One God, One Aim, One Destiny.'"

Tosh stuck out his leg and pointed to his ankle, reminding Crosby of his tattoo. "It's this ideology of unity that draws me to Rasta.

"Now, if you consider Selassie as the same God as Jesus or Allah, or just God *period,* then Rasta becomes a much more universal message. And that's what makes it possible for the music of Marley and Tosh to be embraced by people worldwide. They sing about God, be it Jah or whoever, they sing about love. They sing about spirituality, faith, strength, positive energy, 'upfulness.' These are things for people of all races and ages. So Rasta deals with the human experience, not necessarily just the black experience."

Tosh and Crosby were so involved in their conversation that they did not even acknowledge the waiter delivering their heaping plates of food.

"And nothing represents that more than the fact that Bob Marley, the greatest Rasta prophet of all time, is half-white!"

"Really?"

"His father was an English Naval officer."

"I didn't know that," said Crosby.

"It kind of makes it ironic for those nay-sayers who claim that Rasta is strictly for blacks."

"True," said Crosby, poking his fork into his food.

Tosh twirled a clump of his lo mein around his fork. "Most Rastas, though, admit that a person's skin color is arbitrary. They'll cite lyrics from Bob's song, "War," which he took from a famous speech of Selassie's where he says that the color of a man's skin is of no more significance than the color of his eyes."

"So," said Crosby, "if Rasta is universal, why do you feel uncomfortable saying you are Rasta?"

"Well, accompanying all these concepts that I've been telling you about is a disciplined lifestyle that most Rastas adhere to. For example, Rastas don't eat pork. In fact, most bredren are total vegetarians. They eat strictly *ital.*"

"What's ital?"

"Ital is like the Rasta word for kosher, more or less. It's fruits, vegetables, nuts — that sort of thing — all fresh, natural, unprocessed food."

"No Spaghettios or beef jerky, huh?"

"Right. Plus, they don't drink."

"Oh."

"So I'm not exactly the most orthodox Rastaman, you know what I mean?"

Crosby nodded. "I never liked restrictions, especially with food. That whole 'No Meat on Fridays' thing always bummed me out. Why ruin the best day of the week?"

"Yeah, but it's pretty cool. Many Rastas have in-depth knowledge of the chemical and mineral nutrients in plants and foods. In fact, Rastas traditionally treat illnesses strictly through their use of diet and herbs."

"Herbs, or 'herb?'"

"Well, I mean herbs. You know, all different kinds. But their use of ganja is included in that. That's another reason why I don't like to call myself a Rastaman."

"Why? You smoke herb regularly."

"Yeah, but I smoke it recreationally, you know? Rastas use it to aid in meditation. Meditation is a big part of the Rasta way of life."

"You mean they don't blow a bong and fire up the Nintendo?"

Tosh ignored Crosby's joke. "I've tried to meditate," he said. "I took a meditation class when I was in school."

"What happened?"

"I kept falling asleep."

"Well, what are you supposed to do? What's supposed to happen?"

Tosh paused. "Come to think of it, I'm not really sure."

*   *   *   *

The sweet scent of ganja mingled with the musky aromas of patchouli and amber, saturating the warm, humid air inside the reggae club with a blend of earthy odors.

Tosh navigated through the crammed crowd, jockeying for an optimum position to enjoy the show. He situated himself near a stack of amps about twenty feet from the stage just as the band emerged.

Raz's brother Daniel breathed into the microphone. "Greetings." His long dreads dangled down his back as he adjusted the microphone stand. "Dis one's fe de Sistren," he said.

With that casual introduction, the concert began.

As the keyboardist laid down a gentle skank, Crosby appeared with a jubilant smile and a pair of chilled Red Stripes. "Never thought I'd find you."

Tosh motioned to the stack of speakers. "I'm always near the music."

"What's the matter, you can't hear it by the bar?" Crosby kidded. "It took me so long to track you down, our beers got warm."

Tosh sipped his Jamaican lager, still cold enough to enjoy. "I can hear it, but I want to feel it. Mi like to feel de music, mon."

And feel it he did.

Unlike the concert a few days earlier at the festival, where the joyful sounds sailed up into the sky unrestrained by any borders, inside the club the voluptuous music reverberated off the ceiling and walls and hung in the thick smoky air, surrounding Tosh like a pool of hot oil.

Tosh felt like a wire conducting electrical current as the music passed through him. The pulsating bass rhythm vibrated the soles of his feet. It crept up through his calves and thighs and lingered in his hips, prompting him to swing to the beat.

When it reached his chest, Tosh's heart seemed to pump in unison.

Drawn in, Tosh stepped closer to the bellowing amp. He felt the music kiss his face with the pucker of an angel and realized the literal truth of Bob Marley's song, "Trenchtown Rock:"

"The one good thing about music — when it hits, you feel no pain."

*   *   *   *

When the show ended, the air and the crowd thinned out, leaving behind Raz and Kris like seaweed washed up on the beach.

They had spent the show back stage, mooching cigarettes from friends of the band.

"What do you think?" asked Raz.

"Awesome," said Tosh. "Awesome band."

"Why don't you come and meet 'em?"

Tosh and Crosby followed Raz and Kris into a small room adjacent to the stage, even more smoky and cramped than the club had been. Big Youth played on a sound system as people milled about, laughing and smoking. Kris detoured with a lady friend (and former client,) so Tosh and Crosby slipped onto an old couch in the corner while they waited for Raz to track down his brother.

Crosby lit a Djarum.

"Where did you get the clovie?" Tosh asked with a hint of jealousy.

"Bathroom."

"What, did you find it on the floor?"

"No," said Crosby, exhaling a cloud of candied smoke. "Some guy was selling them."

"In the bathroom?"

"Yeah. He was like a matron guy, you know, and he had a little table set up, selling smokes and cologne and condoms and stuff like that. Didn't you take a leak?"

"Nope." Tosh held his hand out and Crosby passed him the clovie. "I didn't want to miss any of the show."

Tosh held his hit in longer than a cigarette, but not as long as a joint, until he felt a worthwhile head rush. As he licked the sugary residue off of his lips, Raz appeared with his brother and a handful of beers. Tosh held the clove cigarette out to them, a silent offering.

Raz gestured no. "They make your lungs bleed."

"Don't remind me."

The guys got acquainted with Daniel as they downed their brews. He lived with his wife and young son in a cabin in the mountains a few hours outside of San Francisco, earning a modest living through his music, which he described as a cross between reggae and bluegrass.

"Don't take a lotta cash to live up there," he explained. "Livin' ital, we grow most of our own food."

The rest of his band lived around the Bay area, where most of their gigs were, so Daniel usually made the trip to the city with his wife and son.

"Where are they now?" asked Tosh.

"Home," said Daniel. "Kinda got me a predicament."

"What do you mean?" Raz questioned.

"The youth is ill, Raz. So's Tara. I've got both a them sick at home. I wouldn'ta left 'em if I didn't have the gig, but we needed the green."

"Everything O.K.?"

"Yeah, it's nuttin' serious. Just a bad cold or virus or somethin'. They're takin' herbs and all, Echinacea, golden seal and the like."

"But you want to get home to them."

"Well, yeah, I do. That's the problem."

"Van broke down?"

Daniel nodded. "This mornin'. Just outside a Oakland."

"You've got to get some new wheels, brother."

"As soon as I get me a gold record," Daniel joked. "Gonna take a few days to get the parts in. I was hopin' you could lend me yer truck till the van's ready. I'll be back around in a coupla days."

Raz shook his head regretfully. "You know I would, Dan, but I got a big job coming up. I need the pick-up for work."

Dan understood, but he didn't like it. He pinched his brow, trying to figure out another option. The concern showed on his face. "Doggone the luck of it all."

Tosh broke the moment of silence. "Hey Dan, me and Cros can drive you home."

The reggae singer perked up with hope.

"We'll run him up there, right, Cros?"

Crosby shrugged. "Sure. We don't have anywhere to be."

"That's mighty kind of y'all, but I wouldn't wanna put y'all out none. Y'all on a cross-country vacation, right?"

"It's not a problem at all."

Daniel smiled. "Well, I'm much obliged, bredren."

"The only thing is," said Tosh, holding up his empty beer bottle, "I don't know if it's a great idea for either of us to drive right now."

"How do ya feel 'bout me drivin'?" Daniel asked. "I don't drink, so y'all can kick back while I truck us up to the mountains."

Crosby cracked open another beer. "I think we feel pretty damn good about it."

*　　　*　　　*　　　*

Crosby leaned back on a pillow against the rear windows of the van and kicked off his sneakers. Resting his open beer on the bed beside him, he removed his shirt and tossed it over by his backpack. "Could you put on the fan?" he called up front.

Daniel looked at Tosh, riding shotgun next to him. "Fan?"

"I got it," said Tosh, reaching for the switch. "We have an oscillator in the back corner."

Daniel nodded. His dark-rimmed, Buddy Holly-type glasses gave him sort of a nerdy retro look, completely contrasting with his stringy beard and Rasta hair. A coral ring wrapped around one especially matted lock, while beads of different sizes, colors and textures randomly dotted the others like stale Jujubes embedded in a mop. Daniel's brown dreads had streaks of blonde like Tosh's, but they were slightly thicker and a few inches longer. They appeared much longer, however, due to his short stature, which caused his dreads to hang three-quarters of the way down his back. Daniel wore a zippered gray sweatshirt and faded olive pants made of hemp, with work boots on his small feet.

"So, you live in a log cabin?" Tosh asked him.

"It's a cabin all right," Daniel responded, "but it ain't really a log cabin. Got locust in the ground, hemlock boards on the sides, pine floorin'."

"You build it yourself?" Crosby asked.

"Sort of," said Daniel. "It was a storage barn before, and I fixed it to live in. Dug out a little basement with a pickaxe and a wheelbarrow. Ran some wirin', put some sheet rock up, insulation."

"You dug out the basement with a pickaxe?" Crosby asked.

"Well, tried to keep the buildin' costs down to a minimum, ya know? Everything's built with found materials. It's got a wood burnin' stove that I found under someone's house. It was just sittin' there, rustin'. Cleaned it up, warms up the house real good. Got a stove that I lifted from a junked R.V. Fixed that up, built some cabinets and a counter top. My kitchen table I built out of a piece a bowlin' alley."

"Can you bowl on it?"

Daniel smiled. "No, Crosby. The whole cabin's only eleven by seventeen."

"It's only one room?"

"Pretty much, but it's got three floors."

"Three floors?" Crosby and Tosh both asked.

"Well, we got the basement, where we have all my recordin' equipment. Then, we have a small loft that's supported by a maple tree limb hangin' from the rafters. Sorta looks like a tree top goin' through the house." Daniel laughed. "It's like a tree house, but on locust poles instead."

"What are locust poles?" asked Tosh, displaying his carpentry deficiency.

"Locust? It's a hardwood. Doesn't rot when you put it in the ground. It's usually used for fence posts, that kinda thing."

Tosh looked out the window. The placid glow of the moon hung over the rolling pastures of the northern California farmlands. He could see not a single sign that they had left the Bay area only seventy miles behind them, and no other cars accompanied them on the two-lane highway. "We getting close?"

Daniel looked at his watch. "'Bout another two hours, I'd say. Maybe hour forty-five in this baby."

Tosh couldn't imagine their van being faster than anyone else's vehicle. "This is one hell of a commute," he said. "Why would you want to live all the way out here?"

"Well, for one, I dig that fresh country air. Can't get that in the city." Daniel cracked the window open. "I was born and raised in the mountains. I feel at home there. Plus, it's much cheaper to live. Don't exactly rake in the cash as a reggae musician, you know."

"Yeah, the taxes must be pretty low out there in the middle of nowhere."

"Don't pay any taxes. I don't own the place."

"Well, I'm sure the rent on a storage barn isn't too high," Crosby cracked.

"Don't pay rent either."

"You don't pay taxes or rent?"

"Nope. A friend a mine owns the place. He said if I fixed it up, I could live there."

"Wow," said Crosby. "That's cool. For how long?"

"For as long as I want."

"What about utilities?" asked Tosh.

"Utilities?"

"You know, heat, hot water. Electricity."

"Well, our heat comes from the wood burnin' stove. Wood's free — just gotta cut it. Water's free, too — comes from a spring. I got a few a those five gallon jugs. Jus' hike up to the spring, fill 'em up, and lug 'em down. We heat it on the stove."

"You don't have running water?" Tosh asked.

"It runs. We got pipes hooked up to the sink there. We just gotta go get it ourselves, tha's all."

"That *has* to suck," said Crosby.

"It's not so bad. Spring's just up the hill a little ways. When we hike up there to get it, the jugs're empty, so they're nice and light. When they're full, we're comin' down the hill. So that's pretty convenient."

"I think our definitions of the word 'convenient' vary greatly," said Crosby.

"And in the winter time, we can sled it down. That's kinda nice."

I bet, thought Crosby. *Gotta be Nanook of the North just to fetch a glass of water.* "Are you going to tell us you don't have electricity?"

"Nope, we got 'lectricity."

"Generator, right?" asked Tosh, thinking of Tim, living in a tent in the woods around Lake Nitinat.

"Naa, I couldn't live with that noise alla time. As far as 'lectricity, my wires run over the creek, 'round through the woods there and up over the hill to my closest neighbor's house, 'bout six hundred feet away. I kick him some cash every now and then."

"He doesn't mind?"

"Nope. I had wired his house an' all, so I just hooked mine up to him."

"The power lines won't reach your house?"

"They'll reach. I'm jus' way not into hookin' up with the power grid. I don't want the power company comin' up there, tellin' me what I can do with my trees."

Tosh and Crosby looked at Daniel with curiosity.

"I jus' really enjoy not bein' told what to do. Not having to rely on a lot of other people. I figger, if I can keep it simple, do everythin' myself, then I don't have the need for the money part of it. I don't have to go away from my family and the place I love to be, in order to sell myself — to do something I don't like to do, jus' so I can earn some cash, to come here and pay someone to do *less* as good a job as I can. That's inefficient. I'm jus' tryin' to live my life as efficiently as possible.

"Ya know, I cut wood, split the firewood, carry it in, fetch water. I do alla these things, but I'm in a beautiful environment. And it's quiet. And I can think. And I don't got anyone hasslin' me 'bout none of it. Nobody's ridin' my case 'bout none of it.

"I need to live that way, because when the muse strikes, I gotta be ready. I gotta pick up my guitar right then and there and go with it. I'm just a musician, a reggae musician, folk musician. Ain't no big deal. It's just a job like any other job."

"I'd rather be a musician than, say, a plumber," said Tosh.

Daniel chuckled. "Well, as they say, it's a good job if ya can get it!"

"I admire the mountain people who were born and raised up there," Daniel stated. "They're ninety years old, never owned a car. They're all bent over and cricked. And there's a lil' path up through the hills to the lil' house they built in 1922."

Daniel paused, reflecting for a moment. "I admire that. I aspire to that more than I do to being the next Bruce Springsteen or somethin'."

*   *   *   *

The sky had just begun to pale as the guys turned off of the paved road. They followed a "two-track," as Daniel called it — two dirt paths each slightly wider than a tire with a grass strip in the middle — for about a mile. The winding climb shook the van up a bit, but not enough to wake Crosby, who had drifted off a while back.

Daniel pulled right up to the cabin. "Should we just let 'im sleep?" he asked, slipping into the back to grab his guitar case.

"Might as well. I'm not too far behind him."

Daniel hopped out of the van. "Ya don't want breakfast? I make a mean huevos rancheros."

"I think I'm more tired than hungry, to tell you the truth."

"I got a nice wide hammock under the old oak."

"That sounds inviting." Tosh tucked his pillow under his arm and dragged his sleeping bag out of the van, leaving the side doors open to give Crosby additional ventilation for his a.m. snooze.

Daniel pointed to a grove of trees about thirty yards away from the cabin and Tosh lumbered off toward the hammock. "See ya in a few hours," he said.

"Sleep well."

Tosh laid his sleeping bag over the hammock, a wide piece of canvas that looked like it might have had a previous life in the military. The hammock swung gently as Tosh climbed in. He pulled the other side of his bag over him and sunk his head back into the mushy pillow.

As he closed his eyes, he could hear the birds starting their song. A brisk breeze caressed his face, soothing more than chilling. He fell asleep in minutes.

*   *   *   *

Something tugged on Crosby's sleeping bag.

"Stop," he groaned.

The tugging on his sleeping bag continued.

Crosby did not feel like opening his eyes. "Will you quit it?" he said hoarsely. "I'm awake. I'm getting up."

More tugging.

"What's the big deal?"

A strange smell, reminiscent of a barn. Hay?

"Hey," Crosby croaked. He opened his eyes to find, of all things, a goat gnawing on his sleeping bag. "What the— get outa here!"

Crosby pried the goat's jaws from the sleeping bag but the animal seemed unflustered. It stood motionless, breathing on Crosby's leg. Crosby sat up and shooed it away, but the goat ignored him. "Get out, ya damn goat!"

281

Crosby thought he had finally gotten his point across when the goat dipped his head, but instead of leaving, the goat started snooping, sniffing out an opened bag of nacho chips stashed in one of the door compartments.

"That's it," said Crosby. He got up and steered the goat out of the van with some muscle. "And *stay* out!"

Throwing on a T-shirt and his Vans, he climbed out of the van and shut the doors behind him so the goat couldn't sneak back in for a snack. The sun shone down from directly overhead, so Crosby figured it to be around noon. He looked around and saw no one but the goat, so he headed for the cabin.

Inside, he found Tosh sitting at the table with a steaming mug and Daniel cooking at the stove.

Daniel greeted him with a big grin. "Jah morning!"

"Morning," said Crosby. "That your goat out there?"

"Had a run in with ole Mildred, didja? She's from the horse farm down across the way there."

"Stubborn bitch."

"Yeah, when's Millie's hungry she's darn stubborn. But she's harmless. Just lookin' fer a lil' lunch."

"You wouldn't think a sleeping bag would be appetizing."

"Aw, she probably smelled somethin' on it."

"Beer, most likely."

"Yeah, beer. She likes beer." Daniel pulled a ceramic mug out of the cabinet. "Ya want some tea?"

"Sure."

"Green or Darjeeling?"

"Never had neither. Whichever."

"Try the green," said Tosh. "Good stuff."

Daniel poured a mug of hot water from the kettle on the stove. "I'm fixin' y'all some grub."

"Cool. Thanks." Crosby joined Tosh at the table. "Did you sleep?"

"Like a baby," said Tosh. "In the hammock."

"Very nice."

Daniel placed two plates full of food in front of Crosby and Tosh and they dug right in.

"This is good. What is it?"

"Huevos rancheros, ital style."

"This is eggs?" asked Crosby.

"Well, not really. It's fake eggs."

"Fake eggs?"

"Tofu."

Daniel had sautéed the egg substitute in a blend of tomatoes, corn, onions, chilies and chipotles, along with a healthy amount of fresh garlic and cilantro, a cup of lime juice and a splash of olive oil.

"What kind of cheese is this?" asked Crosby.

"Tofu."

Crosby nodded like he had expected as much and proceeded to scarf down his food. "As much as I hate to admit it," he said through a large mouthful, "this is good. Tofu is good. I like it."

"Damn good tofu," Tosh seconded. "You made this salsa?"

"Sure did. Straight from the garden."

Tosh quelled the sting in his mouth with a bite of a biscuit. "You probably have an awesome garden," he remarked.

"The veggie garden is fruitful all right," said Daniel, "but wait till you see the herb garden."

*   *   *   *

Crosby stood at the edge of Daniel's vegetable garden, terraced on a nearby knoll, marveling at the largest cucumber he had ever seen. "I can't believe it. It's like it aspires to be a melon or something."

"We canned twenty-two quarts a pickles last year," Daniel said proudly.

"Dill?" asked Tosh.

"Dill, garlic."

"Crunchy?" asked Crosby.

"You betcha."

"That's a lot of pickles."

"It was a long winter." Daniel leaned down and inspected a tomato plant. "We should have about the same amount this year. We also got some peppers there, carrots, onions, squash, potatoes, lettuce, spinach, Brussels sprouts and the best beets you'll ever taste."

"Brussels sprouts?" asked Crosby, scrunching his face in disgust. *You have to be a hardcore vegetarian to grow, much less eat, Brussels sprouts,* he thought.

"'Course, I'm always sharin' it all with the deer."

"That's beet," said Tosh, but nobody picked up on his pun.

"You have a lot of wildlife around here?"

"Fair amount." Daniel picked a weed from the ground. "We got wood hens, owls, hawks. Occasional bobcat."

"Have you seen bobcats?" Crosby asked excitedly.

"Once. Those critters're pretty elusive. I hear 'em all the time, though."

"Anything else? Bears?"

"Not too many bears 'round here. Gotta go down to Yosemite for that. Tons a bears crawlin' 'round those parts."

"Anything else?"

"Lotta wild turkeys, buncha them. We've had twenty-four of 'em walk in front of our house since last November."

Twenty-two quarts of pickles, twenty-four wild turkeys, thought Tosh. *Daniel sure loves to keep track of things.* It probably got pretty slow up there, Tosh reasoned, except for all the chores. "You do all the gardening?"

"Yes-I," answered Daniel. "Had a neighbor with a tractor plow up the hill, then I raked it into beds. Every spring, I work it by hand with the pitchfork. I call it my 'Rasta Boot Camp.'"

"Must be a lot of work."

"Yeah. But I'll tell ya, come March or so, I really want to get outa that lil' tiny house. After bein' cooped up all winter, it's good to get the muscles workin', get some fresh air."

"Everything's waking up from a winter nap."

"Yeah, it's beautiful. You can eat the wild grasses sprouting up near the creek."

In other words, he eats weeds, thought Crosby.

"Hey, you guys want that cuke?" Daniel asked, offering them the jumbo cucumber. "I don't think that one'll fit in a jar."

"Hell yes," said Crosby. "We can feed off that thing for a week."

*   *   *   *

With the massive cucumber in tow, Daniel guided Tosh and Crosby further up the hill to show them his "herb" garden, which was tucked away in the woods just over the ridge. In a small clearing courtesy of a fallen oak, Daniel nursed a patch of marijuana plants. Northern California had the perfect climate and soil for such agriculture, Daniel told them, and he kindly gave them a sample from this garden as well.

Back at the shack, Tosh and Crosby didn't waste any time testing Daniel's homegrown. Daniel pulled his bong, a foot-high glass water pipe, out of a hiding place in the wall, which was covered by a framed black-and-white photograph of Bob Marley singing passionately into a microphone, dreads swinging high like they had a life of their own. Daniel packed the bowl with a fat bud from his garden and asked Tosh if he wanted to sanctify the herb before lighting it.

"Sanctify it?"

"Kinda like saying grace before a meal," Daniel explained.

"Thanks for the honor, but I think I'll leave that up to you."

Bowing his head, Daniel proclaimed the herb holy, as fruit of the earth put forth by Jah for the uplifting of humankind. Daniel's blessing of the ganja gave the smoking session an air of mysticism, as if the three of them were partaking in a secret, sacred ritual. The herb was powerful and for a few moments no one spoke, the haze of their initial high causing Tosh and Crosby to feel somewhat unsure of themselves, as if they were inside one of those clear plastic balls with the liquid that had gotten shaken up, and now they couldn't see clearly because of the snow swimming around them. It would take a few minutes for them to adjust to the sudden warping of their reality — to feel comfortable again with their whereabouts, their company and their reason for being there — for the snow to settle down.

Just then, Daniel's wife, Tara, appeared, holding a tray with three tall glasses on it. She spoke with a very soft voice. "I fixed y'all some orangeade."

One glimpse of Tara, with sun-kissed blonde dreads, a sparkling white smile and eyes as bright and blue as the northern California sky on a clear day, melted Tosh and Crosby's mental snow altogether. With the scent of her patchouli and the gentle lilt of her voice, she exuded tranquility and warmth. Tosh and Crosby immediately felt irie.

"You shouldn'ta done that, Queen," said Daniel.

"I thought y'all could use a cold drink."

"You're ill, Queen. You're s'posed to stay in bed."

"I didn't want to be a bad hostess."

"Don't be silly now, ya hear? You need rest. I should be bringing *you* the drinks. How's the youth?"

"He's sleepin'. I think his fever is gone."

Tara sat down with the guys for a few minutes and Tosh and Crosby filled her in on their cross-country trip and how they had met Daniel.

"We are surely in the market for a new vehicle," she said as she got up. "Y'all excuse me. Didn't think mixin' a pitcher of orangeade would be all that taxin', but I'm feelin' kinda tired already. Guess Daniel's right. I better get back in bed."

Tosh and Crosby bid Tara a farewell and "feel better" as she headed back up to the loft. Daniel accompanied her and tucked her in. As he descended the ladder back down to the main living area, he called, "I'm a gonna fix ya up a big pot of that miso soup!"

Daniel dug some things out the refrigerator and a large pot out of the cabinet and began his preparation of the soup, his second cooking session of the day.

"So, how did you start singing reggae?" asked Tosh.

"Well, I started singin' with the choir when I was five, so I suppose I been singin' 'bout God all my life."

"A Rasta choir?" Crosby joked.

"Not quite," laughed Daniel. "The Southern Baptist Church. Didn't miss a Sunday for sixteen years. Wednesday night prayer meetings, the whole thing."

"You liked making music even as a kid?"

"Well, didn't have much of a choice. My parents never really asked me, just made me do it. I come from a pretty religious household. Every meal was blessed, nobody never raised their voice or used tools on Sunday. Never heard loud noises, never saw a cigarette smoked or a beer drank, never heard a curse word. I had a charmed life and didn't even know it!"

Charmed life? thought Crosby. *Sounds like prison.*

"How were you kept so sheltered?" asked Tosh.

Daniel refilled everyone's glasses with orangeade, finishing off the pitcher. "Well, we lived in the mountains, remember? My father is one a eight. All my uncles built houses for each other and we lived together in a kind a village up there in the mountains. You could go to the next person's house and they could feed you or spank you, whatever you needed."

"What a huge family."

"I have twenty-one first cousins. Jake, our lil' one, is the twenty-sixth great grandson on one side of the family."

More counting, Tosh thought to himself.

"That must have been pretty cool," said Crosby. "I have a small family."

"It was nice, but the whole scene got kinda stale. So, when I was seventeen, I packed up and headed off to college. That was a trip, man. I went to the state university there. One heckuva mind-opening experience it was. I met people from all over with all kinds of different belief systems."

"Culture shock."

"Yeah, definitely," said Daniel, slicing some carrots. "I mean, I was just a country boy who didn't know it was any different anywhere else. I had never even met a Catholic before! So, for a while, I kinda resented my parents for forcin' me into that whole Baptist situation down there. Ya have to do that as a teenager, I suppose, rebel a little bit.

"But I loved that part a college. The next thing I know I'm doin' all these mind-alterin', hallucinogenic drugs and my whole world just opened up."

"So how did you get into reggae?" Tosh asked.

"Well, one day I heard this music by this guy, Bob Marley, and I could not believe what I was hearin'. I'm like, here's this Jamaican guy, he's got drums an' bass and these wicked gospel harmonies, an' he's singin' about herb! Naturally, I was intrigued and drawn to the music.

"So I just started listenin' to more and more reggae. I was workin' in the construction business at the time, I was a licensed contractor and all, and one day, on a whim, I just sold a table saw, took the cash and headed down to Jamaica for Sunsplash!"

"Power move," said Crosby.

"Yeah, it was pretty intense. I had never been to Jamaica before — heck, I hadn't ever even been outa North Carolina before — so I really had no idea what to expect. So after the festival, I decided to get outa MoBay. It's a tourist city, you know, with all them resorts an' casinos an' all, so I decided to do a little backpackin' up to the hill country to see what the rest a Jamaica was like, see if I could find me some Rastas."

"You backpacked around Jamaica? That must have been amazing," said Tosh. "What was it like?"

"Well, I couldn't believe it at the time, but it was just like home — just like where I came from — people livin' simply in a lil' village in the mountains, prayin' from the Bible. The whole thing seemed real natural to me. It was not a stretch a the imagination. The thing about Rasta, ya know, it's a biblically-based theology. I could say those verses backwards."

Daniel scraped the vegetables he had diced into the soup pot. "And furthermore," he continued, "me and the bredren there, we had us a reasonin' session. And we found that we all had a whole lotta other stuff in common.

"None of us drank alcohol or smoked tobacco. We didn't eat meat. We all lived ital, all lived vegetarian.

"And at the time, I was wearin' my hair in braids. One a them sistren did it for me at Sunsplash. And I had this long, scraggly beard. And the bredren all were sayin' to me, 'You a Rasta, you a Rasta.' 'Cause I was just like them.

"An' I said, 'I ain't really anything. I'm just a guy, a mountain guy.' It was pretty wild, because it was like I discovered I was Rasta before I knew what Rasta was."

"Are you Rasta?"

"I'm a spiritual seeker," said Daniel. "I'm always lookin' for the truth."

That sounds familiar, thought Tosh. He knew where Daniel was coming from. "What do you think about Selassie? Do you think Selassie is God?"

Daniel covered his soup pot, put it on the stove and turned up the heat. "Selassie did many things that were very forward thinkin' for the African continent and for Africans as people, so he must have had some type of guidance, some type a divine inspiration. Jesus did the same thing, but Jesus had a contingent of media followin' him. In other words, Jesus got good press. And his story has survived for 2000 years."

"That's an interesting way of looking at it," said Crosby.

Daniel grabbed a glass of spring water from the fridge. "Y'all want some?"

He filled the guys' glasses and the three of them took their conversation outside to enjoy the afternoon sun. "There are other systems of belief that are way older," he continued. "The Koran, Taoism, Buddhism. You can't ignore them."

"So you believe in some sort of God then?"

Daniel paused. He took a deep breath, savoring the air in his lungs. "I feel like there's no way I can live out here like I do, and look around and not think that there's some type of master architect. That there's a master plan, so perfectly worked out, so amazingly planned, that who am I to second-guess it?

"I'm not exactly sure what I believe God is, but I think that Jah dwells within yourself and I-self. I think Jah is a part a every human on the planet, all 5.5 billion of us. The one thing that's common in all of us — that's Jah, the life-force, the thing that makes everything tick."

Daniel continued, "Growin' up Baptist, they were always sayin', 'God is out *there*. God is *up* there.' Ya know, God is watchin' you and takin' notes. And there's gonna be a film strip played at your funeral when you're standin' at the Pearly Gates, and it's gonna say 'You did *this* wrong, and this…' I was terrified."

Ras Daniel glanced at his wrist, where a ladybug had just landed. It crawled onto his palm and he brought his hand up for a closer look. "Somethin' that I learned through Rasta, which I identify with, is that with Rasta, God is within. You were born as a child of God, and you'll always be that way as long as ya acknowledge it. Ya don't have to convert — you're there already. Ya just need to *own* it."

CHAPTER 17

In the immortal words of *Schoolhouse Rock,* "Three is The Magic Number." Indeed, it is the way of the universe.

Father, Son, Holy Ghost.
Super conscious, Conscious, Subconscious.
Mind, Body, Spirit.
Past, Present, Future.
Beginning, Middle, End.
Small, Medium, Large.
Win, Place, Show.
Three little pigs.
Three strikes, you're out.
Three licks to get to the center of a Tootsie Pop.

Tosh and Crosby had three gallons of gas left when they pulled off the highway to fill up in some tiny hick town on their way to Yosemite National Park. Josephine had started up without a problem while leaving Ras Daniel's place, but now, after topping off the tank and purchasing some root beers and Starbursts, she failed.

Crosby, poised with the starter fluid, signaled for Tosh to turn the ignition key once more, but Josephine refused to turn over.

"Damnit!" said Tosh. He looked up to the sky. "Please don't leave us here in this God forsaken place!"

"There's no mechanic today, right?" Crosby asked the attendant, a skinny kid in a gray Mobil jumpsuit.

He shook his head. "It's Sunday."

Then, behind the attendant appeared a man. "The Lord's Day," he pointed out, fingering his bushy gray mustache. His long unkempt hair spilled out from under a tattered suede Stetson and framed a face crinkled from the years. He wore faded jeans and a navy T-shirt and his boots had a layer of dust. "Let me see that," he said.

Crosby got out of the van and the man got in. Sticking his nose in the engine, he reached in and after a moment said, "Try her now."

Tosh turned the key and Josephine started up. "Yes."

"All right! What did you do?" Crosby asked excitedly, peering in from his position by the pump.

"Oh, I just jiggled that thing there," the man said, sliding out of the shotgun seat.

"Where? Let me see."

But the man didn't turn back. He strode away slowly, heading for the road.

Crosby looked at Tosh and shrugged. "Let's roll."

As they pulled out from the station, they passed the man walking along the gravel shoulder of the road.

"That guy looks familiar," said Tosh.

"You think? Hold up a sec, Tosh." Crosby leaned out the window. "Need a lift?" he asked the man.

"Nope. Almost there," he replied, without turning his head. Then, he looked at them and said, "For the record — God has forsaken no place."

*   *   *   *

Tosh and Crosby headed for Yosemite National Park on Ras Daniel's advice for some good sights to see. Tosh drove with his shirt off while Crosby, one bare foot out the passenger-side window, leaned forward and flipped through the radio dial.

WHY DO YOU FILL ME UP BUTTERCUP NOW ONLY TWO NINETY NINE WITH THE PURCHASE OF CONTEMPTIBLE SINNERS WHO SHALL FEEL THE WRATH OF SOUTHEAST WINDS OF 12 KNOTS AND HUMIDITY AROUND Z-98 ON THE EIGHT HUNDRED LINE AND BE THE TWENTY FIFTH ABOVE GROUND SWIMMING POOL CHRIST YOU KNOW IT AIN'T EASY.

"Leave that," said Tosh.

YOU KNOW HOW HARD IT CAN BE, THE WAY THINGS ARE GOING, THEY'RE GOING TO CRUCIFY ME.

"You know," said Crosby. "I was thinking about what Ras Daniel said."

"Oh yeah?"

"Yeah. About how people believe God is up in heaven, watching everyone and judging all of us and all that. That doesn't seem right to me, either — just seems like an obvious ploy to keep everyone in line."

"Fe real, mon," Tosh agreed.

"I like what Ras Daniel said about God being within us, the thing that makes us all tick. That sounds close to me."

"Yeah. I've heard that before, you know, from other Rastas. They believe that God dwells within. Something about that seems right, but I'm not sure I understand it."

"Well, I got a theory on it."

"You do?" Tosh was delighted Crosby had been pondering the topic of their discussion. "Let's hear it."

"O.K." Crosby gathered his thoughts. "Everything in the universe is in constant flux, right?"

"Right."

"Things are continually getting born and growing and dying, like whether it be people or animals or dandelions or fungus. Or if it isn't alive, it forms, like the elements. They started as chemical compounds or whatever and came together and reacted and formed into other things."

"I'm with you."

"The bottom line is that everything is constantly changing. Just as the earth is always spinning, everything on the earth is always changing."

Crosby pulled his foot in from outside the window. "To put it simply, shit happens."

"That's simple enough."

"Well, something has to make everything work, and that's energy."

"So, are you saying God is the force that makes shit happen?"

"Actually, I think God *is* the happen."

"I think you lost me, Cros."

"The energy is not causing shit to happen, the energy is the happening. The happening is the energy in motion. Rather than God being the button-pusher who starts the process and sits back and watches, God *is* the process. The process is energy in motion, and God is that energy."

"Wow. That's heavy."

"Ras Daniel says he thinks that God is the force that makes everything tick, but I think God is the ticking. The other way, it still makes God seem like He's removed from us. But as the ticking, the happening, the process, that's how God is within us."

Tosh studied Crosby for a moment. *Damn*, he thought, *you can never underestimate people. I didn't think Crosby had it in him.*

*   *   *   *

Tosh and Crosby entered Yosemite before nightfall.

Tosh steered the old van along the winding road at a turtle's pace, he and Crosby gaping at the grandeur of the landscape. A momentary glimpse in the rear view mirror revealed to him that a line of cars had backed up behind them, so Tosh pulled over to the side of the road to let the traffic pass.

"Phenomenal," he breathed.

Crosby echoed his sentiments with a hallowed sigh.

"Have you ever seen such beauty?" Tosh asked.

"Outstanding. We don't have anything even close to this in New Jersey, man. Truly outstanding."

"Lets hear it for Mother Nature. A round of applause, please."

Sitting in the van, marveling at the majestic Half Dome through the windshield, Tosh and Crosby clapped whole-heartedly. (Crosby embellished the ovation with a few whistles.)

"And this is nothing. Wait till we get to the top."

"Top?" asked Tosh.

"Yeah."

"What do you mean?"

"What do you mean, what do I mean? We're gonna climb it."

291

"You want to climb that?" Tosh pointed to the mountain.

"Of course. What do you think we're gonna do, just look at it?"

"That's fucking Mount Everest! You want to climb it? I don't know a thing about rock climbing."

"First of all, that's Half Dome, a pimple compared to Mount Everest. Secondly, we're not going to actually climb the face of it, we're going to hike the back side of it. Easy climb, no problem."

Tosh breathed a sigh of relief.

"Probably about eight hours."

"What's eight hours?"

"The hike."

"Eight hours? Are you kidding me?"

"Give or take an hour, I'd assume."

"Why? Why do you want to spend all that time walking up a mountain?"

"That's why mountains are there — to be climbed."

Tosh didn't exactly concur with Crosby's reasoning, but he knew it didn't matter. They were going to hike Half Dome.

*　　*　　*　　*

With daylight fading fast, the guys hunted for an ideal place to pitch their tent. Unfortunately, they had to confine their search to limited locations due to the park rules, which called for camping in designated areas only. They managed to find a decent spot under a tree at the base of Half Dome, but had to settle for a lack of privacy.

No big deal, they reasoned, for they planned on getting to sleep pretty early anyhow. Crosby wanted to get up at sunrise to get an early jump on their day of hiking.

After setting the tent and starting the fire, they smoked a bud of Ras Daniel's herb and heated up a pot of his soup to go along with some Spam sandwiches.

"I wish we had some lettuce for these sandwiches," said Tosh. "And tomato. I need some vegetables."

"There's vegetables in the soup," Crosby reminded him.

After dinner, they each enjoyed a can of Schlitz as they relaxed in their newest purchase, a pair of old lawn chairs they picked up for five bucks at a yard sale along a rustic stretch of highway.

"Best thing we ever bought," said Crosby, gazing up at the stars.

Tosh threw on a long-sleeved shirt and flipped the Jerry Garcia tape that had just ended. "Definitely. I would have paid twenty bucks for these babies."

When they had finished their after-dinner cocktails, by the light of the kerosene lantern, Tosh and Crosby packed up the necessities for the next day's hike — mainly clean socks and underwear, jeans and sweatshirts (it could get chilly at the top), their flashlight, some granola bars, a jug of water and sunscreen. Crosby topped off the satchel with a pack of rubbers.

"What the hell are those for?" asked Tosh, eyeing his friend dubiously. "We're going to a mountain top. What do you expect to find, the Swedish Bikini Mountaineering Club?"

"You never know," said Crosby. "Maybe they'll be filming a Mountain Dew commercial or something."

*　　*　　*　　*

The next morning, Tosh and Crosby finally got to use the alarm clock that had terrorized them during the first few days of their trip. It rang at precisely four minutes after six, offering the guys no second chances, no opportunities for snoozing, no extra nine minutes tucked comfortably in the confines of their camping cocoons.

The birds in the tree outside the tent had begun their daily coffee talk as Crosby sprung from his sleeping bag. He immediately rolled up the sack and strapped it to the bottom of his backpack. Then, he collapsed the tent on top of Tosh, who had chosen to ignore the alarm and remained half-asleep with a bandanna over his eyes.

"Rise and shine! We've got hiking to do!"

Like a boa emerging from an unbound burlap sack, Tosh slithered out of the collapsed tent. "No breakfast?"

Crosby skipped over to the van and tossed his buddy a banana. "Still yellow," he pointed out, full of excitement about his new banana-preservation technique: He had hung them from the rear view mirror with a shoelace from his sneaker.

The guys folded up the tent and tied it to the pack.

"What are we gonna do for dinner up there?" asked Tosh.

Crosby rummaged through the van. "I don't know. You wanna do spaghetti?"

"Can we?"

"Why not?"

"It will be like eating plastic."

"We can cook it."

"You want to lug the Coleman up there?"

"We'll build a fire."

"With what?" Tosh motioned to the bald peak of Half Dome. "I don't see any trees up there."

"We'll grab some logs on the way."

At quarter after six in the morning, this seemed like a logical plan to Tosh. He took the box of spaghetti from Crosby and threw it into the backpack, along with their small pot, a few bowls, a box of plastic utensils, a garbage bag and a jar of tomato sauce.

"All set?"

"Let's do it," said Tosh.

They locked up Josephine and set out.

*   *   *   *

Before hitting the hill, Tosh and Crosby stopped by the Park Rangers station for a little advice.

"It's a good day for Half Dome," said the ranger, a fit, middle-aged guy with a wide-brimmed hat and a high-tech wristwatch. "No rain predicted."

"Is that watch a compass too?" Crosby asked him.

The question caught the ranger by surprise and he glanced down at his wrist as if he had forgotten about his watch. "Of course."

"Anything we should know before we leave?"

"How long does it take?" Tosh interrupted.

"About six hours, if you make good time. Be careful on the cables."

"Cables?"

"At the top. The last five hundred feet or so, you need the cables. It gets real steep — too steep for walking. Plus, there's nothing to hold on to. It's all rock up there."

"Cool," said Crosby.

Shit, thought Tosh.

"Other than that, just beware of bears," the ranger added.

"Bears?" said Crosby.

Shit, thought Tosh. "There's bears?"

"Sure."

"A lot?"

The ranger poured a cup of hot coffee into a Styrofoam cup. "We get a few sightings each month."

"Where's the bears?"

"Mainly toward the top, but not above the tree line."

"What do we do if we see a bear?" Crosby asked.

Run like hell, thought Tosh.

"Don't run," said the ranger. "If you run into a bear, you should make a lot of noise. Jump up and down, yell and scream, throw rocks at it."

Throw rocks at it?

"You want to scare the bear away."

Scare the bear, thought Tosh. *Yeah, right.*

"Seriously?" asked Crosby.

"Yeah. These are black bears. They're timid. They're more scared of you than you are of them."

There's that damn cliché again, thought Tosh. "Don't underestimate my fright," he said.

"They're not grizzlies. Black bears are harmless, trust me."

600 pounds, five inch claws, fangs. "I'm sure they're not *harmless,*" said Tosh.

"They won't hurt you. They're just interested in your food."

"Are they interested in us *as* food?"

"No. Black bears are mainly herbivores."

Mainly.

"We haven't had a bear attack in over fifty years."

That means they're due.

"Can we spend the night up top?" Crosby asked the ranger.

"We don't advise it." The ranger poured milk into his coffee. "We only allow fires in designated parts of the park and that is not one. Plus, there's no shelter. If a storm rolls in, there's a high risk of lightning up there."

"But you said there's no rain predicted, right?"

The ranger paused a moment, probably deciding whether to alter his weather report. Then, he let out a little grin, like he knew he'd been caught contemplating a fib. "That's right," he said.

"Thanks a lot."

The ranger held his steaming coffee cup up to his mouth and blew on it. "No problem."

"You really shouldn't use Styrofoam," said Crosby, putting his shades back on. "It's bad for the environment."

*   *   *   *

"*No fuckin' way I'm gonna throw a rock at it,* I'll tell you that," said Tosh. "If I see a bear, that's the *last* thing I'm going to do." He stopped walking to emphasize his seriousness.

"Don't worry about it," said Crosby, plucking a long, straight branch from the ground beside the trail. *This will make a good walking stick,* he thought. "We won't see any bears. The way you've been carrying on, we'll be lucky if we see a damn squirrel."

Tosh had decided to use the information the ranger had shared with them — that bears were scared of loud noises — as a preventive technique rather than a battle tactic. *Why wait until I'm face-to-face with the monster to try it out,* he reasoned. *Might as well put it to good use now.*

So, as he walked, Tosh made sure he created a stir. He sang, practiced his Spanish, attempted bird calls — anything — as long as he was loud.

"Come on," said Crosby, "We got a lot of hiking to do."

They continued up the base of Half Dome, Tosh singing the Bumble Bee tuna song.

"You know, Tosh, part of the joy of hiking is listening to the sounds of the mountain — the birds, the running water. The point is to get *away* from disturbances, not create them."

They hiked the first leg of the mountain with ease. The trail rose gradually, and the California sun had not yet heated up the air. Just enough light filtered through the huge leafy trees to dry the dew on the undergrowth.

Some time before noon, the guys stumbled upon a flat boulder covered with a blanket of velvety moss where they decided to take their first break.

Crosby put the pack down and broke out the water and some granola bars.

"How long you think we been hikin'?" Tosh asked.

"Coupla hours."

"I feel pretty good."

"Me too. It's startin' to heat up though."

After about fifteen minutes, Crosby suggested they search for some logs to burn that night. They had no problem finding useful wood, but the logs made the pack much heavier — a fact not lost on Tosh, whose turn it was to take the pack.

"Wouldn't it have made more sense to cook the spaghetti last night on the stove, and bring the Spam and rolls to the top of the mountain so we wouldn't have to cook?"

"Yes, it would have," said Crosby, stuffing the last log into the top of the pack. "But we didn't think of it."

As the day grew warmer, the terrain in front of them grew steeper and the hiking became more difficult. They took frequent, brief breaks to alleviate the strain as much as possible. Still, as they neared the most challenging section of the mountain, they found themselves with sweat dripping in their eyes, burning thighs and aching feet.

Tosh wanted to plop down where he stood, but Crosby prodded him on. "Just a little further. We'll break soon."

"What are we waiting for?" Tosh complained.

"A better spot. If we're gonna kick back for a little while, we might as well do it in a good place."

"This is good. I can smell the pine trees," Tosh pointed out.

"Just a little further," Crosby urged. "We're getting up there. I'd like to see the view."

The vista they soon encountered was well worth the wait. The path led them to a stone bluff, from which Tosh and Crosby could see a spectacular waterfall in the nearby distance. A swiftly flowing stream gushed over the edge of a nearby cliff, sending white water toppling down five stories of gray-beige rock. Beyond the waterfall stood the stately peak of Half Dome, a stone steeple poking into the baby-blue sky.

"Wow," Tosh puffed.

"See?" said Crosby. "I told you. Let's get over by that stream and see if we can get our feet wet."

The path wound around and, in minutes, Tosh and Crosby had met up with the stream. They inched closer to the edge of the falls, allowing them an immense panorama of miles of monstrous mountains, a parade of gray mammoths. Tall conifers saturated the valley like a wide pine river cutting through the range, while those speckling the rocky mountainsides looked like a dusting of green snow.

After taking in the magnificent view to their hearts' content, Tosh and Crosby headed about twenty yards up stream from the falls and sat down on the flat, stone riverbank.

Crosby began untying his hiking boots. "I've done some more thinking on this concept of God that we were discussing yesterday," he said. "That is, God being within and not sitting up in the sky like a giant Judge Wapner."

"Oh yeah? Let's hear it."

"O.K. Most people conclude that God is omnivorous, right?"

"Omnivorous? They think God eats everything?"

Crosby looked at Tosh with perplexity.

"You mean, omnipotent?" Tosh asked.

"What did I say?"

"Omnivorous."

"Oh. Yeah. Omnipotent." Crosby pried off his boots. "All powerful."

"I think most people would agree that God is omnipotent."

"Well, if God is omnipotent, then wouldn't He steer things the way He wanted them to go?"

"You think everything happens the way God planned it?"

"Well, if that's the case, then God definitely doesn't judge us." Crosby peeled off his sweaty socks and stuck his feet in the water. "But I tend to think that God doesn't have any specific plans. I think he gave us free will to decide on our own."

"Free will," said Tosh, sitting down beside Crosby. "I agree that we have free will."

"O.K., so if God gives us choices, but then threatens us with punishment, i.e. burning in hell forever if we don't choose what he wants, then that's not really much of a choice to begin with, is it?"

"I guess not." Tosh tied back his dreads, letting a little air circulate over his neck. "But if God isn't judging us, why would he have given us the Ten Commandments?"

Crosby thought for a moment. "Well, for starters, how do we know God set those anyway?"

"They were in the Bible."

"And who wrote the Bible?"

"Well, a number of people. Moses wrote the part about the Ten Commandments."

"And why should we believe him?"

"'Cause he was there. What are you saying, Crosby, that Moses lied? That the Ten Commandments are not a mandate from God, but just a scheme to keep the masses in line?"

"I'm not saying anything that drastic, I'm just saying maybe he exaggerated a little. Maybe they're not really commandments. Maybe they're just suggestions."

"The Ten Suggestions?" Tosh plunged his legs into the stream. "That just doesn't have the same impact."

"Exactly."

"Why would God give us suggestions?"

"Maybe because he wants us to be happy. Maybe the Ten Commandments are suggestions for us on how to live joyfully. Or do you not believe that God wants us to be happy?"

Tosh leaned back on the ground. "I believe God wants us to be happy," he said, "but renouncing the concept of a judging God makes me uneasy."

"Why?" asked Crosby. "You should feel relieved. You don't have to please the Big Guy in the sky. You don't have to pass the test. Hell, you don't even have to take the test anymore. There's no more pressure."

"Yeah, but Cros, eliminating that concept voids an answer to a very important question."

"What question is that?"

"If life is not a test, then why are we here?"

Crosby leaned back on the stone riverbank like Tosh and considered the question. He became aware of the cool soothing water rushing by his feet and the warmth of the afternoon sun on his face. He heard the rippling of the river over the rocks and the song of birds in the trees. He felt wonderful.

"Maybe God put us here to think. To feel. To experience," Crosby said. "Why does life have to be some sort of test? Maybe God put us here to simply be."

*   *   *   *

The cables climbing the steep summit of Half Dome were suspended by narrow, four-foot-high poles imbedded in the rock. They ran parallel about three feet apart, straight up the rounded crest of the mountain. Two-by-fours had been bolted to the base of the steel poles and ran across the path to provide more stable footing if a climber wanted to rest his arms, which felt most of the strain pulling the person up.

Tosh looked up and thought to himself, *This is a potentially life-threatening situation. It would not take a lot of bad luck to kill me. With just a little misfortune, say a confrontation with an aggressive stinging insect or perhaps an ill-timed groin pull or ankle twist or something, I could lose my grip on the cables and tumble*

*down four stories and smash on the rocks below and shatter my skeletal system,
puncture my lung, obliterate my spleen, rip my face off and hemorrhage.*

"Looks great, huh?" said Crosby.

Tosh looked at his partner and uttered a lackluster, "Yep."

Suddenly, a recurring dream Tosh had had in the past popped into his head. He
could see himself falling through the air. He could not hear his own screaming
because of the sound of the wind thundering by his ears. Below him, the ground
looked safely far away, but he knew it approached inevitably. As soon as he could
make out details, like baseball fields and trees and barns, he seemed to pick up
speed until almost instantaneously the ground was upon him. At the last second, the
wind eerily stopped, allowing Tosh to hear his terrified screams before he made
contact. Tosh closed his eyes and braced himself for the hit.

To his surprise, Tosh hit the ground and bounced up, landing again, gently, on
his feet. He brushed himself off and the dream ended.

After a while, Tosh had begun to recognize the dream and developed some sort
of split consciousness in his sleep which allowed him to watch the dream as a
casual, somewhat bored, observer, rather than a horrified, unwilling participant.
Instead of accepting the falling as reality with a quickened pulse and clenched teeth,
his reality became a disinterested spectator who knew the outcome already and
waited impatiently for it to end. It was like being forced to watch himself in a movie
he had already seen a hundred times. Not a pleasant experience, but better than
being the one falling.

Looking up at the cables, Tosh knew that if he should fall now, there would be
no bouncing.

"I'll go first," announced Crosby. "No problem."

For a second, Tosh felt grateful. But then he pictured Crosby high above him,
showing off with a look-ma-no-hands gesture. Crosby loses his footing and his
cocky grin turns to an expression of fear as his body comes barreling down the
chute toward Tosh. Tosh can see him coming but there's nowhere to go. Crosby hits
him with the full force of his 175 pounds and then the two of them free-fall until, of
course, Tosh hits the ground first with tremendous impact. He dies instantly,
breaking the fall for Crosby, who gets a bit battered but is otherwise unscathed.

"I'll go first," said Tosh, scurrying ahead of Crosby. "That way you can catch
me if I fall."

Tosh looked back and the expression on Crosby's face showed a little
disappointment. Not because he was at greater risk, Tosh figured, but presumably
because Crosby wanted to be the first one to the top.

Crosby didn't complain but instead offered some advice. "Make sure you lean
forward at all times, dreadlocks."

"Thanks. Anything else?"

"Yeah," said Crosby. "Don't let go."

*   *   *   *

And don't look down, thought Tosh, looking down.

Seeing the ground far below made him unsettled, so he quickly returned his gaze to the incline in front of him. He did not need visual reminders to know how high he was. Yet it bothered him that he could not see Crosby, thanks to the curved slope of the mountain. It reminded him of the way the steep streets of San Francisco vanished from their rear view mirror.

With his foot braced against a two-by-four and both hands still gripping the cable, Tosh craned his neck around again and peered over his shoulder for another glimpse. A moment later, he saw the top of Crosby's San Diego Padres cap, and a moment after that, he saw Crosby's face grinning up at him.

"What took you so long?"

"I can't get enough of this view," said Crosby. "Every ten feet I have to stop and admire it."

Tosh chuckled. "I'm movin' on."

Bending his waist slightly toward the mountain helped keep his weight forward. Focusing his eyes on the path directly in front of him, Tosh clenched the cables tightly and pulled himself up. He moved briskly but not hastily, concentrating on his every move, for he knew that if he didn't, it could be his last.

The possibility of death improved his concentration remarkably, he noted, eliminating any possible distractions. Thoughts of brick-oven pizzas, D-cup breasts or fat hairy buds did not dare creep into his consciousness.

Scaling the Dome, Tosh was all business.

*   *   *   *

One step from the summit, Tosh paused. "Cros?"

"Yeah," gasped Crosby, slightly short on breath. He paused a few steps below Tosh and looked up.

"You can do the honors."

Crosby nodded a thanks, inhaled deeply, and climbed the last few feet, brushing by Tosh on the way. As he abandoned the support of the cables and strode on to level ground, he announced grandly, "One small step for man, one giant leap for mankind." Then, he thrust his arms up in the air, tilted his head back and performed a flamboyant little dance, like a defensive back celebrating an interception return in the end zone.

Tosh expressed his jubilation with more humility, falling on his knees and kissing the ground. "Thank you, thank you, thank you," he breathed.

With its barren stone landscape and celestial loft, the top of Half Dome had a Mars-like vibe, though it was more tranquil than creepy. The vast plain in the sky promised to serve up a strong dose of wind, but as the afternoon wound down, only a benign breeze nudged the eye-level clouds gently by.

Surprisingly, Tosh and Crosby found fairly comfortable accommodations, discovering a patch of sand amid the rock and scrub in which to pitch their tent. Further blessing them, the spot enjoyed shelter thanks to some surrounding stones — five flat, round boulders, the type of rocks the Jolly Green Giant might like to skip in the ocean.

With the tent in place, starting a fire came next. Crosby and Tosh set out to scrounge up some kindling, scouring the area for flammable material. Only a scattering of scrub lived atop the rock in the sky, so they would have to provide.

"I feel kind of bad about this," said Tosh, breaking off some twigs from a stubby but resilient bush.

"Why?" asked Crosby.

"I feel guilty. Here we are in this awesome, beautiful place and what are we doing? Fucking it up."

"It's just a couple of branches. It's not like we're pillaging."

"We're acting like typical humans — causing destruction to the environment."

"Think of it as pruning," said Crosby.

Suddenly, their solitude was interrupted by a loud human screech.

Tosh dropped his handful of twigs and Crosby whirled around. "What the hell is that?"

They were not alone.

*   *   *   *

Evan Blake had just scaled the face of Half Dome. He had spent the past ten hours clenching slivers in the rock while balancing his entire body weight on ledges the size of a Lego. His hands were scraped and cut, his face and neck sunburned.

To say Evan was glad to be at the summit would be an understatement. With a warm Schlitz in his hand (compliments of Tosh and Crosby) and his bare feet basking in the sun, Evan rested comfortably. According to the look on his face, semi-cooked spaghetti never tasted so good.

"You guys are the greatest," he said. "Thanks for the hospitality."

"Sorry about the spaghetti," said Tosh. "Gives 'al dente' a new meaning."

"We couldn't get the fire hot enough," Crosby remarked. "Not enough kindling."

Evan was older than them, maybe by a decade or so. His black hair on the longish side, he wore sideburns and round glasses. "That's all right. It hits the spot," he said. "All I have is a Power Bar."

Crosby scooped the rest of the tomato sauce on to Evan's pasta. "Climbing the face of Half Dome — you deserve it."

"What would ever possess you to climb a mountain like this?" Tosh asked. "Just for the thrill of it?"

Evan scratched at the whisker stubble on his cheek. "Not purely."

"A dare?" asked Crosby.

"A bet?" asked Tosh.

"No, nothing like that."

"For the sense of accomplishment?"

Evan rolled spaghetti around his fork. "I won't deny that it feels great to tackle something like this, but I've done it before, so it wasn't a new challenge."

Tosh and Crosby looked at Evan with a mixture of admiration and bewilderment.

"This is the deal," said Evan. "I've been working on this novel for about a year now."

"A novel?" Tosh interrupted. "What's it about?"

"It's a hate story."

"A hate story?"

"Yeah, as opposed to a love story."

"Hmmm," said Tosh. "A hate story."

"Yeah. It's like an anti-romance novel." Evan scraped the remaining tomato sauce from his plastic bowl. "It's about the deterioration of a man and woman's relationship. A couple who at one point had been in love, or what they thought was love — neither of them were actually capable of feeling an emotion as deep as that — who grew to unconsciously despise each other. And, despite their secret ill feelings toward each other, they continued to stay together."

"Why would they do that?"

"They were addicted to each other."

"Addicted?"

"You mean obsessed?" Tosh posited.

"Nope," said Evan. "They weren't obsessed with each other, they were addicted to each other, just like being addicted to drugs. They couldn't live without each other, but in an unhealthy way."

"Can you be addicted to a person?" asked Crosby.

"They were moreso addicted to the things that the other person provided for them — money, sex, prestige. These were two shallow, vain people who constantly needed their egos masturbated. They strictly used each other."

"Couldn't they find those things with someone else?"

"Yeah, but throw jealousy into the mix. Whenever things got so ugly that it seemed like they would have to break up, jealousy was the glue that kept them together."

"Sounds like a match made in heaven," said Tosh.

"More like hell. These two characters embody all of the worst human traits."

"Why would you write a story like this?"

The Cosmic Burrito

"I'm not sure," laughed Evan. "I think it's an adverse reaction to all the trashy romance novels I read as a kid."

"You read trashy romance novels as a kid?"

"Well, I had them read to me. In bed."

"Like bedtime stories?"

"Exactly. I had this babysitter who constantly read those romance paperbacks to me. I guess she was selfish or something and she didn't want to bore herself by reading me children stories, so she just read me her crappy novels. Or maybe she just wanted to see my reactions. In any case, no *Green Eggs and Ham* for me."

"No offense, dude," said Crosby, "but that's kind of weird."

"Oh, I know," said Evan. Then, after a beat, "She taught me about sex, too."

"She did?"

"Yeah." Evan nodded and ran his hand through his tangled hair. "She molested me, man."

Tosh and Crosby both stared at Evan, not knowing how to react.

"I guess I should say it was wrong and it screwed me up and all that. But you know what? It was great. I liked it."

"You did?"

"Totally enjoyed it."

"That's even weirder," said Crosby, "I think."

"I didn't know there was anything wrong with it. All I knew was that it felt good."

"Did you tell anyone?"

"Nope. It was our little secret."

"That's one hell of a babysitter," said Crosby.

"She was definitely my favorite." Evan put down his empty bowl and got up and stretched. "I still think about her now and then."

"What happened to her?" asked Tosh.

"She went to college in Nevada and I never saw her again."

"Probably a hooker in Vegas now," said Crosby. He gathered all the empty bowls and piled them into the garbage bag they had brought along.

"So, Evan, what does all this have to do with you climbing the mountain?"

"Oh, yeah. So, I'm working on this hate novel, and I've got the whole story set up. I'm like two hundred pages into it, and suddenly, I'm stuck."

"Writer's block?"

"Yeah. Something. Everything was rolling along beautifully. I was writing effortlessly, just making things up as I went along. Then, one day, all of the sudden, I had no idea what to do next. I just couldn't figure out where to take it. I felt empty, completely stuck. After a couple weeks of staring at my computer screen with nothing to say, I got totally frustrated, sick to my stomach even. It was torture.

"My friend said that I should put it aside for a little while to clear my mind, and then when I come back to it, I might see things differently. A fresh approach could bring in new ideas, he said. So I tried not writing, but I couldn't really get away from it. Even though I wasn't sitting down in front of the computer, I was so used to thinking about it, analyzing it and planning it every day, that I couldn't get it out of my mind. Wherever I was — in the car, at work, jogging — I kept mulling over the same ideas, like a broken record inside my skull, driving me crazy.

"Then, I got an idea. Not about the story, but how to clear my head. Climbing."

"How so?" asked Tosh.

"When you're mountain climbing, you have no time to think about anything besides the task at hand. Every breath you take, you have to be completely focused on the mountain. You have to think about your every move — which crack to grab hold of, where to place your foot. It takes total concentration."

Tosh and Crosby could relate to what Evan was saying because of their recent climb, even though the cables were a cakewalk compared to the face of Half Dome.

"Were you able to clear your head?" asked Crosby. "Did your plan work?"

Evan smiled. "Well, I hadn't thought about the book until now."

Crosby frowned. "Sorry."

"No harm done," said Evan. "Today made me feel better."

"We'll talk about something else," said Tosh.

"And tomorrow," Evan added, "I have to climb down."

*   *   *   *

Standing on the bluff, Tosh, Crosby and Evan peered over the gorge in front of them. Across the ravine, another flat-topped mountain rose a step higher than Half Dome. Beyond it, brilliant orange glow gushed up from the horizon like a well spewing sunflower oil. A slight breeze rippled by their ears, the only murmur as they stood in awe of the absolute tranquility.

"Oh, man," whispered Tosh.

Crosby shook his head, incredulous of the beauty before them. "I love California."

"So sweet."

"Kansas was fun, Canada was beautiful," said Crosby, "but *this*, this is amazing."

Evan breathed in the twilight. "God works wonders, eh?"

Tosh nodded. "No doubt."

"Don't think I'm weird," said Crosby, "but I feel like we're really close to God right now. I don't know why — I just do."

"It's 'cause we're up so high. It's like we're closer to heaven," Tosh chuckled.

Evan laughed. "Yeah, that's it."

Crosby put his arm around Tosh, a brotherly show of affection. "God is within, right?"

"God's everywhere. He climbed this mountain with me," said Evan. "You think I could have done that alone?"

"We have this theory on God," said Crosby. "Tell us what you think." Crosby related to Evan the 'God is the happening' concept that he had postulated earlier to Tosh.

"I believe that God is within," Evan stated. "I also believe He's in the sky, in the trees, in the oceans and streams, in chocolate pudding and in a big pile of cow manure."

"What?"

"Pudding?"

"Yes. I believe God, as the Creator, is in *all* creation," explained Evan. "But I wonder if we, as humans, can truly comprehend what God is. I feel that God is so awesome, so overwhelming, that God is beyond our grasp.

"That's why I don't seek to define what God is. Your theory is interesting, but it attempts to explain God. What's more important to me is my relationship with God, how I communicate with Him. That's what really counts."

"You mean prayer?"

"Sure, prayer is one way."

"It's the only way I know of," said Crosby. "Hail Marys, Our Fathers and all that."

"That's a misconception. Actually, if you ask me, that's a pretty lame way of communicating with God."

"Why is that?"

"Well, it works for some people, I'm sure, but not for me. I mean, don't you think that those prayers are kind of stale?"

"What do you mean?"

"Can you imagine how many times God has heard the Our Father? He must be bored to death. That kind of prayer is so unoriginal — speaking to God in words that are not even your own. To me, it's not even really speaking to God — it's like reciting Him a poem or something."

"God bored? You make it seem like God is one of us," said Crosby.

"God is not one of us. He's part of us," said Evan. "God is part of everything in the universe, because they are all His creations. God can be bored — why not? God created boredom."

"You have a point there," Tosh remarked.

Evan continued. "Only God is immeasurably greater than all of His creations. He is the sum of the whole. I feel that we, as mortals, can not even conceive of His greatness."

"Mere mortals!" hissed Crosby, mimicking a cartoon fiend.

"But that doesn't mean we can't talk to Him like we talk to each other," Evan stated. "Who says we have to make it so formal all the time? I talk to God whenever I feel like it, and I treat Him like He is my best friend. We are all God's children, and we're all different, so it makes sense to me that we would speak to Him differently."

"Do you think God answers you?"

"I know He does."

"How? Does He talk to you?" Tosh thought of his experience at the reggae festival when God had spoken to him. He had written the whole thing off as the mushrooms, but maybe there was more to it.

"Sure, sometimes."

"What does He sound like?"

"Wouldn't it be cool if God sounded like Cheech Marin?" Crosby kidded. Then, with a half-decent Spanish accent, he added, "Hey man, quit thinkin' 'bout boinkin' in church! You only mek eet to church twice a year as eet ees, try an' be ho-lee."

"It's not like I hear voices in my head or something," Evan explained. "It's just my own voice, my own thoughts. It's not earth moving or anything like that."

Earth moving? Like the sky opening up and God patting me on the ass? It was the drugs, thought Tosh.

"But I believe that God puts those thoughts there," Evan continued. "God creates ideas and gives them to me.

"I believe He speaks to me in other ways, too. Sometimes He sends signs. The trick is to be aware, so you can receive the signs. They can be bold, but they can be subtle as well. So if you're not aware, you can miss a lifetime worth of signs."

"What type of signs?" asked Crosby. "Give me an example."

Evan thought for a moment. "O.K. This one's pretty major, but they don't have to be. They could be less significant.

"About a year ago, I was on my way home to my apartment. It was a Saturday afternoon. I was a couple miles from my place when one of my favorite songs, 'Jessica,' by the Allman Brothers, came on the radio."

"Awesome song."

"Yeah, and you know how it's a really long song? Well, I wanted to hear the whole song. It was a gorgeous day, I had the windows rolled down, and I was feeling good. So I got off the highway before my exit so I could take the side streets for the last couple miles. That way takes a few minutes longer than the highway and I didn't want my ride to end until the song was over. I park in an underground lot, you know, and I didn't want to be sitting down there in the dark, exhaust-filled garage listening to the Allmans. It's just not the same as sunshine and a warm breeze."

"I know exactly what you mean," said Tosh, thinking back to his blissful ride through eastern Wyoming.

"So I take the extra few minutes to get home, and when I get there, my apartment is on fire."

"Holy shit," said Crosby.

"Actually, it was the apartment next to mine, but my walls were getting hot. So I grab all my most important possessions, which included my laptop and Dickie, my cat, and got the hell out. My apartment ended up getting scorched."

"That really sucks, man," said Tosh.

"No doubt," added Crosby.

"It was horrible, but I am thankful the way things turned out. Because I found out later, that on the highway at that time, the way I usually go, there was a five car pile-up. It turned the highway into a parking lot. I never would have gotten home in time to save Dickie. Not to mention my computer, which had the only copy of my novel on it."

"Damn," Crosby said. "Don't you have any back-up copies?"

"At the time, I didn't," said Evan. "Now, I have them all over the place. My car, at work, my girlfriend's."

"Good move."

"So, you can call the Allman Brothers song good timing, a lucky break. Or, if you're like me, you take it as a sign. God speaking to me, giving me a warning."

"You know," remarked Tosh. "That totally relates to the 'Everything happens for a reason' theory."

"Sure does," said Evan.

"How do you know that God sends those signs?" asked Crosby.

Evan looked perplexed. "Who else would?"

"Maybe a guardian angel," said Tosh.

"Ahhh," Evan smiled. "Perhaps. But who do you think controls the angels? Who do they work for?"

"True, true."

"God's the supervisor," said Crosby.

"I've never thought about God in those terms," said Tosh. "I never considered having a personal relationship with Him. I always viewed God as pretty inaccessible, like a distant King or something."

"I always thought we had to worship Him," said Crosby.

"Well, that's what you've been taught. Most people think the same thing, and not only in our culture. We've all been taught to fear God.

"Look at the animal sacrifices — and human sacrifices for that matter! I can't think of anything more ludicrous — that the giver of life would want us to kill something for Him. Can somebody please explain the logic in that?"

"If God wanted something dead, He'd make it dead Himself," Crosby pointed out.

"Sure," said Evan.

"So, you don't think we have to worship God?" Tosh asked.

Evan mulled it over for a moment. "Worship is the wrong word. It's too strong. It implies servitude. I don't believe we are here to serve God, though plenty of people will argue that.

"Think of Him as your father. We are His children and He is our father. Treat Him with love and respect, and He will love and support you. In fact, He will love and support you no matter how you treat Him, because He is God and His love is unconditional."

"How do you know all this?" asked Crosby.

"I know it," said Evan, "because it's what I believe. It's called faith."

*   *   *   *

The guys headed back to the remaining smolders of their evening fire and continued their discussion about God.

"I guess I don't have any faith," said Crosby, somewhat ashamed. "I just picture screaming Evangelists trying to ram religion down my throat. I've never been religious. Even as a kid, I hated going to church. It seemed like a waste of time. During the sermon and all that, all I thought about was girls. I've always had more interest in sex than in religion."

"So have a lot of priests," quipped Tosh.

"I'm not religious either," Evan said.

"What do you mean?"

"Faith in God does not make you religious. Following religion makes you religious. Faith in God makes you spiritual. It's a different thing. You can have a complete, loving relationship with God without being religious."

"You can?"

"Sure. Religions are merely systems of belief. They're most concerned with perpetuating their doctrines and maintaining their survival. And in doing so, they'll have you worrying about extraneous details."

"Like not eating meat on Fridays," said Crosby.

"Exactly. Religions focus more on the process, rather than the result. They're about who you worship and how you pray.

"I don't like people telling me what to think and how to live my life," Evan continued. "I'll make my own decisions, especially about something as important as God."

"And how can one religion be true and all the others be false?" asked Crosby. "That's what I want to know."

"No one religion is true, but all religions have common elements — at the core of all religion lies spirituality. If you take religion and strip away the technicalities, the restrictions and the pomp, you're left with the pursuit of truth, which is spirituality. Religions constrict. They limit your way of thinking. But spirituality expands. It opens your consciousness to another reality — a side of life beyond the world at face value."

"What side is that?" asked Crosby.

Tosh knew. He looked at Evan. "The side with all the answers."

*   *   *   *

The next morning, Tosh awoke to the irritating sensation of a fly's legs tickling his forehead. And his wrist. And his tricep. And his heel.

He threw his sleeping bag off of himself and grunted in disgust. It was no use trying to sleep anymore.

Oddly, Crosby, usually the early riser, continued to lie undisturbed. Had the damn fly left him alone or had he just not felt it?

Tosh exited the tent in his boxers. By the looks of things, dawn had passed a little while ago. The sun burned brightly in the eastern sky and Evan had already packed up and split, presumably back down the face of the mountain. What a nut.

Tosh's first instinct was to go back into the tent and wake Crosby, but something made him halt — a sudden sense of true solitude. It dawned on him how uncommon it was to be the only living, conscious being around. He crept over to one of the flat boulders and sat down.

Remaining still, Tosh took in his surroundings. Curiously, there was very little to look and listen to. With no breeze, trees, birds or bees, he couldn't see any movement or hear any sounds, save the occasional jet airplane in the distance.

There were no ringing phones, no doorbells, no sirens and no barking dogs. No intruding roommates, no nagging mothers or pestering little sisters. No lawnmowers, leaf blowers or radial saws.

How relaxing, thought Tosh. *No distractions. Great place for a nap, except that I just woke up.*

Tosh felt like he should take advantage of his unique situation.

Maybe I should try to meditate, he thought.

He focused his gaze on a patch of thicket. Recalling a technique he'd been taught during his previous introduction to meditation (the class he quit not even halfway through), Tosh concentrated on his breathing. He began counting his breaths on the exhalations, counting up to four and then starting over, making sure not to modify his breathing pattern.

One, two, three, four.

One, two, three, four.

The goal was to be aware of nothing but his breathing, and for Tosh to involve his entire being in the activity. If any thoughts, feelings, impressions or sensory perceptions crept into his consciousness and interrupted his routine, Tosh was to let them go and gently bring himself back to focus.

One, two, three, four.
One, two, three, four.
One, two, three, there's a fly on my knee.

309

Tosh wiggled his leg and the fly skidaddled.

One, two, three, four.
One, two, three, four.
One, two, three, four.
One, two — shit, there he is again.

Tosh wiggled his leg, but the fly did not budge. *Damnit!* He shooed the fly away with his hand and resumed counting.

One, two, three, four.
One, two, three, four.
One, two, three, four.

He's on my head. I'm going to ignore him, Tosh thought.

One, two, he's still there. Motherfucker. Three, four.
One, two, three, four.
One, two, three, four.
One, two, three, four.
One, two, three, four.

The fly landed on Tosh's jaw.

One, two.

The fly spoke: "*Only morning and what a day it's been already some guy cleaned a couple of trout over on the river and left entrails only thing better than the eyes are the stomachs I'm telling you man so salty yum yum yeah so then I fertilized some eggs nothing like a little lovin' in the morning right oh yeah sex in the a.m. on a fresh pile of dog doo I think it was poodle poo but not one of those tiny yip-yip poodles one of those huge ones that look like the little guys bulked up on steroids oh baby that fly was a looker she had the hairiest legs and the pile was still warm and soft nothing like it in the world I'm telling you man it's the greatest sensation then I had me some pancakes thanks to this little kid kids are the best God's gift to flies I'm telling you man you can take your time 'cause they never shoo you away pancakes soaked in delicious maple syrup Aunt Jemima I think it was stuff's great I love sweets but its sticky and that can be a bitch you know what I mean noticed his nose was running so I cruised up for a taste kids I'm telling you he didn't even know I was on his face then I swooped down on some guy's sweaty neck whew you could taste the curry that stuff stays in your system for days do you like curry I don't like curry but I'm not that choosy hell I suck the moisture from shit you know that hey*

310

man what's the big idea you trying to kill me man you'll never catch me you're too slow I got eyes in the back of my head you know what I mean man I see you coming from a mile away you'll never swat me with your bare hands what are you a moron you must be a moron moron moron mor—"

Tosh wiped the crumpled fly carcass from his hand and went to wake Crosby.

* * * *

Tosh and Crosby packed up their sleeping bags and tent and hit the cables without eating breakfast. Crosby took the pack and led the way, feeling fresh after a night of substantial sleep and a hangover-less morning — for a change he had no alcohol to work out of his system.

Tosh found descending the summit much easier than climbing, especially without the pack. He allowed Crosby ample space below him and moved at a swift pace, letting the cable slide through his hands while taking quick backwards strides. Before he knew it, they were down.

"Piece of cake," he bragged, barely breathless.

"Let's haul ass down the mountain," said Crosby. "And try to hit the road by noon."

Within minutes, they crossed the tree line again. It was another clear day and the morning sun filtered through the green canopy, forming pockets of light and shade. Tosh and Crosby moved nimbly and quietly, surveying the ground in front of them, checking for rocks, logs or ditches — obstacles that could sprain an ankle. No one spoke or stopped until they saw the bear.

Crosby spotted it first, just off the path about twenty yards down the mountain. He stopped in his tracks as his jaw dropped open.

With his head down, Tosh failed to notice Crosby had stopped ahead of him. He kept his brisk pace, spurred along by the steady beat of "Guns of Navarone," an old ska tune he kept humming under his breath.

Tosh practically bowled Crosby over. "What're you doin', man?" he huffed.

Without taking his eye off of the bear, Crosby pointed.

"What?" asked Tosh, a little annoyed. "What the hell's the mat—"

"*Bear*," Crosby whispered.

"Bear? Where?"

"There." Crosby pointed again.

Tosh followed Crosby's finger. "Oh my God," he gulped.

Despite its bulk, the brown bear was difficult to see when it remained still, standing in a dim shaded area and further camouflaged by the rust-colored bark on the trunks of the broad trees.

"It's big."

"Uh, yeah."

Tosh and Crosby continued to whisper. They couldn't tell if the bear hadn't noticed them or just chose to ignore them. Either way, it seemed complacent enough, sniffing the ground with a purpose.

"What should we do?"

"I don't know. I guess we should start yelling at it."

"Shit." Tosh hated that idea. "Fuck."

"That's what the ranger told us to do."

"I know, I know. I was just hoping you wouldn't say that."

"The ranger wouldn't mislead us," said Crosby. "Ready?"

Tosh wished he could tap his heels together and disappear. "Ready," he reluctantly agreed.

"HEY YA BIG BEAR, GET OUTA HERE!" screamed Crosby. He jumped up and down and waved his arms.

Tosh followed with "BOOYAKA BOOYAKA! SCRAM!"

Startled, the bear picked its head up and growled. The fur on its back stood on end.

Tosh and Crosby immediately stopped their verbal assault and started a hasty retreat.

"Wait!" Crosby called after a few seconds. "Tosh, wait!"

Tosh stopped. He glanced behind him at the bear and saw the bear hadn't advanced. It stood poised, agitated.

"We're not supposed to run," said Crosby. "We can't show our fear."

Tosh certainly didn't want to encourage the bear to come after them. "O.K. What do you suggest?"

Crosby bent down and picked up a stone. "The ranger told us to throw rocks, too, remember?"

Tosh cringed. "I hate this idea. I have to say I really hate it."

"The ranger wouldn't mislead us."

Tosh felt encouraged that the bear hadn't budged. But at the same time, it didn't exactly run away whimpering either. And he definitely didn't like the sound of that growl.

"Don't try to hit it," said Crosby. "Just try to scare it. Remember, he's probably more scared of us—"

"—than we are of him. Uh-huh, sure." Tosh grabbed a couple stones about the size of golf balls. "Try to scare it," he said.

"Yeah. Ready?"

Crosby screamed, "AAARRGGHHH!" and fired the first shot. It landed in front of the bear.

"GET THE FUCK OUTA HERE, YOU BIG OLD SCARY BEAR!" Tosh yelled. His rock hit a nearby tree.

The bear growled again and began to charge, lumbering forward.

The instant Tosh and Crosby realized the bear was in motion, they turned and ran, scrambling back up the path with their stomachs in their mouths.

Keenly, Crosby grabbed hold of Tosh and wrestled him behind a nearby boulder about the size of a Volkswagen Bug.

"What're you doin'?"

"We can't outrun the bear! We're better off hiding!"

The guys squatted with their backs up against the boulder.

Would the bear eviscerate them with its four-inch claws, claws sharp enough to slice the bark off of trees? Or would he pounce on them with his massive bulk, forcing the air out of their lungs and breaking their backs, leaving them paralyzed while he gnawed away on their flesh? Maybe he'd only get one of them, leaving the other to suffer the pain of letting his best friend die while he helplessly stood by.

Tosh could feel his heart pounding. Sweat dripped down his face. He looked up to the sky and with conviction, burst, "Jah, please hear me, God, please don't let this bear kill us, please, please, please. I know it sucks for me to start off our relationship asking you for a favor, but I'd really appreciate this one. I need you. I need you big-time here."

Tosh pictured God, in the form of one of those white religious statues, hearing his request, springing to life and sending a telepathic message down to the bear, kind of like Aquaman speaking to the fish during those old Saturday morning *Justice League* cartoons. He then pictured the bear hearing the command, pausing, looking around bewilderedly and returning to the spot where he had been sniffing.

Crosby peered over the edge of the boulder. "He's not comin'!"

Tosh breathed a huge sigh of relief. "Oh, thank God."

"Yeah, I guess we should." Crosby glanced down at Tosh. "Good thing you spoke to him and not me. We'd probably be gutted by now."

"The ranger wouldn't mislead us," Tosh mimicked angrily. He was pissed. "I knew that sounded like a bad idea."

Crosby ignored him, still keeping an eye on the bear over the edge of the boulder. "It's a she!" he whispered.

"How do you know?"

"It's got a cub. Up in the tree. We must have scared it. I didn't see it before."

"What's she doin'?"

"Looking up the tree at the cub."

"No way that bear is leaving the cub behind."

"Nuh-uh, no way," agreed Crosby. "I say we lay low and let the cub settle down. Maybe then they'll split."

"You sure you don't want to chuck rocks at it?"

Crosby made a face at Tosh. "It was the ranger's idea, not mine."

*　　*　　*　　*

After about ten minutes, the bears must have thought that Tosh and Crosby had vanished — or else they realized the two clowns hiding behind the rock didn't cause much of a threat — because the cub made its way down the tree trunk and the bears casually strolled into the woods.

Tosh and Crosby kept a watchful eye over the edge of the boulder.

"Cub's cute," said Crosby. "I'd love to have one as a pet."

"Yeah. It would probably destroy your house though."

"I'll say. Would have to keep him in the yard."

Tosh and Crosby remained behind the boulder for a full five minutes after the bears had moseyed out of sight. They were taking no chances.

"I didn't really think we were in trouble," Crosby stated.

"Yeah, right."

"I was just running 'cause you started running."

"What-ever," said Tosh. He opened the pack on Crosby's back.

"What're you doin'?"

"Hold still," said Tosh, rummaging through the pack. He handed Crosby a napkin. "Here."

"What's this for?"

"To wipe the shit out of your pants."

*　　　*　　　*　　　*

Tosh and Crosby hightailed it down the mountain without any further complications.

On the way, they encountered a beautiful doe standing in the middle of the path. Remaining still, she looked them right in the eyes for a long moment before scampering off.

Tosh took the deer to be a sign from Jah that everything was cool. He spoke to God again. "Thank you, Jah. I mean it. I appreciate your support. I really do. You *rule.*"

Then, realizing what he said, Tosh laughed to himself. *He's God. Of course He rules.*

*　　　*　　　*　　　*

As what was becoming usual, Josephine wouldn't start without her dose of starter fluid.

"I think our van is becoming a junkie," sighed Crosby. He sat in the back, unpacking the backpack and putting things back in their places.

"It's the entity," Tosh reminded him. Driving the van out of the confines of Yosemite, he felt good about their experiences on Half Dome. They conquered the mountain, cables, bears and all.

"Get out the map," said Tosh. "And figure out where we're going."

"We're going to hell in a bucket," Crosby sang, the chorus from the Grateful Dead song, "West L.A. Fadeaway."

Tosh looked at his friend in the rearview mirror and smiled. He understood Crosby. Affirming the call with a nod, Tosh completed the chorus, "But at least we're enjoying the ride."

CHAPTER 18

Of the smorgasbord of snacks stocked at the majority of mini-marts, only a few are not mainly sugar, fat, preservatives and coloring: basically, fresh fruit and other natural items. Peanuts, pistachios, pumpkin seeds and other trail-mix fodder do not fall into that category, for, although organic, they contain enough fat to fill a Jenny Craig waiting room.

Of the billions of calories manufactured by the food-processing industry, of the hundreds of thousands of foodstuffs sitting on shelves in varying degrees of staleness in mini-marts across the country, only one has true nutritional value.

It is not Gummy Worms.

It is not Nutty Buddies, Krumpets or Funyuns.

It is neither Twizzlers, Twinkies, Ring Dings nor Ding Dongs.

The Three Musketeers don't have a gram of nourishment among them.

Now and Laters are healthy neither today nor tomorrow.

M&M's may or may not make friends, but they will definitely make cavities.

This special snack is not Pringles, Munchos, Snickers, Snowballs, Doritos, Eskimo Pies, Milky Ways, Toasted Almonds or Pez.

It is beef jerky.

Contrary to popular belief, beef jerky contains only zero to two grams of fat per serving – it's practically dietetic!

And in addition to its favorable dietary status, beef jerky has a rich cultural heritage, having played an important role in the development of our nation. Beef jerky provided the pioneers with their primary form of sustenance. Back in the days of wagon trains, the settlers had to dry their beef to keep it from spoiling. (Maggots make for bad traveling partners. They eat all the food and they are not very adept conversationalists.)

"Grab me some beef jerky, will you, Cros?" Tosh asked his friend as they pulled into an A.M./P.M. Minimart on their way to L.A.

"No problem." Crosby hopped out of the van and went into the store to pay for the gas and purchase the treats.

Not wanting to risk getting stuck, Tosh kept the van running while he filled the tank. After checking the oil (it needed a quart), he ran the squeegee over all the glass, expending a generous amount of elbow grease on a particularly gnarly bug carcass splattered on the left headlight. "Is that a grasshopper?" he wondered out loud.

"Mini-mart, my ass," Crosby exclaimed as he returned to his perch in the shotgun seat. He threw down a plastic bag on the engine cover. "Not with those prices."

"I think the 'mini' refers to the size of the place, not the prices," Tosh pointed out.

"Obviously."

Tosh put an old Aswad tape in the tape deck and steered the van back on to the highway.

Tapping his foot to the chunky reggae beat, Crosby plucked the tape case from the engine cover. "'Ass-wad?' What the hell kind of name for a band is that?"

"It's pronounced 'Oz-wod.' It means 'black.'"

"In what language?"

"I'm not sure. Arabic, I think."

"Are they Arabs?"

"No. They're from England. That was a time, you know, when black consciousness was really taking root in England."

"Then why didn't they just call themselves 'Black?'"

"Black? That's not too original, is it?"

"It makes the point."

"Yeah, but you've got to remember, coming from a band's perspective, they're looking for a word that's unique, a word that's more mysterious. 'Black' doesn't have much intrigue."

"Reminds me of Spinal Tap. Remember their black album cover?"

Tosh laughed, recalling the comedic movie, a fake documentary about a clueless British rock band.

Crosby slipped into a Cockney accent and quoted the movie: "'It's as black as black can be. It's like nothing could be more…black.'"

"Cros, you of all people should appreciate Aswad's imagination. You're an artist."

"Well, they could have at least chosen a language that didn't look like 'Ass-wad' in English." Crosby ripped a plastic wrapper open with his mouth.

"Whaddaya got there?"

"Slim Jim. Don't worry, I got you one."

"I'm not eating that crap."

"What are you talking about?" asked Crosby, wiping grease from the meat stick on his sock. "You told me to get beef jerky."

"Let's get something straight right now," said Tosh. "Slim Jims are *not* beef jerky!"

Crosby looked at Tosh skeptically. "Since when?"

"Since always. Read the ingredients."

Crosby pulled the plastic wrapper back up over the meat stick and scanned the label. "Beef, mechanically separated chicken — *mechanically separated chicken??* That's disgusting!"

"Tell me about it. You know what that means?"

"What?"

"It means that Slim Jims are meat by-products, nothing but lips and assholes chopped and formed and held together by that — that membrane."

317

"Membrane?" Crosby scrutinized his snack with newfound concern. "I hate that word."

"Yeah," added Tosh. "Especially when it has to do with eating."

"I've been eating these things for years!" Crosby said with alarm.

"Slim Jims are not real meat. They're poseurs – beef jerky wannabes."

"What are you talking about?" Crosby asked crankily, obviously distraught with the realization he had been ingesting less desirable chicken parts throughout a good portion of his life.

"Slim Jims are all Hollywood and no substance. They're the glitz and glam of meat snacks. They have all that corporate money behind them — lavish ad budgets — but they're not quality meat. Beef jerky, on the other hand, is choice cuts of lean beef. Straight-up meat — no fillers. You can see the muscle fibers."

Crosby took a last look at his uneaten Slim Jim. He removed the rest of the wrapper and with a frown, tossed it out the window. "I never knew the difference."

*   *   *   *

Venice, California. Community of extroverts — stationary circus.

Aside from its curious assortment of businesses and vendors — so-called psychics reading tarot cards, palms and auras, body piercers, portrait painters, hair braiders and people peddling cheesy T-shirts, Graffix bongs, string bracelets, hemp necklaces, faux Rolexes and an array of useless dust-collecting chachkas — the asphalt boardwalk attracted all sorts of oddities: Shirtless, steroid-shooting muscle heads pumping iron, a tattoo-covered, dreadlocked preacher with a boa around his neck, a harmonica-playing, Mohawked unicyclist wearing a yellow jumpsuit, a skinhead skateboarder towing a chihuahua in a red wagon and some lanky dude on a pogo-stick wearing nothing but a banana-hammock and a jester hat.

"What a parade of freaks," Crosby quipped. "Only in California."

"Reminds me of Seaside, actually," said Tosh. "What is it about boardwalks that bring out the freaks?"

"Beats me. Look at that dude in the yellow jumpsuit. What does he think, he's in Devo?"

Parked in a sand lot adjacent to the boardwalk, Tosh and Crosby sat in their lawn chairs alongside the van, stoned on Ras Daniel's weed. They had eaten most of Daniel's cucumber for lunch, making sandwiches with American cheese, ketchup and mustard. "It's like eating a cheeseburger without the cheeseburger," Crosby had noted.

Midway through the afternoon, the guys were joined by their present neighbor — Angus, a full-time resident of the parking lot who lived out of a camper. For rent, Angus paid a monthly parking fee. He told Tosh and Crosby that the camper used to sit in the back of a pickup, but when the truck died, he sold it to a wrecker.

"Looks like our van's headed for a similar fate," Crosby cracked.

Angus wore less-than-perfect, rust-colored polyester trousers, a thin, white tank-top undershirt and a painter's cap with 'Surf Naked' printed on it. "Whaddaya say we get a beer?" he suggested.

"Now?" asked Tosh. "It's 3:30 in the afternoon."

"I don't have to work, do you?"

"Nope."

"Well then. I always say, 'A drink makes a new man outa ya.'" Angus lifted his cap to allow some air to hit his head. "But then the 'new man' wants a drink, and that puts you in a quandary."

Crosby got up from the lawn chair and went into the van. "What do ya want, Angus, a Schlitz or a Busch?"

Angus, sitting in his own lawn chair, craned his neck around. "No, no, boy. Let's head over to the bar. Happy Hour's just startin.'"

*   *   *   *

The B.M.W. Lounge — Angus' local watering hole. A run-down joint that made Wilma's, the dive in San Francisco, seem like a Friday's. It had no windows or clock, dark concrete walls, tattered, three-year old Monday Night Football posters, a lifeless Addams Family pinball machine and an autographed picture of Magic Johnson that hung askew. In the corner stood a life-size cardboard cutout of Elvira that looked as though it had been gang-raped. The moderately-sized color television behind the bar had a snowy picture and was tuned to a game show. Only the bottles of alcohol looked like they had seen the outside world recently, and that included the customers.

Angus' drinking buddies filled the bar. The fact that Happy Hour hadn't started yet didn't seem to faze them.

"Three drafts, Jesse," Angus directed the bartender.

Jesse, a large man with a graying semi-afro who walked with a slight limp, filled the mugs and slid them down to Angus with the delicate touch of an expert shuffleboard player — the glasses clinked together lightly, spilling just a sip.

"Not bad," said Crosby.

"Jesse played two years for the Atlanta Falcons," Angus informed them.

"Oh, yeah?" asked Tosh. "What position?"

"Place-kicker," Jesse answered.

Everyone in the bar laughed.

"Linebacker. Don't let him fool you," croaked a sweaty man with disheveled red hair, later introduced to Tosh and Crosby as Billygoat, named as such because he ate everything that passed before his eyes, including the scraps which got caught in his beard.

"I played mainly on special teams," Jesse said.

"Co-captain one year, right, Jesse?" asked Angus.

319

"Till I blew out my knee."

Angus sighed. "Damn knee. Coulda been All-Pro."

"At least it kept me outa the war."

By the time Tosh and Crosby finished their first beers, the initial shock of the despair of their surroundings had worn off and the guys settled in. Tosh fed the jukebox a fin and supplied tunes for the duration, a complete seventies soundtrack of disco and funk featuring records by Kool & the Gang, Donna Summer, K.C. & the Sunshine Band and the Bee Gees.

"Too bad we left our leisure suits at home," said Crosby. "We could have gotten laid."

"Yeah, uh-huh, sure," said Tosh, figuring any women to enter the bar would have a drug problem, a venereal disease or both. The place was obviously a breeding ground for addiction, an incubator for indolence, a harbor for depravity.

Yet, in a way, Tosh liked Angus' drinking buddies. He wouldn't add any of them to his address book, but they were hospitable enough, discounting their lack of hygiene. And, at the moment, Tosh and Crosby themselves wouldn't win any prizes for cleanliness.

"What's B.M.W. stand for?" Tosh asked Jesse. "Bavarian Motor Works?"

"Nope."

"Bob Marley and the Wailers?" (He didn't really expect that to be the case.)

"Nope," said Jesse, wiping the bar. "It stands for Brother Man's Workshop."

"My cat ate a rabbit once," said Jewel, a red-nosed fellow in worn khaki pants and a wrinkled Hawaiian shirt. Unlike the rest of the gang, his clothes were almost fashionable, albeit a little soiled.

"He ate a rabbit?" asked Crosby. "Did he like it?"

"Guess so. He ate the whole thing."

"Paw-licking good," said Crosby.

"Gave him gas something fierce."

"Really? Did it smell like carrots?"

"Nope," said Jewel. "Smelt like shit."

"The only pets I got is ants," said Angus.

"Do you have an ant farm?" Crosby asked.

Angus gave him a crooked look. "They live in my camper," he said. "I got two sets of ants. My night ants and my day ants."

"How so?"

"Well, the ants at one end of the camper prefer beer. They always go after the beer cans. But when I leave a soda can on the table, I get ants coming from the other side. I don't drink soda at night, see, so I got my night ants and my day ants."

"Do you work?" Tosh asked Angus.

"Work?" Angus laughed. "Hell no. I won the lottery."

"You won the lottery?"

"Sure did. Fourteen years ago."

"How much did you win?"

"Don't really know, tell ya the truth. I had ta split it with nine other guys."

"Why?"

"Well, we all chipped in."

"What did you each spend, a dime?" asked Crosby.

Angus gave Tosh the same crooked look that he had given Crosby moments earlier. "What's wrong with yer friend here? He drunk?"

"I think they chipped in for a bunch of tickets, Cros," Tosh said.

"What did you do before you won the lottery?"

"Worked in a factory."

"Doin' what?"

"General Motors assembly. Before that I was a vacuum cleaner salesman."

"Where was this?"

"Oh, here and there. Mainly the Midwest."

"Is that where you're from?"

"Yeah," burped Angus. "Michigan."

"So what did you do when you won the lottery?" Crosby asked.

"Quit my job, bought the camper and headed west."

"To L.A.?"

"I didn't know where I was goin'. It was all new to me," said Angus. "Traveled up and down the coast a few times, from Tijuana to British Colombia. Then I found Venice."

Angus polished off the last sip of his beer. "When I found Venice, I knew I'd seen it all. I figured it ain't gonna get any more interesting than this. Might as well stay put."

"Tell him the Cedarville Junction story, Angus." Billygoat turned to the guys. "This is a good one."

Angus motioned for Jesse to bring him a new beer. "All right, Cedarville Junction, here goes. This is back when I was sellin' vacuums door to door. They're reconditioned vacuums, O.K.? I'm buyin' them for three or four bucks an' sellin' them for eighteen. I'm in this little town in Iowa or someplace like that, an' this lady wants one, but she tells me she shouldn't really make a purchase like that without first consulting her husband, who was the manager of the bank. So I tell her no problem, why doesn't she give me the eighteen bucks, take the vacuum, an' I'll go smooth things over with the hubby at the bank. She was kinda reluctant but I told her it would be no problem, I'd do that for her. So I get to the bank an' I find the husband an' I tell him that his wife wants one of these vacuums but she doesn't have the eighteen bucks. He's kinda busy but I tell him I got a train to catch that evenin', so he gives me eighteen bucks an' I leave a vacuum with him. Later on, he gets home an' realizes I swindled him, sold him two cleaners. So he calls the train station an' tells the guy there's a vacuum cleaner salesman gettin' on the train, tell him to wait, I wanna talk to him. So the conductor finds me just as the train's leavin' an' says Mr. So-an'-so called here an' he wants to talk to you. An' I say, 'I know what he wants, he wants one a these vacuum cleaners. Tell you what, why don't you take a vacuum an' give me the eighteen dollars an' then you can get the money from him — he's the manager of the bank.'"

All of Angus' friends cracked up.

"Sold three cleaners that day!"

"Tell him the toilet story, Angus," piped Jewel.

Tosh and Crosby weren't sure they really wanted to hear the toilet story.

"O.K. Toilet story, here goes," warbled Angus. "There was this girl that I liked, that I wanted to court. So I get invited to come over to her parents' place for dinner. I guess they wanted to size me up, ya know? So while I'm there, I have to take a dump real bad. And I'm tryin' to avoid it but it gets worse and worse, so finally I give in. Now, they lived in this tiny little apartment, an' I made a big stink in the bathroom."

"You were dropping wolf bait?" asked Crosby.

"Yeah. It was bad an' I was really embarrassed, so I lit a couple matches to try an' hide the smell. So, while the match is burnin' down, I'm lookin' in the mirror, checkin' to make sure how I look. Then, I feel the match get hot an' I quickly toss it in the toilet, except in my haste I missed an' it landed on the toilet seat. Now, back then, they had these nylon toilet seats. You ever see a pair of stockin's burn? They burn right up."

"Vaporize," said Crosby.

"Just disappear," Angus continued. "So it burned the toilet seat right off. Didn't leave a trace."

Picturing this, Tosh and Crosby started giggling.

"Yeah. So, naturally, I'm even more embarrassed now. So I walk outa the bathroom an' tell the girl an' her parents that I'm double parked an' I better go move my car. I walked out the door an' never went back."

Even though they had all heard it before, Angus' friends laughed as if it were the first time they were hearing it.

"Thing is," said Angus, "think about what those people musta thought. Till this day, they probly say, 'Remember that weird boy you dated who came in here an' stole our toilet seat?'"

"Good thing you never ran into her again," said Crosby.

"Speaking of toilet seats," said Tosh, "where's the bathroom? I gotta drain the lizard."

Billygoat directed him to the men's room which, as Tosh expected, gave the port-o-johns at the reggae festival a run for their money. He made sure not to touch anything in the bathroom except for himself.

After relieving himself, Tosh exited to find Crosby and Billygoat over by the pinball machine. He joined them.

"It works?"

"Just had to be plugged in," said Billygoat.

"Wanna play?" asked Crosby.

After seeing the bathroom, Tosh didn't even want to touch the pinball machine. "I'll pass."

"Suit yourself," said Crosby, dropping some change into the slot. "The Addams Family. This is awesome."

"Too bad it's not the Munsters," said Billygoat.

"The Munsters? No way!"

"What's wrong with the Munsters?"

"Please," said Crosby, as if this point was common knowledge. "Herman was such a dweeb. Gomez Addams clearly outclassed and outwitted him. And Morticia was a nugget, totally sexy."

"Wednesday was pretty cute," Tosh added.

Crosby turned to Tosh, and with complete seriousness, said, "I love Wednesday Addams. I wanted to marry her."

"What about Grandpa?" Billygoat protested.

"Grandpa was cool, I'll give you that," said Crosby. "But the Addams family had Uncle Fester, Cousin It, Thing. They would be an awesome family to marry into."

"Thing could be the ring bearer," said Tosh.

"They had Lurch, Kitty..."

"Who's Kitty?" asked Tosh.

"Their cat!" said Crosby as the pinball shot by his flippers. "Damn."

"My turn," said Billygoat, stepping around to the front of the machine.

"They had a cat?"

"Remember, the lion?"

"Oh yeah!"

"You can't even compare the Munsters to the Addams family, I'll tell you right now," continued Crosby. "The Addams were an eminent, upper-class family. The Munsters were trash."

"They weren't trash," chided Tosh. He motioned with his eyes to Billygoat, who was concentrating hard on the pinball machine, trying to remind Crosby to watch what he said because of the company they were in. After all, The B.M.W. was no country club. "Herman was a bus driver. He worked hard."

"Let's just say they were lower class," Crosby whispered.

Tosh returned to his stool and looked at the cardboard cutout of Elvira. He wondered how many times a man sat there, staring at Elvira, wishing she would come to life. He'd bet that most of the guys in the bar would trade their next drink for that cardboard cutout to be real flesh and blood.

Tosh knew everyone in the bar was a loser, and he knew that they all knew they were losers. Except for Jesse. Tosh could see the way the others looked up to him. Jesse had possessed a special skill. He had been blessed with God-given talent and because of it, he had amounted to something — a professional athlete, a gridiron star. Jesse had held the American dream, if only for a brief while. The rest of these guys seemed like they had nothing to live for.

Then again, who could tell?

All these guys in the bar had a story to tell. Maybe another one of them had achieved some degree of success. Maybe someone else had flirted with fame. Like Angus.

Angus had actually been given a lucky draw. He won the damn lottery! He could have done a lot of things with his life, but he chose to live that way, spending his time and money drinking every day in a squalid pit of a pub.

Around the corner of the bar, Jewel sat with his head hung low. Tosh wondered about his story. Where did he grow up? What did he do for a living? What path had led him to become a daily customer of the B.M.W.?

"Hey, Jewel," said Tosh. "That your real name?"

Jewel looked up from his beer. His hair was slightly unkempt and his constantly contorted face had the disoriented expression of a drunk. Yet there was something compelling about Jewel, Tosh noted. He had a sparkle in his eye, an infectious smile.

"Yep, that's my real name," said Jewel.

"That's a cool name."

Jewel smiled sheepishly. "Guess my mama thought I was a gem."

"You live around here?"

Jewel nodded affirmatively.

"You work?"

Jewel cast his eyes into his beer. "Lost my job."

"What did you do?"

"Spent thirteen years on a oil rig down in the gulf."

"Gulf of Mexico?"

"Yep. Lived in Nawlins."

"New Orleans. That must be a crazy city, huh?"

Jewel nodded and made a slothlike toasting motion with his beer.

"What did you do before that?"

"Vietnam," Jewel answered.

That one word said it all, Tosh knew. To most Americans, it held more meaning than any other word in the English language, a lifetime worth of confusion and pain.

"Were you drafted?" asked Tosh.

Jewel shook his head. "Enlisted. I joined the Marines."

"Wanted to serve your country, huh?"

"Well, my brother was in the Marines, see. I wanted to join, but they'd only take one person from every family, so I couldn't get in. Then my brother got shot, honorable discharge, and I told them they had to take me, 'cause now my family didn't have no one in the war."

Tosh wanted to ask Jewel what 'Nam was like, but he felt apprehensive because he knew a lot of Vets didn't like to 'go there.' He decided to leave it up to Jewel, figuring, if Jewel felt like talking about it, he would.

But Jewel didn't elaborate.

Tosh let the conversation lull for a few minutes, trying to figure out if Jewel minded being interviewed. He didn't seem annoyed by Tosh's questions, yet, at the same time, he didn't volunteer much information.

"You got a family, Jewel?"

"I got a daughter, but she don't wanna see me."

"Why's that?"

"She says I got a bad reputation."

"What does she mean, because you drink?"

"Naa." Jewel fidgeted in his seat and cracked an awkward little smile, like a child admitting to mischief. "I spent some time in the state pen. You know, I got out, then I went back in."

Tosh did not expect to hear that. "What did you do?"

"I killed my brother-in-law."

*   *   *   *

Jewel's tone had a hint of shame, but overall it suggested that the whole episode was more of a hassle than a grave mistake.

Tosh tried not to let his shock show on his face. He played it cool, but he definitely felt uneasy sitting face-to-face with a murderer. What would stop a drunk Jewel from knifing and robbing him or Crosby on a dark street later on that night? He told himself to stay alert.

"You shoot him?" Tosh asked, like he asked that question all the time.

"Yeah, but he shot at me first."

"That sounds like self-defense to me."

"That's what I said, but the judge didn't see it that way."

"How'd he see it?"

"He said that I wanted to kill him, because I shot him two times — in the head and the heart. Of course I wanted to kill him. I wouldn'ta shot him the first time if I didn't want to kill him."

"I hear you, man. Excuse me," said Tosh. He got up to join Crosby by the pinball machine.

*   *   *   *

Tosh threw the empty box of Trix into the garbage can at the edge of the parking lot. On his way back to the van, Angus popped out of his camper with no shirt, no shoes and his fly down.

325

"Hey, Tosh," said Angus. "Wanta beer?"

"No thanks, Angus. I just had breakfast."

"Let me know if ya want one. Picked up a twelve of Meister Brau on the way home from the B.M.W. last night."

"Thanks. I'll do that."

Within the hour, Tosh, Crosby and Angus returned to their lawn chairs to spy on the Venice Beach ensemble. A guy in a toga and a turban roller bladed past them, strumming a guitar.

"Almost time for a beer," said Angus.

"Angus, you do this every day?"

"Just about."

This guy won the lottery, thought Tosh, *and he's spending it all on beer.*

Tosh figured, if he won the lottery, he'd probably spend a significant portion on beer, but not all of it. He'd give some money to friends and family, maybe donate some. He'd try to take full advantage of the sweepstakes — travel the rest of the world, experience as much as possible.

Angus hadn't enhanced his life very much, sitting in his chair, watching the people pass by. He basically did the same thing now as he did every day on the General Motors assembly line, except that now, the line changed every day. It used to be the same old car parts coming down the line. Now, Angus never knew what to expect.

But what did Angus do with his observations? Did he keep a journal? Did he draw any conclusions?

With the amount that Angus drank, probably not.

A spandex-clad dwarf cart wheeled by.

"People are strange," croaked Angus.

Most likely, Angus had just stated his grand conclusion. *Not even an original,* thought Tosh. That conclusion had already been made years ago by another Los Angeles resident, a man named Jim Morrison.

*   *   *   *

Tosh and Crosby needed to upgrade their L.A. experience. Watching nonconformists and drinking with underachievers and murderers had been interesting, but Tosh and Crosby knew L.A. had more to offer.

The plan was to spend the afternoon checking out Beverly Hills and then look for a party in Hollywood that night, maybe find some big-breasted blonde bombshell actress/model chicks to pound some Schlitzes with. Perhaps they'd stumble upon a record biz bash, sneak their way in and shmooze with Madonna wannabes.

Both neighborhoods were just a jaunt up the freeway from Venice Beach. The Grateful Dead sang "Mama Tried" as Tosh pulled the van on to the highway.

I turned 21 in prison doing life without parole, No one could steer me right but Mama tried, Mama tried, Mama tried to raise me better but her pleading I denied, And its only me to blame 'cause Mama tried.

Singing along, the song reminded Tosh of Jewel. He couldn't believe that the guy with such a sparkle in his eye had the icy nerve to kill. Tosh wondered if the woman who had named her son Jewel had shown him love and affection, taught him good values and supported him in trying times. Where had things gone wrong for Jewel?

Had his parents neglected him? Had Vietnam corrupted him? Had his job screwed him? Had life constantly shit on him?

Or was Jewel doomed to fail because of the cards he had been dealt? Was he born belligerent, predisposed to kill one day?

Stoned and jamming to the tunes, Tosh and Crosby failed to realize they were heading in the wrong direction.

"It's been a while," said Crosby over the din of the Dead. "Don't you think we should be in Beverly Hills yet?"

"Hasn't been that long," Tosh answered. "We've only listened to like four songs."

"Yeah, but 'The Other One' is like eighteen minutes long."

Hmm. "Good point," said Tosh. "Let's see what this sign says. 'Lawndale/Gardena.' Check the map."

Crosby picked the road atlas off the floor and flipped through it, searching for the enlarged map of Los Angeles and its vicinity. "Oh, shit. We're totally heading in the wrong direction. We're heading south."

"Didn't you say south?"

"I said north. Take the San Diego Freeway north."

"I thought you said south."

"I definitely said north."

"Well, they sound the same," sighed Tosh. "They both have that 'th' sound at the end."

"Whatever. We can take Route 110 north. That will take us where we want to go."

By the end of the next song, Tosh and Crosby had found the exit for Route 110. "Beverly Ills here we come."

*   *   *   *

Route 110 had a massive traffic jam. Cars, trucks and busses moved at a crawl.

The van, of course, had no air-conditioning, and moving at a snail's pace created no breeze, so the mid-day SoCal sun heated the van up like a tin of Jiffy Pop in a campfire.

"We can walk faster than this," said Crosby.

327

"Maybe we should. It'd probably be cooler outside this sauna."

At the moment, the only thing to cheer about was the Grateful Dead singing "N.F.A./G.D.T.R.F.B.," and that quickly turned sour.

"This is ridiculous," said Tosh. "'Going Down the Road Feeling Bad' is like the world's greatest driving song. We should be cruising down the highway, breeze blowin'..."

"Feelin' bad," Crosby added.

"Exactly! This song makes me move. I gotta be movin'."

Tosh bopped up and down in the driver's seat while Crosby, with his arm hanging out the window, tapped the door.

"This is torture!" exclaimed Tosh. "We've got to be driving! I can't listen to this song in traffic! It's not right. It goes against nature! I want to cry."

Rather than change the tape, Tosh and Crosby got off the freeway. Graffiti, steel bars on windows, packs of probably pistol-packing people quickly told them they had made a bad decision.

Tosh and Crosby tensed up.

"We're definitely going to attract some serious attention," said Crosby. "Just being here, we either look like we're buying drugs or we look completely naive. Either way, we're dead."

"Quick, put in a some reggae," Tosh instructed.

"I wish we had rap," said Crosby, fumbling through the tape case.

"It probably won't make a difference, but at least reggae'll put out a good vibe."

"We'll probably have some gang crawling up our ass within minutes. This has gotta be somebody's turf and I'm willing to bet that we're not welcome here."

Tosh turned around to Crosby. "Bob Marley. Find Bob. Love songs. Mellow."

"Just keep driving. Look for signs for the freeway."

They approached a yellow light. Tosh tried to speed up, but the light turned red just before they could make it. He came to a halt at the edge of the intersection.

Waiting for the light to turn green, Tosh and Crosby stared straight ahead, ignoring the teenagers loitering on the corner. The pedestrians passing by the van gave them disapproving looks, so Tosh tried to seem less stiff and nervous by pretending to fiddle with the radio.

Crosby buried his head in a book, which turned out to be the road atlas. Realizing the road atlas made him appear even more blatantly lost, desperate and pathetic, he promptly dropped it and went to the back of the van.

"Where are you going?"

"The windows are tinted back here," said Crosby. "At least you got dreadlocks."

"Yeah. Driving a van covered with hippie stickers and with a surfboard on top. I'm sure I'll blend right in."

"You got a dollar?" asked some guy at Tosh's window.

"For what?"

"'Cause I want one."

The light turned green and Tosh gunned it.

"Roll up your window," said Crosby, coming up front to roll up his. "Where's the signs when you need them?"

They came to another red light and Tosh stopped.

"We shouldn't stop for anything," said Crosby. "We should've just driven through."

"What, and kill somebody?"

While waiting for the light to change, the van stalled.

Tosh tried to start her again, but Josephine rejected him. "Oh fuck, not here."

"I told you we should have kept going," said Crosby, grabbing the starter fluid.

"How was I supposed to know she was gonna stall?"

The light turned green. Crosby doused the carb with starter fluid while Tosh turned the ignition, but Josephine remained stubborn. The cars behind them started beeping.

"Come on!" urged Crosby. "It's not working!"

People were passing them, shooting them angry glances.

"Can we be any more conspicuous?"

A couple of menacing-looking dudes approached them from the corner, not likely coming to lend a hand.

"I'm getting the scuba knife," said Crosby.

Tosh felt his heart pounding once again. "Jah," he said under his breath, "we need you again. Help us out here, please. Just get us out of this mess and I'll owe you one. Two — I'll owe you two! Please Jah, protect us."

Tosh turned the ignition key and the van started. He turned to Crosby. "Wow — that worked!"

One of the dudes tapped on Tosh's window. "Whussup?"

Tosh gave him a nod and hit the gas.

"Don't stop for anything," said Crosby, knife in hand.

"I can't believe that," said Tosh. "How do you explain that?"

"I don't know," Crosby answered. "But that's twice in one week. I wouldn't go to the well too often."

*   *   *   *

The guys got back on the freeway heading south. The northbound traffic still backed up for miles.

"Screw Hollyweird," said Crosby.

"What do we want to go there for, anyway? It's the heart of Babylon."

"Take this to the San Diego Freeway."

"Yeah, San Diego! Beaches, the zoo, the Padres."

"Yeah," said Crosby. "Fuck Hell-A."

329

*   *   *   *

Tosh and Crosby motored along Route 5, down the California coast.

"It feels good to have God on our side, huh?" asked Tosh. "Like a secret bodyguard."

"Yeah, well you better keep in touch. Don't wanna blow him off like an old girlfriend or something."

"I will," said Tosh. "Maybe you should start, too."

Crosby spit a wad of tobacco juice out the open window. "I don't know, dude. I just feel really stupid talking to God."

"Talk to him in private. How can you feel stupid in front of yourself?"

"I just feel like I'm deluded or something."

"It's just a matter of faith, I think. Like Evan said. If you truly believe it, you wouldn't be deluding yourself."

"I have a question," said Crosby. "If God is within us, why do we talk to him? Wouldn't he already know what we think and feel?"

Tosh pondered Crosby's query. "That's a good question, Cros. Maybe not, though, because it's not like he's in our heads, our minds."

"Where do you think he is, then?"

"He's in our souls, I guess."

"What exactly do you think our soul is?"

"Well, I don't know for sure. I would say that the soul is the essence of our being."

"What do you mean by 'essence?'"

"You know, our core. Our spirit, our energy."

"The energy that makes us tick, right?"

"Yeah," said Tosh. "That energy."

"So then, maybe our souls and God are the same thing."

Tosh looked over at his friend. "You may be on to something there, buddy."

CHAPTER 19

The sun beat down hard on Mission Beach. Tosh and Crosby baked and sweated, scratched and burned. Umbrellaless, they could only seek relief in the water, which was as salty as an anchovy and a mite cold.

Bong hits kept Tosh relatively serene. They didn't help Crosby. Restless and ornery, he stumbled to his feet. "I can't lie in this heat any more. The sun is hot overhead and the sand is hot under my feet. I feel like a piece of toast. I'd pay a hundred dollars for a cool breeze."

"You don't have a hundred dollars," lamented Tosh.

"We're at the beach. There's supposed to be a cool breeze."

"Well, there isn't."

"Damn brochures," Crosby grumbled. "I'm going to walk up to the street."

"It's even hotter up there," chirped Tosh without even opening an eye. "The van has got to be an absolute oven."

"There's no way I'm going to the van. Are you kidding me?" Crosby shot. "No way. I'm not even going to open the van door until it's dark out."

"Maybe you can find some shade."

"Those palms sure don't do the trick. Love the coconuts, but they lack in the shade department."

"Indeed," sighed Tosh.

"I am going to find some air-conditioning. I have to get out of this heat. I'll find a store or something and pose as a shopper."

"Shop slow."

"Definitely. I'll browse. I will browse like I've never browsed before."

And off he went up the beach; a slow, deliberate crawl, a turtle trekking the Mojave.

*   *   *   *

Tosh sat up. Had he been sleeping? Where was Crosby? How long had he been gone?

The image of toast lingered in his mind. Was it a dream? It made him very, very thirsty. His tongue stuck to the top of his mouth and his throat felt dry.

He gazed out at the ocean, longing to open his gullet wide and guzzle a few gallons of the cool blue liquid sloshing back and forth. *What a tease*, he thought.

Tosh got himself to his feet and scoped the territory for immediate beverage assistance. A Godsend! About ten yards away lounged a slender woman with dirty blonde hair. Normally, this itself would be something to get excited about, but due to the circumstances, Tosh focused on the large, round cooler sitting on her blanket. A lone silver cup accompanied it.

Tosh tiptoed over to her. Reclining peacefully in a white one-piece bathing suit, she seemed unaware of his presence.

"I will give you one thousand dollars for the contents of that cooler!" he boomed with authority.

She opened an eye. Coolly, the woman reached for her sunglasses and sat up. "Really?"

"No. I would, but I don't have a thousand dollars," said Tosh, desperation evident in his voice.

"Oh," said the woman.

As she began to reposition herself, Tosh fell to his knees and placed his palms together, pointed toward the sky. "Please, please, ma'am. Cotton mouth, killing me," he mumbled. "If I could have just a little drop of whatever that is in that beautiful cooler of yours, I will forever be indebted to you."

"Oh, take a drink," the woman said amicably. "Help yourself. Go right ahead."

"Should I use the cup?" asked Tosh, unable to stifle his excitement.

"Be my guest. It might be a little sandy, though."

Tosh grabbed the cup and blew out the few grains of beach that had climbed in. He poured the clear liquid, filling the cup three quarters of the way. "Cheers," he gasped before drinking.

The chilly ice water cleansed his parched throat and restored life to his barren mouth. "Oh, thank God," he sighed as he put the empty cup on the woman's beach blanket.

"No, thank me," said the woman, going for the cup. "God filled the oceans, but that doesn't do you a lot of good right now. I filled the cooler."

"You're right," laughed Tosh. "And I thank you tremendously..."

"Tanya. The name is Tanya."

"Thank you, Tanya. How do you do?"

"Quite fine, and you?"

"Much better now," Tosh replied, wiping the sweat off his brow. "I'm Tosh. Tosh Tyler. Care to take a dip?"

"Sure, Tosh Tyler."

Tosh helped Tanya to her feet and they walked down to the Pacific. Tosh paused at the water's edge to feel it with his foot, but Tanya maintained her stride until only her head remained dry.

A little embarrassed, Tosh tried to save face by diving right in. He ducked under the approaching wave and, when he came up and wiped the water out of his eyes, he found himself face-to-face with Tanya. She smiled.

"Whah gwan?" he said.

"Water's warm?"

"No, whah gwan," repeated Tosh. "It's Jamaican patois. It means, like, 'What's going on?' You know, 'What's happening?'"

"Oh, I thought you said 'The water's warm.'"

"No. Actually, I think it's kind of cold."

"You'll get used to it. Where are you from, Jamaica? The Caribbean's probably like bath water."

"I'm not from Jamaica. I'm from New Jersey," said Tosh. "I just picked up this Jamaican patois thing from listening to too much reggae."

"I didn't think that was possible," said Tanya, diving under an approaching wave. She swam a few feet and resurfaced, her hair slicked back and her face glistening in the late afternoon sun.

"What, picking up another language from listening to music?" Tosh asked.

"No, listening to too much reggae."

Tosh smiled. *Who was this woman?*

*   *   *   *

Crosby stepped up his pace on the hot sand just as the hallucinations began. His feet burned badly. Glimpsing a waft of smoke by his feet, he heard a distinct sizzling sound and felt reasonably sure that the flesh was burning off his soles.

He hightailed it the rest of the way off the beach, his heart pounding and sweat dripping into his eyes. He dabbed at the perspiration with his balled up T-shirt, feeling like he might pass out. "*Air*, I need air," he gasped.

The beach ended and turned to pavement that was even hotter than the sand, but Crosby could not tell at that point because delirium had set in. Extremely light-headed, he stumbled toward the nearest building. He looked up and saw the word **PHARMACY** as everything else around him spun. As he blindly fumbled with the door handle, someone pushed it open and exited. Crosby brushed his sweaty body against the old guy exiting and fell into the store.

The cool air-conditioning hit him like a train. He quickly regained his composure enough to get to his feet. Shaking off a once-over from a few nearby people, Crosby nonchalantly headed to an empty corner of the store.

He found himself in the greeting card aisle. *Perfect*, he thought. *I'll look for a card.*

He picked up a card that read, "For a Wonderful Niece." Inside, it said, "For a girl who smiles so bright, for a girl who laughs...*" and then the words began to jump about, letters dancing a mambo, courtesy of a combination of the bong hits that he and Tosh had shared and the quasi-heat-exhaustion he had just lived through. *This won't do*, Crosby thought. *I think I'm going to puke.*

To save himself from the embarrassment and discomfort of vomiting, he instead pretended to read. Giving himself about fifteen to twenty seconds per card, he moved through nearly the entire rack. After five minutes or so, the air-conditioning managed to restore his equilibrium, though it didn't sober him a wink. (It was some good weed.)

333

With his newfound strength and the confidence that he would keep down his last meal, Crosby decided to take up reading again. Staring at the cards bored him profoundly and made him feel illiterate. Now that he had relief from the heat, he sought entertainment.

Reading, however, proved to be a mistake again. The first card he chose featured, on the cover, a small, orange, pear-shaped fellow with skinny little legs exclaiming "Aren't you sick and tired of all this hoopla about birthdays?" On the inside of the card, it read, "I know I Yam."

Maybe it was the pissed-off expression on the Yam's face. Perhaps it was the silliness of the pun. It could have been the bong hits, but most likely it was a combination of all three. It wasn't a particularly funny card, but it set Crosby off into a rambunctious fit of hysterical laughter.

When the fit abated, Crosby noticed an agitated old woman peering at him from the end of the aisle. *Employee,* his senses warned. He forced the smile off his face and immediately grabbed another card. To his regret, the woman made her way down the aisle with a sense of purpose.

"Can I help you?" she asked sternly.

"No thanks. I'm just browsing," Crosby quickly responded.

"In a pharmacy?"

"I'm shopping for a card," corrected Crosby.

The woman scowled and closed the card in Crosby's hand. It read, "For My Beloved Wife on our Fiftieth Anniversary." She took the card out of Crosby's hand and put it back in the rack.

Before he could plead a case, she said, "Didn't you see the sign on the door?"

"No," said Crosby.

"Well, it says, 'No shirt, No shoes, No service.'"

Crosby shook out the crumpled T-shirt hanging from his waistband and pulled it over his head. The woman motioned toward his bare feet.

"One out of two isn't bad," Crosby pleaded.

The woman pointed to the door.

"What if I buy some shoes?" said Crosby, feeling proud of his quick thinking. "Where is your footwear department?"

"Aisle three," the woman huffed. She turned her back and shook her head, obviously distraught that this young, half-naked, smelly hooligan outwitted her.

Crosby knew he was on borrowed time. In his back pocket, he felt only change. That would never be enough to purchase even the most inexpensive pair of flip-flops.

From the counter, the woman watched over Crosby, making sure he went directly to the flip-flop aisle, which he did. Dreading his return to the southern California heat, he milked the moment, trying on several pairs. When the woman seemed like she would tolerate his stalling no more, Crosby slipped on a pair and left the footwear department.

Now he was legally cleared to shop.

*   *   *   *

"Neu-ro-psy-chology?"

"Yes, neuropsychology," repeated Tanya, her smile forming tiny crow's feet at the edge of her bronzed face. "The interrelation between the nervous system and different mental states and processes."

"Wow."

"Yeah. It's pretty fascinating."

"Where do you study that?" asked Tosh, quickly realizing this was not just some beach babe basking in the sun.

"The University of Hawaii."

"Nice." Tosh brushed off some of the sand that had dried on his shin. "Must be tough to get anything done with all the distractions."

"Distractions?"

"Well, you know. The gorgeous weather, the beaches. It must be tough to spend all that time doing research in the library or laboratory when the beach is always calling."

Tanya looked at Tosh with a mixture of bewilderment and amusement. "I manage to get some time on the beach," she said. "Every once in a while I do need to get out and take a little rest and relaxation, and it's nice to live in such a serene setting. But honestly, my work is so exciting, most days I wouldn't want to be doing anything else. Nothing makes me happier." Tanya squirted a dab of suntan lotion on her nose.

"That's really cool," said Tosh. "You are really lucky, you know that?"

"How's that?"

"You're lucky that you've found something that you love to do."

Tanya contemplated this for a moment. She asked, "Isn't there anything that you love to do, Tosh?"

"Well, yeah, lots of things."

"So then I guess you're lucky, too."

At first puzzled, Tosh saw where Tanya was coming from after a moment. "No, I mean you're really lucky that you have found a career that you love," he clarified. "You can get paid for doing what makes you happy."

"Yes I can," Tanya said matter-of-factly.

"Most people don't love their jobs. They do it just to get paid."

"You know, I never really thought of it that way. It's funny, but the fact that I get paid is kind of incidental. I don't really consider it a job. It's what I *am,* it's my purpose."

335

Tosh watched Tanya closely as she spoke. Her speech had a casual tone, yet she came from a deeper place. Her eyes seemed to be searching, at times looking right through him. It was as if only part of her consciousness took part in the conversation, and the other part had a different agenda.

"Every so often, someone hands me a check, which I use to buy the things I need to live. But I am so deeply involved in what I'm doing..." Her voice trailed off and became drowned by the sound of the tide. "What do you do, Tosh?"

"Me? Uh, nothing, really. I mean, I just got out of school. I have no idea what I'm going to do."

Tanya didn't say anything for a moment. She looked out at the ocean. "I never had any question about it," she said.

"You knew from the beginning what you wanted to do?"

Keeping her gaze on the horizon, she continued, "I just never thought about what I wanted to do. I just did."

"Really? You never thought about it?"

"No, more like I just followed my instincts." Tanya focused her attention back on Tosh. "Growing up, I always yearned for knowledge. I had an insatiable desire to know. Seeking answers has led me to where I am. It has dictated everything I do. There weren't any considerations, really. Everything has just fallen into place around my search."

* * * *

Browsing the topical ointment aisle, disaster struck once more.

Crosby tried to look purposeful, but the marijuana caught up with him again. Spotting the familiar Preparation H, he snickered harmlessly to himself. But when a distressed, middle-aged man sharing the aisle with him selected a product called Anusol, Crosby lost it. His full laughter drew an embarrassed glance from the hemorrhoid-sufferer and a furious one from the lady behind the counter.

"Are you finished, sir?" she asked angrily.

"Uh..."

"I think you are finished."

"I just need a..."

The woman waited for a few seconds. "What is it that you need? Or are you just loitering?" She said the L-word with venom. "Because I will call the police."

"No," Crosby reassured her. "I really do need a..." Looking down the aisle at the counter, he noticed the candy section. "A lollipop."

"A lollipop?"

"Yes. Do you sell Charms?"

"Very well. Come with me to the counter and buy your lollipop and get out of here." Again, she said the L-word with venom.

At the counter, she said, "We have no Charms. I'm sorry sir..."

"Damn. None?" Crosby interrupted. "I really need a lollipop. Do you have Tootsie Pops?"

"No."

"Blowpops?"

"No."

Time was running out. "No Blowpops? I really need a lolli..."

"No Blowpops."

"Damn. I'll take a Dum-Dum. Anything."

"A Dum-Dum? You must be desperate," said a voice.

Crosby turned to his right. Next to him stood one of the hottest girls he had ever seen in his entire adult life, a sun-tanned blonde beauty. Her obscenely high-cut denim shorts exposed the rounded flesh of the bottom of her butt. A half-shirt revealed a taught, ab-ridden stomach. She smiled at him and whispered, "Do you have any rolling papers?"

Shell-shocked by the sudden appearance of such an attractive girl and the fact that she was speaking to him, Crosby had a momentary problem deciphering reality. He had heard the question, but he could not tell whether the girl had actually said it or if he had imagined it.

"Do you have any papers?" she whispered again.

Now Crosby knew for sure the blonde was speaking to him. The angry clerk stared at him from behind the counter, her nostrils flaring.

"Ah, no," he muttered.

The blonde turned her attention to the lady behind the counter. "Do you sell rolling papers here?"

"No we do *not*, young lady," the clerk fumed. "We do not sell such items here."

"Why not?" chimed Crosby. He knew his time was up. "It *is* a drug store."

"Out! Both of you! Now! I'm calling the Police."

"Police? What're you nuts?" said the girl. "Lady, you can kiss my ass."

*   *   *   *

"I am in heaven," said Tosh. "Thank you so much."

Tanya applied Hawaiian Tropic (spf6) to Tosh's shoulders, rubbing the coconut-scented lotion into his reddening skin with the fingers of a trained masseuse.

"You know, Tanya, I have always had a desire for knowledge, too."

"You're an inquisitive one?"

"Totally." Tosh spread some lotion on his temples and forehead. "I remember having trouble sleeping as a kid because of it. I'd lie in bed awake at night, thinking about these crazy questions, like 'What happens when you die?' and that kind of stuff. It would make me all upset and I'd call my mom into the room."

Tanya rubbed a little lotion on the back of Tosh's neck. "What would she do?"

"Hell, I don't know. My questions must have really stumped her. She probably just changed the subject and got my mind off of it so I could sleep. I mean, how do you answer questions like 'Why are we here?' and 'How can space go on forever?'"

"Those are difficult concepts for children to grasp."

"Not only children," exclaimed Tosh, turning around to face Tanya. "For everyone! I still wonder about all that stuff. At least *your* search for knowledge provides you with useful information and concrete answers. But the questions I have can't be answered. And it bugs the shit out of me."

Tanya sat back and crossed her legs, Indian style. She listened intently.

Tosh continued, "I can't stand the fact that I have questions that will never be answered. I wish someone could just explain it all to me – why we are here, what God is and all that.

"Tell me, why is everything the way it is? O.K., maybe it's just random and there is no real reason for it. I can accept that, though I'd say it's a pretty remarkable phenomenon. I mean, the odds had to be pretty slim, don't you think, for all of this to occur?

"But what about outer space? Now that really freaks me out. Badly. It goes on *forever?* That's ridiculous. The whole concept of infinity just blows my mind. I mean, it's just far beyond my conception. It really pisses me off. I can't take it. It makes me feel very uneasy, very nervous and weird. I still can't think about it to this day."

Tosh realized he had begun to go off the deep end right before Tanya's eyes. "See what I mean?" he said with an embarrassed smile.

*   *   *   *

Outside the pharmacy, the sun had crept over the Pacific. Crosby squinted at the rolling-paper girl in its still bright light. "Nice lady," he cracked, not wanting her to slip away.

"Bitch," said the rolling-paper girl.

Crosby could not help but stare at her. Only a thin layer of worn cotton separated him from those beautiful mounds of flesh on her chest. He ached to touch them, to run his tongue over the peaks and valleys of her abs, to cup his hand under the firm half-moon that peeked from underneath her denim shorts.

The rolling-paper girl lit a cigarette.

Trying to keep the ball rolling, Crosby thought of something to say. "So, do you want a little help smoking that weed?" Clever and original, no. Appropriate, perhaps.

"Oh, no. That's all right," she said, as if Crosby had actually offered to do her a favor. "My friend and I just have a little roach, and we can finish it off ourselves."

"Oh," said Crosby, the disappointment evident in his voice. "Well, if you only have a little roach, why were you looking to buy rolling papers?"

An absent glance to the ground, a devilish smile, and away she went.

Damn the luck of it all, he thought.

Just then, the clerk came tearing out of the pharmacy. Looking left and then right, she spotted Crosby right away. "Give me back those flip-flops!" she screamed, lumbering toward him.

"Oh no," he gasped.

Like a mule, Crosby kicked the sandals off his feet in the direction of the oncoming grizzly, hoping to impede her. The contraband flip-flops catapulted through the thick air with force, but she skipped out of the way with shocking agility. Barefoot, Crosby scampered away toward the beach.

Once fairly sure the enraged drug store clerk was not trailing him, Crosby slowed down to a walk. He headed toward the water, trying to remember where he had left Tosh. Using his forearm to shield his vision from the horizontal sun, Crosby kept his eyes peeled. With a little luck (for a change), he spotted his buddy in the distance, off to the south.

Tosh was rapping with a blonde!

Unbelievable, thought Crosby. *As soon as I leave, the chicks come over.* "Let's see what's going on over there," he said to himself.

*   *   *   *

Tosh and Tanya remained silent for a while. The lilting sound of the waves crashing on the beach soothed Tosh. A breeze started to pick up and the sun seemed to lose a little intensity as it inched its way down from its perch in the cloudless sky.

Tosh broke the hush. "When I was a kid, I used to imagine that the entire universe was in God's play room and the earth was laid out like a model train set. Every day He would open the door and check on us, make sure things were going as He planned. If not, He would reach in and fix it. If someone was in trouble, He'd stick his giant hand in and help him or her. If He saw someone doing something bad, he would pluck them out and stick them in a jar."

Tanya shooed away a seagull that had snuck up on them. "If you really think about it, that childhood concept says a lot," she posited. "Not only does it depict the nature of God as omnipotent and basically benevolent, it also states that there exists a degree of order in the universe."

"I never really analyzed it before," said Tosh, "but I guess it does kind of make reference to some sort of overall plan."

Tosh scratched some of the sand out of his dreads. "I don't know, it was just something I made up as a kid. I guess it comforted me to think that space did not go on forever. It went really far, but it had an ending in God's room."

He picked up a handful of sand and let it sift through his fingers. "I wish it would work for me now."

"It doesn't have to."

339

"What do you mean?"

"These questions you have, Tosh, about the organization of the universe and the meaning of our existence, they have answers."

"They do?"

"Sure," said Tanya. "They've been answered for a long time."

"Come on," Tosh said skeptically. "Really?"

"Yes."

Tosh couldn't believe what she was saying. "Then how come this isn't common knowledge?"

"It is."

Tosh felt like he had missed one hell of a train. "Well, no one told me," he murmured.

"These answers that you seek have been around for thousands of years, Tosh. But they're not widely accepted because they're not scientifically proven. Most people won't believe things unless they have concrete evidence in front of them. Especially in this culture, people have a hard time dealing with abstract reality."

"How come I don't know this? Why don't I have these answers?" Tosh asked, like a jealous mother cheated out of a juicy secret at the P.T.A. meeting.

"Well, have you ever looked for them?"

"No." Tosh suddenly felt kind of stupid. "I just figured they didn't exist."

"There you go," said Tanya.

"Where do I look?"

"You can start at the library. There have been hundreds of books written about this stuff."

"So you're telling me the meaning of the universe is *at the library?*"

Tanya laughed. "That's just the beginning. It's not just in books, it's all around. Be perceptive. You already have the knowledge."

"That's a good thing," said Crosby, announcing his arrival at the seaside discussion. "Because I had my library card revoked."

Tanya looked up.

"Overdue books," said Crosby. "No more privileges."

"This is my buddy, Crosby," said Tosh. "He's a slow reader."

"It's nice to meet you. My name is Tanya."

"The pleasure is mine," said Crosby, plopping down in the sand next to Tosh. "Mind if I take a drink?"

"Not at all." Tanya bent to fetch the cup, but Crosby already had the cooler pressed to his lips.

"Wait a minute," said Tosh, "Did you say that I already have the knowledge?"

"Yes."

"I do?"

"Everyone does."

Tosh looked at Tanya quizzically.

"I say it's common knowledge because everyone already has the answers inside them. The mind has infinite — sorry, I know you hate that concept — but the mind has infinite capabilities. These answers are locked inside your mind. Reading and research will help you understand certain things and it will help you find which path may be right for you."

"Which path?"

"Yes. The path that leads you inside yourself. To not only find, but to truly understand these answers, you have to look inside yourself."

"Look inside yourself," repeated Tosh. "What does that really mean? It sounds cliché. How do you look inside yourself?"

"You open your mouth up real wide in front of a mirror," cracked Crosby. "No, I'm sorry. I'm just kidding. Go on."

Crosby realized that Tosh and Tanya were involved in a deep conversation and, although he didn't know how they got there, he figured he would shut up and tag along for the ride.

"Inside yourself, you can find understanding, you can find truth, universal truth," Tanya continued. "But you can't do it in a normal state of consciousness. The mind won't let you."

Tosh leaned in closer to Tanya to hear her more clearly over the sound of the waves and wind.

"Our consciousness denies access to these most powerful, wonderful parts of our mind. We're conditioned this way by society from the day we're born."

Like the way society corrupts our psychic abilities, thought Tosh, remembering his conversation in Victoria with that woman named Darla.

Tanya continued. "People use different ways to access these mysterious realms of the mind. Meditation, for one."

"I've tried meditation," said Tosh. "I couldn't do it."

Tanya smiled. "It takes a lot of practice."

"Yeah, yeah, I know," Tosh sighed.

"I'm serious. This isn't riding a bike we're talking about. It requires focus and dedication."

"Why do they make it so difficult?"

"Who's 'they?'" Crosby interrupted.

"The proverbial 'they,'" said Tosh. "You know, whoever designed this whole process. Whoever developed our existence and everything that goes with it. God, I guess. Why did God make it so difficult to find these answers?"

Tanya looked at Tosh and Crosby with amusement.

"Let me guess," continued Tosh, "I'll find that answer with all the others."

Tanya laughed. "That, you will. But it's really no more difficult than a lot of things, like playing guitar, for instance. Do you think Jimi Hendrix played 'Voodoo Chile' the first time he picked up a guitar?"

Tosh frowned. "I suck at playing guitar, too."

"How long did you attempt to meditate?"

"A few weeks."

"A few weeks? Did you try it every day?"

"Like twice a week," Tosh said meekly.

"Oh, please, Tosh. That's nothing. That's like not even trying at all. It takes a long time."

"Really?"

"Yes. But you don't have to have special powers or talent. You just have to have commitment. I'm telling you, Tosh, anyone can do it."

"I know a guy who meditates," said Tosh. "And he's just a regular guy. At least, he was. I don't think I'd call him regular now."

"Who's that?" asked Crosby.

"That hermit I met by Nitinat. He told me he meditated so much he didn't even need to eat."

"What?"

"He said he didn't need to eat because he obtained his energy by soaking up the cosmic energy around him, or something like that."

"Yeah, right," said Crosby. "Whatever."

"He seemed sincere," Tosh said. "But it just doesn't seem possible. I mean, it was fascinating but very hard to believe."

"Hard to believe, yes," said Tanya with a been-there-done-that look. "And that, my friends, is why things are the way they are today."

*　　　*　　　*　　　*

The three made one last plunge into the Pacific before the sun laid down for the night. The intense afternoon heat had dwindled, and the air and water felt about the same heavenly temperature. A dazzling sun hovered just above the horizon.

"So, Tanya," continued Tosh, "you really think I can learn to meditate?"

"Sure."

"And all I need is commitment, huh?"

"Yes, but don't underestimate how difficult commitment can be. For most people, that's the hardest part." Tanya ducked under an approaching wave. "It's difficult to stay with something that doesn't show immediate results, especially in this rat race. With so many things to do, people are afraid of wasting time."

"Maybe I'll just keep out of the rat race," said Tosh.

"Go for it!" encouraged Tanya. "But that's easier said than done. It basically means abandoning society, you realize. And to do that, you either need to be almost entirely self-sustaining or, how do they say it, 'independently wealthy.'"

"Well, you can scratch 'independently wealthy,'" quipped Crosby. "We're independently poor and after this trip, we'll be independently broke."

"Yeah," agreed Tosh. "I guess that leaves self-sustaining." Ras Daniel came to mind. He had successfully avoided the rat race and seemed to lead a pleasurable life.

Tanya added, "Either way, I'd recommend starting with getting rid of your television."

Then again, Ras Daniel counted wild turkeys for fun. Tosh wasn't ready to kick his television out. He'd fight to keep his commitment *despite* the rat race. "Then, in reality," he said to Tanya, "meditation is not so easy after all."

"I never said it was easy. I just said that anyone can do it."

"Tanya," said Crosby, "you said that people use different ways to access these other realms of the mind. What are some other ones besides meditation?"

Tanya pulled off a piece of seaweed that had clung to her arm. "Well, drugs are another."

"Drugs?"

"You mean like acid and mushrooms?" asked Tosh.

"Yes, psychedelic drugs."

Hmmm.

"I know that Leary used to preach that psychedelics could do some pretty freaky stuff," said Crosby, "but what's the deal with that?"

"Some people believe that they can achieve a higher consciousness by taking certain drugs," said Tanya. "But I always felt that was the lazy man's way."

Tanya continued to say that drugs were risky, they had harmful side effects and they drained the body of energy, whereas meditation actually energized the body and was natural, with no chemicals being put into the body, but Tosh had stopped listening. His heart began to race as he thought of his God-speaking-to-him-and-patting-him-on-the-ass experience while he was on mushrooms at the reggae festival. He had twice written it off as a hallucination, but maybe it was more. Maybe he had misinterpreted it. Could he have flirted with this higher consciousness?

"I don't understand that," said Crosby. "How can people believe that those drugs take you to a higher consciousness? Whenever I'm tripping, I can barely speak."

"That's true," said Tosh.

"Well, actually, that would make perfect sense in keeping with the theory," Tanya said. "Remember, to access these higher realms, you need to get around the normal thought processes. You have to put aside the everyday workings of the mind. You need to shut it down. That's why you have trouble with routine social interactions while you're under the effects of the drugs, because your mind is operating on a whole different level."

"Oh," said Crosby.

"My God," said Tosh, now really excited. "I may have had a taste of this higher consciousness."

Crosby looked at Tosh with raised eyebrows.

343

"Really?" Tanya asked.

Tosh told them the story. "What do you think, Tanya?" he asked.

"It doesn't matter what I think," she said, smiling. "It happened to you. It was your experience. What do you think?"

"I'd like to believe that it was more than a hallucination."

"Yes, own it."

"Own it," said Tosh. *I've heard that before.* "What do you mean by that?"

"You know, live it," said Tanya. "Make it real."

*   *   *   *

Tanya got out of the water. She told the guys she had to leave because her uncle was scheduled to pick her up just after sunset. "So Crosby," she said, squeezing salt water out of her long blonde hair, "Tosh wants answers. What do you want?"

Floating in the waist-deep surf, Crosby stood on his hands. His buoyancy helped to keep his balance for a minute. Then, like a windmill, he let his feet fall and his arms and head emerged from the blue-green water.

"What I want," he said, "is a cure for cancer and AIDS, an end to acid rain, animal testing and global warming, tropical reforestation instead of deforestation, the legalization of marijuana, food for the starving, shelter for the homeless, freedom for the oppressed, racial harmony, world peace, a rewarding career and a supermodel, but right now I'd settle for a slice of pizza."

*   *   *   *

Tosh watched Tanya stroll farther and farther away up the beach. *Quite a woman*, he thought. She had injected him with energy, a bristling vibrancy that he could feel running through his veins.

"My balls itch," said Crosby. "On second thought, screw the pizza. What I really want is a shower."

"Yeah, my dreads itch," Tosh responded, without taking his eye off of Tanya.

"I would give my left nut to wash my right one," said Crosby. "Salt water just doesn't do the trick."

"Soap would be nice."

"I don't know about you, but I can smell myself."

"Patchouli. Patchouli will take care of that."

"I'd rather smell myself," said Crosby, sniffing his arm pit to check the conditions.

Tanya became smaller and smaller as she moved further on up the beach. She had just about reached the end when Tosh felt coldness on his feet. He looked down to see the rising tide swirling about his toes.

"No wonder that lady in the pharmacy disliked me so much. She hated my stench."

Tosh looked up to grab a final glimpse of Tanya. Under the darkening sky, she had disappeared. In her place sat a red pickup truck.

"I think I'm at the point where I should maybe stay out of public places," Crosby continued, scratching his crotch.

Tosh took a few steps toward the truck as its headlights ignited to meet the dusk. It slowly began to pull away.

Suddenly, recognizing the truck, Tosh started running toward it.

"Where are you going, dude?" Crosby called out. His words went unanswered.

Tosh ran by a man with a pair of binoculars, peering out at the boats on the water. He halted in the sand and yelled to the man, "Let me borrow those for a sec, will you? Quickly, it's an emergency!"

The man obliged without a word or a moment of consideration.

Through the binoculars, Tosh had a closer view of the rear of the pickup. Through the orange glow of the lingering twilight, he could make out the clear black-and-white lettering on the bumper: **NEVER DIE WONDERING**.

*   *   *   *

Tosh and Crosby gathered their sandals, towels and beach chairs and headed back toward the van.

"I hope Jo didn't melt," said Crosby.

"Yeah," said Tosh. "It's probably still lethally hot in there."

"I'd sleep on the beach tonight if I knew I wouldn't get mugged. Don't know if it's safe around here at night, you know?"

Tosh stopped in the sand. "Cros, I gotta tell you something weird."

"What's that?"

"You know when I grabbed those binoculars from that guy? I wasn't checking out Tanya's ass."

"You weren't?"

"No."

Crosby looked at Tosh with a touch of anxious suspicion. Hesitantly, he asked, "You were checking out some guy's ass?"

"No. I was checking out the truck. Her uncle's truck."

Crosby breathed a sigh of relief. "Yeah, so?"

"I thought I recognized it — and I did. We've seen it before."

"When?"

"In the middle of Montana or Wyoming somewhere."

"How can you tell it's the same truck?" Crosby asked.

"It had that sticker on it – Never Die Wondering. Remember? We were trying to make sense of that saying. Ring a bell?"

Crosby picked up a clam shell from the beach, the remnants of a gull's dinner. "Yeah, I remember. But I don't think it's the same guy."

"Oh, come on. How many old red Ford pickups do you think there are with that crazy bumper sticker on them?"

"Not many, but probably more than one. We're in San Diego, man. That's a far way from Montana."

"I know. That's what's so weird. You think the guy is following us?"

"Naa," said Crosby. "Why would anyone follow us?"

"And even if it is another guy," posited Tosh, "don't you think it's weird that we'd see two trucks like that with the same crazy bumper sticker?"

"It's probably just a coincidence."

"No way. No such thing as coincidence, remember?"

Crosby threw the shell toward a garbage can, but the breeze caused it to flutter down before reaching its destination. "So what do you think it is?"

"Do you remember what Evan said? About how God sends signs? Maybe God is trying to tell us something."

"Oh boy," sighed Crosby. "O.K., well, what do you think God is trying to tell us?"

"Never die wondering, I guess," said Tosh. "But what the hell does that mean?"

*   *   *   *

Tosh and Crosby cleaned up as best they could under the public rinse and then headed across the street to score a couple of slices of pizza for dinner.

"Canadian bacon," Crosby repeated to the Italian guy behind the counter.

The pizza man mumbled something, but neither Tosh nor Crosby could understand him.

"That's right," said Crosby, "and green peppers. Don't forget the peppers."

"What do you feel like doing tonight?" Tosh asked as the pizza man prepared their slices.

"Something mellow. I'm fried."

"Me, too. Musta been the sun."

"Want to go to the zoo? San Diego is supposed to have a good zoo, I think."

"I don't think the zoo is open at night," said Tosh.

"Why not?"

"I don't know. I guess the animals go to sleep at night."

"Are you kidding me? They sleep all damn day," said Crosby. "They can't sleep at night, too."

"I'm telling you, Cros, I've never heard of a zoo being open at night. Maybe it's because it would be too dark to see the animals."

"I'm sure they have lights. It's not Wrigley Field. Hey — there's an idea! Baseball. Maybe we can catch a Padres game."

"That sounds cool."

"Hey buddy," Crosby asked the pizza man, "are the Padres home tonight?"

"Zoo no open," the pizza man answered.

"We'll check the paper," said Tosh.

The pizza man handed them their slices on paper plates and again mumbled something incomprehensible.

"The doctor said it should clear up by Thursday," said Crosby, "if I don't pick the scabs."

*   *   *   *

On the way to the Padres game, misfortune struck. While attempting to make a left turn, Josephine stalled in the middle of an intersection. Unwisely, Tosh and Crosby fiddled with the engine instead of first getting the van out of the flow of traffic. This prompted a messy gridlock which in turn drew the attention of a nearby police officer. After helping Tosh and Crosby push the van out of the road, the pissed-off, sweaty cop wrote them a nasty ticket.

"It's for obstructing traffic," said Tosh, scrutinizing the summons.

"I thought people down here were supposed to be laid back," said Crosby.

"Apparently that's a myth." Tosh rubbed his eyes, tired from a day of squinting and salt water. "I guess cops in Southern Cal are no different than anywhere else."

"Do you think Ponch would have given us a ticket?"

"Who?"

"Poncherello. You know, Erik Estrada from *CHiPs*. The TV show. "

"Oh," said Tosh. "Probably. He kinda had an attitude. Probably would have been a hard-ass."

Crosby rummaged under one of the van's benches for the herb. "His partner was cool, though. John would have given us a warning and let us go."

"Ahh, we deserved a couple of tickets for those lights, anyhow," Tosh reasoned.

Josephine's condition had been worsening ever since their ghetto scare in L.A. The van had picked up the annoying habit of stalling whenever she came to a halt. Tosh and Crosby had already run two red lights trying to avoid this inconvenience, and with this most recent development, even slowing down for turns seemed risky.

As much as he hated to do it, Crosby admitted they had a definite problem. "I don't know, Tosh, I think we're in trouble."

"Do you think we can fix it?"

"I doubt we can, but that doesn't mean it can't be fixed. We'll find a pay phone and call someone first thing in the morning."

"So, I guess the Padres game is out of the picture."

"Looks that way."

While Crosby packed the pipe full of California's finest, Tosh opened the blinds an inch and peeked out the window. He saw nothing but white lines and pavement.

"Dude, we're in San Diego, the surf capital of the United States. There's reggae all over town—"

"Babes everywhere—"

"And we're hanging out by ourselves in the Wal-Mart parking lot. This really sucks."

"Tell me about it." Crosby lit the pipe and took a hit. "Our funds are getting low, anyway."

"Yeah, I know," grumbled Tosh, taking the pipe from Crosby. He held the smoke in his lungs for as long as he could and then exhaled out the rear window, opened an inch for ventilation. "And on top of it, I've got God sending me cryptic messages."

"Let's just smoke this salad and hit the hay," said Crosby. "I'm whupped."

The guys passed the salad bowl back and forth until just a few burnt croutons rested at the bottom.

Crosby took a few swigs from the water jug and passed it on to Tosh. "Don't sweat it, man. We'll figure it all out tomorrow," he said, snuggling into his sleeping bag. "Good night."

"Night."

Tosh polished off the water and threw the empty container into the garbage bag draped over the shotgun seat. Planting himself on the back bed, he leaned back and eyed the photograph of Bob Marley hanging on the wall of the van. The reggae legend looked completely content as he sat on a ledge with his hands folded in his lap, dreadlocks framing his half-shut eyes and easy smile. The picture gave Tosh a peaceful feeling, as if Bob was saying, "Don't worry, mon. Every t'ing gonna be all right."

Tosh closed his eyes. Things weren't so bad, after all.

*   *   *   *

Things were bad.

The guy at the filling station could not tell what ailed the van's engine. "It could be a lot a different things," he said, wiping his hands on a rag. "I hate ta tell ya this, but from what yer tellin' me, ya could have a crack in the engine block."

"Is that bad?" Tosh asked.

"That's bad," said Crosby. "Real bad."

"Well, in any event," continued the grizzled mechanic, "I can't really tell ya what the problem is without takin' 'part the engine."

"How much is that going to run us," said Crosby, expecting to be displeased.

"Roughly six hunnerd dollars."

"That's bad," said Tosh.

"Do we look like we have that kind of dough?" asked Crosby.

"I dunno what you look like," the mechanic said matter-of-factly, "but I do know that takin' 'part that old van's engine is gonna take me a lotta time and that's what I get paid."

Crosby and Tosh frowned at each other.

"Look, fellas, I don't mean ta be a curmudgeon, but I dunno what ta tell ya. I can't really cut ya too much a break. Ya know, I got a family ta feed an' all."

"Don't worry about it," Crosby said.

"You're not a curmudgeon," added Tosh.

The mechanic's greasy hands fingered his greasy whiskers. "Well, think about what you boys want ta do."

"So you're telling us that it's going to cost us about six hundred dollars to fix the engine?"

"No, I'm tellin' ya that it's gonna cost ya six hunnerd dollars to take the engine 'part and tell ya what's wrong. Then, I dunno. Depends onna problem. Ya got a cracked block, yer gonna need a new engine. That could run ya coupla grand."

Tosh and Crosby hung their heads.

"I'm sorry, fellas. Think about what ya want ta do. I got some work I got ta 'tend ta." He adjusted the dirty cap on his head and walked back to the garage.

"What's a curmudgeon?" asked Tosh.

"Beats me."

"What the hell are we going to do?"

"Not much of a choice," said Crosby. "Either we move to San Diego and live in our tent or we find another way back home."

"We got a lot more of the country to see. I don't want to go home."

"Neither do I, bub, but what can we do? We can't drive around the rest of the country without stopping. Besides, our cash is getting low, remember?"

"Maybe we can cut some lawns or something."

"Cut some lawns? We don't even have a lawnmower."

"I don't know. Maybe we could ring some doorbells and see if anyone wants us to do some yard work. There's got to be a lot of weeds around here. The weather's always warm."

"Are you for real? You want to be a migrant landscaper?"

Tosh shrugged. "This is southern California. You never know."

*   *   *   *

Crosby shot down the lawn mowing plan.

It seemed like they were out of options, so the guys explained their plight to the mechanic, hoping for a suggestion. The mechanic told them he had a friend who rebuilt engines as a hobby. His friend bought old cars and fixed them up, so he might be willing to buy the van off of them for a few hundred dollars.

349

Tosh and Crosby did not want to sell Josephine. Selling Josephine definitely meant the end of the trip, unless they planned on scoring some cheap bicycles at a garage sale or something. And considering all the crap they were carrying, that wasn't really an option. It would take supreme ingenuity to transport Crosby's wind surfing gear by bicycle.

But besides facing the end of their long-awaited journey, Tosh and Crosby hated to let go of that van. She was not only their home, but their traveling partner, and they had become attached to her. Tosh and Crosby had wanted to keep her around for years to come, sort of like an heirloom.

Selling the van was an emotional decision, but really, what choice did they have?

*   *   *   *

"Didja make up yer mind, yet?" asked the mechanic, sitting on a stack of tires, smoking a cigarette.

"Yeah. Call your friend," Crosby told him.

The mechanic took a swig of his Dr. Pepper and strolled into the office. After a couple of minutes, he returned and said, "My buddy'll be down in an hour or so. He's hanging his laundry out to dry."

"He live around here?" asked Tosh.

"'Bout thirty-five miles west." The mechanic finished off his soda and crushed the can. "Got a dart board in the back, if you're interested."

"No thanks," said Crosby. "We've got plenty to do. I guess we'll start packin' up our stuff."

"O.K., then. I'll be under that Pontiac if you need me." The mechanic headed into the garage to resume his work.

Tosh and Crosby opened up all of Josephine's windows for full ventilation and began the solemn duty of sorting through their stuff, trying to determine what to bring home and what to leave.

"Pepper Pot?" joked Tosh. "Should we pack the Pepper Pot?"

"I hope this guy likes canned goods. He's going to inherit a decent supply of food."

"Maybe he'll throw us an extra twenty bucks for all of it."

"Yeah. I'm sure."

They emptied out their backpacks and reorganized all of their clothes. Tosh took down all of the pictures and posters that were hung inside the van while Crosby dumped the ice from the coolers. He put the coolers in the sun to dry and took the five beers that remained and set them in the shade under the van. "We'll save these for later," he said to Tosh.

Soon, the mechanic reappeared with his friend, a burly fellow with unkempt black hair and a beard. Despite the San Diego summer sun, he wore a black leather vest and a Harley Davidson hat.

"This here's Chuck," said the mechanic.

"What's up, Chuck?" said Crosby, offering his palm.

"Nothin' much," Chuck replied. He smiled and shook Crosby's hand. "Hit a critter out on Route 6, some kinda rabid squirrel or something. Little guy darted out in fronta my wheel."

With round eyes and a reddened nose, Chuck's Hell's Angels garb contrasted with his cheerful, chubby face. He looked like a young biker Santa Claus. "So, you boys want to sell me a van?"

Crosby threw his thumbs back over his shoulders. "This is it."

"What is it, '74?"

"'73," said Tosh.

Chuck gave the van a rudimentary look-over. "I'll give ya two hunnerd."

"Two hundred? That's it?" asked Crosby. "How about five?"

"Two," said Chuck.

"How about four?"

"Two," Chuck repeated.

"Three?"

Chuck pulled out a wad of bills from his pocket and counted out three fifties, two twenties and two fives. "Here's two hundred."

"Fair enough," sighed Crosby.

"Hey, Chuck," said Tosh. "Got a question for you."

"What's that?"

"Do you like Pepper Pot?"

*   *   *   *

Tosh and Crosby watched their final west coast sunset with their ankles in the Pacific.

Chuck had offered to give the guys an extra twenty for the groceries, but they told him to keep the cash and asked if he could give them a lift to the beach instead. Chuck obliged and stuck the twenty dollar bill in Crosby's shirt pocket anyway.

Although the deep orange sun looked majestic over the horizon, Tosh could not enjoy the moment because he could not stop dwelling on the fact it was the last time he'd see the sun set over the ocean. At least for a while.

Nostalgia sucks, he sighed.

Tosh felt dejected. He was pissed about having to sell the van, didn't want the fun to end just yet and dreaded returning home to bland suburbia to try and figure out what to do with his life.

"Do you feel cheated?" he asked Crosby.

351

"Well, at first I did," said Crosby. "But come to think of it, I think two hundred bucks was pretty fair. The van was old, man. Even with a good engine, it wasn't worth a lot."

"No, not about the van. I mean, do you feel cheated about having to end our trip so suddenly?"

"A little," said Crosby.

"You know what sucks? Everything we've done on this trip has been by choice — for no other reason except that we chose to do it — and now, in a way, we're being forced to end the trip. I wish we could have driven through the south, checked out the Grand Canyon and Texas and New Mexico — Mexico, for that matter — just driven until we were good and ready to go home. I pictured us pulling into our driveways with a van full of stories. The explorers returning in glory."

"We may not have our van, but we have the stories, Tosh. No one can ever take that away from us."

"That's true."

Crosby looked at a seagull landing nearby. "Ah, fuck it, Tosh. Shit happens, you know? All good things come to an end, right?"

"That's what they say."

"I'm just taking a tip from Willy and trying to focus on all the positive things about going home," said Crosby. "Just think, we could take long, hot showers whenever we want. Every day. Twice a day. We could eat home-cooked meals, well-rounded meals that don't come from a can."

"Yeah, that'll be nice."

"We could watch sports on TV and rent movies. We could play roller hockey on the tennis courts."

"Yep."

"But best of all, Tosh, best of all, we can sleep in beds again. Do you remember what a soft, mushy bed feels like? No sleeping bags, no bugs, no rocks. Pure air-conditioned, uninterrupted sleep. You have to admit, that's going to be sweet."

"Uh-huh."

Tosh agreed with Crosby verbally, but his voice had no enthusiasm. And for Tosh, words without passion were words without meaning. They were hollow. "Come on, man, lighten up," Crosby consoled him. "Big deal if we didn't get to see the whole country. We'll see it some other time. The south isn't going to disappear."

Tosh smiled at his best friend.

"So what if we were forced to come home, dude? We fulfilled our goal of driving cross-country! That's awesome. And hell, we did more traveling this summer than most people get to do in their lifetimes."

Crosby is right, thought Tosh, and he began to feel thankful. Thankful to have had the opportunity to take the trip. Thankful the van made it as far as it did. Thankful even, they had found a suitable vehicle they could afford. And thankful to have such a good buddy like Crosby to share the experience with.

Tosh reflected on their journey. They had made that map come to life. Lines became roads and words became towns, and in those towns they had met a diverse mix of people, people who had shared their stories and beliefs. That's what taking the trip was all about.

And because of it, Tosh felt like he had a different understanding of things. All this stuff that Tanya had told him about the answers existing had him juiced up. He looked forward to returning home to pursue this "truth." Yoga? Meditation? What would be the way for him? Tosh didn't know yet, but the important thing was that he was out of the woods, on a path toward something he hadn't known existed. Every ending is a new beginning, isn't that what they say?

And speaking of new beginnings, what about this new view of God? Although Tosh had a recent penchant for prayer in times of panic, he wondered about the validity of his communication with God. Despite his drug-induced vision at the reggae festival and the Never Die Wondering messages following him around the country, Tosh still found it hard to believe he had a personal relationship with God. If God actually did exist, could he really have a tète â tète with Him any time he wanted? Tosh took comfort in the idea and wished he could embrace it.

Evan said it was a matter of recognizing the signs and then just accepting them. Tosh could now recognize them, but he was having trouble accepting them.

Own it, Tanya had said.

I guess I just have to stop wondering about it, thought Tosh, *and just believe it. Wait a second...stop wondering...Never Die Wondering...*

"Oh God," said Tosh. "Duh."

*   *   *   *

"So, you think it's a call for faith?"

"Yeah, but not only in God."

"What else?" asked Crosby. "Faith in pizza?"

"No, you ass. Faith in the truth."

"What truth?"

"Don't you remember what Tanya said yesterday about the mysteries of our existence having answers? If we just allow ourselves to accept these ideas instead of being skeptical, if we give them some consideration instead of automatically discarding them as impossible...that truth."

"I don't know, Tosh."

"What don't you know? It all makes so much sense. It's clear to me now."

"I don't want to rain on your parade," said Crosby, kicking sand out of his sneaker, "but Never Die Wondering could mean, like, don't waste your time thinking about it all, because it just doesn't matter."

This stumped Tosh for a moment. He felt nauseous, like his stomach had leapt into his mouth.

"You know, Tosh. Maybe this truth does exist. Maybe we can know the answers to the universe, but then what? Will it change anything?"

"Why do you have to be so cynical? Can't you give it a chance?"

"I am not being cynical. I'm being realistic."

"You're being close-minded."

"No. I believe that these answers might exist, but all I'm saying is, what good are they to me? Are they going to put food on my plate and clothes on my back?"

Tosh thought of the hermit Tim, photosynthesizing his life away in the woods around Lake Nitinat. "Maybe they could. You never know, Cros."

*   *   *   *

Tosh and Crosby sat on the hard plastic seats of the bus station watching a television tuned to Geraldo Rivera.

"At least we'll get to see more of the country this way," said Tosh.

"Yeah, a lot more. About eighty times more because that's how much longer it will take us to get home."

"We don't have to worry about cabin pressure."

Crosby pouted. "It just sucks. I used to get antsy on the ride to school, and now I'm going cross-country in a bus."

"These busses are more comfortable."

"Still a bus," Crosby huffed.

"Look, we'll just smoke a bowl, kick back and watch the country pass before our eyes."

"That's what really sucks, Tosh. It's just a tease. We'll be able to see everything, but we won't be able to experience it. After what we've just done, we're going to want to get out and meet people and touch things and smell the air. We're gonna feel trapped inside. Man, I'd rather just eat a microwaved meal, watch a bad movie on a small TV from far away, and be done with it."

"Well, flying is not an option, Cros. We don't have the cash."

On the television, Geraldo prodded a transsexual English professor. The lusty literarian pulled a red magic marker from his/her brassiere and scrawled a giant F on Geraldo's tie. The audience hooted and howled and hollered while Geraldo played up his misfortune.

"This is what we've been missing," hissed Tosh. "This is what we have to look forward to."

"No, we won't have time for this garbage. We have to find jobs, remember? That's what we have to look forward to."

Oh God, thought Tosh. *That issue again. Never did resolve it.* "I have no idea what the hell I want to do."

"Me neither."

"I've got to find something fulfilling. I want to feel like I'm doing something meaningful."

"That would be nice, Tosh, but I'm more concerned with making a living to tell you the truth."

"Uggh, then there's the job search process. Figuring out what you want to do is hard enough, much less finding a job doing it."

"I've got to get my resumé together."

"Resumés, cover letters, searching the want-ads, interviews."

"I've got to get a new suit."

"I've got to cut my hair. Shit."

Crosby looked at Tosh's tangled, dirty-blonde mop. It seemed like his dreads got even fatter during the course of the trip. "You're gonna cut it?"

"Got to. No other way to get these babies out but shave 'em."

"A buzz cut? No way. Never thought I'd see the day."

"No one will hire me looking like this. I'll have to be a baldhead to find work." Tosh knew he would have to lose his dreads one day and he had prepared himself for the inevitability. He accepted this reality, but it bummed him out. He'd been growing those dreads for a couple of years and every day they looked a little better. "I wish we could be our own bosses. Start a business and work for ourselves."

"Yeah. Me, too."

Crosby looked up at the television. Grated cheddar cheese filled the screen. It was a commercial for Taco Hell.

What a load of crap, thought Crosby. *It's junk food.*

"Some people think that's Mexican food," he said to Tosh, pointing to the screen. "Sad."

Tosh shook his head. "Ignorance."

"We should open a burrito stand, man."

"Yeah, right."

Crosby thought about what he had just said. Why not? Tosh could manage a business. They both had experience cooking. And no one knew Mexican food like he and Tosh. Not even the Mexicans. Burritos were Tex-Mex, after all.

"I'm serious," Crosby said. "Don't you want to continue our search for the Ultimate Burrito?"

"Sure, but that's kind of a hobby, you know?"

"It doesn't have to be. What better way to continue our quest than by experimenting ourselves? We're qualified, don't you think?"

Tosh thought about it. He liked the aspect of searching for the Ultimate Burrito in their own kitchen, but he wasn't sold on the idea as a way to make a living. "I don't know, Cros. There's a lot of Mexican restaurants out there. Tough competition."

"Look who's being skeptical."

"I'm just being realistic."

355

"Skeptic. You should hear yourself," Crosby scowled.

Tosh knew Crosby was right. But did he want a career as a cook? He'd been doing that every summer down at the beach, and it sure didn't feel very fulfilling. "I just wonder if I'll be satisfied serving food all my life," said Tosh.

"Dude, we'd be restaurant owners. That's prestigious, man."

"Aaa, we'd essentially be cafeteria workers, glorified cafeteria workers. You don't want to be a cafeteria worker, do you?"

"Tosh, those are two completely different things. Cafeterias have no creativity. When you own a restaurant you have to design dishes and decorate the place. You've got to give it character, a vibe. It's artistic."

"Yeah, but you really only do that stuff in the beginning. After that, you just run the place. That is not very fulfilling."

"Whatever, Tosh." Crosby gave up. Sometimes his friend was too idealistic. "Then go win a Nobel."

"Fine. I will."

The two sat silently for a few minutes. Crosby shifted in his chair, peeling his sweaty hamstring off the plastic chair. "How much longer till this damn bus leaves?" he asked.

"What if we did a little more with it?" asked Tosh.

"What do you mean?"

"Well, we'd have to set our place apart from all the others, you know. Maybe if we did something really funky, like have meditations and stuff. Readings, yoga."

"In the restaurant?"

"Yeah. It could be like a burrito stand slash metaphysical center."

Crosby looked at his friend like he had just vomited a pygmy nut hatch.

"Maybe you could put your artwork up. Add some other artists, make it like a gallery, too."

Crosby liked that idea. "I could do that."

"And we can have live music - reggae bands!"

"And Latin music," said Crosby. "Merèngue."

"Salsa," added Tosh. "'Have some salsa with your salsa!'"

"This is great! We can do this, dude."

"We could really create a special place, man. People could come in, munch a burrito and search for the truth. We'd be stimulating people's tastebuds *and* their minds. Filling their bellies and their souls! I could get into that." Tosh slapped his buddy five. "Let's get home."

"Hey dude," said Crosby. "What do you think we should call the place?"

About the Author

At a very young age, David Shiffman was coaxed into eating a poisonous wild mushroom by a flirtatious playmate. Though the incident led to a decade of mushroom-hating, his years living at the unruly Phi Who fraternity at Penn State University changed his perspective on mushrooms and in turn, opened his mind up to the wonder of the universe.

David has spent the past decade writing for various music publications, writing, directing and producing an Off-Broadway comedy, acting in various commercials, plays and films and spending what little money he has made on his extensive music collection, which he has dubbed, "Rootsdude Sound System." He has a feverish passion for reggae music, Rasta consciousness and island culture. David plays ice hockey religiously for Team Rasta, a recreational team he founded and manages. His favorite food is Mexican beer, especially Pacifico.

Printed in the United States
22735LVS00002B/237

9 780759 665866